WHAT A TANGLED WEB

Reviewers Love Melissa Brayden

"Melissa Brayden has become one of the most popular novelists of the genre, writing hit after hit of funny, relatable, and very sexy stories for women who love women."—*Afterellen.com*

Two to Tangle

"As usual, Brayden delivers with great dialogue, likeable characters, and emotional turmoil."—*Bookvark.com*

"Melissa Brayden does it again with a sweet and sexy romance that leaves you feeling content and full of happiness. As always, the book is full of smiles, fabulous dialogue, and characters you wish were your best friends."—*The Romantic Reader*

"I loved it. I wasn't sure Brayden could beat Joey and Becca and their story, but when I started to see reviews mentioning that this was even better, I had high hopes and Brayden definitely lived up to them." —*LGBTQreader.com*

Entangled

"*Entangled* is a simmering slow burn romance, but I also fully believe it would be appealing for lovers of women's fiction. The friendships between Joey, Maddie, and Gabriella are well developed and engaging as well as incredibly entertaining...All that topped off with a deeply fulfilling happily ever after that gives all the happy sighs long after you flip the final page."—*Lily Michaels: Sassy Characters, Sizzling Romance, Sweet Endings*

"Ms. Brayden has a definite winner with this first book of the new series, and I can't wait to read the next one. If you love a great enemies-to-lovers, feel-good romance, then this is the book for you."—*Rainbow Reflections*

To the Moon and Back

"*To the Moon and Back* is all about Brayden's love of theatre, onstage and backstage, and she does a delightful job of sharing that love... Brayden set the scene so well I knew what was coming, not because it's unimaginative but because she made it obvious it was the only way things could go. She leads the reader exactly where she wants to take them, with brilliant writing as usual. Also, not everyone can make office supplies sound sexy."—*Jude in the Stars*

"Melissa Brayden does what she does best, she delivers amazing characters, witty banter, all while being fun and relatable."—*Romantic Reader Blog*

Back to September

"You can't go wrong with a Melissa Brayden romance. Seriously, you can't. Buy all of her books. Brayden sure has a way of creating an emotional type of compatibility between her leads, making you root for them against all odds. Great settings, cute interactions, and realistic dialogue."—*Bookvark*

Beautiful Dreamer

"I love this book. I want to kiss it on its face…I'm going to stick *Beautiful Dreamer* on my to-reread-when-everything-sucks pile, because it's sure to make me happy again and again."—*Smart Bitches Trashy Books*

"*Beautiful Dreamer* is a sweet and sexy romance, with the bonus of interesting secondary characters and a cute small-town setting." —*Amanda Chapman, Librarian (Davisville Free Library, RI)*

Love Like This

"I really have to commend Melissa Brayden in her exceptional writing and especially in the way she writes not only the romance but the friendships between the group of women."—*Les Rêveur*

"Brayden upped her game. The characters are remarkably distinct from one another. The secondary characters are rich and wonderfully integrated into the story. The dialogue is crisp and witty."—*Frivolous Reviews*

Sparks Like Ours

"Brayden sets up a flirtatious tit-for-tat that's honest, relatable, and passionate. The women's fears are real, but the loving support from the supporting cast helps them find their way to a happy future. This enjoyable romance is sure to interest readers in the other stories from Seven Shores."—*Publishers Weekly*

"*Sparks Like Ours* is made up of myriad bits of truth that make for a cozy, lovely summer read."—*Queerly Reads*

Hearts Like Hers

"*Hearts Like Hers* has all the ingredients that readers can expect from Ms. Brayden: witty dialogue, heartfelt relationships, hot chemistry and passionate romance."—*Lez Review Books*

"Once again Melissa Brayden stands at the top. She unequivocally is the queen of romance."—*Front Porch Romance*

"*Hearts Like Hers* has a breezy style that makes it a perfect beach read. The romance is paced well, the sex is super hot, and the conflict made perfect sense and honored Autumn and Kate's journeys."
—*The Lesbian Review*

Eyes Like Those

"Brayden's story of blossoming love behind the Hollywood scenes provides the right amount of warmth, camaraderie, and drama."
—*RT Book Reviews*

"Brayden's writing is just getting better and better. The story is well done, full of well-honed wit and humour, and the characters are complex and interesting."—*Lesbian Reading Room*

"Melissa Brayden knocks it out of the park once again with this fantastic and beautifully written novel."—*Les Reveur*

Strawberry Summer

"This small-town second-chance romance is full of tenderness and heart. The 10 Best Romance Books of 2017."—*Vulture*

"*Strawberry Summer* is a tribute to first love and soulmates and growing into the person you're meant to be. I feel like I say this each time I read a new Melissa Brayden offering, but I loved this book so much that I cannot wait to see what she delivers next."—*Smart Bitches, Trashy Books*

First Position

"Brayden aptly develops the growing relationship between Ana and Natalie, making the emotional payoff that much sweeter. This ably plotted, moving offering will earn its place deep in readers' hearts."
—*Publishers Weekly*

By the Author

Waiting in the Wings

Heart Block

How Sweet It Is

First Position

Strawberry Summer

Beautiful Dreamer

Back to September

To the Moon and Back

Soho Loft Romances:

Kiss the Girl

Just Three Words

Ready or Not

Seven Shores Romances:

Eyes Like Those

Hearts Like Hers

Sparks Like Ours

Love Like This

Tangle Valley Romances:

Entangled

Two to Tangle

What a Tangled Web

Visit us at www.boldstrokesbooks.com

What a Tangled Web

by

Melissa Brayden

2021

WHAT A TANGLED WEB

ISBN 13: 978-1-63555-749-7

This Trade Paperback Original Is Published By
Bold Strokes Books, Inc.
P.O. Box 249
Valley Falls, NY 12185

First Edition: March 2021

CREDITS
EDITOR: RUTH STERNGLANTZ
PRODUCTION DESIGN: STACIA SEAMAN
COVER DESIGN BY JEANINE HENNING

Acknowledgments

I'm a person who knows what it's like to carry true passion for my job. I'm lucky enough that I've experienced it a handful of times throughout my life and hoped, in writing this book, to capture that kind of passion in the pursuits of both Madison and Clementine, who both love what they do. I also hope that joy is a little bit contagious and that you relish their journeys to a brand-new passion, each other.

It's never easy to say good-bye to a group of characters, and the Tangle Valley gang was a definite favorite of mine to write. I hope you've enjoyed your time with the series as much as I did. I learned so much about wine tasting, wine making, Willamette Valley, and what goes into making a vineyard run smoothly. I can't wait to visit again!

Many thanks to: Alan for not only all of the cheerleading and support, but for teaching me everything I needed to know about the hospitality industry. My mom for being a lifesaver in helping me carve out time to work in the midst of a pandemic with a toddler at home. My publishing friends (all of you) with special shout-outs to Nikki, Georgia, Rey, Carsen, Paula, Kris, and Fiona for pulling me along, making me laugh, and acting as my sounding board. You guys rock. To the fabulous folks at Bold Strokes for inspiring me, working with me, and helping me get better at what I do. There is no better place to work. Ruth, my editor, for seeing the forest for the trees when sometimes I couldn't and for always breaking it to me kindly and with humor. To my readers, how I wish we could sit down and chat over a glass of wine, or coffee, or both. I'll bring the snacks. I have very much enjoyed the conversations we have gotten to have along the way, however, as well as the emails, messages, and posts you've sent my way or tagged me in. I'm most grateful.

For the innovators.

PROLOGUE

G rapes don't sleep," Maddie murmured, bleary-eyed and bent over her pad full of scribbles. Her calculations littered the page, her own mathematical madness. "So why should I?" She took another sip of hot cocoa from her thermos.

It was after midnight at Tangle Valley Vineyard, smack dab in the middle of lush Oregon wine country. As winemaker, Madison LeGrange was at home with the extensive hours, if not a little exhausted. They produced four varietal wines at the vineyard along with a handful of rotating blends, which meant there was always more to do. She'd pulled another long day, but with new assistants to train, machinery to keep clean, grapes to care for, and a calendar to maintain, she'd had her hands full. Plus, everyone needed something, and the quiet of the evening gave her a chance to knock out some of the items on her to-do list without interruption. This wasn't her first late night, and it wouldn't be her last.

"Um, what in the world are you doing out here so late? Again," Joey Wilder asked, peeking around the open door to Madison's office with a stern look. "I saw the light on in the tank room, so of course I stomped over to investigate this crime against slumber. Here you are. Guilty, as suspected."

Madison blinked a few times at Joey, while her brain acclimated to communication with others. Her neck ached, and she was hungry, having missed dinner. These days, she preferred to lose herself in her work. Life felt easier that way. "Just making plans for harvest since we're almost there. Our yield should be good. I'm also getting my day organized for tomorrow, and"—she held up her notebook—"working on leveling out the acidity in the chardonnay." She flipped open her planner. "Oh, and do we still have that private tasting happening on Thursday after lunch?"

"Yes, I'll play hostess, but I'd love it if you could make an appearance. Maybe say a few science-like words about the creation of the magnificent wine and make them feel special. But you know what?" She closed Maddie's notebook for her. "We can talk about that tomorrow when regular people talk about work things, Maddie."

"What? You don't like now?" She grinned widely.

"I don't, strangely. After we've slept, I'm all yours. We'll be like the rest of society."

"Definitely, but while you're here, I was thinking about the pinot harvest, and if we schedule on—"

"Madison. Look at me. Into my eyes." Madison obeyed and found her best friend's baby blues. "I love you, but I'm going to have to murder you and hide the body, *Dateline*-style. This next part is important. Please make sure I'm the beneficiary of your life insurance."

"Wait." Madison balked. "You can't murder your best friend and then take the money."

"Can so. Will do it, too."

"Then I will Dateline you right back."

Joey frowned. "Are you even listening? I already Datelined *you*. There's no double Datelining. It's impossible."

Madison tossed her pencil onto the desk, angry to have lost the murder competition. "I will be faster next time. With the Dateline. Mark my words, buddygirl," she said, employing her childhood nickname for Joey.

"Marked and highlighted." Joey pointed at the desk, the scene of the overworking. "I'm serious, though. You've always been a workaholic, but this has gotten out of control, even for you. Wanna talk about why, because I have definite ideas."

"Of course you do, but I'm fine." Madison shrugged off the concern, while at the same time copping to it because Joey was right. She likely needed to slow down. She had a demanding job, yes, but she had been pushing extra hard lately because nothing felt quite right. Almost as if something hadn't clicked into place that should have.

"You've been this way ever since Gabriella and Ryan got back together. Have you noticed?"

"Yes." It definitely hadn't been easy to have her ex-girlfriend who worked just across the vineyard fall in love with someone else while she watched, but she'd survived and had made her peace. Everything had worked out as it was supposed to, and Madison actually believed Ryan was perfect for Gabriella now that she'd seen them in action. She could also see that she and Gabriella were not a good match in the romance department. "I think I just needed a temporary distraction when that all hit. But I'm great with Ryan and Gabs now."

"So you just forgot to turn it off?"

Madison frowned because she didn't exactly know. "Yeah, maybe."

"Is there some kind of party in here that no one invited me to? Ryan fell asleep on the couch, and I saw the light on from my front porch."

As if they'd summoned her, Gabriella Russo—her ex and their best friend—stood behind them with her hands on her hips and pink bunny slippers on her feet. With all three of them living in such close proximity on the property, it was hard to have any real privacy. When your work light was on, people took notice.

Madison raised an eyebrow. "Well, it's not a pink bunny soiree, but join us."

"A shame, then." Gabriella shot them a smile. "What's the actual occasion for this early morning gathering? I'm not caught up."

"Madison is overworking herself," Joey said. "It's after midnight, and she's still at this damn desk. I've threatened murder. We're waiting to see if it worked."

Gabriella nodded. "Murder Madison at Midnight. Has a ring. Could be a book." She raised a shoulder and nodded at her ingenuity.

Madison's mouth fell open. "Coming from the innocent in the bunny slippers. Et tu, Brute?"

Gabriella puffed with pride. "You heard the boss lady, and I have her back. To bed with you."

Madison stared at her serious-looking friends, gave in, and closed her laptop. "Fine, but you guys can't threaten me every day. Good wine doesn't just appear in the bottle. There are actual processes involved. Plus, my mojo."

"Yes," Joey said. "You wave your magic wand all over the grapes, which is why I hired you. For your fairy dust."

Joey Wilder had been her closest friend since early grade school when they'd been assigned seats next to each other in Mrs. Davidson's homeroom class. Hell, Madison had practically grown up on Joey's family's vineyard, which made it extra special that she was now their head winemaker. There was something special about the place that made Madison move all the way home from the Finger Lakes of New York when Joey called up and offered her the job.

As they walked the path from the barrel room, where Madison kept her office, she took a cleansing breath of the fresh night air, invigorated to be outside and have the autumn chill against her skin. "Damn. I love this place at night."

Gabriella smiled over at Madison, her arms wrapped around herself. "There's a sort of magic, isn't there?"

Joey nodded, staring off at the acres of vines. "I used to think it was just me."

Madison stopped walking to take it all in, and her friends joined her, leaving them standing in a small circle. "Do you ever stop and wonder about the forces that brought us together? We're standing here, right now, for a reason."

Joey nodded. "All the time. When I lost my dad, I thought the world had ended, and I had no idea what would happen to Tangle Valley. But then you two arrived, and I get to work with my best friends. I can honestly say that you saved this place." She shrugged sentimentally. "And me."

Gabriella bumped Joey's shoulder with hers. "I know I feel every bit as blessed. I get to make my food at Tangled every day and then step outside to all of this gorgeousness." She swept her hand in the direction of the farmland. "Don't get me started on how much I love my cottage. And I say things like *cottage* now because I live in a small town." She sighed. "But working with you guys? That's the best part."

"Why are we all sappy under the sky in the middle of the night?" Madison asked with a laugh. Moments like these, while special, weren't exactly her comfort zone. "Who are we? Let's trade insults and get back to normal."

Joey linked her arm through Madison's. "We're the best. That's who we are, so you're just gonna have to suck up the emotion, my stoic friend. Becca may be the love of my life, and that one over here"—she jutted her chin to Gabriella—"has Ryan. But this?" She reached for

Gabriella's hand, while still linked up with Madison. "*This* combination has been my rock, okay? So you let me say it. I know I can count on you two for anything." She laughed at her own sentimentality. "And now I'm even *more* sappy under the stars in the middle of the night. Stop me now."

"I like sappy JoJo," Gabriella said.

Madison shifted uncomfortably because a lump had lodged in her throat. Dammit. "Now let's take our magic selves home because I'm up early with the grapes. We harvest soon, so I'll be testing."

"Deal," Joey said.

They walked the short distance to the Big House where they dropped Joey to flit away to Becca, who'd moved in officially a few months prior when their relationship hit the forever zone. Madison and Gabriella then continued down the path toward what she had come to think of as Cottage Row. The Wilder family had built a series of small homes for their most important staff, those who might be needed at off-hours. A nice perk. She and Gabriella each had her own modest but nicely appointed digs. They arrived at the Sunrise Cottage first. Madison's.

"Want me to walk you home?" she asked Gabriella, who lived maybe fifty more yards down the path in the Spring Cottage.

"Nope. Me and my slippers need alone time. Much to discuss."

Madison grinned. "Should have known better. You said Ryan's staying tonight?"

"Yeah, but she's passed out already. Gotta drag her off the couch and listen to her talk nonsense in her sleep. One of my favorites. She told me to hand her the damn hammer the other night and then asked me to wash the rabbit. We don't have one, so I was surely a disappointment."

"Yeah, work on the fake rabbit washing, maybe."

"Way ahead of you. Night, Maddie."

"Night, Gabs. See ya tomorrow."

She let herself into her cottage and flipped on the lights, comforted by the familiar gray, soft orange, and white decor picked out for her by Joey before her arrival. The cottage was essentially one large room, containing the kitchen, living area, and dining room. One large bedroom and bathroom stood just down the hall on the left. Joey had updated the hell out of the place, which had been an unexpected bonus.

Madison dropped her keys, fell onto the gray couch, and finally played the voice mail that had come in earlier that day from her investments guy. Yep. She had one of those now, which was a little mind-blowing because that meant she now had funds available to invest. At first, working as a winemaker in a male-dominated industry had been intimidating. To combat it, she'd worked her ass off and then some, studying, learning from every noteworthy winemaker she came in contact with. Cold-calling wineries and asking to tour their facilities and chat up their staff. But now she'd established herself and came with clout. She'd been featured in a handful of magazines and trade publications, and in addition to her job at Tangle Valley, she was a sought-after consultant for a top-dollar hourly rate, lending her knowledge to vineyards who reached out.

"*Ms. LeGrange, Oscar Mimms. Sorry to have missed you,*" the investment guy said in too loud a voice. "*I've been looking over potential options and have some ideas about diversification. Can we set something up for next week?*"

She made a mental note. She wasn't the kind of person who knew a ton about finances, and she wanted to be responsible with her savings, as it seemed to be growing quite a bit. She lived rent-free and was able to save most of her paycheck, minus a few bills.

"I'm thinking about finances on my couch on a Friday night." She paused. "I'm boring. And I'm talking to the ceiling. How did I get here exactly?" A pang of regret struck. Joey's words played back in her head. She was falling into a sad pattern. Other than Joey, Gabriella, and their girlfriends, Madison didn't have any kind of social life. She didn't date. She didn't explore outside interests. In fact, she'd made her world pretty small these days.

She poured herself a glass of Bordeaux from a little boutique winery she'd fallen in love with in Paris a few years back. She received a shipment from them every six months now, and it was well worth the trouble. Dark cherry, spice, licorice. Dry tannins. Perfect. She let the wine settle over her tongue and linger in the back of her mouth, savoring. Wine was romantic. It was mysterious. It was rich. Deep. Complex. When made right, she never tired of its study.

But there had to be more out there, right? She rotated the stem between her thumb and two fingers, embracing the coolness of the glass she'd kept chilled. Madison couldn't help but wonder about what the world might have in store for her if she opened herself up a bit more.

She downed the last bit of her wine. Couldn't hurt to peek her head out a little bit, right? Take a few risks.

Maybe it was time to explore her carefree side. After all, she only had one life to lead, and hers might be passing her by. She walked in circles through her living room as she worked it through, picking up courage with each lap. Until finally, "Be bold," she murmured, a small smile creeping onto her face with her new sense of direction. She liked how it felt. She went a bit further, enjoying this now. "Make big choices. Talk out loud to no one in your kitchen if you want to. Why the hell not?"

Madison fell into bed close to two a.m. with that small smile lingering as she wondered what the future just might have waiting for her.

CHAPTER ONE

It was the perfect day for making fresh biscuits. That was for damn sure. The breakfast rush at the Bacon and Biscuit Café had finally trickled off in the late morning hours to just an odd customer here and there. Clementine Monroe exhaled and grinned, enjoying the moment to catch her breath and looking forward to pausing for a meal herself. She'd learned to eat something quickly between breakfast and lunch, stealing time when she could. She wasn't complaining. She adored her job managing the small café that specialized in just what the name advertised: all kinds of bacon and biscuits with a few more items dotting the menu for the sake of variety. Muffins, croissants, banana bread on occasion—when there was time. All baked fresh in-house by either Clementine herself or one of her carefully trained part-time employees. All the menu items were amazing, each in its own right. Though, in her opinion, none really compared to the hot, fluffy biscuits that melted in your mouth.

There was something about breakfast food that she found to be magical and heartwarming at the same time. It was the perfect start to the day, and her job allowed her to be part of that. Not only that, but she loved the small niche of the market they'd carved out for themselves. The Biscuit was now a fixture in town, and Clementine was a part of that. In many ways, it made her feel important, when not a lot in this life did.

She rubbed the back of her neck to ease some of the tension from morning service as she watched four of her regulars pick up and go. Maude, Thelma, Birdie, and Janet gathered each morning at the table by the window. The women were retired, as well as widowed or divorced, which left them with way too much time on their hands to gossip and meddle in the affairs of, well, everyone who lived in Whisper Wall. She'd seen them scheming firsthand from her spot behind the counter, discussing everyone else's business over coffee and biscuits at their very own white-haired gossip party that happened daily. The town had nicknamed them the Biddies, and damn, they'd earned it. They hid their meddlesome ways behind a veil of endearing grandmotherly smiles and well-wishes. Clementine fell for it every time and genuinely liked the spitfires. Especially Ms. Birdie Jenkins, the most gentle of the foursome.

"Your usual, Clem? Not even sure why I'm asking," Frankie said, tossing his spatula and catching it like the wannabe showman he was. They'd worked together so many years now, that they could predict each other's next thought. He was a newer transplant to town and about ten years her senior. Yep, Frankie Delacourt Jr. knew how to make the most delicious food, and she was honored to work alongside that kind of genius behind a grill. Frankie knew it was her stolen moment to eat a quick bite and catch her breath as service shifted from breakfast to lunch. Not much would change, just the adding of a few additional menu items to scratch the midday itch. BLTs. Sausage wraps. Biscuits were always available no matter what time of day. But she preferred to stay in the breakfast lane as much as possible.

"Yep, let me try a little of that new strawberry jam we ordered. See if we can live with it."

He shrugged. "I'll put it on the plate, but it's no better than the last stuff in a jar Rothstein had shipped in." She deflated, still not understanding why they couldn't make the jam fresh, in-house, the way they did the biscuits. The customers would go crazy for the recipe Frankie had perfected. Clementine didn't have a ton of skills in life, but understanding what menu items their regulars would love and pay more for was definitely one of them. Plus, the tourists in town for wine tasting rarely cared about price point. It's what people did on vacation, spend money.

"I have no idea why he won't listen to my suggestions. He's never here. He has no idea about this place and what makes it work." She was interrupted when the bell chimed and Stephen Finch, the handsomest gay cowboy in the land, strode up to her counter. He and his husband lived on the Moon and Stars Ranch just outside of town, growing vegetables and taking care of a dozen or so rescue dogs until they could find them loving homes. Good folks. Stephen grinned and ambled her way, flashing his movie star smile. He had no hat with him today, but he did have on the boots, and that made her grin.

"Hey, Clementine," Stephen said. "I'm in need of food."

"I figured as much, as you've presented yourself at my counter. I'm a detective these days."

"Very astute."

"I thought you'd think so." She grabbed a white sack, popped it open, and waited for Stephen's order so she could pass it back to Frankie. It was all for show because she already knew what he'd ask for. He and Monty liked the classic butter biscuits. Everyone did. They'd take a half dozen and top it off with an order of candied maple bacon for Stephen and an order of jalapeño bacon for Monty. Two to-go cinnamon coffees with extra sugars. She knew this, yet she waited. Four seconds later, Stephen delivered that exact order. Clementine grinned and called it back to Frankie, reaffirming that she knew her customers.

"Busy today?" Stephen asked.

"We had a pretty good run this morning. People will circle around again come lunchtime for their BLTs and butter biscuits with ham and honey mustard. Those go fast."

"Ever thought of staying open for dinner service?"

Clementine didn't hesitate and shook her head. "No, no. We're a breakfast place, and we know it. We kill at breakfast. We've done okay for lunch, but dinner just isn't our vibe."

"Gotta admire your fierce sense of breakfast culture."

Clementine kissed her fingers and placed them over her heart. "Breakfast is everything, Stephen. Don't forget it." She was being lighthearted but also meant it very much. She loved everything about the early morning and the delicious food that came with it.

Frankie hit the bell and handed over two full white sacks that smelled like heaven on earth. Clementine took a deep inhale as she handed them over to Stephen.

"See you sooner than I'd like to admit," he said and tipped the hat he wasn't wearing. She tipped hers back, grinned knowingly, and accepted her brunch on a hot plate from Frankie. He was right. The jam was just the same as all the others. Boring. Lackluster. Forgettable. It was a total shame to have passion for her job, know all the right moves to make, and not have the power to exercise them. She shook her head and popped the last bite of her biscuit. What she wouldn't give to make this place her own. She'd reorganize the menu, slimming some of the excess items that rarely got attention, change the paint color inside, and most importantly, bring in more local, fresh ingredients. That was most important to a place like this. Mr. Rothstein wouldn't budge on any of those requests, yet he had no idea about the day-to-day operations and how her suggestions would truly benefit the café. She couldn't imagine owning a place as wonderful as the Biscuit and taking so little interest in its success and growth.

"Verdict?" Frankie asked.

"Uninspired and mediocre."

He leaned against the counter. "Like my ex who left me for my brother on Valentine's Day in 2003. I hated 2003."

"Yeah. Still sorry about that year. Ouch, right?"

"Not as sorry as my brother was in the long run. She was a piece of work. Ripped his heart right out, and I enjoyed every minute of it."

She laughed at Frankie's dark enjoyment of the situation, though they both knew he was just being a clown. The guy had a huge heart, just one of the reasons she loved working with him. In fact, she loved working with all of the Biscuit's employees. Most of the part-timers only stuck around for the short term, college students who'd go on to other things or cities, but they were all good people. Together they made a great team. No matter what the combination. She checked the clock and switched to lunch prep, already feeling energized after her caloric refuel.

The door dinged, and she called out, "Welcome to the Biscuit. Be right with you."

"No problem," a smooth, even voice said. Clem knew it well and went still. Goose bumps appeared on her skin. She turned around, and sure enough, just as her body had predicted, there stood Madison LeGrange, her high school crush who had been back in town for almost a year now. Still with the same beautiful curls a third of the way down her back. Light brown with blond highlights most likely from the sun. There were those same big blue eyes that had a tendency to sparkle when she was happy. Madison was gorgeous, and Clementine had always thought so. She had tried not to get caught staring at her in the classes they'd shared in high school. Beyond that? She was brilliant, and that's the part that really did Clem in. She remembered dreamily watching eleventh grade Madison in calculus class, constantly explaining the assignment to the other students with confidence and patience that she longed for. Madison was always so far ahead of everyone else in class, but friendly enough to help out. However, Clementine could count on one hand the exchanges they'd had that had lasted over five minutes. Madison made her nervous. Stripped of her conversation skills. Always made her cheeks feel warm. All of those things were in effect in this moment, making Clem feel fifteen years old and awkward all over again. Never failed.

She tucked a strand of her hair behind one ear and tried to jumpstart her voice with a clearing of her throat. It worked. "What can I get for you?" She forgot to smile and amended the oversight, which probably came off as fake and weird. She'd work on it.

Madison stared at the menu hanging over the counter. "How about a chive biscuit with jam and a medium cinnamon coffee to go?"

"Perfect. That'll be just a moment." She rang Madison up and poured the coffee she'd just brewed ten minutes ago, reminding herself to breathe normally, even if Madison's blue eyes appeared even more blue because of the color of her shirt.

"Busy morning?"

Okay, apparently, they were going to chat. No problem. "It was. We ran out of bikes …bacon"—she shook her head—"*biscuits*, I mean." What in the world? "Not forever or anything. We have them *now*. Just didn't have any for about twelve minutes. Just a hiccup."

Madison grinned widely. "You're lucky there was no riot. This town is obsessed."

"Not going to complain about that." This was going better. See? She could be a person. Kind of.

Madison leaned in. "Confession. This place is my favorite spot in town. I don't make it in here enough, and when I do, it just reminds me to come more."

"I'd love that." She closed her eyes. "*We'd* love it. The business would. Because the money helps. To keep us going." So much for being a normal human. She'd settle for awkward at best.

Madison frowned and even that was a beautiful sight to see. "This place isn't in trouble, is it?"

"No. No." She shook her head, put her hand on her forehead,

and closed her eyes briefly. "Doing well. In the black for years now, according to Mr. Rothstein. I don't think he'd mind me saying so."

"Oh, good." Madison's expression relaxed. She had a slight tan even in autumn, likely from tending to the vines at Tangle Valley. "In that case, I feel better. Can't imagine life without the Biscuit, ya know? It's part of our DNA around here."

"You definitely won't have to." Frankie handed her order over the large counter that separated the kitchen from the restaurant, and Clem presented it to Madison along with her coffee. "Hot and fresh. Enjoy."

Madison held up the bag and grinned. "Thanks, Clementine. Good to see you." She'd only taken a few steps when she glanced back over her shoulder. "I don't know if you're doing something different with your hair, but it's really cute today. Thought you should know." She didn't wait for a reply, which was good because it took Clem a moment to absorb the compliment. Her hand then moved to her hair, which had been cut, just days before, to her shoulders. No one had mentioned the slightly shorter look, which was no big deal, but to have Madison say so now was...surprising. Not unwelcome. A little jarring. It made her step a little lighter and the day feel a little easier, though, being noticed that way.

By three p.m., when she'd locked up for the day and strolled behind the restaurant to her car, a white Honda Civic she'd bought used five years prior, she grinned to herself because it had been a good one. Service had been smooth, the food Frankie turned out was wonderful as always, and she'd enjoyed her time with the customers. The highlight had definitely been the kind exchange with Madison, however. What a silly person she was to place such focus on a minor moment in the scheme of life, but here she was. She drove through town center, glimpsing the familiar businesses as they passed outside her window. The salon, a few sandwich shops, Pizzamino's, and—of course—the handful of tasting rooms set up for visitors to sample the local wines all in one swoop.

Next, she passed through the cute little subdivision made up of one-story homes all in a row, set apart from the farmlands and vineyards that flanked the town on all sides. She used to imagine her family living in one of those little houses growing up, so quaint and pretty. Many of her classmates had, and she'd secretly envied them. The mobile home park where she'd grown up instead was two and a half miles north.

Nearly three from the elementary school and three and a half from her high school. Clementine knew the hilly walk well. These days, she avoided the stretch of road she used to call home altogether. The place dredged up too many unpleasant memories too heavy to shake. She'd grown up poor, yes, but there had been worse for her to contend with at home.

She drove on, taking in the scenery and reflecting on the town's divide, only noticeable to people like her. Whisper Wall was mainly made up of middle-class farmers, grape growers, wine industry folks, and small business owners. Laborers tended to live on the outskirts. Most of those homes lay in the smaller school district located several miles north of Whisper Wall, but not Clementine's. She'd gone to school with the kids who lived in town, town kids as she called them, and had never felt like more of an outsider. Good times.

She took a right on Sunburst Lane instead and followed it to her nondescript apartment complex with the generic name Windmill Run, though neither the sign nor decor had anything to do with windmills in the slightest. Red brick adorned the six three-story buildings, all identical in style and structure. Tan doors and black iron staircases that never quite seemed to go together accentuated the outside. Clementine lived on the second floor in a two-bedroom apartment she shared with her sidekick, Toast, an ambitious white and brown cat with an affinity for playing hockey in the kitchen with oranges. He'd actually gotten quite good at ball control, batting the orange between his paws like a professional, weaving around corners and cabinets. Though she was his only audience, he seemed to appreciate her cheers of encouragement. Yep. She and Toast, making their way in the big, bad world together.

"Why are you looking at me like that?" she asked her cat as she perused her mail. He quirked his head from his spot on the back of her comfy recliner. "Cat got your tongue?" She smiled to herself because that one never got old. "It's not dinnertime yet, no matter how much you will it." Toast hopped down and trotted off into the bedroom, having been refused what he wanted, petty little guy.

Clementine spent that evening at her kitchen table, knocking out her monthly bills, pleased to see that, once again, she had a little bit left over to set aside. "Nice," she murmured, checking her savings account, which got a tad bigger each month. She had big plans and wasn't one to get discouraged if it took her a while to get there. If she kept going, she'd eventually have enough to make a solid offer to Mr. Rothstein on the Bacon and Biscuit. Every year, he became increasingly more distant and hands-off, leaving the day-to-day running of the business to her. Since the restaurant didn't interest him, maybe he'd accept her offer and move on to other things. Her plan was to put down a good portion of up-front money and hope he'd finance the rest over the next few years. If not, there was always a bank loan. She'd made steady progress already, and if she kept her spending down, she'd continue to make strides. It was becoming more and more of an actual possibility that she could do this.

With a full and hopeful heart, she read a little of her book before bed and turned in for the night. No one to say good night to or check in with, but that was okay. Clementine kept to herself for the most part and didn't mind her quiet life. She had her customers, her cat, her apartment, and maybe one day a piece of something bigger, her own business. As she drifted off to sleep, it was with the hint of a smile tugging at her lips. The future was bright.

❖

Tick-tock. Tick-tock. Tick-tock. Madison winced. The miniature mouse clock that topped the desk of her financial advisor was the loudest she'd ever heard. She sat in Oscar Mims's office alone while he tended to things before their one p.m. meeting. What kinds of things? She wasn't exactly sure, but surely paper shuffling and coffee stirring were among them. *Tick-tock. Tick-tock.* She blinked at the annoying mouse, confused because weren't mice known to be quiet?

"Sorry about that," Oscar said, shutting the door behind him with a thud.

"Not a problem. Me and this mouse were getting to know each other."

"Annoying damn thing. I'd toss it, but my eight-year-old gave it to me for Father's Day, and I'd feel like the worst kind of human if I did."

Madison smiled. "So here you sit, tortured daily by a timekeeping mouse."

He nodded as if that understanding hit him hard. "I've never thought of it that way. Tortured."

"Well, I didn't mean to upset you." Madison winced. She'd meant the quip to be lighthearted, but sometimes she was a little too matter-of-fact. Something she was working on. Not everyone had her thick skin. Mouse guy probably just wanted to run his numbers and go home to his family for pork chops and macaroni, and now she'd upended his sense of peace.

"No. I'm just noticing it more now." A pause. *Tick-tock. Tick-tock.* His eyes went wide.

"Yeah. Me, too. Pretty impressive, though. The gusto."

He grabbed the mouse, tossed it into his drawer, and slammed it away, muffling the sound and looking pleased with himself. He exhaled, relieved. "Now, on to business."

Oh, she'd enjoyed that. "Onward."

He clicked around on his laptop, studied the screen, and looked up at her. "You have some extra funds, I see. Not doing much of anything for you."

"Yes. My income has picked up quite a bit in the past three years because of the consulting work I've done. I don't have much of a life, and not much time to travel, so the money is just sitting there. Rarely spent. I'd like to do something with it."

"Exactly." He smiled. "Why not put it to work for you? My advice is diversification." He turned his laptop around to a rather tepid PowerPoint presentation that eventually caused her eyes to glaze over as he spoke, making her long for the tick-tock of that pesky mouse. Yes, there were high risk funds and low risk funds and mutual funds and stocks and CDs and bonds, and she wasn't sure she had a strong opinion about any of them.

"What about something local?" she asked finally. "Is there any way for me to invest in something that, I don't know, has meaning to me?"

"Well, of course." He sat back in his chair. "That's the kind of diversification I'm talking about. A portion here, another there."

She liked the sound of that. If he wanted her to mix it up, then that's what she would do. "Why don't you handle all of the on-paper stuff and I'll look into something a little more personal. Something I can see."

He gestured to his computer with a sparkle in his eyes. "Are we talking high-risk investment?"

"I'm not feeling the lucky vibe. Let's stick with moderate, Oscar."
His joy was snuffed out like a tiki torch at the end of a luau. He
nodded. "Moderate it is. Let's go over what that means."

She sighed and settled in for more information, mentally drifting
back to Tangle Valley and her work there as Oscar droned on. She
needed to get started on a juice sample to test the sugar levels of the
grapes before harvest and crunch those numbers along with the pH
readings. They were so close to picking. That much she could already
tell just by the way the fruit hung on the vine.

"And if you're good with all that, we just need to sign some
paperwork."

She perked up and accepted the pen, proud of herself for being
responsible and putting her bored money to work. Her parents would
approve. She'd have to give them a call in Florida and let them know,
surely disturbing their golf addiction brought on by retirement.

"And as you've requested, I've set aside a decent sized portion
for whatever local donation or project you might come across in the
coming year."

She slipped her messenger bag onto her shoulder. "Thanks for all
your help today. I apologize for wrecking your relationship with your
clock. I actually feel pretty bad about that."

"Bygones," he said.

Madison bid him farewell, hopped in her blue truck with the white
stripe, and drove herself back to Tangle Valley, not even stopping to
take in the gorgeous view of the property at the top of the hill on her
way in. There was too much to do to ogle. She spent the rest of the
afternoon gathering grapes for her sample, selecting fruit from every
eighth vine to get a good variety, crushing the grapes by hand when
she was finished, and using a hydrometer to calculate the sugars. This
part always got her fur up. Excitement pooled in her midsection where
she tended to carry her emotions. A quick calculation told her exactly
what she wanted to know and had already predicted. They would likely
be picking the pinot next week. For her, it would be like Christmas
morning with a lot of work tacked on. Madison scrunched her shoulders
with anticipation, excitement, and nostalgia. She remembered harvest
times at Tangle Valley from when she was a kid, following Jack Wilder
around his vineyard like a pesky puppy, soaking up most anything he

said to anyone, taking actual notes that she had saved in her keepsake trunk. Now, here she was, head winemaker, ready to tackle the pinot, the crown jewel of the vineyard.

"You're smiling like a lunatic."

She didn't even look up from her notepad where she jotted the numbers she'd just collected. She knew Joey's voice. "The grapes are calling out to me. *Madison! Madison!* the grapes say. *See you soon.*"

Joey joined her at the long tall table at the back of the barrel room. "So we're on track?"

"Next week should do it. I'll let your uncle Bobby know to schedule the pickers."

"Good. He's lost in his own lusty love land lately."

Madison closed her notebook and looked up. "Lusty Love Land should already be a theme park. How is it not? I'd buy a ticket."

"I'd get a season pass," Joey said. "Missed opportunity right there. Regardless, Bobby is already there. He asked a guy to look in on the irrigation system and totally spaced. Stood him up. Found out later, he had taken Loretta to breakfast." Madison grinned, loving this story. Bobby and Loretta had worked together at Tangle Valley for decades and shocked them all earlier in the year when it was revealed they were caught up in a secret affair. Even more shocking, it had blossomed into love. "Last week, he left the fans on overnight when we didn't need them."

Madison frowned. "Yeah, I didn't love that part."

"He's gone on Loretta, and it shows. Emphasis on *gone.*"

"Those two are so unlikely, yet so perfect—it's film-worthy."

Joey raised a finger. "That's why I forgive him. The cute is not lost. I've wrangled the cute and keep it in my back pocket for when I want to wring his Uncle-Bobby-neck. It's the only thing that saves him."

"Well, at least you're self-aware."

"I appreciate you noticing," Joey said with her serious face on. "But we are offtrack."

"That's normal."

"I'm here to finish our conversation from last night before the adorable bunny slippers interrupted us."

Madison sighed. That meant Joey wanted to talk about her state of mind. "If you're checking in on me, I'm fine. Truly."

"You're fine. Your arms, your legs, your face. But how's your heart?"

Madison gave proper weight to the question, pleased with the answer. "I think time has revealed a lot. I wasn't back in love with Gabriella. I just went into this confused mode when I saw her falling for someone else, and instead of recognizing that I was working through this new transition, I think I mislabeled what I was feeling." She shook her head. "Thank God she saw things clearly because we never would have worked. Chalk the whole thing up to confusion and nothing more. She and Ryan are definitely meant to be. Watching them these past six months…" She shook her head. "No one is better suited."

Joey raised an eyebrow in challenge.

She laughed. "Except you and Becca. Clearly a tie between two perfect couples."

"Nice save." Joey exhaled, slow and measured. "About the rest, I was hoping you'd say that. That's kind of what I assumed was happening all along, but you're the only one with access to your brain."

"It's a good brain, too. Shame you don't have that key."

"I'd have paid a lot of money for it in twelfth-grade physics." Joey let her hand trail along the table as she walked. "Come by the tasting room for a glass when you finish up. We can celebrate the grown-up grapes, make them little graduation caps."

Madison grinned. "They'd be so honored." A pause. "And JoJo?"

"Yep?" Joey's blue eyes sparkled expectedly.

"Thanks for checking in on me. And for, you know, being my person or whatever." God, she felt uncomfortable.

"Are you being sentimental right now?"

"Definitely not."

Joey placed the tip of her index finger on her cheek. "I seem to remember someone letting me bawl my eyes out in their lap not too long ago, so I think that goes both ways."

"That it does," Madison said with a grin. "I just don't see that ever happening the other way around. Not really my style."

"Mm-hmm," Joey said, rolled her eyes, and headed out.

Madison finished her work, and just after five made her way to the tasting room, modern and gorgeous, with a towering ceiling. Gabriella was already seated at a table across from the bar, sipping a glass of dolcetto, her favorite. Joey didn't even ask and poured

Madison a glass of their current award-winning pinot noir. They knew each other well.

"Well, look who's ventured from the wine cave." That was Gabriella's recent nickname for the barrel room.

Madison looked around expectantly. "I'm here for the news of the day."

"A Biddy in training," Joey said and joined them with a glass of the pinot for herself. "I can help. Gabriella here is in dire straits about next weekend's dinner special at Tangled." The twelve-table restaurant was open for dinner service six days a week with lunch added in on the weekend. As executive chef, Gabriella deserved all the credit for the restaurant's outlandish success. You had to plan ahead to eat there, making reservations at least a week or two in advance. Joey shook her head. "It's high food drama."

"Tuscan rubbed ribeye or apple smoked pork chop," Gabriella said, with absolute anguish in her eyes. You'd think they were deciding the fate of a patient on the operating room table.

Madison decided to logic her. "What do people gush about more?"

"The pork," Gabriella said. "They practically lick the sauce off the plate."

"I think we have our answer. I'm a wizard."

"You do cut through to the important stuff," Gabriella said. She swiveled to Joey. "Any news from the tasting world?" Joey loved her job managing the tasting room alongside Loretta and their staff of part-timers. She was the perfect ambassador for Tangle Valley wines and a wonderful tasting guide, given her girl-next-door charm and wine knowledge all wrapped up in one human. People loved shooting the breeze with her as they sampled.

"I did pick up an interesting tidbit from Thelma, who stopped by to grab a bite from the food truck, who heard the tidbit from Maude, who heard from Birdie."

"Oh, wow," Gabriella said. "That's a Biddy trifecta right there."

"I thought so, too. The operation is top-notch. Anyway, she says that the Rothsteins have put their house on the market."

Madison squinted. "That's odd. Their place is perfect. A fantastic view of the hillside. Why would they move?"

Joey sipped her wine. "Exactly my question. Apparently, Mrs.

Rothstein's mother isn't in the best shape, and they're heading back east permanently."

"Whoa. They're a Whisper Wall fixture." Madison shook her head. "They're not closing the Biscuit, are they?"

Gabriella sat up straighter. "Well, that can't happen. I need the Biscuit."

Joey frowned. "We all do. I wish I could tell you more."

Madison placed a finger straight down on the table. "Put your ear to the ground, Wilder. We need the details."

Joey offered a salute. "I'll see what I can find out. How did your finance thing go?"

"Fine. There was an annoying mouse clock, but by the end we decided I would invest in some moderately risky funds Oscar picked out for me, and I set aside money to invest in something more meaningful." Gabriella smacked her arm. Hard. "Ow. Why would you haul off and hit me?"

"Because it's all coming together." Her eyes were huge. She tapped her temple and made an explosion gesture that had Madison intrigued. "You buy the Biscuit."

She blinked and laughed. "Because that makes sense."

Gabriella pressed on, her excitement undeterred. "It's perfect. You want to invest in something that's meaningful. What's more meaningful than everyone's favorite morning spot? You love the Biscuit."

"And we want to save it," Joey said, jumping in. "If the Biscuit is closing, you have to buy it. Decided." Joey and Gabriella clinked glasses as Madison balked.

"No, no, no," she said calmly. "I won't be buying a café. Are you insane? I have zero experience with running a restaurant and no time to learn or give to the place. I work *here*."

Gabriella shrugged. "You don't see Mr. Rothstein behind the counter, do you? That's why you hire amazing people like Clementine Monroe. Because they know what they're doing and will take your business to amazing heights."

Madison laughed and shook her head. "Not gonna happen. Plus, the Rothsteins might hold on to the place and run it from afar."

Still, when Madison ran into the Rothsteins on the cereal aisle two days later, she couldn't help but inquire, after a few pleasantries.

They'd been friends of her parents back in the day, and she felt comfortable enough to ask the question. "Is it true you two are moving out of Whisper Wall?" Madison asked as she made a grab for Frosted Flakes. "We'll be so sad to lose you."

"We'll miss your wine," Mrs. Rothstein said, adjusting the vegetables in her cart to make room for the giant handful of cereal boxes Mr. Rothstein had just dumped haphazardly inside. "But it's true. We'll be leaving for our new life in New Hampshire in under a month."

"That's so fast. What about the café? I might secretly have a personal interest in protecting my butter biscuit habit."

Mr. Rothstein chuckled quietly, always a low-key guy. "You and half the town. I've put out some quiet feelers to see if anyone might want the place. If that doesn't work, I'll make a larger go of it and officially put it on the market."

"Oh, wow. So it's for sale?"

He nodded. "If there aren't any takers, I'd hate to close up shop, but it might just fall that way. Let me know if you know of someone."

"Tell them we're in a hurry," Mrs. Rothstein tossed in.

"I think I do know of someone."

Mr. Rothstein's eyebrows rose, and Mrs. Rothstein leaned in. "Who would that be?" he asked.

"Maybe me? I'd love to learn more about what you're asking." Madison couldn't believe the words had just left her lips. Was she honestly doing this right now? The truth was she hadn't been able to shake the notion of snatching up the place ever since her conversation with her friends in the tasting room. It was insane and impetuous, but also maybe not.

The Rothsteins exchanged a look. "Maybe we should sit down and have a conversation," Mr. Rothstein said. "What do you say?"

"A little conversation can't hurt, right?" Madison said, feeling uneasy but also weirdly excited. This actually felt like a realistic prospect now that she'd expressed interest out loud. And why not? She had the funds just sitting there, and she couldn't let the Biscuit just fold up and lock its doors. The staff was amazing. The place was incredibly popular with the community. All things considered, this was at least an opportunity worth exploring, even if its scope was larger than she'd originally planned for herself.

Honestly, what did she have to lose?

CHAPTER TWO

Clementine's hands were shaking. She'd heard the news first from Brenda Anne at the Nifty Nickel gift shop. She didn't quite believe it. Not fully. Next, Patsy at Patsy's Boot and Scoot mentioned she'd also heard about the Rothsteins selling. That made the whole thing feel a little more real. Finally, that morning, Clementine heard the rumor again, this time from all four Biddies, who nodded wholeheartedly, confirming it all. Oh yes, Rothstein was moving and the Biscuit was on the market.

"Oh yes. It's quite true," Maude said, around a bite of her warm croissant. Clementine refreshed their coffees and nodded along. They didn't offer table service at the Biscuit, but she liked going out of her way for the regulars to make their time at the café a little more comfortable. "No question. Times are a-changing, and the Biscuit is no different. Now we have that chain hotel, and we're losing our gems one by one."

"I don't think we'll lose this place," Thelma said, frowning. "Will we? I couldn't bear it."

Janet raised a nervous finger. "I hope it stays and that the new owners don't change much. I like our table and our daily breakfasts. What if they turn it into one of those hipster coffee shops with couches and cigarettes in front of the shop. Will I have to take up smoking?"

"Maybe," Birdie said, also looking worried. She was, by far, the sweetest of the Biddies.

"No one is picking up a nicotine habit." Clementine grinned, her spirits taking flight at the firm confirmation from the four people in town who knew everything. "I have a strong feeling that the Biscuit is sticking around, you guys, and holding on to its best features and improving its weaker ones." She winked at them on a high. "Just you wait."

It was actually happening. She sashayed her way back behind the counter, her mind racing in the best sense. As she slid the newest batch of gorgeous, plump biscuits out of the oven, she took a moment to sort through all her thoughts, tame them into some sort of order. This was all happening way sooner than she'd ever imagined, but that didn't mean she couldn't make her plans work. She'd need to get in touch with the bank to get her loan application moving in case Rothstein wasn't able to finance her beyond the money she had to put down, but she'd done lots of research on the process and felt confident that with her work history at the Biscuit and in-depth knowledge of the business, coupled with a decent down payment, they would back her. They had to, right? She couldn't entertain any other outcome. Next, she would need to let Mr. Rothstein know that she was all in. Honestly, it surprised her that he hadn't notified *her*, of all people, before anyone else. She was the manager, and this would affect his employees most, but honestly, the way Rothstein did business had never made much sense to Clementine.

"What are you grinning about?" Frankie asked.

"I heard some interesting news, and it has just been confirmed." She eased the sheet of biscuits onto the cooling rack, winking at them as a welcome-to-the-world gesture. Something she did with each and every item out of the oven. Everything at the Biscuit tasted better when made with love. She whirled around. "Ready for this? Rothstein is selling."

"Get the hell out." His eyes went wide. "You gonna do it?"

She shrugged, unable to contain her smile. "It's now or never." She made a *yikes* face and refrained from pinching herself.

He shook his head in amazement. "Clem, with you making the decisions and me on this grill, this place can be everything we've talked about. Local, fresh, fantastic food."

She had goose bumps. "It's so close." She gave herself an uncharacteristic hug of reassurance. "Frankie, I've never owned anything. Do you understand that? And that's about to change."

He knocked her one on the shoulder. "Can't think of anyone more deserving. Hell, this place is entirely you anyway. You give it the heart, and everyone knows it."

"Well, I couldn't do it without my team backing me, and you're my number one. Sorry I'm getting all sappy. It's a big day."

"I can take it." He beamed right along with her.

That afternoon, she filled out all the necessary online paperwork and received a call of confirmation from the bank that she'd hear back from them soon. "What are my chances, do you think?" she asked Minerva, the friendly voice on the phone.

"The application doesn't look too shabby. Good credit and a solid work history with the establishment. Plus, our officers root for small businesses." Clementine grinned, trying not to get too excited. "It's not a tiny amount, though."

She swallowed, nerves creeping in. "No. That part I get."

"We'll review the application and all the materials you provided us and be in touch with probably a few follow-ups."

"I appreciate that."

That night, Clementine took a deep breath and left a voice mail for Mr. Rothstein to call her, indicating her interest in purchasing the café but saving the crux of her pitch for their discussion. She would make her case and submit her formal offer, her speech all prepared. She'd practiced it eight times in her kitchen with Toast as her mildly bored audience of one. As for her offer, she'd researched the hell out of what a place like the Biscuit would go for in Whisper Wall by crunching their monthly intake and future projected sales and felt that her offer was more than fair. Rothstein was smart. He would see that.

She'd sat by the phone all night, but the call never came. Sleep hadn't come easy with something so exciting hanging in the balance. She was eager to make it real. The next morning, she was surprised to see Rothstein enter the shop with a big smile on his face. Well, that certainly boded well. She geared up, wiping her hands on a nearby towel and standing up straight, ready to do this. "Good morning, Mr. Rothstein," she said, matching his grin.

This was it. She pressed her hands against her apron and smoothed it down, reminding herself of all of her talking points.

"Morning, Clem. Smells amazing as always. Can I steal a hot scallion biscuit and medium coffee?" No mention of her phone call. Her stomach did about eighteen somersaults. She ordered it to relax.

"Easy enough," she said. She put together his order and stole a glance at him as he waited. "Did you happen to get my voice mail last night about the café? I thought maybe that's why you stopped by."

"I did. It's admirable you're so passionate about the place. But I'm afraid it's already sold."

She froze and her skin prickled. The information hadn't quite made it all the way into her brain because it didn't compute. His words made no sense. An overwhelming feeling of dread descended, and her limbs felt numb. She turned to him, his coffee cup only half poured, the carafe suspended in the air. "Sold?" Her eyebrows drew in and everything moved slow, like they were trudging through mud on a hot day.

"Yes!" He continued to beam, clearly having a great day. "Very unexpected, but I signed the paperwork yesterday with my attorney. Meant to talk to you about it sooner, Clementine, truly, but it's just been a whirlwind. Moving across country after thirty years is not something I recommend."

"Right." She blinked several times, trying to force her brain to think clearly. This couldn't be true. What was she going to do now? Two minutes ago, she had her dream right there in her grasp, and now it had been cruelly snatched from her. She felt heavy, like a stone sinking slowly to the bottom of the lake.

Rothstein nodded toward the half-poured cup in her hand, and Clementine swallowed, attempting to regain functionality, her footing. Finally, she located the will to finish the pour and handed him his coffee with a shaky hand. "I was surprised to hear you'd be interested, though. That'd be a big leap for someone like you. Luckily, you're off the hook."

Her gaze fell to the counter where it remained. She remembered back to her childhood and how staring at the ground had been her crutch on those days in school when she just wanted to remain invisible, when the town kids were making plans for parties she often wasn't invited to, talking about their summer camps she could never afford, or enumerating the details of the brand new pair of jeans their mom had bought for them. The worst. Clementine would drop her head and try to shrink herself to as small as possible, a habit that, until this moment, she thought she'd broken. "I didn't want to be off the hook," she said quietly, raising her gaze.

"What's that?"

WHAT A TANGLED WEB

She touched the cool granite countertop, and the sensation helped anchor her. She'd lost her gumption, her grit. She was that loser kid again and she couldn't shake it. "Nothing."

"Biscuits are great today," he said around a hearty mouthful. "You make these?" He held the second half up in reverence.

She nodded.

"You folks amaze me," he said, talking with his mouth open. "I owe you all for making this place what it's become. Do you know how many people begged me not to close when news got out? Too damn many to count. That's a testament to you and your staff."

"Thank you, Mr. Rothstein. Who is it?"

"Who is what?" He squinted, still mauling his breakfast as crumbs fell onto the counter and his shirt.

"Who bought the Biscuit?"

"Oh, that Tangle Valley woman who does the wine out there. Madison LeGrange. Her dad was a golf buddy of mine. She's smart as a whip. Not to worry."

For the second time in five minutes, Clementine's world skidded to a halt. Why? How? It made no sense that Madison would have any interest in a small business like this one. She had her hands full with her job at Tangle Valley, with all of her magazine articles and guest appearances at vineyards across the West Coast. She was well-known in these parts. Clementine had heard folks talking all about her for years now. "I don't understand. Madison makes wine."

He shrugged. "Wants to branch out, I guess. I don't think she'll be in your hair too much."

That's right. She'd be reporting to Madison now. She worked for *Madison*. The idea was just as surreal as it was awful. Clementine felt like all her hopes and dreams had been shriveled into an unattractive ball and slam-dunked into the wastebasket of life.

She swallowed the burst of emotion. Nothing ever changed. Nothing she did, no amount of hard work, would ever propel her forward. She was Clementine Monroe, stuck, and always would be.

She eyed Mr. Rothstein. "So, the papers are already signed? This place is all Madison's?"

"That's right," he told her.

She shifted her weight and leveled a stare. "Then that will be three dollars and seventy-nine cents for your breakfast."

❖

Madison hadn't told many people that she'd gone rogue and bought the Bacon and Biscuit because honestly? She hadn't fully broken the news to herself yet. Half excited, half terrified of what she'd gotten herself into, she did what she always did and walked around her cottage in circles as she worked through her emotions. Walking in circles and talking out loud to herself was literally the only way to solve any and all problems.

"You now own a café and have zero experience with food preparation or small business ownership. On the flip side, you're a quick study and can read a few books that will help get you through the first six months." She paused as she took the corner around her kitchen island. "Unfortunately, you have very little time on your hands to devote to the business because your hours here are already crazy." She held up a finger to argue with herself. "But Mr. Rothstein said that it's a business that runs itself for the most part. You just need to check in here and there. Think of this as a new adventure." She shook her head. "Nope. Level with yourself. You've done this because you're in some weird transition period in your life, kicked off by the Gabriella confusion, and now you're looking a little too closely at your purpose on Earth." She tilted her head side to side. "That part is true. But the reason for the huge decision doesn't have to influence its outcome. This could be a really great thing. Give it a chance before you beat yourself up too much for taking the leap." She nodded decisively and popped a salt and vinegar almond from the dish on the counter. Talking out loud worked better with snacks. She popped another. "You're gonna be okay. Just know what you know, and admit to what you don't." Then she did some more circle walking for good measure. There could never be too much circle walking.

The next day, she arrived at Gabriella's cottage just down the path from her own. Gabriella didn't sleep there too often these days, opting for Ryan's gorgeous lake house instead, but she made a point to cook for her friends every once in a while, and Madison was not going to miss the chance for one of Gabriella's fabulous meals. The mouth-watering aromas hit her the second she walked into the cottage.

"We're not having Italian tonight!" Gabriella told her gleefully from the stove. It was odd for her to branch out from her niche, but then she'd been cooking at Tangled all week, which specialized in Italian cuisine.

"We're having Gouda stuffed burgers, truffle Parmesan fries, and an adorable salad with a red wine vinaigrette. Dessert is giant homemade chocolate chunk cookies with pistachio ice cream."

"Damn. I've come to the right place."

"We're blessed," Joey said with a dreamy sigh. She pointed at Gabriella. "I love her. I'm keeping her forever."

"Um, I'm sitting right here," Becca said, holding a glass of chardonnay.

Joey didn't hesitate. "Which is why I said it. You should know where I stand."

Gabriella beamed. "I'll keep you eating, JoJo. Becca can do the rest."

"God, if that isn't the best of both worlds," Joey said happily.

"So, I bought the Biscuit." Madison placed her hands on her hips and glanced around with a no-big-deal demeanor.

Gabriella's spatula went down to her side.

Becca blinked.

Joey squinted. "That's not a sentence you just say." A pause. "You don't just tell us you bought our favorite breakfast café without even filling us in on the fact that you were seriously considering it in the first place. You missed all the steps." Joey's mouth hung open.

"Definite flag on the business-buying play," Gabriella said, coming closer, her burgers sizzling in the pan behind her. "There was no notice. There was no discussion. Just wham-bam, have one of my biscuits. I own them now."

"Wham-bam is a good descriptor, I admit." Madison shook her head. "It all moved very fast, and I just followed my gut. It felt right, though, at least at the time. Something…" She gestured to the air. "Some unseen force was dragging me down this path, even though it makes no sense. And you guys know how I feel about sense and logic."

Joey didn't hesitate. "You worship at their altar."

"Like a little fact and figures disciple," Gabriella added.

"Exactly, so this is new for me. Please assume the appropriate shocked and impressed status."

The information seemed to settle over her friends. Becca was the first to speak again. "I, for one, am thrilled for you. I didn't even know the place was up for grabs, but kudos to you for seizing an interesting, exciting opportunity."

Joey looked over at her. "That's Becca for *this is so fucking cool*."

"She gets me," Becca said with a grin. "It is."

"What about you?" Madison asked Gabriella. "It was your suggestion, but you haven't weighed in."

"I'm simply surprised that I'm not the only one in the food business anymore. You're an honest to goodness biscuit pusher now."

"Honest to goodness," Madison said. "I probably need a business card or something."

"Or a hat," Gabriella said, for reasons Madison didn't follow. "Regardless, this is good news. The best." She dashed back to her burgers with an extra spring in her step. "What did Clementine say?"

"Oh." She paused. "I haven't talked with her about it yet."

"What?" Joey swiveled. "We've known Clementine for years. You didn't consult with her about the sale? Get her take on the state of the business from the inside, what it requires?"

She should have. It would have made a lot of sense. She realized that now but had gotten caught up in the moment and pressured herself to step out of her comfort zone and take a chance. "I'll drop by there tomorrow. Honestly, I'm really counting on her. Rothstein says she's the backbone of the place. The rock."

"Yeah, you might want to have a sit-down with her soon." Becca straightened. "She's likely going to be concerned about what kind of changes you might be planning to implement, what this transition of ownership means to employment or daily life at the café. If she's your rock, she needs to be in the loop ASAP."

"Listen to Corporate over there," Joey said, nodding. "Change management is her specialty."

"What have I missed?" Ryan Jacks asked, standing in the doorway. Gabriella's smile wattage doubled in her girlfriend's presence. Fresh from work, Ryan still wore her Level Up black polo and jeans. "Things ran late on the reno job on Marshall. Mold. They're not gonna be happy about the delay."

"Ouch," Gabriella said, accepting a kiss from Ryan and lingering. "Hi there."

"Hi," Ryan said, lost in a happy love-filled haze. Madison and

Joey exchanged a *Should we be here right now?* look because the temperature in the room had just risen noticeably.

"You bought the Biscuit," Ryan said, turning to Madison. "I'm absolutely floored and excited for you. Did not see that one coming."

"How did you know?" Madison asked.

"Clementine told me. She was a woman of few words when I stopped in for lunch earlier, but she had enough to mention that much."

Madison's eyes went wide. "Clementine knows."

Ryan nodded. "Half the town does by now. Thelma McDougall was in line behind me, probably cataloging the conversation. She dashed off before even ordering. I have a feeling the gossip was too good, and she didn't want to get scooped." Ryan shook her head. "It's like the Biddies are now competing with each other for the best dish."

"That's dangerous in so many ways," Madison mused.

"The War of the Biddies. Sounds like a PBS series I don't need to see. Or maybe I do." Joey sighed, conflicted. "Regardless, it means you need to talk to Clementine. And soon."

"I would advise that," Ryan said. "She didn't look...thrilled."

Madison frowned. "Really? I thought we'd work well together. She's a nice person who's great at her job. If not a little bit quiet. I figured we'd get past that part."

Joey shook her head. "Gotta disagree. Clementine's not quiet."

Gabriella looked up from her careful plating. "Agree. She can be a chatterbox at softball practice."

Madison thought back on her experiences with Clementine, which were always friendly but brief. "She says a few things and then dashes off whenever I see her. Huh."

"Hmm." Joey smothered a smile. "I can't imagine why that might be."

"She doesn't like me?" That part hurt. They'd never had a single harsh word.

Gabriella shook her head. "Negative."

"What aren't you saying?" Madison asked, trying to keep up. They were talking in code.

"Nothing at all." Joey glanced behind her. "And here come the most amazing looking burgers. Let's eat."

The conversation shifted to the food, the harvest timeline, and the giant tip a table had left for their server after what they called *a life-*

altering meal at Tangled. Now that Madison had articulated her new venture to her friends, it felt more real than ever. Nerves crept in, and since when did she get nervous about anything? For reasons unknown to her, this seemingly innocuous investment mattered.

A lot.

She just hoped she wouldn't screw it up.

CHAPTER THREE

It took Madison LeGrange, former crush and now full-blown enemy of the people, an entire twenty-four hours to show her face in the Bacon and Biscuit after purchasing it. She pushed open the glass door, and the small bell chimed, a crystal-clear sound that Clementine normally relished. It meant people, customers, success. Today, it just meant the person who'd swooped in and stolen her plans for the future had arrived. *Oh, goodie.* She thought about faking a smile but then discarded the idea. She simply didn't have it in her.

"Hey, Clem," Madison said, easing a strand of her light brown curls behind one ear. Not two days ago, Clementine would have internally swooned, and her morning would have shifted into the exciting and flustered lane at a glimpse of Madison and the fear that she'd say something dumb. Exactly none of that happened now. No, the sale of the Biscuit seemed to have muted Madison's entire effect on her. In fact, she bristled at the sight of the person who'd yanked this place away from her without warning.

"You bought the place," Clementine said flatly. Not her most friendly moment.

"Yes. You heard. It probably sounds a little, I don't know, out of left field." Madison winced and bit the inside of her lip, rebounding into a bright smile. "I'm truly excited, though. You have no idea."

"I definitely didn't see it coming," Clem said. Madison would have to be excited all on her own. "What can I do for you?"

She'd caught her off guard. Madison swallowed, and blinked, and glanced around as she tried to recover from the lack of a warm welcome.

It didn't take her long. "I was hoping we could schedule a time to meet formally. Go over everything. I've received a lot of paperwork from the Rothsteins, and I've pored over it before and after the sale." She shook her head ruefully and added a laugh. Clementine didn't join in. "I have a decent grasp on the financial day-to-day and I can even improve upon some of what I've seen."

"Oh, really?"

"Just some shortcuts to be more efficient. Take some of those practices online. Rothstein was a paper guy, and it's probably time to modernize. But I was hopeful you could give me some insight into how things happen here." She held up a hand. "I don't feel the need to interfere, but education is always a good thing, right?" Her blue eyes sparkled with hope.

Clementine rolled her lips in. "Of course. I work for you now."

"Oh. Okay, great. What about tomorrow afternoon after closing?"

Madison was aiming for rapport. She wasn't finding it in this exchange, which clearly had her on her heels, scrambling. It wasn't that Clementine enjoyed freezing Madison out. She had just lost her spark along with the business. Score another one for the rich kids of Whisper Wall. Always eight steps ahead of her. She sighed, understanding there was no way to escape this. The Biscuit closed at two p.m., and it took another forty-five minutes to an hour to reset everything for her early morning opening at six a.m. "Three o'clock would work."

"Great. I'll come here."

"Unless there's anything else, I'll see you then." Clementine stared at Madison expectantly.

"Oh," Madison said, as if a fun thought had just hit. "Maybe I'll take a butter biscuit for the road." She pulled out her wallet.

Clementine pointed at it. "No need. You already own it."

"Right," Madison said, giving her head a shake. "I'm going to have to get used to this."

"Yeah." Clementine didn't hesitate. "Trust me when I say we all are."

❖

"She hates me."

Joey blinked at Madison's declaration as she came around the bar in the tasting room. "She doesn't hate you. Clementine doesn't hate anyone. But most especially not you."

The place was closed down for the day, the last tour bus having lumbered off the property just moments ago. Madison had held her tongue until she and Joey were alone but had to talk to someone about her uncomfortable exchange with Clementine Monroe, someone who'd never been anything but cordial in the past. "Then I don't understand what happened, but my guess is that she is not at all happy that I bought the Biscuit. Maybe she thinks I'm underqualified."

Joey snagged three empty wineglasses from one of the tables and carried them back behind the bar. "I'm willing to bet she's surprised and working through the information. She's an internal processor. Like someone else around here I know."

"You don't think she was secretly involved in a clandestine affair with Mr. Rothstein, and she resents me taking his place?"

Joey nearly dropped the glasses as she set them down. "Wow. No. I most certainly don't think that's a possibility." She squinted at Madison, as if to say *Really?* "Maddie. Clem is gay. Surely you picked up on that."

"No, no, no. I really don't think she is." The possibility seemed so far-fetched. Not Clementine with the big blue eyes and gentle voice and sweet smile. Not that those things disqualified a person, it just didn't seem in the realm to Madison. "This town is small. I would know."

"Um, yes," Joey said, without hesitation. "I get that you haven't been back home for very long, but you've apparently missed a few things. Big ones."

"Get out of here." She balked. "Jo, you can't just go around making everyone gay just because they haven't publicly dated. You have no proof. Clementine just prefers to be on her own. She's always been that way. She rarely attended any events in high school, even. Think about it." She added a laugh to punctuate her point.

"There were other reasons for that, starting with her awful parents." Joey slid a strand of blond hair behind her ear and seemed to consider how to best explain herself. Madison waited. "Plus, I don't need proof, you see. I have intuition."

"Misfiring gaydar. That's what's happening." She shook her head. "You're a victim."

Joey sighed. "Clementine is an intensely private person. We can all agree. But when her gaze wanders? It's not to any man. I've seen it firsthand. In fact, she's seen me see it, and she's blushed and smiled and shrugged her shoulders at me when I have. I don't even think she's hiding it."

Madison stared at the marble of the bar, tracing its swirl. "Huh. No. Really? How have I not noticed this?"

Joey grinned. "No offense here, but there are charts and graphs on your refrigerator. That's your focus. Data. You lead less with your gut and more with your head." She scrunched up one eye. "Except when it comes to grapes. You know those guys backward and forward like you served in the Marines together. I don't know how to account for that exception, but it's true."

"Winemaking is a journey." She grinned. "So at least I have *some* intuition."

"When it comes to Clementine, there's something else you're missing." Joey paused as if she wasn't sure she should continue, and that just made Madison want her to all the more.

"What is it? Why are you arguing with yourself in your brain? Argue out loud instead."

"Listen. Brain arguing saves us a lot of uncomfortableness in life." She swallowed, still considering something. "What I was going to say is that you've also missed that Clementine has had a hard life."

"I haven't missed that part. She lived in that run-down trailer park, and her parents never came to any school functions."

Joey held up a hand. "Oh, then my mistake."

There was something Joey wasn't saying, but they were now wildly off topic. She attempted to reroute them, shaking her head. "So, if there's no lost love being ripped from her clutches, why does Clementine hate me?"

Joey got a sly look on her face. "I don't know, but I'm a woman of the people." She gestured to the empty room. "They come in here, they have a little taste, they order a glass, and they talk. Trust me to find out why the battle lines have been drawn?"

"You're officially hired."

Joey straightened, staring off into the distance. "A Biddy in training. That's me."

Madison went in for a fist bump that Joey happily reciprocated. She then returned to the barrel room to work on the picker schedule for harvest the following week when something crazy hit her. Clementine Monroe was gay. Madison looked up from her laptop in wonder. She flashed on Clementine in high school—young, pretty, but quiet. A loner. She'd found her confidence slowly at the Biscuit and come out of her shell, in her element. She'd blossomed quite a bit, too. Her soft blue eyes were wise, soulful.

Now that Madison knew what Joey seemed to, it was as if her entire perception shifted. She couldn't put the toothpaste back in the tube. She imagined Clementine's smile, and a little shiver moved through her, inspiring goose bumps to rise on her forearm. She laughed off the reaction and focused on the schedule. "The world is weird lately. That's all this is."

❖

"When's she getting here?" Frankie asked.

"We agreed on three," Clementine said and took off her apron. She changed it two to three times a day to stay presentable for counter service. Butter, batter, and grease looked better in the kitchen than on her clothing, and how she presented herself to her customers mattered. They were a small operation but ran a clean, tight ship, and she wanted the world to know. "It's still a little surreal." She slid into a booth in the now-closed dining room. "No more Rothstein to butt heads with."

"I'm not sorry about that part. But listen, it's okay to be pissed about the way it's all worked out," Frankie told her. "You got shafted and it's not okay."

She raised her eyebrows and dropped them. "Just means my destiny is something else, right? I can handle that. Just wish I knew what, because things seem to continue to just pass me by one at a time. Story of my life."

"I know. Life sucks in the worst way, just when you think it's getting good. But listen to me." His dark eyes carried an intensity that got her to focus. "You gotta hang in there till it hits the upswing again. It will." He joined her in the booth, sliding in across from her. "You were excited about the idea of taking over. Hell, I was just as pumped, and it wasn't even me buying the damn place." She offered a soft smile. Her buddy. Her partner in biscuits. Frankie had a way of calming her seas. She'd only had a handful of friends in her life, because it took a lot for Clementine to let people in. But Frankie had taken her walls down slowly and was a solid friend. She trusted him completely. "But here's the thing. Your little bit of wonderful is on the way. If anybody is due a little happiness, it's you. You heard it here." He sat back.

"I hope so."

"Hey, you want to come over this weekend? Jun is making her amazing pork dumplings that I wait all year for. Her family's recipe." Jun Zhen was Frankie's girlfriend of two years. In that time, she'd also become a friend to Clementine. A good listener and a gentle soul, who told it like it was. Clementine opened her mouth to decline but realized that maybe some downtime with Frankie and Jun might do her head some good. Distract her from all this.

"Yeah, if you think Jun wouldn't mind. I'd love to hang out."

"Nah, she'd love it. She's been pushing me to get you to come around for weeks. She's a fan of yours. Says you're good people. Wants me to hang out with more folks like you."

"Well, I am the most boring influence on the planet, so that makes sense." She couldn't disagree with Jun's goal. Frankie grew up much like she had, with not much money, from the stories he'd shared. He hadn't always surrounded himself with the best kinds of pals and wound up in juvenile detention at sixteen for robbing a convenience store with his buddies. He sadly went back to prison in his late twenties for stealing a Cadillac and crashing it into a ravine, after a police chase the city of North Adams, Massachusetts, still talked about. At least, according to Frankie. Once released, Frankie had escaped it all for a new start in Oregon and had done well for himself. He was dependable, kind, and steady.

"Not boring. You're just cautious," Frankie said. "Always have been since I've known you."

"Maybe that's my problem." Clementine drummed her fingers on the table, taking in the smell of bread and bacon from the morning, still lingering. She would never tire of their combination. "I should take bigger risks. Work on my adventurous side."

He frowned, and his dark hair, newly out of the bandana he wore to cook in, fell just shy of his brown eyes in a tousled fashion. "Gotta say no. As someone who's given that a shot and paid the damn price, the way you do things is way better. Trust me on that."

"Late-night reading with my cat it is."

He winced. "I didn't say that. Damn, that sounds pathetic."

"Hey. My life is not—"

The bell sounded, and they turned. Madison stood in the doorway with a wide smile like an excited kid on her first day of school. All she needed was a perfectly organized backpack, which she probably had in the car. Clementine was pretty sure the jealousy that sprang from her had to be visible in the air all around.

"I will never get used to how amazing this place smells when you first walk in the door. It really is magical, isn't it?"

"One of our most popular comments. Brings them back every time," Frankie said, pushing himself up and out of the booth. "Frankie. We've chatted here and there, but nice to meet you officially."

Madison happily extended a hand. "You're kind of a celebrity to me. Your skills on that grill are unmatched."

He smothered a proud grin. "I've had time to perfect my work."

Clementine eyed the two of them, taking in how eager they both were to please, to start their new relationship off on the right foot. She should try to find the will to do the same. "You want to stay for the meeting?" Clementine asked. She wouldn't mind having her second by her side. Reinforcements and all.

"Nah. I'll let you two talk about the important stuff. I just make food and like it that way." He grinned and hightailed it out of there, leaving Clementine alone in the dining room. With Madison. Her *boss*. Still so strange and surreal.

"I guess we should get started," Clementine said, once they were alone. She led them to a booth along the window.

"Great. Let me just…" Madison opened a notebook and took out a pen. She gestured to the page. "I'm old school. I'll transfer everything to digital later, but there's something about basic note taking, scratching things out, scribbling in the margins that helps me focus."

"Whatever works for you," Clementine said.

Madison smiled. Clementine smiled back.

"I guess I can start by going over the basics," Clementine said finally. "Our hours are six to two. Two to three employees work at a time. Frankie and I are both full-timers, and there are four other part-time employees who work on a rotating schedule that I draw up once every two weeks, depending upon their presubmitted schedules. That door revolves a lot, especially when we're hiring younger people who then go off to college. Frankie and I are the solids."

"I hear you. Can we back up?" Madison said, making a circular rewind gesture. "I feel like I skipped a big part of why I wanted to meet with you today, to explain my passion for the restaurant." She shook her head with a smile, marveling. "How much I love it, and how I already trust you and your staff."

"Oh," Clementine said. "Well, I appreciate the confidence." She didn't let the compliment land fully. She was still bristling and preferred to leave it that way.

"And I want to reassure you. It's not my goal to come in and make any big changes."

Clementine exhaled wearily. "Well, that's a shame because there are so many to be made."

Madison blinked. "Oh?" She clearly hadn't been expecting that.

"The look on your face says that you're not really that excited about the concept of an overhaul, but if you're asking, that's what we need. A new coat of paint in here. Some updated decor that makes more sense than five guys on horses," she said, gesturing to the artwork across the room. "We have our menu staples. We live and die by biscuits, bacon, and coffee, but there's so much more we could do to bolster them. I've never been allowed to explore those kinds of options."

"Got it." Madison nodded, astute now. She jotted something in her notebook. "What kinds of things?"

"Well, some of our menu items could be locally sourced, allowing for fresher ingredients, fewer preservatives, and a better tasting product."

Madison squinted. "What's the drawback?"

"Money," Clementine said without delay. "Local means more expensive, and Rothstein never wanted to invest, even though that's what it would be in the long run, an investment. He got us frozen product brought in on trucks from the big suppliers. We work with it as best we can, but we can do better. Is that what you want to do? Or are you more like Rothstein?"

Madison blinked, wide-eyed and caught. "I'm being honest when I tell you that I don't know. I was planning to leave so much of these decisions to you. I've never run a restaurant and I have the vineyard, so—"

"I'm sorry. Then why did you buy it?"

A long pause. "What do you mean?"

"Why did you buy the Biscuit if you have no interest in cultivating the business, nurturing it along, improving upon what you found?" She heard the accusation in her voice and didn't recognize or enjoy it. She had never been a confrontational person, but she honestly felt like there was very little to lose at this point, and she was hanging on by a thread. Everything she'd been working toward and dreaming of was now gone. Life felt as aimless as Madison seemed right now.

Madison held her composure. "I was looking to invest in something important to Whisper Wall, and there's no place like this one. It felt like a new adventure." She paused and sat back in the booth with her thoughtful face on. Clementine knew it well. "Listen, I know I'm not the expert here. That is, by far and away, you. But I'm someone eager to see the Biscuit succeed and know how lucky I am to have a team like yours behind me."

"Does that mean you're willing to listen to my input?"

Madison nodded. "Of course."

"Then I'd like to start with making our jam in-house from fresh fruit. No purchased jars. I'd like to bring in our bacon from Morton's Meats and let the public know we're buying local. We can discuss more improvements later if that goes well. What do you think?"

"Okay." More worried scribbling.

"Now, what about the bank drops? What days will you be making deposits? It's best not to have a lot of cash in the safe."

"Me? Oh. I didn't…Yes, that's something I could handle. Bank drops," Madison said with a slight wince. More scribbling.

Clementine nodded. "Great. This might be a good time to discuss my salary."

"Right," Madison said, her cheeks dusting with color. She'd not been as prepared for this meeting as she'd likely thought. "Can you put the details of what you're asking in an email, and I can review it against our monthly bottom line?"

"Of course. Be happy to. You'll have it before the end of the day."

"Great." Madison opened her mouth and closed it again. Her

confidence had clearly been shaken, and that got through Clementine's steely exterior. Madison LeGrange was not a bad person. In fact, up until the whole debacle, she'd been one of Clementine's very favorite human beings. She just wasn't sure she could set this aside.

Madison was staring at her and seemed hesitant.

"Was there something else?" Clementine asked.

"Are you maybe…mad at me? You've been so different ever since you found out I bought the café. Not confrontational, but…okay, maybe a little confrontational."

Clementine exhaled, looked at the ceiling and back at Madison. She felt it all rushing forward. "I'd been saving up for years. I had the paperwork ready to submit to the bank. I was finally about to have something that was mine, and I was this close." She pushed her thumb and forefinger together.

Madison went pale. "You wanted to buy the Biscuit?"

"Guess you were faster. How about that tour you mentioned that you wanted?" Clementine stood, moving them out of confessional central.

"Oh. Um, all right. Do you want to talk about this some more? I had no idea that—"

"No. I really don't."

The meeting had gone as well as could have been expected. If her goal had been to give Madison a taste of what she'd gotten herself into, she felt like she'd succeeded. After hitting the high points of the operation, Clementine took Madison on a formal tour of the small building. The kitchen, the cupboards, the walk-in freezer, the trash system, the safe, and the closet of an office. "For paperwork, ordering, and any employee conversations that need to happen privately," Clementine told her.

"This was much more informative than the tour Mr. Rothstein gave me. Very organized. Everything seems to have a rhyme and a reason. Great systems in place."

"Well, Rothstein doesn't actually know a ton of what we do around here. Part of why he wouldn't agree to the changes we've asked for over the years."

"We?" Madison asked. "Frankie agrees?"

Clementine nodded. "Everyone does."

"Gotcha. Well, thank you for the orientation. Is there anything that needs my attention imminently?"

"Leaking faucet in the men's restroom. And the back corner of the roof in the storage room leaks when it rains."

Madison slid a strand of lazy curls behind her ear, showing off her neck. "I suppose I should get used to that sort of thing."

"Oh yeah," Clementine said, eyes wide. "I'd say it never ends around here. Building is old."

"I'll call a guy I use."

"Much appreciated, ma'am."

"Oh no, no," Madison said with a friendly smile. "No need for *ma'am*. We were classmates. Contemporaries."

"Except you're my boss now. That changes things quite a bit."

Madison waved her off. "That's just a technicality. We're friends, right?" She offered a perfect smile, cover-worthy. Clementine hesitated, shifting her weight, struggling to step across the battle lines she'd drawn ever since she'd learned of the sale. "Except for the whole restaurant-stealing thing," Madison tossed in.

"There is that," Clementine said, holding her ground. "I'll let you get out of here and on with your day. Don't worry. Your investment is in good hands."

"I have no doubt," Madison said and headed for the door. She offered one last curious glance over her shoulder as Clementine watched after her, still not able to absorb that this was her reality and it sucked. Stuck in place. Always and forever the runner-up.

❖

Madison dropped into the chair at her customary table toward the back of the tasting room where Joey and Gabriella had already gathered. Gabriella would be gearing up for service at Tangled soon and already wore her white chef's coat, starched and ready. Joey would be winding down now that they were closed for tastings, with just a little leisurely cleanup.

"Rough out there today," Madison said. Joey poured her a glass of chardonnay from the carafe on the table. She felt like the day had been never ending. With temperatures warmer than she was used to for

October, her walk through the fields had tired her out physically. The meeting with Clementine clung to her mentally, leaving her feeling like she'd been side-swiped by a truck and then backed over. A one-two doozie.

"You've made it through," Gabriella said and patted her arm. "I still have about five hours ahead of me."

"Well. I'm here to brighten your day with the gossip you requested." Joey's turquoise-blue eyes sparkled as she turned to Madison. "Nailed my first outing as an unofficial Biddy and came home with the info." She sat back proud and waited.

"You're a rock star, but I already heard from Clementine why she's less than thrilled with me."

"Then you know that it was the stealing of the Biscuit." Joey shot a glance at Gabriella as if to catch her up. "She wanted it for herself. Badly. Apparently, it's been a dream of hers for years to own the place, which we all kinda knew but never took seriously. But *she* was. Very serious. Clem was planning on making Rothstein an offer, but before she knew it, he decided to up and move away without notice and sold it to you-know-who before Clementine even had a second to get her financial world in order. She's crushed. May never recover." Joey exhaled, exhausted.

"That's awful." Gabriella smacked Madison in the arm. "You stole her dream? Why? Why would you do that to Clementine? She's the nicest."

"Hey," Madison said, rubbing her arm. "Are you kidding me right now? First of all, assault. Second of all, you're the one who told me to buy the place. It was you who planted the entire seed."

Gabriella sighed. "Oh no. That's true. But I didn't know about the dream killing at the time. I'm not in favor of it generally."

"Neither did I. And I'm not a killer of anything." Madison raised her shoulders to her ears. "I don't even like to fish."

Gabriella frowned "Who does? So boring."

Joey held up her hands. "Wildly off topic here, guys. There's a war afoot. Let's focus."

"Now, hold on." Madison turned to her. "There's no war. Just a hiccup that Clem and I will sort out. Our meeting went fine." She sighed, because it did and it didn't. "Though, I will admit there was a chilly blanket over everything that I'm not used to from Clementine."

"The worst kind of blanket, too," Gabriella said and winced sympathetically. "What are you gonna do? Give the business back?" Her hazel eyes were soft.

"What? No. Absolutely not. I'm going to stay the course. Learn as much as I can so I'm helpful to the café's growth and show Clementine that I'm not going to ruin the place she loves so much."

"Just her hopes and dreams for *herself*," Gabriella said sadly. For that, Madison had to hit her in the arm right back.

"Ow."

"Warranted," Madison said in her stern voice that never managed to sound too stern.

"Okay, when you two are done smacking each other around, try this Sottocenere." She handed them each a piece of semisoft cheese. "Italian. Cow's milk. I'm auditioning it for the menu."

"Oh, wow, wow, wow. I love the truffle," Gabriella said. "Will pair beautifully with the pinot noir, and I think it can likely hold its own with the dolcetto, even."

"It very much could," Madison said, studying it. "I love this stuff."

"Sold." Joey nodded as she chewed, savoring the cheese a moment. "I'm ordering some for the tasting room, but what do you think about adding it to our cheese board for special events in the barn? It seems like a good wedding cheese."

Gabriella didn't hesitate. "Definitely add it. Is there more?"

"Is there more?" Joey repeated with an are-you-kidding-me smirk. She held up a finger and dashed behind the bar. "I have to tell you guys, the plans for the barn are really coming together. I think we could book our first wedding in early spring. Well, the first beyond Loretta and Bobby's."

Ever since Joey had taken the reins at Tangle Valley following her father's passing, she'd made strides to take the place to the next level and position it on the map as an important vineyard. She'd started with the addition of Tangled, the restaurant that packed 'em in nightly, and was now in the process of transforming the big barn on the property into the perfect place for events. Weddings, parties, you name it. The rustic barn was gorgeous and would serve as the perfect wine-themed venue, especially once Ryan had finished decking it out with reinforced beams, sliding walls, sophisticated lighting, a sound system, and a beautiful dance floor and bar. Becca even wondered if the Jade might lose a little event business to Tangle Valley, not that she was complaining.

"Well, if you need any bacon or biscuits for your fancy bookings, I happen to have the inside track. In case you didn't know, I'm in the food business now."

"So unexpected," Gabriella mused. "I can't wait to see this whole thing play out. You. Clementine. The café." She exchanged a knowing smile with Joey, who, dammit, returned it. How curious they were being.

"Why are you two grinning at each other like you have a secret?" Madison asked.

Gabriella immediately straightened, smile gone in a flash. "We weren't. That's just our faces."

"Exactly, and you of all people should know our regular faces," Joey said and innocently popped another bite of cheese. "Do me a favor, though. Keep us updated on the Clementine situation."

Madison quirked her head. "Why? You honestly think we're not going to forge a beneficial relationship? I'm incredibly professional and rational. You know that. I'll make this more than work out." Another exchanged look that left Madison annoyed. "I'll have her eating out of my hand."

"Yep," Gabriella said, clearing her throat. "That's exactly why we're interested."

Madison didn't get it but also didn't want to dwell on her troubles. She shrugged. "It'll be fine. Everything's always fine, right?"

"It will be," Joey told her and slung an arm around her shoulders. "It might even be better than that."

Gabriella grinned. "A lot better."

CHAPTER FOUR

It was the first very cold night of the season when Clementine presented herself on Jun and Frankie's doorstep, clutching a bottle of wine. She was no wine expert, but growing up in Whisper Wall, it was hard not to learn the basics. Red was her go-to, and she'd picked up a bottle of the flagship Syrah from Throckmorton Cellars, one of the smaller outfits in town. She'd always liked their style and had a soft spot for their underdog status in the community. She shrugged farther into her jacket just as Frankie swung open the door and stepped aside.

"Get in here. It's cold as balls out there."

"That's one way to put it." She jumped inside and rubbed her hands together. "Cold front came out of nowhere."

"Warm in here. Come in the kitchen and defrost," she heard Jun call. She could also smell the inviting aroma from the crackling fire in their fireplace on the back wall of the living room, making the house feel so homey and nice. In the kitchen, Jun moved about, plating the dumplings and rice for three. "I hope you like these. I only make dumplings once a year and don't have my mother's special touch." Her jet-black hair was pulled into a thick ponytail and Clementine admired its shine. Her own hair seemed lackluster and boring by comparison.

"I can already tell that they're fabulous."

"I can at least tell my mother I made them. Score some points. Do you have recipes handed down?"

"No. None."

Jun lowered her brow. "You never talked about your parents, now that I think about it."

"Yeah, there's a reason for that." She frowned. "I don't know where my mother is, which is probably a good thing."

"I'm sorry to hear that. And your dad?"

"Who knows? He's been out of jail for a year. Living at a halfway house in Portland, last I heard, but who knows about now. He could be anywhere. At least he's not here asking for money I don't have." She shook her head, remembering the little bundle of cash she'd kept hidden in a hole in her mattress so she could maybe have enough money for her senior prom. Tickets weren't cheap, and she would need something to wear. Only she'd come home two weeks before the big night to find her room ransacked and the money gone. Her father had disappeared for a week after that, too, no doubt gambling it away. She hadn't attended prom after all but enjoyed seeing the photos of her classmates all done up. Probably for the best.

Jun gestured to her with her large spoon. "If he ever shows up, you tell Frankie, okay?"

"I will. But he's harmless. Just a selfish pain in the ass who never got his life together."

"Which is why you have to remember that you have a family right here. A chosen family. Who feeds you dumplings once a year."

Clementine smiled, because there weren't too many places where she felt like she belonged. The Biscuit was one. Her softball team, the Muskrats, was another. But Frankie and Jun were becoming her safe place to fall, and that felt nice. She smiled. "Thanks, you guys."

"We Biscuitheads have to stick together," Frankie said, as they shared a fist bump.

Jun joined them at the table for dinner. "I wonder how your new boss is going to handle her new responsibilities alongside the upcoming harvest, which has to be soon, right?"

Clementine chewed the amazing food and considered the question. "I tend to think we won't see much of her. She's already overcommitted and probably thought the Biscuit would just be a place to invest some cash. Our meeting the other day was her wake-up call."

"She's friendly enough, though. Seems smart," Frankie offered, barely looking up from his bowl. He was an eater. That was for sure. He and Jun took turns cooking for each other and had the sweetest relationship. She envied them. She'd had a couple of girlfriends here and there, but nothing overly serious. She didn't invite many people into her life. It was just her way, to keep to herself. Tons of acquaintances. A few friends. Nothing further. But these two people made her wonder *what if.*

"I heard that she and the chef at Tangled used to be an item." Jun set down her fork. "Or is that just gossip? I never know."

"No, it's true," Clementine said. She remembered a time shortly after high school when she heard Madison was dating girls. Her head had nearly exploded, especially in the midst of the secret crush she'd harbored. It seemed so far away now. "Gabriella's become a friend since she joined softball. They used to date."

"Impressive that they're working together now," Jun said. "You think we could do that if we broke up?"

"Baby." Frankie raised his big brown eyes, abandoning his meal dramatically. "You thinking of breaking up with me? With this?" He gestured to his face.

"No, you knucklehead, but do you think we could work together if it ended?"

"Nah. No way I could see you every day knowing I'd been with the best." He touched his chest. "My life would dim. My soul would deplete." He shook his head and returned to his dinner. "I'd shrivel up."

Jun reached out and scratched the back of his head. "You get bonus points for that one. The shriveling was a nice addition."

"Damn, Frankie." Clementine grinned. He always did have a flair for the dramatic and used it to his advantage every chance he got. A sweet-talker, that guy.

He beamed, proud of his work. They spent the rest of the night drinking the wine she'd brought in front of the fireplace and spitballing plans to present to Madison LeGrange, who might be a little more freewheeling with the funds than Rothstein had been.

"I bet she listens to everything you have to say." Frankie gestured with his glass. "She gets that the Biscuit is all you."

She took a sip of her wine. "We'll find out soon enough."

She didn't have to wait long. Madison popped in during the middle of the morning rush as folks were heading into work. At first, she got in the pretty substantial line, going up on tiptoe and peering over the masses at Clem. She clutched her notebook expectantly. Clementine handed Mrs. Mills her half dozen butter biscuits while asking Kevin, who split his time between the Biscuit and the fry shop, to make the two coffees to-go for Mo, who was behind her in line. Next, she gestured to Madison to get out of line and come around the counter.

"Wow. I don't think I've ever been here at this time of day," Madison said, eyes wide.

"Welcome to the trenches." Clementine called back an order to Frankie and slid the slip across the metal counter between them. "Two orders of extra crispy pepper bacon."

"Got it." The snaps and sizzles from the grill were near constant all morning in a very familiar underscore. Frankie worked the grill like a pianist in the midst of a concert. Meanwhile, she worked the counter and had one of her part-timers, today Kevin, on coffee. It was just a basic three pot system: decaf, regular, and cinnamon. But someone had to keep them full and the orders filled. Kevin juggled the job like a pro even if his customer interactions could use a little more energy. He tended to sound bored every second of the day.

"Two medium cinnamon coffees. Piping hot," Kevin deadpanned and slid the to-go cups to Mo, who owned the service station on ninth.

"You guys have this system down," Madison said, in awe. Her blue eyes shone brightly, and she had her curls pulled back today with most of the blond highlights from the sun on top. Underneath, Clementine caught glimpses of browns and a little red. She really should focus on the customers. Yet she felt a little flushed now. Annoying. Old habits and all.

"Well, we've been at it a while. That'll be four dollars and thirty-four cents, Mrs. Helms. What can I get you?" A pause. "Madison?"

"Oh. Dammit. I'm sorry. You meant me. I just wanted to go over some of your requests from our meeting. I had a chance to go over figures and the books from the past year. Twice, actually."

"Of course you did." Clementine grabbed a warm bag to fill with Mrs. Helms's cinnamon biscuits, which were awesome today. "I'm all for talking, but as you can see, eight a.m. is never going to be a good time for it."

Madison swallowed and nodded, her face pinker than when she'd arrived. "God. You're right. I'm about to leap into harvest in an hour and thought we could knock this out, but I wasn't thinking."

Clementine forced a smile and waved at the new customers entering the café. "It's okay. This isn't your world."

"Right. I feel like I'm reminded every time I set foot inside."

Thelma McDougall, next in line to place her order, looked wide-eyed between Clementine and Madison and then grinned like she'd just landed the Biddy scoop of the season. *Tension behind the scenes of the Biscuit.* Wonderful.

"Can you come by this afternoon?" Clementine asked.

Madison sighed. "Sorry. No. Big week for me at Tangle Valley. We kick off harvest on the pinot. That's why I swung by here first. Before I'm whisked away to wine land."

She took a moment to keep her line moving. "What can I get for you, Thelma? The usual?"

"Yes, and an extra order of bacon, but the kind with the spicy kick." She wrote up the ticket and slid it to Frankie. "I just love the spicy kick bacon. Makes me shake my hips."

Madison grinned, and that seemed to break the tension.

"I'll come to you, then," Clementine said. "Once I'm through closing, I'll head over. We can have a quick chat. I'd like to not lose time." She took note of the way Thelma listened intently.

"If you're willing." Even though Madison stole dreams, she was still polite. "I don't want to put you out. But that would be incredibly helpful. My days are insane lately."

"Yet you bought a café." A pause because that was unnecessary. "I'll be there." Clementine looked over at Madison, who still seemed like an embarrassed fish out of water. "Anything else?"

Madison winced and Clem wished it wasn't cute. "Could I place an order for two dozen biscuits, mixed variety?"

Clementine didn't miss a beat. She wrote up the ticket for her employer and placed it at the front of the line. The rest of the world would just have to wait. When Madison LeGrange wanted something, she got it. Clementine wondered, with an internal sigh, what that must be like.

❖

There was nothing like the morning of a good harvest. Madison took a deep inhale, pulling in the sweet, earthy aroma of the day, one of her favorites of the year, when they'd bring the pinot home, clearing nearly nine acres. It would be a long day, but it would kick her into a new phase of production, and she couldn't wait to get started on the new vintage. The crushers and destemmers were ready to go, the tanks primed and ready.

With frost forecast in the week ahead, Madison made the decision to sound the metaphorical alarm and call in their pickers. Would it be more efficient to use a harvester that could pick exponentially more tonnage from the acreage? Yes, but that wasn't the way Madison preferred to do things, and she and Joey were in agreement on that. Each grape would be harvested by a human hand and evaluated, taken care of, and banked. She was shooting for a slightly elevated acidity level over last year's yield. Yes, titration tests on the grapes had been a helpful gauge, but Madison got where she was in the wine business by relying on her most valuable tool. She tasted the grapes daily as they inched closer and closer to the right sugar and acid combination. At last, they were ready. After consulting with Joey's uncle Bobby, who oversaw the day-to-day farming, they'd called in the pickers and kicked off the big occasion in celebratory style. It was a ton of work, but that didn't mean they couldn't enjoy it. Loretta had a table set out in front of the tank room with coffee, hot cocoa, and doughnuts. Madison contributed the warm biscuits she'd picked up, and Gabriella and the high school kids were already well into lunch prep for the workers. Amazing aromas wafted over from their food truck, Jolene, and Madison heard a rumor that her favorite, toasted ravioli, was on the menu. That was motivation alone to work hard until lunch.

"Nice job, Mary," she said to a familiar picker, as she moved between a row of vines. They were making decent time. "Anybody need a bottle of water?" Madison acted as the friendly, supportive winemaker as she moved among the pickers, but honestly, her job along with her team was to make sure that the grapes were being harvested properly, handled with care and without any breakage. She needed to control fermentation, and that couldn't happen until hours later. "Careful about early crushing," she said gently to a teenager with extra eager hands. "Perfect. Like that. Looking good."

Finally, she went to work herself, picking her fair share along with the rest of the team. It wasn't until midafternoon when the second shift arrived that Madison stole a moment to inhale a late lunch and return a few emails before heading back out. She was lost in a whirlwind of ordering supplies when a knock on her office door startled her. She looked up to find Clementine standing in her doorway in jeans, a long-sleeve white shirt, and blue slip-on sneakers. She looked fresh-faced, relaxed, and beautiful. Madison just stared for a moment, captivated. Was it just her or did Clementine's eyes pop even more when the sunlight caught them so?

"Did you hear me?" Clementine asked and slid a strand of blond hair behind her ear. She had it down, which she only did when not at work. It reminded Madison of their high school days when Clementine sat at the back of most any classroom and sneaked away before any sort of socializing happened after class. She'd always been kind, though, when they'd worked together on group projects. Smart, too. She carried her weight.

"Sorry. I totally spaced." Madison offered a self-deprecating laugh, her head fuzzy from the morning and caught off guard by her reaction to Clementine in her very office, looking like that. "It's already been a day. How was yours?" She gestured to one of the three seating options in the room, the two chairs along the wall perpendicular to her desk and the more comfortable one directly across from her, which Clementine selected.

"My day. A haze of dough, flour, people, and credit cards. How was yours?" She seemed softer this afternoon, but then the vineyard had a way of doing that. People relaxed when they came to Tangle Valley. She'd seen it happen time and time again.

"Grapes, coffee, a cheddar biscuit, more grapes, and adrenaline." She offered a wary grin. "Harvest day is big."

"And it's the pinot," Clementine said. "Thin skins, if my time in this town has taught me anything."

"You would be right about that. The pinot requires a lot of extra care and love. It's delicate."

"I look forward to giving it a try once it's ready."

"You'll only have to wait a couple of years." Madison offered a wink.

"You have to have so much patience for winemaking. Luckily, my biscuits plump up in fifteen minutes."

"Which is why they are a wonder of the world. Shall we talk about the café?"

"Okay, but I want to say something first." Clementine moved to the edge of her chair as if preparing for something important. "I realize that no business owner wants to cough up more money, especially when the business in question is already profitable. But I know in my heart that your investment would be a wise one, and I would personally work to show you firsthand. So before you say no to my requests, just consider—"

"I don't plan to say no."

Clementine paused, clearly not expecting that response. "You don't?"

"No." Madison laughed at the look of shock on Clem's face. She clearly wasn't used to getting her way. "You're right. Buying local is definitely the best course of action, especially when you and Frankie, who I trust, think it will make such a difference in the food. I'm also approving your requested salary. You're worth it, and I need you desperately." She frowned. "Maybe I shouldn't reveal that."

Clementine offered the smallest hint of a smile, and Madison felt warm. She liked seeing Clem happy. She still hadn't said anything, though.

"This is all good news, right?" Madison asked.

Clementine gave her head a shake. "Sorry. No. Of course, it's good. I'm just taking it in. What about the small repairs I mentioned?"

"I have a call in to Ryan. She's going to send Billy out. He'll talk paint colors with you, too."

"That would be amazing." A real smile this time. Maybe Clementine was beginning to understand that Madison wasn't the enemy.

"Hey," Madison said, standing. "Want to look in on the harvest?"

Clementine seemed surprised by the invitation. "Sure. I mean, if I wouldn't be in the way. I know you're slammed."

"Of course not." Madison walked her out to the action, where Joey was quick to swoop in and hand her a glass of their most current vintage of pinot.

"To get you in the proper mood for harvest," Joey said.

Clementine raised her glass and grinned. "Well, now I'm ready for action."

She and Joey had always gotten along well, and now Madison wondered why she'd never spent more time with Clem herself. "Follow me," Madison said with a raise of her eyebrow.

❖

Clementine reveled in the fresh air of the autumn afternoon and felt a little bit of her daily stress float off her heavy shoulders. She was on a gorgeous vineyard in the middle of harvest and refused to miss the opportunity to soak it all in. The sunshine. The friendly people. The hum of excitement that seemed to drape everything. The smile on her face was authentic and her joy much needed these days.

"Pinot, as gratifying as it is to grow and sculpt, can be frustrating," Madison offered, midway through their short tour of the vines. Clementine walked side by side with Madison, realizing that they were nearly the same height. If anything, she maybe had half an inch on Madison.

Clementine chewed the inside of her cheek. "I've heard that before. Delicate, right?"

"Very. And the grapes are small. So is the yield." Madison slid her hands into the back pockets of her jeans. There was dirt on the knees, a sign she'd been doing some picking of her own. Yet she still looked beyond amazing in them. Go figure. "Some winemakers add the juices from other grape varietals to bolster their pinot, but I think I'd rather die first."

"You're a purist."

"I think that's a good way to put it. It's by far my favorite grape, and I can't imagine doing anything to betray it."

Clementine laughed. "Well, we all have our loyalties."

Madison didn't hesitate. "Grapes are people, too."

"I work with biscuits all day. You don't have to convince me."

Madison paused their walk and turned to her. They were on their own now, a good distance from the pickers. "You like your job. I can tell."

Something about her recent anger at Madison had somehow counteracted how nervous Madison used to make her. The spell had been partially broken. Now Clementine's reaction was somewhere in between, which made her feel like she had a little bit of control. A strange and perplexing combination, but she wasn't sure she minded. "I love my job. It's simple, sure, but good food and a place you can count on are important. I like offering both to my customers."

Madison began walking again, and Clementine followed. "First of all, nothing you do is simple. Just watching you behind the counter this morning had me shaking my head in amazement."

"Thanks," Clementine said, her cheeks now warm. "I've been at it awhile. You develop systems. Just like the ones you clearly have in place today." She studied the acreage as the sun made its journey lower and lower. "What happens to the grapes next?"

"They'll be sorted and separated from anything that shouldn't go into the wine. Stems, debris. Next, we'll move to crushing."

"Like *I Love Lucy*. See? I know about wine."

Madison laughed, and Clementine felt a tiny bit proud for having made that happen. Maybe her heart was softening as far as Madison went. Not that it should. "That's exactly how we do it. Joey and Gabriella are practicing their stomping now. We pay them in brownies."

"I knew it."

They walked farther, and Madison explained more about her process to Clementine. The skins, the extra dash of acidity this go round, and how frost forecasts kept her stressed and awake at night for the vulnerable pinot. Madison had a measured way of speaking that reflected her logical, scientific brain. But at the same time, her blue eyes sparkled with contagious passion, which made Clementine more interested in wine than she'd ever realized possible.

"There's definitely a lot to it," Clementine said. She took a minute to reflect. "But you're right. There's overlap in our worlds. I work on perfecting our biscuit recipe daily. It's always changing just the slightest bit. Moving toward what I hope is the perfect, fluffy biscuit." Madison was watching her. She shifted her weight. She winced. "Does that sound crazy?"

"It sounds like you understand my world. It's figuring out the perfect combination of ingredients to create undeniable chemistry in a bottle. Or in your case, in a biscuit."

"Our case. You're in the biscuit business, too, now."

She shook her head. "I keep forgetting."

"I don't plan to let you."

Madison exhaled. "You don't hate me, do you?"

"Wow. You just flat out said that." Clementine widened her eyes, caught off guard. They had just been talking about wine.

Madison touched the back of her neck. With her hair up, the elegant column was visible. Clementine didn't mind. The skin there appeared so smooth. "It's been bugging me. Usually, I just swallow that kind of thing, focus on something I can control. It hasn't worked."

"That must mean you care about what I think." Clementine added a laugh to let Madison know she didn't actually believe herself to be that important. Merely a joke.

"No. That's it. I really do care." She met Clementine's gaze in earnest, and it pulled Clem up short. Since when did she matter on a personal level to someone like Madison LeGrange? Her stomach felt weird and her knees like liquid. "I keep thinking about what you said, about buying the Biscuit for yourself."

"Wasn't meant to be. But no, as much as I hate that you got there first, I don't hate *you*. I liked to pretend I did for a little while. Didn't stick. I don't think you did it on purpose." She paused and stared off at the picturesque horizon. "You didn't, right?"

Madison shook her head. "I had no idea you were interested."

"I believe you. And one day"—she glanced at Madison, inching ahead as they walked—"I'll come around."

"One day?" Madison asked, catching up.

"That's what I said. Now tell me about those grapes in that section over there."

Madison followed her gaze and grinned, surely eager to impart more of her knowledge. "Chardonnay. Follow me."

And she did, in awe of Madison in her element. She'd always been interested in wine and the business of making and selling the different varietals, but without any real direct link to the vineyards she'd grown up around, it had always been from the sidelines. Clementine did, however, come with a deep appreciation for the industry that kept them all afloat and of course purchased her fair share of the local product.

Madison led them past the rows of now empty vines to the full ones as she explained the goals of the next few weeks in regard to the chardonnay and what she hoped to accomplish. "We want sunshine for these guys, but not too much. Not as delicate as the pinot, but they still need the TLC." Madison ran her finger and thumb around a small green grape. For just this stretch of time, Clementine let herself enjoy being outside and in the midst of all the excitement and forgot about the real world.

Madison straightened, facing Clementine full on, curiosity on her face. That's when it hit her. She was alone in the middle of a field with Madison. Surreal. Exhilarating. Scary. The old version of her wouldn't have rolled as well with this punch. "What's your favorite wine to drink?" Madison asked.

"I don't know a ton about wine," she said, right off the bat, afraid she'd embarrass herself if they went much further into this conversation. Her good friends, self-doubt and self-protection, were present and accounted for today.

"No one needs you to. But I bet you know what you like. You're an expert at that."

"Red mainly, but it changes, based on my mood. Big reds late at night, but my go-to might be a nice simple blend. I've run into a few good ones at the wine shops in town. I also like a nice glass of the Tangle Valley pinot." She lifted the glass in her hand. "Which is very good, by the way. I think I'll purchase a bottle on my way out."

"On me."

"No. No. I don't want you to have to—"

"I think it's the least I can do. Wouldn't you agree?"

She stood down. "When you put it like that."

They shared a laugh and walked back toward the staging tables at the front of the property. The vineyard was still bustling with pickers and grapes and staff and snacks. As they neared the action, Madison pulled her hair out of the tie, and it tumbled past her shoulders, sun-streaked curls on display. Clementine averted her gaze, something she'd trained herself to do over the years. Invisible was best. Never draw too much attention.

She must have drawn some, however, because Gabriella Russo, her softball teammate and friend, had pretty much hopped onto her back from behind. "No one told me you were here." She made a muskrat face, which of course Clementine made back in solidarity to their team, the Muskrats.

She eased Gabriella back onto land. "Well, I didn't want to bother you at work."

"You would never bother me," Gabriella scoffed, full of energy still, even after what had to have been a long day. "You're Clementine. Maddie show you around the vines?"

She nodded. "I now know all the super secrets of harvesting day."

"I figured she's trustworthy," Madison deadpanned. "So I handed 'em over."

Joey shrugged nonchalantly from a few yards away. "Why not?"

"And now I'll take them back and start my own wine dynasty. Likely tomorrow." She turned to Madison. "Thanks for the tour, and the meeting earlier."

"You're happy? Less likely to curse my name?" She sounded like she was kidding but maybe only halfway.

Clementine relented with a small smile. "We're getting there, boss."

"I accept progress. Oh, and here," Madison said, grabbing an unopened bottle of pinot from the row of them on the table. "Enjoy, and imagine the small changes we talked about for the new vintage."

She held up the bottle in thanks. "Will do."

In a way, Clementine didn't want to leave what seemed to be a fun party. She'd come with a mission, however, and now that it was accomplished, she had no real reason to linger. Yet heading home to her quiet apartment seemed like such a letdown after spending time with the Tangle Valley folks. As she drove back through town, she decided to swing by the library and see if they'd managed to score any of her requests. She found that when life let you down, there was always another world to escape into. All she had to do was crack the spine of a new book and lose herself completely. Even better? Libraries gave books to you for free, at least temporarily. Upon that discovery, younger Clementine had about died from joy.

"I can take it home?" she'd asked Mrs. Morrison, the town librarian in years prior. She'd been reading the book about a chocolate factory alone at a table in the kids' section for hours, and the library was getting ready to close. Looking back, it had probably alarmed Mrs. Morrison that no one had come looking for this wayward nine-year-old for all that time, but then Clementine's parents didn't care much for responsibility.

"You can most certainly take it home," Mrs. Morrison said. "We'll just need to make you a library card all your own."

Clementine frowned, her spirits sinking. "How much does that cost?" She had a dollar in her pocket and was hoping to use it to buy the hot lunch at school the next day rather than eat the peanut butter sandwich they gave you when you brought nothing. It was awful not having a regular lunch to eat like the other kids, but this book was so good. It would be a difficult decision between tomorrow's lunch and this book.

"Library cards are free," Mrs. Morrison had said. To her amazement, she'd taken Clementine's hand in her larger one and led her to the front desk where they'd filled one out together. From that day forward, Clementine was never alone again. She blew through one book after another, making friends with the characters along the way. She was always careful to take care of each borrowed copy, never dog-earing the precious pages. She slept with whichever book she had checked out beneath her pillow, where she could look in on it, make sure it was safe and close. When her mom didn't come home for a week, leaving her with her father, who spoke to her only when he wanted her to cook or run an errand, she assigned herself the mom in one of her favorite stories, imagining Ramona Quimby's mother stroking her hair, or tucking her in at night. In her own house, no one really said good night.

Clementine stared up at the library, still unchanged from all those years earlier. Mrs. Morrison had retired a few years back, but her daughter, Evelyn, with the beautiful red hair and kind eyes, had ascended the library's ranks and taken over. When she popped her head in, Evelyn laughed. They were about the same age. "Let me guess. You want to know if the new Groffman came."

Clementine said, "It didn't. Did it?"

Evelyn leaned down and grabbed something beneath the counter, and to Clem's delight, she straightened with the book in her hand with Clementine's name written across a Post-it stuck on top. "It arrived this morning. I had a feeling I might see you."

"My day just turned into an amazing one." She reached into her bag and pulled out her last two charges, a murder mystery and a romantic comedy. The rom-com had been a little too picture-perfect for her liking. Real life didn't end in neat little bows, but the mystery had been a real page-turner with an ending she never saw coming. Rare. And now the new Groffman was here. She exchanged books with Evelyn with an unmistakable grin taking over her entire face.

Evelyn pointed to the Groffman cover. "You'll have to let me know how that one goes. I might just read it next."

"Well, you won't have to wait long." Clementine knew she'd tear through that book in about two days and then have to wait forever for the next one. Why couldn't her favorites write faster?

"I know. I've met you."

She laughed, always enjoying her exchanges with Evelyn. It was a shame they weren't closer friends with so much in common. She'd always been envious of Evelyn's beautiful red hair and green eyes and welcomed by her cheerful disposition. With Mrs. Morrison as her mom, it was no wonder she was kind and generous to all who came through the library's doors. She'd seen it firsthand. "Thanks, Evelyn. See you soon."

"Enjoy your night." Evelyn laughed. "But I already know how you'll be spending it. Bye, Clem."

It hadn't been a bad day at all, Clementine thought to herself as she drove the short distance to her apartment. She'd gotten the go-ahead on some key changes at the café, got to join in on the excitement of the harvest at Tangle Valley, learned a little bit about wine, and now she'd scoop up her cat, put on her favorite pair of fuzzy socks, and lose herself in espionage and intrigue. Clementine was someone who counted her blessings, and it felt like she had a good few to cling to, in spite of her recent disappointment. She'd count today as a win.

CHAPTER FIVE

It had been a couple of weeks since the pinot harvest, and Madison was finding the ability to breathe again, eager for the world to slow down, and conscious of the fact that she could use a break from the whirlwind of a month. With her assistant winemaker, Deacon, showing more and more promise every day, she reminded herself that delegating more was a real and viable option she should exercise.

She took her morning walk through the vineyard and felt her heart tug protectively at the yellow and red leaves falling from the pinot vines that would now recess into dormancy until the growing season resumed. These vines were her kids in a way, and she was hell-bent on looking after them.

She walked on, pensive this morning, like something was gently nudging her out of her zone, though she wasn't quite sure toward what. She needed to swing by the Biscuit this afternoon and pick up the bank drop, something she did every other day. Clementine seemed to be warming up to her presence a bit more, though it had been a slow process. She remembered walking her through the vineyard during harvest and how alive Clementine seemed. She was energetic, interested, and—well—happy. Madison couldn't explain it, but it had hit her like a drug. She'd thought back on that afternoon a lot. The way the sunlight had backlit Clementine's soft blond hair, creating the most beautiful halo. The gold flecks in her blue eyes shimmered as she asked questions and took in the scene. Madison had not seen that side of Clementine since that day, but God, she longed to.

The Biscuit had closed for the day, so Madison used her key. She heard the customary alternative rock music playing from the kitchen where she knew Frankie and Clementine and whatever part-timer was on that day would be cleaning, closing up, and resetting the café for the next morning's service.

When she approached the counter, she paused for a moment because Clementine, with her back to Madison, was actually jamming out to the music, lost in her own world, hips swaying in a sexy rhythm as she wiped down the coffee stand. She then took a moment to shoulder shimmy, then shoulder shook her way down to the ground and back up again. Madison swallowed, aware of her body's immediate reaction. Where the hell had that come from? Another burst of lust hit, and she blinked, befuddled, grappling.

"Oh, hey," Clementine said, pausing her dance, rag in midair. If she was embarrassed to be caught, she refused to show it. "Here for the cash, I take it."

Madison raised her voice to be heard above the music. "Yeah, but I seemed to have walked in on a fantastic dance party." Behind Clementine, she saw Frankie scrubbing down the grill as he bopped his head to the beat. He offered a wave that she returned.

"Sometimes we let loose a little." Clementine ran her forearm across her forehead. "Good for the biscuits."

"Well, we definitely want the biscuits happy." She gestured to the small closet of an office where they kept the safe. "Be right back."

"We had a good week," Clementine called after her.

Madison found the cash bag and corresponding paperwork, locked the safe, and returned to the front. "Maybe it's the colder temperatures blowing in. People like comfort food."

"True, but I've already accounted for that. Everyone's been raving about the food. Adding an extra half dozen of this. A full dozen of that. The cinnamon biscuits with fresh jam are flying out of the case, and when we serve them straight out of the oven, the customer is back the next day like clockwork."

"It's getting crazy," Frankie called. "We had to reorder bacon midweek. It's Morton's. The fresher product is giving us a lot to work with."

"So it's really making that much of a difference?" Madison asked, happy to hear it.

Clementine turned the music down two notches, allowing it to underscore rather than dominate. "You seem surprised." Clementine raised an eyebrow. "We've been doing this awhile, you know."

Madison held up her hands. "Which is why I agreed to your recommendations. But are we profitable, given the more expensive ingredients?"

"We will be," Clementine said, holding her ground. Madison swallowed back a grin. She was learning to like the spunky version of Clementine. "Give it time."

"That I can do." She gestured to Clem's cheek. "Hey, you got a little flour on your cheek."

"Oh." Clementine naturally swiped at the wrong side, and Madison, without even thinking, reached out and dusted the other cheek with her thumb. Clementine went still, which made her freeze, too.

"Got it," Madison said quietly. She lowered her hand, absorbing the jolt of unnamed energy that had just passed between them. Whatever it was, it was powerful.

Clementine smiled casually and glanced away, but then touched her cheek in the same spot Madison had. Had she felt it, too? It was the simplest of exchanges. A basic touch that happened in the course of everyday life, yet Madison was shocked by the notable effect. She was a scientist and could only equate the exchange to a chemical reaction. "Let's grab dinner together." The words were automatic, out of her mouth easily, like it was something she said every day.

Clementine looked up, perplexed. "Who?"

"Us. We can catch up."

Clementine took a moment. "From what?"

"Exactly." She inclined her head to the side. "What do you say? My treat." She'd caught Clementine entirely off guard, that much was apparent. A small divot appeared between her eyes as she attempted to decode Madison's invitation, when really, it was just as simple as it sounded. Inexplicably, she wanted to spend more time with Clem and had ever since harvest day when she'd taken Madison's breath away.

"Um." Clementine put a hand on her hip. "I guess we can eat. I'd have to change."

"You live at the Windmill Run apartments, right? I can swing by and pick you up."

"No, no." Clementine shook her head. "Let's just meet."

"Fair enough. Cabernet Club at seven?"

"Okay." She still looked uneasy, and Madison wasn't sure what to make of that. "Teddy's food is my favorite," she said of the restaurant's head chef.

"Joey swears by his broccolini." For what felt like longer than it probably was, they stared at each other, the air in the room still not the same as before she'd dusted Clementine's cheek. She wondered distantly if it ever would be again. The world felt like a strange and exciting place all of a sudden.

Finally, Clementine moved them out of it with a raise of her rag, indicating there was more work waiting for her. "Seven o'clock."

With the cash bag in hand, Madison bid the team good-bye and drove to the bank, marveling at the things she was feeling, wondering where the hell they'd come from, but refusing to back away from them. Her life had been anything but exciting lately, and the least she could do was follow this beckoning rabbit down its hole and see what was in store.

The Cabernet Club, a casual spot for lunch in the light of day, always felt decidedly upscale to Clementine when evening brought with it an elevated dining experience. The lights were dimmer, the white tablecloths came out, and the menu shifted from gourmet soups and sandwiches to a handful of impressive entrees. Clementine was apparently first to arrive, so she requested a table for two and waited patiently in her dressy jeans and red top with the poet sleeves. She'd selected her boots with the slight heel and hoped she'd dressed up enough.

"Hi."

Clementine turned from her spot in front of the host's stand to see Madison smiling up at her. Her light curls had been swept up into a twist, and she wore all black except for a silver necklace on top of her slim-fit sweater, making her look devastatingly sophisticated and gorgeous. Clementine took a moment to regain her composure. "Hi," she said finally and gestured to the empty stand. "I think they're putting our table together." She shifted her weight as she balanced her attraction and nerves equally.

"Perfect," Madison said with the kind of confidence she always seemed to exude.

"Right this way," their host said, retrieving two menus and moving toward a quiet table off to the side.

Madison followed him. "You look fantastic," she tossed over her shoulder.

Clementine paused, absorbed, blushed, and walked on. Madison had been one of the town kids, then her high school crush, her mortal enemy in business ventures, and now her boss. Had she somehow backtracked to the crush? Why had no one consulted her? Maybe it was a mixture of all three that made for a complicated dynamic. How was she supposed to unpack all *that*?

There was no time to decide because she swiftly found herself sitting across from gorgeous Madison LeGrange at a nice restaurant on a night in late fall, when the cold made people feel cozy and close.

"What are we drinking? Red?" Madison asked.

"I defer to the expert."

As Clementine perused the menu and picked out the roasted chicken with sweet carrots and mash, Madison spoke quietly with their server over the wine list. "We'll take a bottle of number seven hundred forty-three," she heard her say. Their server nodded and dashed away.

She turned her attention to Clementine. "It's a new blend from Crescent Moon out on Route 20. I've been meaning to try it because I've heard good things about their processes."

Clementine had heard of the small winery but had never been to visit. After the wine arrived and she savored a few sips, she decided she should change that.

"They're really upping their game." Madison sat back, staring at the glass. "Complex. Did you get notes of wood?"

"I can't say I've ever gnawed on a piece."

Madison laughed. "Okay. That's fair. But the essence is there. It's perfect for a chilly night like this one." She let her head drop to the side as she held Clementine's gaze. The candle flickering on the table caused her face to glow. Breathtaking. "Thanks for agreeing to dinner. I thought it might be nice to just…hang out."

"I haven't had the chance to hang out with too many of my bosses."

"Oh." Madison straightened. "Here's the thing. I own the Biscuit, yes, but I don't think of you as an employee. You're still my friend. That part came first."

"This is a social outing, then?" Why did that make her entire body go warm. Madison nodded. "Fair enough." She sipped her wine, feeling shy and unsure, which was typical Clementine.

Luckily, Madison took control. "I remember you really well from high school. We had lots of classes together, but I don't remember seeing you much *outside* of school."

Clementine nodded. "Not many people did. You were a town kid, and I wasn't. It was hard to break through that divide."

"I never enjoyed that weird social structure."

"Part of life around here, I guess. Plus, I stuck to myself. I was shy."

"But smart. Do you remember that project we worked on with that Brendan guy? The one about Mars and its ability to sustain life?"

Clementine laughed. "He was so out of his league."

"We practically shoved him out of the project." Madison shook her head. "You were amazing at the research part. That much I remember. It was so nice to have a group member I could depend on. I usually had to shoulder group work on my own."

She shrugged, remembering those days as nice ones. "I like to read a lot, so research was a good fit." She took another sip of the wine, actually noticing the wood this time to her own amazement. Madison did not mess around with her tasting notes.

"Yes! You always had a book tucked into the pocket of your backpack."

Hold the phone. Clementine sat up straight. "You noticed that? No."

"Of course I did. The titles changed so often, which told me you tore through them."

She'd imagined herself invisible to people like Madison and her crew back then. This was news. "I figured you barely registered my existence."

"Nope. But I wish I'd registered more." She met Clementine's gaze sincerely and her volume dropped. "Big mistake." Madison traced the top of her glass while Clementine tried to imagine if she'd heard that right because her brain had stopped cooperating.

She finally found her words, honest ones. "You were a role model for me in a lot of ways. You were out by the time we were seniors in high school. I couldn't imagine that kind of bravery."

Madison shook her head. "I wish it had been as easy as it looked. My parents weren't thrilled. They still aren't, but they're supportive now. More so, at least. Sometimes I think they expect I'll wake up and change my mind and find some nice guy who plays golf to settle down with. What about yours?"

"I never told them."

Madison's eyebrows rose. "Ever? Even now?"

"The thing you have to understand about my parents is that they're not like other people's." She left it there. "We don't speak, really."

"I'm sorry," Madison said. To her credit, she didn't press for more details, intuitive enough to stay back. But the look on her face communicated so much more. She cared. It wasn't an act or a way to smooth things over with Clementine after the events of the last few weeks. "You're going to laugh, but I didn't know about you. Your sexuality. Shows how oblivious I can be sometimes."

Oh, Clementine enjoyed that part. "Really? Interesting." It meant Madison hadn't caught the stolen glances or flummoxed responses Clementine leveled on her whenever she'd come into the Biscuit. How was that possible? She was flooded with relief, and it offered her a side shot of confidence. Madison didn't have her number, after all. Clementine could wash away that past embarrassment. "I guess I'm not as open of a book as I thought."

"Trust me when I say you're not. You've always been a little bit mysterious to me. Even more now."

"Well, at this point, you're just flattering me." They shared a laugh, and she held Madison's gaze unabashedly. Wow. The exchange was exhilarating in a way she'd never experienced before. Heady and surreal. They ordered their food, Clementine the chicken and Madison the filet, a choice that didn't surprise Clementine at all.

"How did you wind up at the Biscuit?" Madison asked. Clementine noticed that the tables had filled in quite a bit around them. When had that happened? Her glass was close to empty as well. Both signs that she'd been focused. No, *captivated*.

"That's an easy one. I needed a job. Badly. I was young, and Rothstein could see I was desperate enough to work for minimum wage.

I made myself invaluable over the years, but even then, he struggled to pay me decently."

"So you snagged a raise when I showed up."

"Let's just say that I found myself in a position to negotiate and angry enough to follow through." Clementine grinned proudly and gestured to Madison. "No one said owning a business was easy."

"No one said anything about it either way. A blind leap."

"Then what made you do it? Make the leap?"

Madison nodded, absorbing the question. "I needed to diversify my investments. That's what kicked it off, but it became bigger than that." She shook her head. "I wish I could explain it better, and I'm probably sounding like a lunatic, so bear with me." She rolled her lips in as she considered her words. "I think…I was searching for something. Maybe longing to be a part of something bigger? The Biscuit is the heart and soul of this town, and I was just me, on my own. I've felt that a lot recently, and this was another way to connect."

Madison was lonely? No. Never in a million years would Clementine have imagined that possibility. She had her friends, her badass job, and her high profile. To anyone looking on, she had it more than made. "You were trying to fill a hole."

"Maybe so. Either way, I leaped. Might have been a really dumb thing to do, given my lack of experience in the food industry, but it's been nice, and I hope I'm learning as I go."

"Well, you haven't run us into the ground yet, so that's something."

"Any advice?"

"Just keep listening to those in the know." She looked away but pointed at her own face.

Madison laughed. "The Queen of Biscuits? How could I possibly avoid her opinion?"

She snapped her focus back to Madison. "Who told you my name?"

"I'm raking in the info tonight." Madison stole a hot roll from the bread basket and tore off a piece. It was sexy as hell. "This is fun. You are."

Her brain stuttered. "I'm just Clementine."

"Understatement."

The wine had her feeling bold, loose. "Want another understatement? You used to intimidate me back in school. I was never able to just be normal around you. The recent anger has helped. Knocked you off your pedestal." Had she just said that out loud? She closed her mouth, fearful of what else might come flying out.

Madison frowned. "Me? Since when have I intimidated anyone?"

"Please. Do you know how put together you are? And universally friendly and well-liked?"

"Those are bad things?"

"Just unattainable. To someone like me, who owned enough clothes for barely a week and was so shy that it was hard to get out three sentences? You were this ideal. Someone to be admired from afar."

Madison took a moment with that. "I had no clue, and I feel like I'm saying that a lot tonight. How did I miss so much?" She frowned. "I'm sorry."

"That's okay. We're getting to know each other. You didn't do anything wrong." She waved off the idea and sipped her wine, marveling at how they'd actually broken through the surface after all these years.

"If you hating me over the café got us here, well, maybe it was for the best. We should have done this a long time ago."

Clementine dipped her head. "There you go with the kindness again. Don't make it hard for me to resent you when you walk into the Biscuit. It's what gets me up in the morning these days." She added a smile.

Madison immediately seized the bottle and poured Clementine another glass. "Have some more, maybe." Followed by a wink.

Their food arrived, and they took some time to gush about it. The place was top-notch. Clementine watched Madison eat through stolen glances. She'd gone quiet, studying her food thoughtfully as she consumed it, which was so very Madison that it was amusing. Everything was about the intake and processing of information with her. "I feel like you're working out an important equation," Clementine said, as she gestured to Madison's steak, which she'd immediately sectioned off from her potatoes once the plate had arrived.

She blushed, caught. "No, no. Just letting the flavors do their thing." Cue the sheepish grin. "Sometimes I get in my own head about it. Comes from the job. Sorry about that, if it's annoying."

"It's the opposite," Clementine said and went back to her own meal, all the while feeling Madison's gaze on her this time.

"Do you date?" Madison asked, moments later.

Clementine dabbed her mouth with the cloth napkin and set it on the table. "I'm not against the practice."

"That's a bit noncommittal. Don't you think?"

"I've had good and bad experiences with dating. Plus, the pool in a small town like this one isn't huge. I'd have to venture out, and by the time I'm off my feet for the day, the concept seems…too much."

"Yet, here *we* sit." Madison took a delicate bite of steak.

What in the world was happening? Was Madison LeGrange flirting with her? No. Absolutely impossible. Not the girl—correction, woman—she used to think about just before she'd drift off to sleep. Her smile. Her charm. Her devastatingly good looks. Couldn't be happening.

"Are you flirting with me?" Yep. She'd just gone and said that.

Madison offered a sly smile without missing a beat. Her self-assurance astounded. It was also incredibly hot. "Just making it up as I go."

"But we're mortal enemies now."

"We are not."

"You're also my boss."

"You're your own boss. I just own the business."

A pause as they took in the state of things. Clementine pursed her lips. "So, what are you saying?"

Madison gestured to her plate with a grin. "That this steak is incredibly good. And I like tonight." She turned her attention back to her meal before meeting Clementine's gaze one final time. "I think we'll need dessert. What do you say?"

This time, Clementine didn't hesitate. "I'm in."

CHAPTER SIX

It hadn't been a date.

Maybe one-eighth of one. Possibly a quarter if she stretched the numbers. But Madison had enjoyed her dinner with Clementine more than she had anticipated, which had already been a decent amount. Clementine, while beautiful, was the most enigmatic person she'd ever met. Kind on one hand. Feisty on the other. She couldn't leave guarded off the list, however, because Clementine was definitely that, too. Even in the midst of her daily tasting from the tanks that housed the newborn pinot, Madison couldn't seem to concentrate. She watched as the cellar crew pumped the tanks over and pulled a sample into a capsule. She poured out some for herself and her assistant.

"Fermentation seems healthy," Deacon told her, as they tasted the juice side by side. He'd been part of the vineyard sampling to determine harvest dates, and his instincts had been in stride with hers. She saw a lot of potential in Deacon, if he continued to work hard.

Madison let the juices settle in her mouth and moved them around, absorbing the sugars and the early acidity, which would meld as the wine aged. "It's already evolving nicely. Yeah, I'm pleased with this. Not a lot of residual sugar so I think temperatures are good."

Deacon nodded. "That jammy kick is still there, too."

"I was hoping it would hang around." Madison bounced her eyebrows in victory, enjoying having a partner in the process. She let Deacon move on to the dolcetto tanks, while she took time to study the skins of the pinot, making sure they were on target and that she didn't need to press more. The cap, the layer of skins and matter along the top of the tank, was cool enough, and that told her they were in good shape, and she likely wouldn't need extended maceration.

"Oh, look at the studious wine lady." She glanced up from her notebook to see Gabriella standing there.

"Wanna taste the pinot?" Madison asked, handing her the glass.

Gabriella took a sip and closed her eyes. "That is crazy sweet. Wow. In your face about it, too." She shook her head as if to cure herself.

"Not for long," Madison told her with a laugh. "It's showcasing the dark fruit early, giving us a glimpse, which is what we want. Skins are kicking it."

"When's it going to taste like wine? I'll come back."

"It will taste a lot closer after fermentation. But the juice is too young to be structured for quite a while."

"Got it. Next question. Why didn't you tell me you took Clementine out? I had to find out from Instagram, and it's a knife in my gossip-hungry heart. You know I love Clementine. You should have banged down my door." She smacked Madison in the arm, and in typical Gabriella fashion, she did not hold back on power.

Madison stared at her walloped arm in shock. "Well, first of all, I don't have a clue who *you* had dinner with last night, so we're even. Second of all, where did this right hook come from? I could have spilled the juice."

"That's a cheeky response, and you know it."

"We just hung out." She handed off her glass to Justin on her crew and headed out of the barrel room into the sunshine with Gabriella keeping pace.

"So it wasn't a date, or anything like that?"

A quarter date, her brain supplied. "It was not a date. No." She made a point to scoff a little at the notion because she wasn't ready to admit out loud that she had developed a romantic curiosity as far as Clementine went. A social preoccupation. Okay, a crush. She could admit as much to herself. Though she reserved the right to retract the assertation at any point. "We were both at the café and decided to get food. Jointly."

"An impromptu social outing minus the romance."

"That's an accurate description." While it felt weird not to be forthcoming with Gabriella, Madison felt this tug to hold her cards where no one could see them. It's not like she could explain her reasoning if she wanted to. "Wait. What did you see online?"

"You were wearing black, looking like a celebrity, and Clementine wore red, only adding to the clandestine nature."

"There was no clandestine anything. You're such a hyperbolic weirdo. Were you always this way?"

"And in the photo, you were standing beneath the awning of the Cabernet Club like a duo in the midst of a talk."

Aha. They'd been spotted saying good night. A very chaste good night in which Madison had not stared at Clementine's mouth, wanting desperately to kiss it after killing that bottle of wine at dinner. "That wasn't a talk. That was *See you later. Nice meal.*"

"Fair enough. No saucy details, then. I can accept that. But Ryan's having a gathering out at the lake house this weekend because I've convinced her it's too wonderful a spot to keep tucked away from the world, and we're inviting Clementine."

Madison's hands went tingly. "I think that's great."

"Pencil it in. A few handfuls of people. Nothing major. I've taken the night off from Tangled and will put out some of my best snacks. We'll drink and hobnob. I love a good hobnob when it's done right."

Madison blinked. "There's a wrong way to hobnob?"

"God, Maddie. Yes." Gabriella stared at her like she'd missed a vital point, which was not new. "Gotta get ready for dinner service. Your fruity wine is gonna be great someday. I just know it."

Gabriella dashed off, leaving Madison's brain battling between skin maceration, tannin levels, and Clementine Monroe hobnobbing at a lake house party, walking along the water. Guess which won out.

❖

The great big autumn moon was nearly full, beautiful and blue, looming over the horizon as Madison, Joey, and Becca drove the lonely road just outside of town to Ryan's lake house for the get-together. Small lanterns illuminated the driveway up to the gorgeous home made of sturdy beams and dark wood. The lights from the two-story glowed in warm invitation, and the water lapping against the dock not too far away provided a peaceful underscore as they made their way inside. A handful of cars already populated the long drive, which meant they were not the first to arrive. Madison had selected six reserve bottles from Tangle Valley's stock, approved by Joey, and presented them to Ryan, who greeted them at the door.

"Aww, you didn't have to bring anything," Ryan told her. "Just stoked you guys made it." Gabriella's girlfriend was growing on her. They hadn't gotten off to the best start early on, but time had healed all offense, and Madison felt they'd landed in a good place. She forgave Ryan's overt beauty and badass talent with a set of tools. Ryan was a good person and treated Gabriella with kindness, care, and love.

"Look at you," Joey said, taking one of Ryan's hands. Ryan had her jet-black hair pulled into a high ponytail that accentuated her perfect cheekbones. She wore a navy-blue sleeveless shell top that showcased her sculpted arms, and dark jeans that reminded them all why she used to get so many dates from just a curl of her finger. Before she fell head over heels for Gabriella, that was.

"I tried to clean up for you." Ryan flashed a playful smile. "Ta-da. No construction polo."

"Slam dunk," Becca said and kissed her cheek with a smack.

"Speaking of cleaning up. We have casual Becca tonight. I love it." Ryan twirled Becca, in jeans and matching denim jacket, into the room, where she was immediately nabbed by Monty the cowboy, who hugged her warmly. Both Ryan's dog, Dale, and Becca's dog, Skywalker, had been rescues from Monty and Stephen's ranch. Immediately knowing his old friends were visiting, Dale hung at Stephen's side, accepting hearty ear scratches.

This could be fun. She liked the group.

Madison scanned the room of about fifteen people, sipping drinks and chatting at different spots through the open living room and kitchen combo. A couple of people on the couch, a few standing in front of the television, another group chatting around the island in the kitchen as music played from the built-in sound system. She blinked as if an imaginary record player had just scratched because there stood Clementine across the room. Red flirty lipstick, a beige sweater, jeans, and tall boots. Her hair had been curled, and she quite simply depleted the air from Madison's lungs. She laughed at something Ryan's buddy Billy said. He was a frequent customer at the Biscuit, so maybe they were friends. Madison glanced away so as not to be obvious, but it didn't matter. What she really wanted to do was walk straight over there and join their conversation because a gravitational force had grabbed hold of her. Attempting to play it cool, she picked up a Manhattan from the labeled tray Gabriella had set out. Gabriella always preferred to have a signature cocktail going at her gatherings. A nice touch. Madison sipped the boozy drink just as Clementine lifted her gaze to hers. She broke into a soft smile and raised her glass. In a reaction that she didn't recognize, Madison's entire body went warm and her head fuzzy.

"Isn't this great? We've been meaning to get people out here for the longest time," Gabriella said, joining Madison.

"Wow. This hummus is amazing," Joey said, following with celery in hand. "Homemade?"

Gabriella squinted, paused, and tilted her head, waiting.

"Gotcha. Weak question," Joey said.

Gabriella slid into a grin. "You're forgiven because you're nice and my wine dealer."

"She gets away with so much for that very reason," Becca said, placing a kiss on Joey's temple.

While her friends continued to talk about the food, the decor, the company, and the house, Madison caught Clementine slipping out onto the deck. She should at least say hi. Check in on her. See if she needed anything at the café. It was the businesswoman thing to do, and she was, after all, a dedicated new business owner.

"Excuse me a sec," she said and headed outside.

"Where are you off to, huh?" Joey asked. She might have been on to her. Hard to say and she didn't care to wait and find out.

The deck that led out onto the dock that extended over the lake was gorgeous, decorated with white strung lights of varying sizes.

"This is pretty," Madison said, joining Clementine at the rail.

Clementine, who had been staring out at the water, turned. "I didn't hear you come out."

Madison shrugged. "I lean heavily on the element of surprise in most of my dealings."

Clementine nodded. "Oh, I can agree with that."

"You have no coat."

"Neither do you."

Madison glanced down. "I guess we're both going to freeze our asses off to get a look at the pretty water." A pause. "How are things?"

"We had a decent breakfast rush. Lunch was busier than normal, but that's typical for Friday. More people splurge and go out."

Madison nodded. "That's great, but I actually meant how are things with *you*."

Clementine straightened and turned, resting her back against the railing. "Oh. Um…" She seemed to give the question some thought. "I guess I'm good."

It was a lackluster response. "You guess. What would make it better? Because I think we should shoot for more."

"Honestly, this kind of thing is nice. Getting together with everyone in a group. I don't do this a lot." She paused. "Chatting with you on this ridiculously cold deck isn't awful either."

"I guess I'll take *isn't awful*."

Clementine exhaled. "Here's a confession. Sometimes I hide behind my dry sense of humor." Her shoulders relaxed. "The truth is talking with you is actually…really nice. Always has been." Another pause. "I had a really nice time at dinner, too."

Madison smiled automatically, her spirits lifted, giddy, on a high. "I've thought about it more than I should. That's a return confession for you."

The corners of Clementine's lips tugged. "Why do you think that is?"

Madison placed one hand on the deck and faced Clementine, who still leaned against it. A gust of wind hit, and Madison shivered. The muffled sounds of voices could be heard from just inside. "Because I think we're an interesting fit."

Clementine shook her head. "This is a surreal conversation."

"Why do you say that?"

"I've never thought of us as a *we* in as long as I've known you, and you've just grouped us. I'm taking it in."

"And isn't that a shame?" Madison flashed a smile. Her midsection fluttered as the moonlight illuminated Clementine's expressive blue eyes. God, she was more beautiful every time Madison saw her. "I'll just leave it there. See you inside." She tapped the railing.

Clementine offered only a nod, but Madison felt her eyes on her as she retreated to the door.

"Wait. Madison?"

She turned back. "Yeah?"

Clementine hesitated, but only for a moment. "You look really pretty tonight."

The words stopped her in her tracks. Clementine didn't give statements like that away freely. At least not to her. Madison's body flooded with heat, and her skin prickled, sensitive and alert. "Thank you." She didn't walk away just yet. Instead, they stood there, staring at each other under the stars that seemed, in a strange way, to be watching over them. It wasn't uncomfortable or awkward in the slightest. In fact, she wanted to walk right back over to Clementine at that railing and pull her into a kiss she could relive over and over again. In fact, she should—

"You guys okay out here? Kinda chilly." Ryan stood in the open doorway.

Madison turned reluctantly. "We're good. I was just coming in."

"Me, too," Clem said.

Ryan eyed them with an amused curiosity, holding the door open as Madison led the way inside. "Don't let me interrupt," she said quietly to Madison.

"Could you maybe not next time?" She offered a wink and headed off in search of Gabriella's amazing food.

The evening turned into a great time. Laid back with lively moments interspersed. After a good deal of wine, a hard-core take-no-prisoners version of cinematic charades broke out, splitting the remaining guests in half. In a surprise to no one, Becca, who was unfortunately on the team opposite Madison, emerged as the charades ringer, rocking her depiction of *The English Patient* among other titles. The game was tied, and Madison was up, nervous, excited, and feeling competitive. She pulled her slip of paper. Damn. *When Harry Met Sally.* How was she supposed to make that one work? No time to dwell. The clock had started. She focused on her team of six, all gathered on the leather sofa arrangement to her left. She shook hands and flipped her hair, then immediately switched sides and returned the handshake as a much more masculine individual. The guesses coming from her team were nowhere close.

"*Fifty First Dates!*"

"*Pretty Woman!*"

She revamped. She tried eight other *meeting* tactics, only to surrender when there were ten seconds left on the clock. Unless she won this point, the other team would take the game. She had no choice but to go for it. She sat down with an imaginary tray of food that she sampled and with six seconds left she tossed her head back and simulated the best silent orgasm in a deli she could possibly muster. The guesses, completely inaccurate, continued to flood in.

"Taking a shower? What's a movie with a shower?"

"It's sensual. Something sensual."

"*Showgirls. Hustlers.* Is it *Hustlers?*"

"Oh, wow."

Two seconds left.

"*When Harry Met Sally,*" Clementine said simply. Madison paused her performance, grinned, and nodded just as the timer beeped. She joined her team to cheers and high-fives and some good old fashioned trash talking to the other side.

"Let's just be honest," Gabriella said. "Your clues were easier."

"Are you kidding?" Ryan said from across team lines, gaping. "Billy was crawling on his stomach like a worm."

He touched his belly. "Got a little rug burn, too."

"But I like it when you get all feisty," Ryan said to Gabriella. "Shoot me one of those dagger looks again."

That did it. Gabriella was up on her toes and stealing a kiss. "Why does competition make us like this?" she asked.

"Thank God for you," Madison told Clementine quietly. She was feeling a tad tipsy from the drinks. Clementine, she'd noticed, had cut herself off much earlier. Likely because she'd driven herself.

"I thought you did a great job." Clementine shrugged. "Clear from the start."

Madison frowned. "You didn't guess until the last second, though."

"Not like I was going to miss the show." She dropped her tone and leaned into Madison's space. She smelled wonderful, like cucumbers and lime. "Do I look stupid?"

Madison opened her mouth and then closed it. "Not in the slightest. You look…hot." Yep. She'd said that.

This time Clementine didn't blush or go quiet. She didn't even look away. "Thank you," she said with a confidence that tripled Madison's attraction. "I'm glad you think so."

Their flirtation quotient continued to rise with each of them taking it further each time. It had Madison keyed up and preoccupied all night in the sexiest way. Now she couldn't help herself. Her mind went places. She wondered things—like what Clementine wore to sleep, how she liked to be kissed, and what her secret desires might be. She also wanted the everyday details. How many books did she tear through each week? What was her favorite kind of bacon from the Biscuit? Had she ever been in love? As a kid, what did she want to be when she grew up? It had been a long time since she'd been this excited to get to know someone, for what was to come.

"You guys need anything?" Gabriella asked, slinging an arm around Clementine. "Drinks. Food. A dance party? We're here to accommodate."

Clementine kissed her cheek. "The dance party sounds promising, but I'm up early and have to head home. Thanks for having me. Please thank Ryan as well. I love the house."

Gabriella gave her a squeeze. "I will pass that on."

Everything in Madison protested. She didn't want Clem to leave. Hell, she'd make the biscuits herself, if only she knew how. "I wish you didn't have to go," she told Clementine once Gabriella left them.

"You know where to find me," Clementine said. "It was fun tonight." She had a feeling Clementine was alluding to their exchange on the deck and the stolen glances ever since. Okay, the heat that passed between them might have been a factor, too. Damn sure was for Madison, who'd felt it across the entire room.

She smiled. "Me, too. Let's have more fun in the future."

"Walk me out," Clementine said.

Madison didn't hesitate. Once the heavy oak door closed behind them, the sounds of the gathering disappeared, leaving them in the quiet of the country night. Clementine led the way down the driveway to the road where they came upon her white Honda. She turned around when she landed next to the driver's side door. "I'll have this week's order made up in the morning. I'm having them toss in a double order of fruit, because we're low. Do you want to look it over before I send it in?"

Madison stepped into her space and slid a strand of hair behind Clementine's ear, captivated by how beautiful she looked in the moonlight. "I trust you." It had been a bold move, and there was no denying they were in new territory. She'd just declared it.

Clementine swallowed. "Please don't play with me," she

whispered earnestly. "I'm afraid I'm not as strong as I sometimes seem, and if this is just some—"

Madison slowly lowered her hand. "Clem," she said. "No. That's not what this is. I'm sincere."

"Why *now*?"

She searched for the words. "Because I *see* you, and I don't think I can ever undo that. You're smart, and a spitfire"—she touched Clementine's waist with both hands—"and too damn beautiful for me to breathe normally."

Clementine exhaled slowly. Her gaze dropped and landed on Madison's lips, prompting everything in Madison to respond. Her breasts pushed uncomfortably against her bra, and she shifted her weight. Everything in her willed Clementine to lean in, to make the first move, and kiss her already. Her lips ached, longing for the feel of Clementine's, but it had to be her decision.

"Yeah. I think I better go," Clementine said and offered Madison's hand a squeeze.

Madison didn't have a chance to protest or ask her to wait because Clementine was in the car in two seconds flat. She fired the engine and flipped on her headlights before Madison could speak. What in the world had just happened? What had intervened and broken the most magical, wonderful spell?

"Good night," Madison managed, but with the windows up on the car, it was likely a lost farewell. She raised her hand half-heartedly in confusion as Clementine pulled away and disappeared down the dark country road, leaving Madison standing there alone in the cold, grappling with what she'd done to cause it.

❖

When she arrived home, Clementine walked straight to her apartment, head down, thoughts racing, embarrassment dialed to overload. Tonight had been such a fantastic night. She didn't receive a ton of invitations to gatherings like that one, but lately, her friendship with Gabriella had become a nice link to a social world beyond the café. She'd been on a high all evening from the great conversation, the laughs, the food, the new cocktail she'd tried and loved. But even more exciting was whatever was happening between her and Madison.

It occupied most of her brain capacity and just felt a little too good to be real. She wasn't able to trust it. How in the world could someone like Madison have true interest in someone like her? What was the catch? The doubt acted as an additional guest at the party, tapping on her shoulder again and again, no matter how forcefully she tried to ignore it. It felt like the universe playing some kind of joke on her, that Madison, who was leagues out of her reach and always had been, was suddenly interested, and not just in general, but romantically? No, no, no. There had to be some kind of miscommunication, only she couldn't seem to locate one, and if Clementine wasn't mistaken, they'd been moments from kissing before she let it all come crashing in on her. She'd freaked the hell out and fled like a bank robber from the scene.

She plopped down, dejected, into her oversized reading chair and examined the moment that could have been. She'd behaved irrationally back there because she wasn't sure what else to do. "I got inside my own head," she told her cat, who clearly didn't care. He continued licking his oversized paws. "She must think I'm deranged. Feral. How am I supposed to handle this now?" Her attention was now on the ceiling, because it likely held more answers than Toast in this moment.

She lay in bed that night with her arm tossed over her head, lost in a haze of overthinking. Maybe this had been her wake-up call to sidestep whatever this thing was with Madison. First of all, they now worked together. Kind of. Second of all, that was a sad excuse and she knew it. Third, she wasn't qualified to date Madison LeGrange, widely respected winemaker and beyond beautiful person. Hell, she shouldn't even get past the first interview for that position. She was Clementine from the dusty trailer park up the street, bound for nowhere exciting, and noticed by no one. All that would come of an attempt to date would be more embarrassing moments like tonight, and who wanted a fresh collection of those kind of cringeworthy exchanges in their memory bank? Certainly not her.

Decided. Exit the highway. Get outta there.

To avoid the stress she was already feeling and the eventual humiliation, she should take a step back and breathe. Treat Madison like her boss and acquaintance, and remember her very comfortable, if not a little boring, place in this world. At least her heart rate would slow down and her brain could relax and go back to normal. She would miss the way Madison made her feel, though.

Special.

Pretty.

Like she mattered.

She closed her eyes as sleep began to whisk her away. Her final thought was of Madison's smile, her lips, her eyes when she laughed.

CHAPTER SEVEN

"W e have to stop remodeling all the buildings on this property. We keep losing our movie rooms," Madison said glumly from her spot on the floor of the old barn. She watched the credits roll on the first Avengers flick. It had been her night to pick, and neither Joey nor Gabriella had seen the franchise, so it was time she did her due diligence and introduced them. Becca and Ryan, also superhero fans, had joined them for the viewing. She was full of Gabriella's amazing popcorn and two glasses of the dolcetto and feeling a little melancholy about having to move out for the remodel.

"Where should we set up next?" Joey asked. "I don't want movie nights to die just because we keep stealing our own hangouts from underneath ourselves. Why do we do that again?"

Madison didn't hesitate. "Because your entrepreneurial spirit cannot be quelled."

"Jack Wilder in heaven is nodding along with you on that one," Joey said. Her dad always did have a hard time holding Joey back from all the ideas she had for the vineyard.

Becca stared up at the rafters of the beautiful old barn. "This place is going to make a lot of memories for the people in this town, though. I can just envision the dancing, the food, the special occasions. Photos with the vines in the background at sunset. It's already breathtaking." She looked over at Ryan. "I can't wait to see it once you get your hands on it."

Ryan stretched and stood. "When you say that, I feel like I need to get started on this transformation right now, so you guys are gonna have to scurry on out of here with your popcorn." She paused. "But maybe leave me some, because that clarified butter is unreal."

"My butter gets me hot women," Gabriella said from atop a bale of hay. She yanked Ryan back down next to her, and they snuggled up the way they often did when within twenty feet of the other. The image of the happy couple right there in front of her—correction, two happy couples—dragged Madison's mind right back to the one topic she'd been trying to escape, Clementine.

"Is it a bad idea to date someone who works for you?" she asked her friends. It was really the only reason she could come up with for why Clementine had done an about-face when they'd started getting too close.

Joey and Becca exchanged a look.

"I knew it," Gabriella said. She turned to Joey. "It was only a matter of time."

"What?" Madison asked. "Can someone not ask a hypothetical question without drawing an arrow sign?"

"No," Joey and Gabriella said in unison.

Madison sighed. "Fine. I can speak to this. No, I don't have any plans to date Deacon, but I feel like I should have my ducks in a row should the situation ever change."

"Oh, she's good," Becca said, pointing at Madison. "You're good."

"Thank you." She surveyed the four individuals all staring back at her. "Thoughts on the topic?"

"I've never done it," Ryan said, "but I would certainly hesitate. The consequences are much greater when there's a working relationship and something goes wrong. Plus, there's the whole power dynamic."

"So you think it's a bad idea."

"Don't listen to her," Gabriella said. "I was her *client*, and she had no problem kissing me on the jobsite. Now look at us. If you suddenly become interested in *Deacon* one day, then I say go for it. We only live once, Maddie."

Joey held up a finger. "*Go for it* might be a strong sentiment. How about you dip your toe in, and go from there. Deacon is someone who's not always had an easy time of it. Deacon should be handled with care, which is not to say he's anything but wonderful and gorgeous and kind."

Madison squinted at the three warring opinions she'd just been handed, realizing they only had her more confused.

Becca offered a reassuring smile, proving once again how intuitive she was. "I have a feeling your instincts on this are better than you think. My advice is trust your gut. If you and Deacon have something developing, let it happen organically without outside pressure or scrutiny, and figure it out as you go. You've never struck me as unprofessional in any way."

Gabriella nodded. "I defer to Becca."

"Same," Ryan said. "I think as long as power isn't an issue, and that's made clear, you might be okay."

Madison exhaled and met Joey's gaze. She smiled back, and that offered her encouragement. Joey knew her best, knew her heart, and would never steer her wrong. Clementine was a tenderhearted person. She was beginning to understand that more and more.

Madison didn't have any reason to swing by the Biscuit that next afternoon, but she damn well came up with one on the drive over. Yep, she'd decided to inspect the work that had been done on the restroom the week prior, even though Clementine had already assured her that Ryan's guys had done a fantastic job. Maybe she could even check out the paint samples Billy had dropped off. Swinging by was a totally normal businessy thing business owners did. Also, it was good practice to show her face, let the staff know she cared.

The café appeared empty when she used her key and let herself in. It was an hour after closing, but there was no sign of dancing today. Dammit. Apparently, she'd missed her window.

Clementine scared her out of her skin when she popped up from the floor behind the counter and kicked her hip out. "Well, hey there."

Madison's hand fluttered to her chest and she bent at the waist, trying to grab hold of her wits again. "Oh, wow, okay." She held up a hand, asking for a minute, and gave her head a shake before straightening. "Were you hiding back there? Why in the world would you do that to me?"

Clementine glanced at the floor and pointed at the now empty display cases beneath the counter. "Cleaning the cases. Standard daily procedure. Watching you freak out like a five-year-old was purely bonus." She had her hair partially pulled back, which really accentuated the shape of her face. Sigh. Why did she have to be so pretty? It made it hard to concentrate on much else.

"The display case. Right. Should have caught that." Her heart rate had finally settled.

Clementine smiled. "You're still sort of new at this. To what do I owe the honor?"

"Oh, um…" She closed her eyes, trying to remember the story she'd decided on, but the scare and the hairstyle had pretty much wiped her short-term memory. "I just thought I'd stop by. No big deal." She walked casually into the room like she owned the place, which of course she did.

Clementine eyed her suspiciously. "You sure you're okay? Want some water?"

Madison scoffed. "Totally fine. What can I do to help?"

Clementine placed a hand behind her hip, studying her. "Really? Okay." She grabbed a dry rag and tossed it to Madison. "You can wipe down and sanitize the coffee station and prep it for a new pot tomorrow. Cleaning supplies are there." She pointed to a bottom cabinet.

Madison eyed her subject, a pretty standard triple coffee machine, and went to work with the rag and bottle of spray she'd located. They worked together in silence before Madison turned to her. "No Frankie today?"

"Dentist appointment. His tooth has been bothering him, so he sped out of here after giving the grill a rubdown. I'm covering the rest for him."

They were alone.

The smart thing to do would be to bring up the other night, discuss things the way two mature adults would, yet Madison continued to work, giving the task her full attention. In fact, she lost herself in a furious haze of scrubbing. She was nothing if not committed.

"I think that coffee pot might need a break," Clementine said, looking over Madison's shoulder as she scrubbed her heart out. "In fact, it's feeling a little abused."

"Sorry," Madison said, straightening. "I just wanted to make sure it was up to…" But her voice died because they were now facing each other with very little space between them. She hadn't expected that. Clementine inhaled. Blinked. But didn't move away. Madison could see her pulse beat. Her neck was so smooth and elegant. She wanted her lips pressed to the skin there, imagined burying her face in the curve and kissing lower. She shook her head, remembering Ryan's words. She was the boss, and things could get dicey if she wasn't cautious. She had to make sure that Clementine's feelings were—

Lips were on hers. Clem's. And they were soft and insistent and wonderful. Madison savored the kiss a moment before giving back, and oh, did she ever give. Slightly up on her toes for better access, she angled her mouth over Clementine's, moving her lips in a glorious give and take. Her body sprang to life, wanting and needing and anxious to touch and explore, to the point that she thought she'd explode. She parted her lips, and Clementine's tongue was in her mouth as she was walked backward until pressed against the counter. Good God. The world had surely stopped moving. More kissing. The really excellent kind. She had Clementine's face in her hands, and Clementine's hands were to either side of Madison's waist, though her thumbs were inching higher with each passing moment, and Madison couldn't help but cheer them on.

And then, all of a sudden, it was over.

"I shouldn't have done this," Clementine said, breathing deeply, dropping her hands. Oh, the loss. "I'm so sorry about that."

"I wasn't protesting," Madison said. A pause, as she waited for their brains to catch up. They were still standing so very close to each other. "Please don't undo the past two minutes. Is this because I'm your boss and now I've crossed a line?"

"What?" Clementine asked, pulling her face back enough to see Madison. Her cheeks were flushed and her eyes dark with lust, mirroring Madison's own experience.

"I'm kissing you, and you technically work for me." She squinted one eye. "I don't want you to feel pressure. I'm sorry if you did. Your job won't be affected by whatever this is in the slightest. Ever."

Clementine seemed to relax now that Madison wasn't. "You're cute when you're flustered. Plus, no. I'm the one who kissed you," Clementine pointed out. Her voice still sounded breathy, and Madison loved it. "Now we're both apologizing."

"What's wrong with us? Let's stop and do this just a little bit more." She pulled Clementine's mouth to hers for another few scorching moments that made everything in her jolt to life.

"Madison," Clementine whispered, millimeters from her mouth. "I can't believe I'm kissing you."

"In the Biscuit," she supplied.

Clementine closed her eyes and laughed, putting more space between them. "In the damn Biscuit."

Madison tilted her head to the side. "But it turns out we're really, really good at it."

"So good," Clementine said, returning and placing her forehead against Madison's. "Too good."

"I don't know that there's such a thing."

Clementine straightened. "Trust me. There is." She said it reluctantly, like she spoke from experience. Madison didn't like what the sentiment might foreshadow. "There's a big part of me that doesn't think this is a good idea."

The words slugged her like a punch in the gut. Not what she wanted to hear, and her mind went to work trying to piece together what was going on. "And the other part of you?"

"I think you just met her."

Madison nodded, trying to remain diplomatic between the two warring Clementines, even though she had a clear favorite. "Well, if it's not the working relationship giving you pause, what is it?"

Clementine opened her mouth and closed it again, seeming to be at a loss. Madison stepped in.

"Are you seeing someone else? You can level with me."

"No." She sighed and gathered herself for an explanation. "Sometimes I feel like this"—she gestured between them—"might take me out of my depth."

Madison smiled, happy to hear that there wasn't a rival in their midst. "What about this? We take it slow. If you want to put the brakes on, we will. But I want to get to know you more. Let me?"

"Slow," Clementine repeated. "Were you not here for the last ten minutes?" She shot a glance to the counter they'd just been kissing against.

"You have a valid point. But I think we're more than capable if we put our mind to it."

Clementine sighed. "Look at you standing there." Madison smiled. "You might be trouble for me."

"I don't want to be," Madison said. In fact, all she wanted was to make Clementine smile back, make her life easier, happier.

A buzzing sound from somewhere behind Clementine hit. Her

cell phone danced its notification across the counter before Clem scooped it up and clicked on to the call. Madison, in an attempt to offer Clementine privacy, moved into the dining room while picking up cues that someone wasn't doing so great.

"And they're going to get you in tomorrow?" A pause. "No, it's fine. We'll make it work. Don't even worry about it." Another pause. "Let me know how it goes, and hugs to Jun."

"Everything okay?" she asked, as Clementine set the phone down.

"Frankie's tooth was a mess. He's got a root canal scheduled for tomorrow morning. He's in some pain, so they're working him in." She shook her head. "I gotta find someone to cover the grill, but it's an awful week for it. Two of my part-timers are on fall break and unavailable, another only works lunch service, and my last always requires notice because he balances two jobs."

"I can help out," Madison said and shrugged. "Deacon can handle things at Tangle Valley for one morning, right? And then your part-timer can take over at lunch."

Clementine stared at her like she'd announced she was enrolling in astronaut school. "You want to put on an apron and bag bacon and biscuits?"

"It actually sounds fun. Plus, it's like helping myself if you think about it. It's my job."

Clementine chuckled. "Sure. I'll work grill, and I'll be happy to put you to work behind the counter."

"And we'll get to spend the morning together. I'll get to walk in your shoes."

"Oh. Are you sure you're ready for that?"

"More than." Madison couldn't stay away any longer, her eyes on the neckline of Clementine's long-sleeve T-shirt. "Do you have somewhere to be right now?" she asked, blinking innocently.

Clementine grinned and allowed Madison to pull her close. "I have a few minutes."

With that green light, everything in Madison heated, and she met Clementine's lips, making the absolute most of those few minutes and even stealing a few extra. No one could argue with her ambition.

"If I had known this was the way you kissed," Clementine murmured against her mouth.

Madison's hands slipped beneath her shirt to warm skin at the small of her back. "Then what?"

"My head would have exploded," Clementine said, going back in hungrily for more.

Hopeful, happy, and drunk on lust, Madison reluctantly headed home, prepared to go to bed early so she'd be all set for her new role behind the counter at the Bacon and Biscuit. She stared at herself in the bathroom mirror. Her curls were a little extra wild when she ran her hand through them, her lips still a little swollen, and her spirits on a high. "Damn," she said with a smile. She could really get used to this.

❖

Holy hell in high-tops. Clementine shook her head in mystification as she drove from the Biscuit home to her apartment. She'd lost her mind and kissed Madison LeGrange in the middle of the day like a downright lunatic. Clementine imagined saying that sentence to her teenage self and watching her world erupt in chaos and disbelief. She had no idea what had come over her, but she'd completely deviated from the plan. But when she'd found herself standing in front of Madison, who looked so stunning it made her chest hurt, she found herself taking action. And damn if it hadn't rocked the world as she knew it. In fact, nothing looked the same. Not the café, the green of the grass along the roadside, or the outside of her apartment once she stared up at it. Everything hummed with a new kind of energy, anticipation of what might just be something wonderful waiting for her.

"Hey there, Miss Clementine." She smiled. Her downstairs neighbor, Slow Joe, stepped out of his apartment, blue flat cap in hand. He was likely heading to the Scoot for a beer, his usual midafternoon outing in retirement.

"Hi, Joe," she said, pulling him into a hug. This was not customary. She was well aware, but she was feeling extra exuberant this afternoon, and Joe was the recipient.

He chuckled and patted her back. "Someone had a good day."

She released him, realizing she was smiling without putting forth any effort. What a concept. "I had the kind of day that you remember, when the events stand out in stark contrast to the rest of the days'."

"So many of mine blend. You're lucky." He waved his cap in farewell. "Oh, wait a sec. I forgot to tell you." Clementine turned around. "You had a visitor. A nice guy popped by looking for you. I let him know you were at work and would be home this afternoon."

"You didn't recognize him?" The town wasn't that large.

"He looked familiar but I couldn't say much more. Short brown hair, about six feet. Younger than me. Older than you."

"Huh. Well, thanks, Joe. Enjoy your beer."

"I might scoot, too. Thelma McDougall is going to be there."

She raised an eyebrow. "Joe, do you have your eye on a Biddy? That's dangerous. You'll be plastered all over the online tabloids of this town before you can blink."

He winked. "I'm on the lookout for a little fame and notoriety these days. Spice up my life."

"Not a bad point." Clementine laughed, enjoying her neighbor who reminded her of everyone's favorite grandpa. "Onward then. Don't say I didn't warn you."

He headed off to get his scoot on, and Clem wondered about her mysterious visitor. Didn't sound like her father, thank God. She stayed on guard, just in case. Maybe just a solicitor masquerading as a friend? They were more and more creative these days.

She checked in on Frankie, who let her know that root canals sounded to him "like no fucking fun" but felt confident he'd be in to work the day after. She wanted more than anything to spill her guts about what had happened, to confide in someone, to share her shock and excitement. Somehow, she couldn't bring herself to do it. Instead, she held on to the moment for herself, tucked it away, like a happy little secret. She'd truly *connected* with someone today, and more than that, it was the last person she'd ever have expected a short time ago. Just when she started to think nothing noteworthy would ever happen to her, life stepped in and threw a curveball.

Maybe her plan had been hasty. Maybe instead of running, she should gulp in a breath and let whatever was going to happen simply happen. She watched Toast bat around the orange she'd tossed him. He zigged and zagged and improvised each step of the way, which felt like the perfect blueprint. She could be like Toast.

Follow the orange and see where it goes.

❖

The neon *Open* sign was off at the Biscuit when Madison pulled in at five thirty the next morning. While the outside sat dark and quiet, the warm glow of the lights inside said that things were already cooking, literally. Given her round-the-clock job, she wasn't shy about early morning hours and actually enjoyed catching the worm.

"Good morning," Madison said, when Clementine opened the front door and let her in.

"Morning, Hostess of the Day. Biscuits are in the oven, and I've got you all set up at the front."

"Is that my title?"

"Yes. I just made it up."

"I can work with that."

Clementine slipped her a printed-out list of responsibilities that Madison gave a once-over. "Okay, okay. I think I can handle this."

"I got here early and already prepped the grill, which I'll be manning today, so we could do a brief training session. It's nothing too difficult. You should be fine for one day."

Madison scoffed. "I plan to do you proud." A pause. "I also had a thought about pastries. Have you ever considered doing giant cinnamon rolls?"

Clementine frowned. "Not exactly."

"Think it over. I think now that we've nailed the biscuit, maybe we move into other territory."

"I will definitely give it some thought."

Clem took the next fifteen minutes showing Madison how the cash register worked, how to correctly bag the biscuits and other items from the menu. She was to handle coffee on her own until their third coworker arrived at nine for the big rush. Grill orders went over the back counter and had to be written out a certain way. Okay, her head was beginning to spin. This might be harder than she had anticipated, but surely once she found a flow, they'd be good. She tried not to think about the lines she'd seen there midmorning in the past, and focused on one task at a time.

"You feel good?" Clementine asked, as she pulled a tray of hot biscuits from the industrial oven and slid another one in. The wonderful aroma of the fresh baked goods almost brought Madison to her knees.

"I do. What can I get you?" she asked.

Clementine frowned. "Me? I'm good." She organized the trays of uncooked biscuits like little soldiers waiting for their turn in battle.

"No. Not you. I'm practicing. See? How can I help you?" she asked an imaginary customer. "What'll it be? Can I interest you in an order of our candied bacon? How are you today? Staying warm? Our biscuits will help with that."

During her performance, Clementine had come around to stand next to her at the counter. "Impressive. And I like the smile. Always have."

"Are you flirting with me, ma'am?" Madison asked, still in character. "I'm going to have to get my manager out here."

Clementine laughed and headed back to the grill. "Isn't that *you*? Are you going to call yourself? And yes, I might have been flirting with you again. My apologies."

"I think you shouldn't chastise yourself too vehemently," Madison said with exaggerated sympathy. "The Hostess of the Day has been putting out flirtatious vibes of her own. It should probably be noted on her performance review."

Clementine shook her head as she dipped the bacon. Her cheeks were dusted with pink. Adorable. "Oh, it will."

Things felt different between them today. The kiss had unlocked a new level to their relationship, and things felt light and fun. Tension filled, too, but in a good way. Unfortunately, a new kind of stress arrived just half an hour later when the first trickle of customers arrived. Madison wasn't the fastest at bagging the biscuits, but Trevor, the wine store salesman, was patient enough. She felt bad when Mrs. Fillmore, her second-grade piano teacher, had to wait while she ran her credit card three times because she screwed up the first two attempts. Each time Madison hit a hiccup, more people entered her line, which just made her more nervous, which made her make more mistakes, which made her line longer again.

Clementine was steady as a rock on the grill. She turned the tickets around lightning fast while kneading biscuit dough in between. They had yet to fall behind on supply. "You doing okay?" Clementine asked, coming around the counter to check on Madison, who stared woefully at the line of about eight people.

"I can't seem to make it go down," she whispered out of the side of her mouth as she handed Nadine Montgomery her change. "Enjoy those cheddar biscuits."

"My favorite. Morning, Clem."

"Morning, Nadine." Then Clem turned to her and said, "Why don't you let me take a few. While I do that, will you pull the tray of biscuits out when the timer beeps and help me bag? I've cooked a bit ahead, so we should be good for ten minutes."

"That I can do." Madison stepped to the side and watched the expert in action. Clementine turned on the charm and chatted up each customer as she simultaneously rang them up, passed the tickets to Madison, and assisted on coffee fulfillment. Amazing. The coordinated multitasking was a thing to behold. Clementine then handed off their orders and receipts and moved on to the next customer. In no time at all, she'd taken care of the crazy line, and worked it down to a much more manageable wait for their customers. Madison had never been so smitten in her life.

"How did you do that?" she asked, marveling, once they'd hit a lull.

"Let's just say we all have our skills. You make your wine, and I keep the people of Whisper Wall happy in the mornings."

That's when Kevin, the college-aged server from I Only Have Fries For You, walked in and tied on an apron. She leaned close to Clementine's ear. "I didn't know Kevin was on today. I never know what he's thinking."

She whispered back, "I Only Have Fries for You picks him up in the evenings, and I use him in the mornings. He's not great on register because he's rarely friendly, but he's great on coffee and counter assistance. He'll be a big help to you."

"Hey, Kevin. Good to see you," Madison said with a wave. She only knew the kid, who had to be around nineteen or twenty by now, from her interactions with him as an uninterested server at the fry shop.

He looked up, completely unfazed. "Hey. Heard you bought the place. Amazing." Only he said it in a monotone voice that communicated anything but amazement. Yep, there was the Kevin she knew.

"I did and am happy to see Clementine has you on staff." A minor exaggeration, but Kevin was apparently efficient.

He glanced around, took in the scene, saw her apron. "You're working the counter. Huh."

Clementine nodded. "Frankie's out, so I'm covering grill. Madison agreed to step in."

"Big of you," he said and organized his coffee station to what was likely his own system. Two new customers joined the line, which made her happy to have his help. But by the end of the big breakfast rush, Madison's hands shook. The line was brutal and never seemed to quit. She'd never quite experienced that amount of in-the-moment pressure.

"I feel like I failed them," Madison said to Clementine as they reset for lunch. Clementine had been nice enough to make her a warm bacon biscuit to eat before she left for work at Tangle Valley. Clementine and Kevin would cover lunch on their own, and she had to say she was relieved for that. "The people of Whisper Wall. I'm not used to failure. I might need to pace and talk this out."

"Does that help?" Clementine quirked her head.

"Always."

"Well, you didn't fail anyone. Everyone was fed, and no one yelled. I call that a win at the Biscuit during rush hour."

"I have newfound respect for you." A pause. "And I may need to stop in during peak biscuit buying time more often."

"A fan of long lines?"

"I like watching you work. You're very impressive. The multitasking prowess alone has me humbled."

"Really?" That seemed to catch Clementine off guard. "No big deal. I just happen to like my job and have a lot of experience."

Madison took Clem's hand and gave it a squeeze. "Well, you rock at it." They exchanged a smile, and the moment felt like a much needed exhale. No, it was more than that. Madison, though exhausted, stood in front of Clementine with a very full heart. One of her favorite feelings of all time.

"You're on Instagram," Kevin said behind them, as he stood on a ladder and changed out the posted breakfast menu to their more petite list of lunch offerings.

"I am?" Madison asked. That was new. The Biddies had always been highly tuned in to the lives of her friends but generally left her alone. She had always chalked it up to her mundane life not making the cut. Not a ton to document other than temperature readings, grapes, and stem sorting.

"Saw it on my break. It's wild. You're incredibly famous," he deadpanned.

Madison pulled out her phone and scrolled her feed. And there it was. The Biddies had arrived in the middle of the breakfast rush, and though she only vaguely remembered helping them, she was aware of their morning dish session happening at their customary table facing the window in front. It went on for over an hour. One of those wily spitfires must have snapped this photo when Clementine stepped in to tame the line. It was a shot of Clementine speaking quietly in Madison's ear. There was a relieved smile on Madison's face and the caption: *Sweet Nothings or Trouble at the Office?* was clearly there to provoke speculation. Huh. Madison had never been the center of either of those things and wasn't sure how to feel. Honored? She was, a little. Clementine stared at the post over her shoulder.

"Well, that's not good. I don't know what to do with those Biddies."

Madison shrugged and turned her face to Clementine's. "It upsets you?"

Clementine thought on it. "I figured it's not something you would want out there. People thinking that you're carrying on with me."

From the look on her face and total lack of confidence when she said it, Madison understood. Clementine assumed Madison wouldn't want people to know about them. She took Clementine's hand and pulled her farther into the empty dining room, giving them space to speak out of Kevin's earshot. "Do you think I'm ashamed we've... connected?"

"Oh. Um, honestly? I don't know." She smoothed her apron, seemingly overcome with a shy insecurity. "But it wouldn't shock me. I mean, Madison, you're sought after. A big name around here. I don't have any of that."

The idea actually made Madison angry, but she held it in for now, needing to set Clementine straight, first and foremost. She needed reassurance, and as unfortunate as that was, Madison could give it. "Listen to me. That's the most ridiculous thing I've ever heard," she said and added a smile. "Everyone knows and adores you. Trust me. I hear the entire town singing your praises on the daily. My best friends alone think you're the kindest person on the planet and might like you more than me."

"I don't know about all that." Clementine stared at the floor, vulnerability on display. It was endearing, but also crushing that she struggled with hearing positive affirmations. It meant Clementine thought very little of herself, and that was awful. Who had done this to her? Madison wanted to take it all away and make her see how interesting, and beautiful, and smart she was. "I'm just me."

"Well, if the people in this town are whispering about you and me, I have zero problem with that." That seemed to surprise Clem. "Let them. They're not wrong, are they?"

"I just figured you were a private person who maybe wouldn't want people to—"

"Know how into you I am?"

Clementine closed her mouth and absorbed. "Yeah. That." A small smile crept onto her lips.

"I have to head back to work now." Madison flashed the photo on her phone again. "But this doesn't scare me, okay? Very little does."

The smile on Clementine's face blossomed, and it made her eyes light up. Madison would hold on to that image for the rest of the day. A new favorite daydream. "Fair enough."

While she wanted more than anything to lean in and kiss Clementine good-bye, this probably wasn't the right moment for that. "I'll call you." She backed up. "Or, you know, you could call me."

"It's a novel idea. I'll give it a shot. Say hi to the wine."

"It loves it when people send messages." They shared a smile, and Madison headed out, excited to get back to the work she was passionate about, but also a little sad to leave the café, where today she'd felt like part of the team.

"Why are you so happy?" Joey asked a few hours later when Madison slid into her favorite chair by the window in the tasting room. Her workday had been hit and miss because she lacked focus. Her mind drifted to the café kissingfest of the day before, to sexy Clementine working the counter that morning, and to the sweet smile right before she left. It all had Madison wondering about the next time they'd speak, laugh, or touch. It couldn't come soon enough. She felt like a damn kid.

"Remember when you first started wondering about you and Becca?"

Joey fanned herself. "She tossed my life in the air and mixed everything the hell up."

"Consider my life in the air," Madison said with a nod of her head.

Joey threw a victorious fist in celebration.

CHAPTER EIGHT

Less than a week later, as Clementine quietly wiped down each of the café's tables alongside Frankie, who was always nice enough to help her out with the dining room, she decided to go for it. Spill her guts. Madison had called the night before to see if Clem was free for dinner at Tangled. Apparently, they were having their monthly pairing dinner, and Madison was able to snag a table.

"Guess what? I have a date this weekend."

"No shit?" Frankie straightened and looked at her with wide eyes. Okay, so it had been a little while since she'd dated, but he didn't have to look like she'd just announced that she was joining a boy band. "Is it with that library lady? With the red hair." He clapped his hands. "Totally called that. She's got the library glasses even. I told Jun, I think Clementine likes that library lady. You're always there."

She scoffed. "Evelyn? No. Frankie, Evelyn is happily married and has two children. How do you not know that? She brings them in for breakfast at least once a week. And I spend time at the library because I love to read."

"Just the books?" He squinted. "Then who is the date with?"

Clementine swallowed. This was the first time she was sharing any of this out loud, and it felt like a big deal. She decided to play this one breezy, nonchalant. That's what regular dating people did. "Madison," she said simply.

"Get the hell away. Are you kidding me? No." He pulled his face back and placed his hand on the lucky blue bandana he tied around his head to cook.

"I'm serious."

"I thought you absolutely hated her after she up and bought the Biscuit. You went on and on. Spoiled. Inexperienced. All of it. I listened to you nonstop."

Clementine sighed, trying to think how to explain. "I liked her a lot before, though, and *then* I hated her, and after that, it was in between. Now, it's…a date. A real one. Do you think I'm crazy?"

"Hell, yeah, I do." He paused. "Doesn't seem like you guys go together."

She returned to her wipe down, the comment landing. Apparently, she wasn't the only one who thought Madison was out of her league. The sentiment took hold and didn't let go. But she didn't fault Frankie. "Well, I'm going anyway. Just to see. Might turn into nothing."

He watched her. "Not that she's some hotshot and you're not," Frankie said, backpedaling. "You're awesome. You know I think so."

"It's fine. I wouldn't have put us together either."

"Okay, but just so you know, dude, that's not what I meant."

She offered him a reassuring smile. "Yeah, yeah. I know." She didn't.

Frankie headed home first, and Clementine lingered in the quiet of the café a few moments longer, trying to pull herself out of it. The really nice popular girl had kissed her back and asked her out, and that was all that mattered, right? She sighed, grabbed her backpack, and headed out the back door to the parking lot behind the building, stopping short when she saw a man leaning against the tail end of her car.

"Can I help you?" Clementine asked.

The man straightened and turned. She knew that smile. Everything in her chilled and stilled. The world was on pause. Holy hell.

"Hey there." He shook his head. "Well, get a look at you. Wow. All grown up. How about a smile for your old dad, huh?"

"What are you doing here?" she asked, shifting her weight. She crossed her arms in front of her, in defense mode already. He looked entirely different than the last time she'd seen him. His sandy brown hair was short now. No beard. His shirt was tucked in for a change, and he was slimmer, physically fit even. Strange. But it was still him all right.

"I hesitated to stop by," he said, running a hand through his hair. It had always been thick and full. A little less so now, but still there. "I know it screws with your life to have to deal with me, but that's not why

I'm here." He held up his hands, palms up. "I just wanted to see you. Let you know how I'm doing, which is pretty great, by the way, and check in on you. Something I should have been doing all along." He gestured to her. "You're my kid. My blood."

"I'm fine. Thanks for stopping by," she said and walked around him to the driver's side door.

"Hey, hold on a second. Please?"

She paused, hand on the door. This man had not been good to her, and she owed him nothing. Yet there was this little part of her that still listened when he spoke. Why was that? Why couldn't she shake that unwelcome hold? "What is it?"

"I was just wondering if you might be free for a cup of coffee. We could catch up. No strings. No obligation beyond that." He shoved his hands into the pockets of his crisp Levi's. "Just a chat."

She exhaled slowly, always on guard. She didn't trust him and desperately wanted to sidestep the turmoil he would undoubtedly introduce. "I have a lot going on."

He glanced behind her at the café. "I can tell. What did this place used to be called?"

"Snappy's Snack Shack. This place does much better than that one." There she went, trying to impress him again. She was still seven years old, looking for approval.

"That's right. I remember that place. I'll have to pick up a biscuit sometime."

Sometime? How long was he planning to linger? Her stomach turned, and nervous energy shot through her veins, swift and powerful. "Sounds good. I better go."

"About that coffee?"

"Can I think about it? Like I said, my schedule is nuts lately." She should just say no and put an end to it. Why hadn't she done that yet?

"Course. Here's my card. Call, text. Whatever." He fished around in his wallet, pulled out a business card, and extended it.

Clementine just blinked for a moment, because since when did her father have a business card? He couldn't have landed a job if it killed him last time he'd been in Whisper Wall. He'd moved from vineyard to vineyard as a day laborer, picking, farming, or cleaning, until he proved himself time and again to be not only lazy and dishonest, but a thief, too. No one would touch Len Monroe in these parts, which is why he'd finally moved on. That is, until he'd gotten tossed in jail for who knew what. She took the card. Landscape Architect and Maintenance. He was self-employed, apparently.

"Business is great," he said, pointing at the card. "It's not like before, Clem. Nothing's the same. I've gotten things together." He stood tall. "I'd love to tell you about it."

She was afraid to hope. She didn't know what it was like to have a parent who actually contributed to her life, society, or anything helpful, really. Her mom had skipped out on them when Clementine was an adolescent, and they'd not heard from her since. Lenny was different, though. He liked to pop in and disrupt her world like a kid with a magnifying glass who wouldn't let the ants work in peace. What if all that changed one day? Nope. She couldn't go there. "Probably not a good idea."

"All I'm asking is a chance to explain a few things. Just think it over." He backed away from her car to give her space. "It's really nice to see you, Clementine. You're doing well for yourself. I can tell."

"Thanks." She nodded and with one last stare at the man whose brown eyes were shaped just like hers, she got the hell out of there, arguing with her beating heart to slow down. She was safe. She was in control, and this man had no power over her. Now she just had to convince herself that the last part was true.

❖

Madison had insisted on picking Clementine up for their date personally and driving her back to the vineyard grounds. When Clementine opened the door wearing a black cocktail dress, Madison's mouth went dry, and she was grateful for the plan because she couldn't imagine missing this moment. She forgot her greeting and just grinned like an idiot instead. She'd never seen Clementine in a dress that she could remember, and she now realized what a shame that was.

"Hi," Clementine said. "You found me." She was smiling, too, which made Madison feel like less of a smiling lunatic, but her words must have still been on a conference call or something because she couldn't find them.

Madison nodded and understood finally that Clementine was referencing the apartment. "Yes, I found you. Really nice. The bricks."

Clementine looked to her right at the red brick exterior of the building. "Bricks, indeed. I find they hold the building up nicely." She quirked a questioning look at Madison. Madison didn't blame her.

She swallowed and tried to explain. "I'm sorry. Your dress. You look so pretty."

Clementine grinned and glanced down. "I wasn't sure how dressy tonight would be. Do you think this is okay? I can change into pants."

"No. Better than okay."

"Great." Clementine disappeared briefly and returned to the door in a long black coat with a sash. She looked sophisticated and...hot.

For the first time, Madison was super aware of the fact that she drove a dusty blue truck, which was great for vineyard life, but less than impressive on a night out with someone you wanted to impress.

"Oh, uh, sorry about the truck."

"Why?" Clementine looked around the inside of the cab, searching for the flaw. "What's it going to do to me?"

Madison laughed. "No. I just wish it was...sleeker. Not so great for driving others to nice restaurants."

"I'm not sorry. It seems very capable of delivering us both." A pause. "You look beautiful." Her voice was smooth and confident, and it made Madison break into goose bumps. She gripped the steering wheel to steady herself. Clementine, with just a simple sentence, affected her like no one ever had. Even in the dim light of the truck, the coat and dress looked amazing on her.

Madison had opted for black pants and a navy blouse she was told brought out her eyes. But she'd never been great with fashion. "It makes me happy you think so."

"I have a thing for curls."

"I have those." Madison was now glad she'd worn her hair down, letting the curls fall freely, unruly as they could sometimes be.

"Indeed you do," Clementine said, holding her gaze. The temperature rose, and Madison exhaled slowly.

They drove to Tangle Valley as the last shred of daylight disappeared altogether. Riding in the truck next to Clementine through the darkened streets of Whisper Wall had her energized and excited for the night ahead. In fact, she'd been looking forward to tonight all week. It was a colder evening, and Madison had the heat all the way up, which only added to the coziness of the drive.

The warm lights from Tangled beckoned, and once they were inside, one of Gabriella's culinary students led them to a table in the corner of the restaurant, where two glasses of pinot grigio waited. "I love everything about this place," Clementine said, once they were seated. The lights were noticeably dim, and the candle on the table flickered, casting a small shadow. Romantic. "The size, the decor, and I can't wait to try the food if it's half as good as what she puts out in the food truck. God. Gabriella is in a league of her own."

Madison smiled. "It's better. The menu tonight features all new dishes. She's trying out a variety of new techniques and seemed really excited earlier today when she described them. All over my head, of course, so I just nod and act impressed because I am."

"She never stops studying. I admire that. So, if I'm not mistaken, you two…"

"Used to date, yes." Madison sipped her water, because it was awkward talking about your ex while on a date with someone new at that same ex's restaurant. "Long in the past, though. And it wasn't a great match, destined not to work."

"Madison, you don't have to feel weird about it. I don't. We've all dated people."

"No?"

"Of course not. I'm not a jealous type, anyway."

"Prosciutto and Parmesan risotto to start you off," their server said and slid a plate in front of each of them.

Clementine took a bite and nearly melted off her seat. Madison's fork hung in midair, en route to her mouth, because she was not missing the moment of sheer enjoyment on Clem's face. "Is it good? Be honest."

"It's okay," Clementine said with a sly shrug and went in for another bite. Madison joined her but all the while stole looks at her date, struck by how much she appreciated the meal. Every once in a while, Clementine would look down at her plate and give her head a shake—as if it was too good to be real.

Madison leaned in. "I've had two meals with you now, and I think the verdict is in."

"What have you decided?"

"That you have an appreciation for food that I can get behind."

"Guilty. What's your favorite food?" Clementine asked and placed her chin in her hand. They were on the second course of the night, the wedge salad, which—bless Gabriella—came with not only pepperoncini but fried pepperoni.

"I can't pick."

"Yes, you can. You're all about data. I guarantee you have a rating system. Just open your mouth and tell me."

That's when she caught that Clementine's eyes were on her mouth. "I can't with you staring at my mouth like that." She took a sip of wine and set her glass down. She leveled a stare. "Makes me want to use it other ways."

She watched Clementine's face turn slowly red, and that's when she heard the comment out loud. "Oh no. I meant kissing, for the record," Madison said and felt her own face heat. God. Clementine was laughing, so that was good. She couldn't help but laugh with her, and then as embarrassment ramped up, she couldn't stop. "I promise. PG-13 intentions."

"I was about to remind you, Ms. LeGrange, that we're on a first date." Clementine looked around. "In public."

Madison took a sip of the chardonnay that had arrived with the salad. It bought her a moment to regain control. Finally, she let her shoulders drop and took a deep inhale. "So this is going well."

That sent Clementine laughing all over again, and Madison was right there with her.

"Well, I hope you're not laughing at my food." Gabriella. They turned to see her standing at their table, wearing her chef's coat and looking like a culinary badass.

"Definitely not," Clementine said, beaming. "You killed it, and we're only halfway through."

"Not as much as you're killing that dress," Gabriella said. She kissed her friend's cheek. "Gorgeous." She hovered between them, close to their ears to not be overheard. "You know who else is killing it? Brenda Anne."

Madison craned her neck, realizing that as caught up as she was with Clementine, she'd pretty much ignored the other eleven tables in the room and had very little idea of who had joined them for the dinner.

"Well, well," Madison said. "She's with a man. You think that's a date?"

Gabriella nodded. "It has to be. They've been canoodling all night. Talking close. Holding hands. Shooting each other little looks. It's a whole love story happening right in front of us as we cook."

"I'm so happy for her," Clementine said, a hand to her heart. "Of everyone I know, she deserves it most." Madison knew just what she meant. Brenda Anne owned the Nifty Nickel, a cute gift shop in the center of town, and had a quirky charm that made people want to stick around. She was also the town's unofficial concierge, recommending restaurants and wineries to all interested tourists, who automatically trusted her. But her life had been relatively solitary. Well, until now.

"I don't think I've known of her ever dating before. This is huge." Madison scanned the room. "The Biddies would be furious to know they're missing this."

Gabriella nodded. "They'd go insane."

Clementine laughed. "Don't worry about them. They'll be in the café tomorrow morning discussing it in detail. Someone will fill them in. Who's the guy? A tourist?"

Gabriella folded her arms. "He's handsome, whoever he is, and a little bit older than her. She's a smitten kitten."

Madison couldn't see the guy's face, but Gabriella was right. Brenda Anne was beaming, which was really sweet.

Gabriella straightened. "I better get back in the kitchen and make sure my chefs aren't in the weeds. Enjoy, you guys. Parmesan lamb chops in a white wine cream sauce is next with a side of garlic fingerling potatoes, paired with the pinot. *Bam.*"

They thanked Gabriella profusely again, and she was off.

Once they were alone, Madison turned to Clementine to comment on the next course, but found she'd gone still. Pale, even. "Hey," she said, squeezing her hand. "Are you okay?"

Clementine still hadn't moved, her eyes trained across the room. Madison followed her gaze right back to Brenda Anne and her date, which didn't compute.

"Clem, talk to me."

Clementine blinked and gave Madison's hand a squeeze. "I'm sorry." She took a sip of water, as if her mouth was suddenly dry. "I just blanked on whether or not I turned my oven off." She tried to smile, but it was a feeble attempt. "I'm sure I did. It's fine."

From that point on, dinner felt different. Clementine was quieter and lost in her own thoughts. She didn't celebrate the food in the same way either, even though it was excellent. Finally, midway through their dessert course, she caught Clementine gripping her spoon tightly in her fist at the same moment Brenda Anne and her date rose from their table to leave.

"Are you and Brenda Anne in some sort of argument?" Madison had never known Brenda Anne to beef with anyone, nor Clementine, but she was grasping.

Clementine waited until the couple had disappeared through the door before turning to Madison, hesitation all over her face. "It's my dad."

Madison blinked. "What about him? Did something happen?" She tried to remember what she knew of Clementine's parents, but honestly, not a lot.

"He seemed okay tonight, living it up with Brenda Anne."

That's when it struck and her head swiveled in the direction of the empty table. "Wait. That was your *father* over there? The handsome guy with Brenda Anne?"

"The handsome guy." Clementine raised a resigned shoulder. "I haven't seen him in a few years. He just showed up earlier this week out of nowhere, which is what he does." She met Madison's eyes. "He has a way of worming his way in." She sighed. "I would hate to see Brenda Anne mixed up with him."

"She looked pretty mixed up already." Madison frowned. "I'm really sorry. I had no idea."

"Don't be. Just part of my life. I should have known it was only a matter of time." She sat back in her chair, resigned. "I had hoped he was just here for a day or two before moving on, but now it seems he might be hanging around."

"You want to get out of here?"

"Can we?"

Madison signaled for the check, and their server approached. "Ms. LeGrange, Ms. Wilder has already taken care of your meals."

She shook her head. Damn Joey, never letting her pay for anything, which was silly when the restaurant only had so many tables. "I'll be sure to thank her," she said.

"She doesn't have to buy my dinner," Clementine said, alarmed. "I don't work here. I don't mind paying."

"You can argue that point until the sun rises and sets again. She's not going to listen. That's Joey. Plus, she very much supports us."

"Us?" Clementine raised an eyebrow. Might have been playful. Definitely sexy.

Madison didn't waver. "There's an us. We just haven't defined what the us is. We go on dates now. That's part of us."

Clementine nodded. "We make out."

"We do. We sometimes argue, though that kinda plays up the whole tension factor."

"It can be hot, kissing the enemy."

Madison grinned, everything heating pleasantly. "I'm not going to complain about it."

"Good." Clementine was starting to relax, flirt with her again. Madison had no problem distracting her from the stresses of her father's arrival on the scene. Selfishly, however, she wanted Clementine's attention for her own reasons.

"Do I have to take you home after this?" Madison asked.

Clementine bought herself time and delicately sipped the last of the dolcetto, a slam dunk served with the flourless chocolate hazelnut cake. Chocolate and red wine happened to be Madison's favorite combo, and the spiciness of the dolcetto highlighted the hazelnut to perfection. "Where were you hoping to take me?" Her voice was quieter, signaling that the question made her nervous. Madison didn't want that.

"Well, you've seen the vineyard by day. What if we took a frigid stroll by night? Clear skies always make for a nice walk."

"In frigid temperatures?"

"Only adds to the adventure."

"You're crazy."

"I'm feeling a little out of sorts, yeah," Madison said, holding their eye contact. There was no denying her meaning. Clementine had her on her toes, trying to understand these new feelings and still concentrate on her job, her life, when all she wanted to do was find out what was happening with Clementine and hers. If she was having a good day, and what drew her to the cat she'd mentioned several times. The idea that they'd lived in such close proximity on and off since they were kids was mind-blowing to Madison. So much time wasted, not noticing someone who had such an unforgettable effect on her. She bristled at the thought.

"I'd love to take this arctic walk."

"Yeah?" She inclined her head to the door, eyes still on Clementine. She didn't want to look away because she was too beautiful to be believed. "Let's do it."

Madison walked them along the perimeter path until they reached a break in the small white fence that separated the walkway from the vines. "Chardonnay," Madison said and took Clem's hand. The wind hit, and they went still, bracing against it.

"Will the grapes be okay tonight?"

"We're not expected to freeze, so ice shouldn't be an issue. But I'll keep an eye on the weather reports. I don't want frost on these guys." She ran her thumb and forefinger over a grape. "If we get it, Bobby will blow it off with the fans."

"A rescue mission."

"Exactly."

They were quite a distance into the vineyard, far enough that the sky took over, and the buildings began to vanish. This was her happy place, and she loved that Clementine was here to experience it with her. Plus, the stars must have heard they were coming and put on their show, appearing bright and plentiful.

"Wow," Clementine said, tugging on Madison's hand and pulling them to a stop. "You were right about nighttime out here. It's"—she shook her head, searching—"startlingly beautiful. Worth the Eskimo simulation."

Madison beamed, happy to hear that Clementine liked it out here as much as she did. "When I walk out here at night, I'm always reminded how small I am in the scope of the universe, but also how important. I'm part of it. We all are."

"I like that." Clementine stared up at the night sky. "Small and big at the same time."

"Just goes to show you that nothing is ever just one thing."

Clementine raised her hand to Madison's cheek. "If your hand was not freezing, this would be a really romantic moment." Clementine laughed and dropped her hand, only for Madison to lift it up and put it right back. "The kinds of things I'm willing to do for you."

"Icicle cheeks?"

"Are my new favorite." The bright sky illuminated Clementine's blue eyes, and Madison couldn't resist her. She leaned in for what she thought would be a simple kiss, but once her lips met Clem's, she wasn't in any hurry to continue their walk. She had the softest mouth, and their ability to kiss left Madison staggered. She'd always believed she had experienced mad chemistry before, but this was a new level. Every part of Madison trembled against that kiss, reaching for more, longing to take it further.

"Definitely warmer this way," Clementine murmured against Madison's mouth. "We might be on to something." They were, too. It was called amazing kissing in a vineyard at night, not to be confused with amazing kissing in a café after closing. She couldn't wait to add to that list.

Breathless and turned the hell on, Madison pulled her mouth away. "We should have done this years ago."

Clementine smiled and touched her lips. "You wouldn't have had a ton of convincing to do." They grinned at each other, and Clementine looked behind her. "Let's keep walking. I like it out here. The penguins should be by soon."

Madison chuckled and led the way. "There's something about the dark, isn't there? That makes things easier to say."

Clementine nodded. "It's a safety blanket. No glaring spotlight to make you feel like you're on display. You can hide."

"I think that's exactly it. When Joey and I would have sleepovers, we'd lie in our sleeping bags on her floor or mine and just put it all out there, confess all our secrets, knowing everything we said was secure, safe. It was okay to be sad or angry or happy. Just voices in the dark." She looked at Clementine. "I can't stop thinking about you."

"Oh." Clementine swallowed.

"Maybe that's not cool in a modern dating world where you're not supposed to show your cards early on. But I'm not hip enough to know all the rules." She rolled her lips in. "I'm just me, and the darkness gives me the courage to tell you that. You should also know that I'm not someone who expresses my feelings a ton, so this is a moment."

Clementine watched the ground as they walked. Finally, she looked over at Madison. "I don't think you have to worry about rules or what's considered cool when you're with me. I've never been considered cool, and I'm just finally learning to be okay with that." She held up a hand when Madison opened her mouth to argue. "You don't have to argue otherwise. It's okay. I was the girl from the trailer park who learned not to hope for much, but here's the thing." She looked up at the sky. "Me standing with you here in the dark has me starting to hope. For an us. Is that crazy?" She touched her chest. "My heart is beating a million times a minute." She paused their walk and turned toward the vines, taking a minute.

Madison came up behind her and encircled her waist. With her chin on Clementine's shoulder, she spoke to her quietly. "Please dare to hope. Every step we take forward feels to me like I'm finally headed in the right direction, and for so long, I've been lost."

"You?" Clementine asked. "You always seem so together, like someone who has it all."

"Sometimes you don't know what's been missing until you find it."

Clementine turned in her arms. "I'm terrified. I wasn't going to do any of this. Even after we kissed, I was planning to back away because, Madison, things like this don't normally happen to me, and I very much expect this to be temporary."

"But what if it's not?"

The wind picked up, and they braced, holding on to each other for warmth, Clementine's body pressed to hers. Madison closed her eyes and memorized the moment. Things were changing between them, slowly but surely, and she didn't want to miss a second.

"Maybe that's the part I'm most afraid of. Then what?" She met Madison's gaze. "What if I'm in over my head."

"What if the town is invaded by circus performers?"

Clementine's eyebrows leaped to her forehead. "I think I'd enjoy that."

Madison gave her a playful squeeze. "But you see my point."

She nodded. "You want me to stop planning on the worst, which, you should know, goes against every part of my being." She offered a rueful laugh, but the sentiment was anything but funny.

"I don't want to be another disappointment," Madison whispered. "Don't you see that?"

"I'm trying. Some moments that works better than others."

Madison nodded, trying to be understanding yet reassuring, a balancing act. "Can you try and extend me a little bit of trust? I don't need all of it. How about just a quarter?"

Clementine's lips tugged. "You want me to one-quarter trust you?"

"I do. I can submit my request in writing. Or we can…kiss on it."

"Well, I already know that I like your lips," Clementine said wistfully.

"They like you." She grinned. "A lot."

"And I like your smile. The moonlit version has definite perks. The only downside of tonight is that I can no longer feel my hands or feet. I one-quarter trust that they're still there."

Madison frowned and took Clem's hands in her own. "We should probably head back. Do I have to take you home?"

"Where do you want to take me?"

"My cottage is just over there, but I don't want you to feel like—"

"Your cottage? Well, this is incredibly forward."

Madison opened her mouth to explain. Her intentions were honorable, after all, unless Clementine didn't want them to be.

A cheeky grin from Clementine thwarted her effort. "You're too easy to tease. Let's go. I'd love to see where the winemaker lives, and I'm hopeful there's heat." She slid her hand into Madison's.

"Have you met us?"

"Nice one," Clementine said, as they strolled the vines beneath a skyful of stars.

CHAPTER NINE

Madison, she learned, lived in the Sunrise Cottage, which appeared absolutely quaint on the outside. Three steps led up to a small porch where Madison'd placed two chairs. A gray door marked the entrance. Clementine set her hands on her hips. "It's like the Wilders grew this place out of the ground. It matches everything else on the property perfectly."

"My thoughts exactly," Madison said. "My place is closest to Joey at the Big House over there, and just up the path you'll find Gabriella, Bobby, Loretta and the rest of the live-ins. Just a handful."

Clementine trailed Madison up the steps. "You guys have your own community out here. I'm surprised you ever leave."

"We have to. For biscuits." She flashed a smile. "Follow me."

Clementine would have followed Madison anywhere that night. Not only had Madison turned what could have been a very upsetting evening into the most romantic date she'd ever been on, but Madison had also managed to get Clementine to relax, drop her guard even. Not many people had that effect on her.

"This is very you," Clementine said, as she moved into the main portion of the cottage.

"You're not the first person to say that. Gabriella's cottage has a very similar layout but has been decorated to the brim. Flowers, blankets, curtains, and candles. Mine is, well, more suited to my aesthetic. I don't know if that's a good or a bad thing."

The decor was minimalistic, but clean and comfortable. "Definitely not bad. My apartment has lots of cuddly, secondhand furniture, but it's run-down as hell." Madison's cottage was subtly decorated with touches of oranges and gray. A couch and a chair, but they didn't take up much room. On the wall in front of her was a painting of a long, empty sidewalk flanked by tall trees in autumn. Above the couch was a landscape of a mature oak, offering its branches to shade a boy reading a book at its base. There weren't any knickknacks or personal photos visible, even though Madison had good friends and her parents in Florida. The surfaces were clean and clear of clutter. That checked out. The stark organization felt very Madison. A series of charts hung on her fridge in the open kitchen that Clementine had to assume had something to do with wine and chemistry and who knew what else? A signal to Madison's mathematical, analytical side. She touched one of the charts.

"Keeps my brain going," Madison said, gesturing to the fridge. "I rotate them every other week. I'm a nerd."

Clementine smothered a smile. "You are, but you embracing your nerd-dom makes you cool. I always envied how smart you were." And how beautiful, and kind, and effortless. It had taken Clementine some time as a teenager to understand that she didn't necessarily want to *be* Madison as much as she wanted to be *with* Madison, to experience all of those things about her up close and personal. And now, here she was. The interesting thing? Madison LeGrange actually lived up to every overexaggerated fantasy Clementine had had about her, which was no easy feat. No, Madison definitely wasn't perfect, as evidenced by the reckless manner in which she purchased the café, but Clementine wasn't drawn to perfection. She was, however, drawn to Madison, the real version of her, whom she liked a great deal.

"Did you enjoy high school?" Madison held up a bottle of pinot noir, and Clementine nodded.

"Yes and no," Clementine said, as Madison poured two glasses. "I was quiet. Everyone was mostly friendly to me, and that made school a nice refuge from home, where that wasn't generally the case."

Madison frowned and handed her a glass. "I'm so sorry."

"It's okay. Makes you stronger, if nothing else." Clementine lifted a shoulder. "I've learned to look for silver linings."

"Well, that makes you a better person than me. I'd be resentful as hell."

"There's some of that, too." She took a sip of the wine Madison had passed her and let the smoky flavor settle. "But I didn't have true friends at school and was well aware of it. No one called me up on the weekend for a movie or to go to a party. I was mostly a figure in the background."

Madison frowned. "That was our loss. Entirely."

She exhaled. "But when I started working at the Biscuit, I really found my voice. I got to know more and more of the people in town, and they got to know me. I was a face that people *expected* to see every morning. I was a part of their day, and that meant I mattered. That was huge."

"I like this part of the story more, because it's true. It's exactly how I've always felt as a customer. I looked forward to stopping in. More so now, obviously." She paused, changing directions. "I know you're still not thrilled with me for buying the café, but in this moment, with you in my kitchen, it's feeling like the smartest decision I've ever made."

"What do you put on your sandwich bread?" Clementine pivoted out of the compliment out of habit, but it was also a legitimate question.

Madison didn't flinch. "I'm a mayonnaise kind of woman." A pause. "Is there a right answer?"

"Mustard people alarm me."

"Huh. I'll be on the lookout for them."

"You'd be well advised."

"Also?"

"Yep?"

Madison set down her glass. "You totally sidestepped my having-you-here-in-my-kitchen declaration."

Busted. Madison was kind, but that didn't make her timid. She said what she thought and didn't let much slide. She kept Clementine on her toes, which might actually be good for her.

"I know. Let me try again." She sighed. "I'm happy to be in the kitchen." She looked around. "It's a very nice kitchen."

Madison approached her. "Mm-hmm."

"In fact, it even looks serviceable. You can make a good sandwich here. With mayonnaise." Madison took Clementine's drink and placed it on the counter. "We're both lucky to spend time here." She grinned just as Madison's lips descended on hers, and God in heaven, her heart sang and her body yearned, waking the hell up all over again. How was Madison so good at making that happen? She angled her mouth over Madison's for better access, allowing Madison's tongue entrance and nearly sinking to her knees, as they were about to give out on her. Madison wrapped her arms around Clementine's neck and was up on her toes, which took care of their subtle height difference and brought Madison even closer. Chest to chest, Clementine could feel Madison's breasts pressed to hers, and it was the most amazing feeling she had ever experienced. Her underwear was instantly wet. She backed Madison up against the kitchen counter, their legs staggered, which provided even more friction. *God, yes.* She pressed against Madison's thigh, then did it again, needing more, hungry for purchase. The sensations coming from between her legs were unreal, and it had only been a few moments. And were they actually doing this? How far were they going exactly? Her brain tried to catch up but wasn't working properly. She lifted her thigh, pressing it to Madison's center this time and making her gasp.

Buzz. Buzz.

They ignored the annoying phone notification, and Madison switched their positions, pressing Clementine against the counter. The new dynamic had Clementine even hotter. She loved Madison's ambition and had no problem letting her be in charge. Well, sometimes.

More distant buzzing.

"What if there's an emergency?" Clementine asked, breathless.

Madison pulled Clem's mouth right back in for another searing, openmouthed kiss. "There's no emergency."

The buzzing stopped. And then started again. Damn.

"There was, last year. Didn't part of this vineyard burn down?"

That did it. Madison pulled away from the kiss, closed her eyes, and sighed. "Okay, but this better be good." She stalked over to the phone, held it up, and showed Clementine. Gabriella. "Hey, what's up?" A pause. "I don't sound weird." Clementine smothered a smile because Madison's voice was a little breathier than usual with a hint of a rasp. She'd done that, and the pride was immeasurable. Another pause. "I'm just relaxing, you know." Madison turned to her and mouthed, "I'm sorry."

Clementine replied with a smile.

"We loved it. Both of us. Sorry we didn't get to tell you personally."

A pause. "Why would I just say that if it wasn't true? I've always been honest with you about food…Mm-hmm…Yes." Silence. "I didn't catch that little hiccup, no. The cinnamon worked, regardless. Don't worry."

Madison let her head fall backward in exasperation, but to her credit she was friendly to Gabriella, even if a little short. The conversation continued, and with each second that passed, Clementine felt her wits creep back in a little at a time. She took a seat on the couch and exhaled slowly as Madison chatted. Maybe leaping into bed wasn't the best idea. In fact, she'd never really been a leaper in regards to anything. Why was she starting now with someone that felt important?

Madison clicked off the call. "Turns out it was *not* an emergency."

"Gabriella checking on her food?"

"Bingo. Tell me we didn't lose the mood."

Clementine smiled. "I have a feeling we could easily recapture it, but maybe this isn't the time. It was such a great night, and—"

"Say no more. I get it."

Clementine stood and squeezed Madison's hand. "Shall we go?"

"Yes. Truck is still at Tangled, so we can take the path. Kiss me first?" Madison said as they moved onto her porch.

Clementine grinned and did just that, savoring the softness of Madison's lips. She'd dream about them later. "Thank you for tonight, for everything. I nearly self-destructed at dinner, but you were there to catch me. Thank you for that."

Madison grinned, looking beautiful and sexy beneath the halo of the porch light. "I will always catch you. Every time."

Clementine nodded. "Good, because it's a really nice feeling." She held her gaze for a final beat, and then with her hands in the pockets of her coat, they headed off into the night, side by side.

"Oh, wait," Madison said, patting her pocket. "My keys. I'll catch up."

"No problem. I'll chat with the grapes."

As Clementine walked the quaint path in silence, her thoughts shifted to the moment Madison had picked her up at her apartment, and like a recounting of the night in fast motion, she saw everything replay. The looks, the words, the kissing. God, the kissing. She was worked up all over again and missing Madison, her touch. Her smile. She paused in the middle of the path, and in that exact moment a blast of cold air hit her like a damn wake-up call. She blinked, turned around, and stared at the cottage down the road, only hesitating a moment before stalking right back down the path.

Madison opened the door just as Clementine arrived in front of it. Her lips were on Madison's before she could speak. Up against the open door. And then the wall, as Madison kicked it closed behind them. She pulled back and looked questioningly into Clem's eyes.

"I changed my mind," she said. "Is that okay?"

"More than okay," Madison said, grinning as her eyes dropped to Clementine's lips. The hunger on display had Clementine's body practically vibrating with anticipation. Her dress was slid down her shoulders to her waist right there in front of the door. Madison's gaze dropped to her bra and all it revealed. She kissed her way down the center of her cleavage, then pulled both cups down entirely, exposing Clementine's breasts and taking a moment to marvel. She lifted one to her mouth and sucked its nipple as Clementine's eyes slammed shut, pinpricks of pleasure hitting all over. She held on to the wall for support, her mouth open as she searched for air. Yeah, this had been a good idea. Madison's tongue, her teeth, all teasing Clementine mercilessly as her arousal climbed. "God, look at you," Madison breathed, switching her attention to the other breast. Their pace was slow. So much to be discovered about each other. Clementine had her hands in those beautiful curls as her hips began to push out and her need climbed. Madison, sensing her request, pulled her dress to the floor, and she easily stepped out of it, leaving her clothed in just her panties and displaced bra. Madison was instantly on her knees. She kissed her way up Clementine's legs to her thighs, using her thumbs to part them slightly and placing an openmouthed kiss on the square of underwear between them that nearly brought Clementine to the floor. Madison curved her fingers into the waistband of her panties and lowered them just a tad, revealing the sensitive skin of her abdomen, which she kissed and licked until Clementine simply couldn't anymore. "I'm losing my balance," she whispered, her knees shaking.

Madison didn't hesitate. With dark blue hooded eyes, she took Clementine by the hand and led her the short distance to her bedroom. A lamp across the room offered a small amount of light. She stood in front of the bed and faced Madison, who immediately slid Clementine's underwear down her legs, reached between them, and explored.

"God," Clementine said, as she was touched so very intimately.

Madison's fingers continued to softly explore, pushing through wetness and gently massaging. Her hands on Madison's shoulders, she began to move her hips in rhythm with Madison's slow exploration. She tried to pick up speed, but Madison held strong, determined. She'd not yet been inside, and Clementine's desire for her there was unreal. "Take me," she whispered in Madison's ear as her hips rocked in a dizzying plea. "Please. I need you." Her breasts were swaying, she could tell. Madison looked down at them in satisfaction. Her stroking became more insistent, and that was good. That was very good. Clementine pushed herself against Madison's hand, nearly there, starving for more. Madison wrapped an arm around Clementine's waist to anchor her, and thrust her fingers inside in one motion. Clementine heard the moan strangle in her throat. On the brink of what she wanted, no longer in control, she held on as Madison slid in and out of her, slowly at first and then with command. The pressure inside her was fierce, and when the release came, Clementine went still and taut as the pleasure overtook her. Madison hadn't stopped, and that kept the sensations pulsing through her in overwhelming intensity. Finally, spent, sated, and wondering where she was, Clementine fell backward onto the bed. "I'm gonna need a minute." Madison afforded her maybe that and not a second more before she knelt in front of Clementine and took her in her mouth. Clementine gasped, convinced she was done. "I can't," she murmured, just as familiar stirrings hit. How was this possible? With her tongue, Madison worked intoxicating magic, and before she knew it, Clementine was on the brink again. The second orgasm came fast and furious. Clementine braced against its impact with no choice but to submit to the wonderful payoff. "How?" was all she could manage.

Madison smiled up at her. "My ambition has never steered me wrong." She climbed up the bed, and Clementine joined her among the pillows, a much more comfortable spot. Madison stared down at her naked body. "And I had a lot of motivation. You're beautiful."

That's when Clementine realized that Madison still wore every single stitch of clothes that she'd arrived in. Wildly unfair. Clementine wanted nothing more than to see her, touch her, and take her wonderful places. With her desire taking over, she found Madison's lips and kissed them, sinking into the wonder of her mouth, sliding her tongue inside, and climbing on top.

"Oh, hi," Madison said, her eyes sparkling up at Clementine.

"Oh, this is good," Clementine said, nestling in, loving her new vantage point. With one hand between them, she unbuttoned Madison's pants and watched as her eyes darkened. "I'm taking these off you," Clementine informed her and did just that. "These, too," Clementine said, running a hand over the slim-cut navy briefs. Madison nodded, wordlessly. She ran both hands up Madison's thighs to her shirt, which she quickly pushed up, revealing breasts nearly bursting out of a pink bra. She kissed the top of each one, moaning quietly, so enraptured she hoped this never ended. At the same time, she needed more, pushing the shirt the rest of the way off and reaching behind Madison to expertly unclasp her bra. Lying there naked, and breathing in short breaths, Madison was devastatingly sexy. "Wow," Clementine breathed, trailing one finger from Madison's chest to her stomach. She didn't even know where to begin, except she did. With her hips between Madison's legs, she kissed her mouth hungrily and began to rock against her.

Madison closed her eyes and moaned. She opened her legs, allowing Clementine better access. "Oh my God," Madison murmured.

Clementine loved every second of this. She buried her face in Madison's neck, kissing it softly. She paid attention to Madison's cues, how desperate she slowly became. She took her to the brink and then withdrew her hips to a quiet whimper from Madison, who clung to her in need. She turned her attention to Madison's breasts, round and perfect. She pushed them together and went to work with her mouth, swirling her tongue around first one nipple and then the other. Madison's were sensitive, she learned, and her hips bucked with the attention. Clementine followed the curve of her body lower, kissing her stomach, her abdomen, and then the insides of her thighs softly, slowly. Madison tilted her hips, asking, squirming beneath Clementine, who smiled and obliged. She settled in between her legs and with her tongue touched her softly. "Oh, yes," she heard Madison hiss. She traced a lazy pattern, circling Madison's most sensitive spot, teasing and pulling away as Madison rocked her hips and whimpered. Finally, she kissed her fully, using her lips to tug and suck gently. With her fingers, she pushed inside, taking Madison, pumping, following the fast-paced rhythm Madison set for her as her tongue went to work.

Finally, Madison bowed and went still, crying out loudly, her back arched. Clementine watched the display in amazement, memorizing the beauty. She crawled up the bed and placed a kiss on the underside of Madison's jaw.

Madison turned to her and cradled her face. "That was other-wordly."

Clementine smiled, proud of the endorsement. "I kind of thought we'd be good together, given the way we kiss, but I think I under-estimated."

"We are combustible," Madison said, turning into her and kissing her lips. "Chemistry in a bottle. God."

"What should we do now?"

Madison got a very serious look on her face. "I have an idea."

"And what's that?"

"Chocolate chip cookies. The absolute best chaser for sex."

"Chocolate, huh?" Clementine asked with a laugh. This was adorable.

"Uh-huh. I love it so much. Don't go anywhere, okay?"

Clementine watched as Madison scampered out of the room without a stitch of clothes and returned moments later with a plate with two cookies.

"I heated them in the microwave."

Clementine stole a cookie and melted at the gooey chocolaty center. "Okay, I'm calling it now. Best night ever."

Madison, mouth full of cookie, kissed her lips. "You can say that again."

"Best night ever," Clementine repeated, popped the rest of her cookie, and snuggled up to the sexiest woman she'd ever met.

❖

Madison woke to the sound of rain pelting against her window and a wonderful warmth against her side. She was happy. That much she knew, though her brain hadn't woken enough to fully understand why. She moved toward the warmth, opened her eyes, and then remembered. *Clementine.* Their wonderful night together. She grinned and stretched her one free arm since Clementine slept on the other one. She softly kissed Clem's exposed shoulder, careful not to wake her. They'd been up so late, and this was Clementine's one morning a week to sleep in. Her day off. As she listened to the soothing sound of the rain, Madison watched Clementine sleep. With her blond hair fanned out across the pillow and the sheet tucked beneath her arms, she looked angelic and beautiful. How were her lips so perfect? She remembered kissing them last night, and how it startled her, yet again, how well they fit against hers. She must have fallen back asleep, which was rare for her, always an early riser, because the next thing she remembered was movement against Clementine's body and then a pair of slate blue eyes looking across the pillow into hers.

"How is it morning already?" Clementine asked in a sleepy voice. She lifted her shoulders to her ears, stretching. "I slept really hard."

"You have a morning voice," Madison said with a smile. "I love it."

"Yeah?" Clementine kissed Madison's shoulder. "You know what I love? Waking up here, with you. Also? You're still naked." She eased the sheet down Madison's body, leaving her topless and staring up at Clementine who'd propped herself up on her forearm. Oh, she liked morning Clementine a lot. She was smooth. "It's raining," Clementine said softly as she traced the outside of Madison's breast with her finger. Madison took a slow inhale because that did tantalizing things to her. The stirrings low in her body shifted into overdrive.

"I noticed that."

Clementine pressed her lips against Madison's neck and then raised her gaze to her mouth. "I've always been a sucker for rainy mornings. They feel like a hall pass to be lazy." She placed a soft kiss on Madison's lips and returned her focus to her breasts, tracing smaller circles, this time around her nipple. Madison's stomach tightened, and her breathing went shallow. She changed her position, no longer comfortable. That didn't help. Not with Clementine touching her so intimately like she had all the time in the damn world. Madison's eyes fluttered closed when Clementine slowly took the nipple in her mouth and sucked. She saw stars, and the aching between her legs was not something she could easily ignore. Clementine pushed herself into a sitting position and slowly pulled the sheet down, watching as the rest of Madison's naked body was revealed to her. She ran a hand from

Madison's waist, across the curve of her hip, to her thigh as goose bumps broke out on Madison's arms, and she raised her hips ever so slightly.

"Okay, I think you more than like the rain. I might like it a whole lot more now, too."

Clementine offered a small smile. "Confession. It might be a little bit more than the rain that gets me going."

Madison moaned and swallowed as Clementine trailed her hand down to her inner thigh, trying to hold on to her composure and losing. "Totally allowed." With a small smile Clementine climbed on top, ground her hips against Madison once, and kissed her way down Madison's body, taking her sweet damn time, driving Madison insane. The room had gone quiet, with the exception of Madison's quick breaths and the drops against the window. Every part of her was fully awake and at the mercy of this wonderful torture. Clementine crawled farther down the bed, parted Madison's legs, and settled fully between them, the anticipation almost enough all on its own. She touched Madison softly with her tongue, and Madison's hips bucked as pleasure shot through her like a rocket. She heard herself whimper quietly. Holding her legs in place, Clementine settled in and began to do wondrous things with her mouth. Sweet heaven, was that a figure eight? No clue. Her eyes practically crossed as the pressure built steadily and with purpose. What she wouldn't give to enjoy this longer, but at the same time, she longed desperately for the release that was heading her way like a speeding train. Clementine, on the other hand, had no such sense of urgency. Her skillful attention was meant to prolong the experience, and what an experience it was. Clementine had moved on to using her lips now, Madison realized distantly, kissing and sucking gently. Madison forgot where she was, the year, her goddamn name. Her hips moved in rhythm with Clementine's mouth as she edged closer and closer until, with a cry, she careened over the edge into blissful explosion, gripping the sheets as she rode out the ripples, her hips moving rapidly with the staggering payoff.

When her conscious thought returned, she was aware of Clementine lying next to her, naked and gorgeous and looking intensely proud of her accomplishment. "You deserve some sort of certification," Madison said. "No. Retracted. You might need to teach the course."

"What can I say?" Clementine lifted a shoulder. "I have a few passions."

"Biscuits and morning sex?"

"How did you know that?"

Madison laughed. "Just a few clues I followed."

The grin on Clementine's face faded, and she touched a strand of Madison's curls. "You're so beautiful. Sometimes I can't wrap my mind around it."

Madison's insides went soft. The thing about Clementine was that no matter what she said, you knew she was being truthful and speaking from the heart. She'd never encountered that dependability before Clem. "As flattering as that is, I think you stole my line. Because I couldn't take my damn eyes off you last night over dinner. Or at the café. Or really anywhere I see you. You drive me crazy."

"I didn't know that," Clementine said. The blush hit her cheeks in a matter of seconds and spread down her neck. Adorable.

"Well, don't ever forget it," Madison said, sliding on top. She stared down at Clementine and swept a strand of hair from her forehead tenderly. A clap of thunder hit, and Madison looked over her shoulder. "Oh, look. Still raining." She slid her thigh between Clementine's and raised it playfully, grinning. "That means the lazy morning continues, right?"

Clementine's lips parted. "I mean, rules are rules."

Another clap of thunder. Louder this time. Now this was a soundtrack Madison could work to. Mornings would never look the same again, she thought, as she took exactly what she wanted.

CHAPTER TEN

Madison's stomach rumbled as she waited in line in front of Jolene, the resident food truck at Tangle Valley. She was moments too late and found herself behind a group of tourists from one of the daily wine buses that worked the area. She had a million things to accomplish that afternoon, including two job interviews to replace a member of her crew who got an offer in Sonoma, but for the first time in a long while, she didn't feel stressed or pressured at the number of items on her to-do list. Everything that needed to get done would get done, right? Not a big deal. Lately, life felt a lot bigger than just her job and absolutely wonderful. Completely unexpected, she had this new exciting woman taking up half her focus. Okay, *more*. She'd daydreamed about Clementine naked in her bed for half her work morning. She grinned lazily because their weekend had been more than memorable. She felt lighter today, more energetic, and ready to take on the world on her own terms. She shook her head because, yes, she was a damn walking cliché.

"Well, look who's here to patronize my truck," Gabriella said, climbing down. She no longer worked in Jolene full-time now that Tangled had opened to such success, but she did check in on the culinary students she charged to run it. They had a pretty impressive system happening.

"Like I'd ever miss Goodfella day." Gabriella's perfect little slider—with salami, pepperoni, prosciutto, mozzarella, roasted red peppers, and a vinaigrette she waited all week for—was worthy of rock star attention.

Gabriella folded her arms and grinned. "It's developing quite a following from the locals. Powell Rogers is here every Monday when we pop open the window. Takes back two extra to the car dealership for his second lunch at three p.m."

"I can't believe that's never occurred to me," Madison said. "I'll take eleven."

"Eleven? I'm impressed."

"I'm starving."

The line moved forward, but Gabriella stuck around to shoot the breeze with Madison while she waited. "You're glowing, you know. Kinda like you were two nights ago at the restaurant. Tell me I'm wrong. I dare you."

Madison raised a shoulder and kept her gaze on the menu board that hung above the truck's window. "I glow now. It's what I do. Will you have arancini tomorrow?"

"I can't discuss arancini with you when you're being coy and know it. You better stop being coy. Right now." Madison casually looked in Gabriella's direction. "You're doing it again. This time with your coy eyes. That means things are going well with Clementine, aren't they?"

"They are," she said, losing the nonchalance and relaxing into a sincere grin.

Gabriella squeezed her forearm and her matchmaker-face-of-victory appeared. "I can't even tell you how badly I want to do about six cartwheels down that hill."

"The wine bus would love it. Probably throw dollar bills. I don't think there's any reason not to."

"Don't tempt me, Maddie. What else?" She was nearly to the front of the line.

"It's jarring."

Gabriella squinted. "Why would you say that?"

"I'm not used to things working out so well," Madison explained. "My life has always been good, fulfilling, but also pretty even-keeled without a lot of excitement." She exhaled. "Lately, I'm excited for each new minute. I'm having to get used to it. It's not me. I feel like…you."

The playfulness fell right off Gabriella. "You're tugging at my heartstrings here. That's amazing, even if it does feel scary right now. I think that's normal."

"And I hear how that sounds when I say all of this to someone

I was once in a relationship with, but I want you to know that I was excited about us, but in a different way. It's hard to explain."

Gabriella placed a palm flat on her chest. "I'm not taking it personally. I promise." She dropped her head to the side. "Believe me when I say that I'm so happy for you."

"Thank you. There's just this click with me and her."

Gabriella nodded. "I know the click. I've not too long ago experienced it for the first time myself. Once you click, nothing else compares."

"What can I get you?" Chelsea, the gossipy twelfth grader, asked from the window of the truck.

"Eleven sliders, please," Madison said.

Chelsea blinked.

"You heard the woman," Gabriella barked. "She has a lot on her plate. Gotta keep her energy up." She turned to Madison, who shook her head and held up a more reasonable three fingers to Chelsea. "Can we all catch up with wine and pizza with crispy pepperoni soon? And I mean really crispy. I want to hear more about your exciting life while I eat crispy food."

"You want the dish. No pun intended."

"No, no, no." A pause. Gabriella leveled a stare. "I *need* it."

Madison laughed. "At least you're up-front about it."

"Always. So we'll talk soon?"

"Deal."

"I'll tell Joey."

❖

The Nifty Nickel was moderately busy when Clementine arrived. The quaint gift shop was one of her favorites to peruse, full of seasonal decor, knickknacks, greeting cards, and all sorts of Whisper Wall mementos for tourists to take back home. She walked slowly, taking in the various displays, feigning interest in a wine country wall calendar until the customer count dwindled down to just her. Brenda Anne, whom she considered a friend, stood behind the counter, studying her laptop, when she approached. Clementine put the small cornucopia centerpiece she'd discovered on the counter.

"Well, hey there, Clem. I didn't see you sneak in. A stealthy little ninja is what you are. That's right." Brenda Anne beamed the way she always did.

"Just checking out the autumn wares."

"This centerpiece is my absolute favorite," Brenda Anne said, admiring it. "We got ten of them in last Wednesday, and I only have three left. Super tickled about that. Always give myself a little pat on the back when that happens. You know, for my scouting skills." She shook her head. "I don't know what I'm saying, a pat on the back. I give myself a brownie, that's what."

"Now you're talking. I got a dozen from the Dark Room the other day that I highly recommend."

"Oh, that place. Good golly, it's dangerous. I'll stop by after work. Never could stay away from a good brownie."

Clementine shifted her weight as Brenda Anne rang her up, something she did when she was nervous. She wasn't here to purchase a centerpiece. That was simply her cover. "Hey, I saw you at Tangled the other night. Fantastic meal, wasn't it?"

"God on a tennis court. It was. I haven't stopped thinking about that cake. It haunts me in the nighttime hours. You know, right before bed? My weak spot on the clock."

"Oh, me, too." She swallowed. "I saw you were there with Lenny."

Cue the immediate blush. "Yes, Len. He's new to town. Did he tell you people call him Lenny? He hadn't mentioned that."

"He's my father."

The smile on Brenda Anne's face dimmed to fifty percent of its wattage. "Oh. I had no idea, but of course, that makes sense. Len Monroe. I just figured it was coincidence."

"No. He hasn't been in town for years now, so it makes sense you wouldn't know about our connection." Brenda Anne had moved to town and opened the Nickel maybe six or seven years prior and wouldn't have crossed paths with her father, who had been long gone at that point.

"Well, he is just a dream," Brenda Anne said, melting into a puddle. "I can see why you've turned into such a wonderful person, Clementine."

Damn. This was going to be hard. "Here's the thing."

Brenda Anne frowned. "Your face is worrying me."

Clementine passed her a wan smile. "I don't know where things stand with him now. I haven't seen him in years, but the least I can do is warn you that he hasn't always been the most reliable of people."

"Oh." Brenda Anne looked like someone had just stolen her joy. Clementine hated that it had been her. "I appreciate you looking out for me, but he seems so gentle. Really put together. He has his own business, even."

"All of that may be true now. Like I said, it's been years. I just want you to be careful is all." She attempted to explain. "And that's just me being cautious. As your friend." There was so much she wanted to say. To scream. Whether time had passed or not, she didn't trust that man, and the idea that sweet Brenda Anne might get mixed up with him was a recipe for disaster that turned her stomach.

"I'll be cautious," Brenda Anne said. "To be honest, things *have* been moving rather fast between us."

"Yeah. You looked pretty cozy at the restaurant."

"We met at the Scoot on a Tuesday night. Half-price beer night, you know. And we hit it off right away, and things have been…wonderful."

Clementine understood the sentiment, recognizing a very similar parallel in her own personal life. She knew how amazing it felt to be excited about someone, but that didn't mean she wouldn't offer Brenda Anne the facts. "Did he tell you he's been to prison?"

"Yes, but honestly it was such a huge misunderstanding. He's been through so much."

"Is that what he said?"

Brenda Anne pursed her lips. "He moved in with me two days ago. At least temporarily, until he can get his own place." She rushed to explain. "It's just that he's been living out of a suitcase at the motel just outside of town, and I know how that can wear a person down."

"Right," Clementine said, a sense of dread overwhelming her. The situation was much worse than she'd imagined, but what was there for her to actually do about it? She sighed. The centerpiece sat in a twine-handled bag on the counter. She lifted it carefully. "Just remember what I said. Keep it in your back pocket."

"Will do," Brenda Anne said. "But I think you might be surprised."

"I hope so."

Clementine held her bag up in gratitude. It wasn't until she landed on the sidewalk in the center of town that she allowed herself to breathe again, sucking in air as if she'd forgotten what it was.

"Funny running into you here."

She swung around, face-to-face with her father and his familiar brown eyes. "I can't say the same. You moved in with Brenda Anne."

His gaze shifted to the shop. He obviously didn't realize she knew so much. "No big deal. Just for a little while. The bed at the motel is killer on my back."

"And hers is preferable. I get it. Listen, she's a really nice woman. A friend of mine. Don't do this."

He balked. "Listen, I know what you're thinking, and I understand why. But I promise you, all the shenanigans are in the past. I don't want to make trouble for anyone. Not her. Not you. Not me."

She shoved her hands into the pockets of her jeans. "If you say so."

"Let's have that cup of coffee. I can explain everything."

"Fine. When?"

"How about tomorrow afternoon when you get off?"

"Sure. Come by the café at three. I'll keep a pot on."

He grinned. "Definitely. I will be there." He nodded to her. "See you soon, Clementine. Looking forward to it."

"Yep. See ya."

He disappeared inside the Nickel, and Clementine stared up at the sky, reminding herself that she could only control her own actions. Somehow, that didn't make her feel much better. What she craved more than anything was to find Madison and escape all of this. About now, Madison would be in the middle of her workday, concentrating on figuring out some formula or another, which would make her bite her lip in concentration—the sexiest. Maybe later she'd give her a call. After the way they'd spent the weekend, it seemed a little crazy that she'd be nervous or hesitant to reach out. Yet here she was, concerned she'd bother Madison or disturb her. Her confidence could definitely use a makeover, but some things never changed.

❖

Madison had hoped she'd hear from Clementine today, but her phone had remained mostly quiet. She didn't mind being the one to always reach out, or send a text, or do the inviting, but she wondered if that would ever change. Would Clementine relax enough to blow

Madison's phone up? Or show up unannounced on her doorstep? Now that was something she could really get behind.

"Why are you off in another land?" Joey asked from her spot across from Madison in the tasting room. Loretta was guiding the last batch of visitors through their tasting experience, which allowed Joey to relax with her friends. "Dreaming up new fermentation schemes?"

"She's dreaming up new Clementine ones," Gabriella said and placed a bowl and a basket of warm crostini on the table.

"What's that?" Joey asked, peering inside.

"A new dip I'm trying out for snacking purposes. I find it's important to have a good arsenal of snack recipes at the ready. Try it. It's a warm dill and garlic combo."

Madison loaded up a crostini and took a bite. The spices were perfectly balanced, and the warmth of the dip was like a hug from the mountain gods. "I vote it into the snack arsenal posthaste."

Joey nodded around a bite. "Bring it over every day. I promise to sell more wine if this is my happy hour reward." She turned to Madison. "Speaking of rewards, Gabs says you have updates for us, and I'm here in blissful snack heaven and craving news."

"That's fair," Madison said and sipped from her glass of pinot.

"Why are you so even about it?" Gabriella slugged her in the arm. She was going to need to invest in padding one of these days if they planned to remain friends. "I'm like bouncing in my seat like Italian Tigger."

"Because she's Madison, and that's how Madison handles good news, bad news, any news. In stride." Joey pointed at her. "But inside her brain, she's just as excited and bouncy. Her face just refuses to play along."

"No. But I'm happy. Really happy." She offered them a smile and felt the blush creep up on her cheeks. It earned a collective *aww*.

Joey looped an arm through Madison's. "So things are progressing?"

She nodded. "We've had a couple of dinners. A couple of make-out sessions at the Biscuit."

"That's a town scandal, right there. The best kind." Gabriella shook her head and marveled.

"She stayed over this weekend." Madison kept her expression even.

This time Joey slugged her. "Get out of this tasting room. Why didn't you run over to the Big House with a banner? Fly a skywriting plane over the vineyard? Smoke signals. Something."

"I realize I'm late with the friend gossip, and you guys hate that," Madison said, holding up a hand. "But I wanted to keep this for a little while, just me. Enjoy it before the two of you declared a national holiday because Madison was finally dipping her toe into the dating waters."

"I think there were more than toes involved," Gabriella said, her hazel eyes twinkling in victory.

"Oh, there were, too." Madison said with a grin from behind her glass. "I don't want to kiss and tell—"

"Then you might be in the wrong tasting room," Joey said quite seriously.

"But our chemistry is shocking, to say the least. I wish I could map it on paper for you, to fully illustrate. I don't know how to quite capture it in logical terms. I keep trying."

Gabriella patted Madison's hand. "I like science, too, Maddie, but sometimes it's okay to just feel it. Take the ride without pulling it all apart and seeing how it works."

She shook her head. "That's hard to do. I don't usually fly blind." It was the one hiccup in this whole thing. Feelings were invisible and hard to quantify, and that had never been her style. She banked on data, certainties. She watched the final guests depart the tasting room as she pondered her inability to fully grasp the intangible hold Clementine had on her. People had written thousands of books on matters of the heart and the theories behind them. Maybe she should buy one.

Joey nodded. "You like to be in control. Love doesn't allow for that."

"We might be a bit ahead of ourselves," Madison pointed out. "I'm not ready to declare myself in love or head over heels. I'm just... happy. And okay, I can admit it, out of my element with the lack of control factor."

Joey circled her glass thoughtfully with her finger. "You have to just take the ride."

Gabriella leaned in. "And sometimes that ride jostles you the hell around and makes you cry, but in the end, you don't want to get off."

"Who doesn't want to get off?" Loretta asked with a cheeky grin as she dried a rack of glasses. It pulled a collective gasp from the group. She was everyone's surrogate mother, yet she floored them with her unexpected one-liners at least once a week. Madison should have gotten used to them by now. "Here's my take," Loretta said, coming around the bar. "When the universe decides to wallop you with a romance that has you off balance and feeling a little light-headed, you take it as a compliment, a blessing. You say, *Thank you, Universe,* and pretend you're a little drunk and enjoy the buzz." She tossed a towel onto her shoulder and sauntered back to the bar.

"You heard it here," Joey said, extending her arm in Loretta's direction. "From my future aunt. Speaking of, did you settle on a caterer?" Joey called over to Loretta, who would soon wed her uncle Bobby in a highly unexpected matchup.

"I have. She's sitting right here."

Gabriella beamed. "Tangled got the gig officially. I'm going places."

"Have you checked their references?" Madison asked Loretta. That's when she saw her friends' heads turn in the direction of the tasting room door. She expected to see Becca moving toward them as she'd be off work around this time, but when her skin tingled at the sight of Clementine, she knew her day had just taken a turn for the better.

"Hi," Clementine said tentatively. "I was looking for Madison, but I can…" She gestured over her shoulder toward the door.

"No!" Joey and Gabriella shouted in unison as if someone was stealing their snacks.

"Come sit with us," Joey said, hopping into the empty chair next to hers, leaving the one next to Madison open.

Gabriella took it one step further and raced over to Clementine to escort her to the table. Madison was on her feet and beamed at Clementine as she approached, wearing jeans and a snug black sweater that accentuated her shape and made her blond hair pop.

"We're just shooting the breeze. Hey." Their eyes connected, and on cue, the world slowed down and felt so much better.

"A glass of pinot for you, Clem?" Loretta asked.

"Is that what everyone else is drinking?" She glanced around, clearly not wanting to make anyone go out of their way.

Loretta gestured to the bar. "Yes, but I got the whole lineup here. No trouble."

"Have whatever you want," Joey said.

Clementine studied the bottles along the bar. "Oh, um, do you have the dolcetto?"

"Got it right here," Loretta said and poured her a glass.

Gabriella smiled. "A girl after my own heart."

The group settled back in, but they switched the topic away from Madison's love life, for obvious reasons, and chatted instead about plans for Wassail Fest.

"We'll be there with warm biscuits," Clementine said of the café's booth. Then she looked to Madison in question. "I mean, that's what we've done in the past. You might have other plans now."

"I don't think I can come up with something better than warm biscuits on a cold day. I defer to your expertise."

"Why, thank you," Clementine said, meeting her gaze happily. They lingered there a moment until she realized that all eyes were on them and everyone was smiling like proud parents at a child's first recital. Madison laughed and shook her head. Becca arrived shortly, carrying two large pizzas with extra crispy pepperoni, and just as they started to dig in, Ryan joined them straight from work. The happy voices overlapped as they ate and chatted, the sounds of their laughter full and rich. Madison surveyed the group. This all felt weird, and when she said weird, she meant amazing. She wasn't used to having a plus-one in the midst of the two happy couples. She was always the loner, the tag-along friend, and used to it. She hadn't been on the lookout for a romance when things had combusted with Clementine, but she could imagine getting used to *this*.

Once the crispy pepperoni had been consumed, the group dispersed in their different directions. With Clementine's hand in hers, Madison led them out of the tasting room to the edge of the closest field, buying them space, alone time.

"So, hi," Clementine said. The setting sun was all but gone behind her, with only the brilliant pinks lingering for extra glow.

"Hi."

Clementine closed one eye sheepishly. "I showed up and crashed your get together. A head-on collision."

Madison kissed her cheek, balancing the leftover pizza box in one hand. "I've never been happier to see you, and that was already a high bar."

"Really?" Clementine made a *yikes* face. "You weren't at home, or in the barrel room, and when I found you were with your friends, I wanted the floor to swallow me whole. I didn't realize you'd be in the middle of something." She sighed. "And then everyone was forced to invite me to stay."

"First of all, they're your friends, too, and they wanted you there. They don't fake that kind of stuff. Neither do I. Secondly, you don't need an invitation, okay? You're always welcome to swing by. I'm saying so formally. So do the swinging."

Clementine nodded as if trying to convince herself. She exhaled slowly. "I'll try and swing here and there. Since it's a formal invite and all."

"That's all I'm saying."

"Do you have a minute to talk business before I go? Nothing major, just a rundown of the week's events."

"Sure, can we do it at my place? We can lounge. It's been a day."

"Yeah, sure." Clementine got a twinkle in her eye. "Let's lounge."

A few minutes later and they were out of their shoes and relaxing on Madison's two gray couches that came together and formed the shape of a V. Madison sat on one couch and Clementine, interestingly, selected a seat on the other. When Madison raised a questioning eyebrow, Clementine scoffed. "This is a business meeting. I have to be professional."

"Fine. Let's assume our roles." Madison sat up straight.

"First of all," Clementine began, "I lost an employee to studying for finals as the semester winds down. Denise, with the brown hair? She usually covers the Thursday and Friday midmorning backup. She gave her notice."

"Does that happen a lot?"

"The part-timers tend to turn over more often." Clementine slid a strand of hair behind her ear. The little things she did always caught Madison's eye. She loved those little mannerisms. "I'd like to offer Kevin more hours."

"Oh. Yeah. That would be all right."

"I wasn't asking permission. As manager, those things are generally my call."

"Oh." Madison winced. "Sorry. I thought you were asking."

"You are in charge, but I would normally just update Mr. Rothstein about things like employee changes. Would you like to be consulted on hiring decisions?"

"I trust you."

"Good," Clementine said with a soft smile. "I thought about your cinnamon roll idea—to make them a front and center menu item?—and while it's definitely your call, I think it's a mistake."

Madison frowned. "Why? Cinnamon rolls are amazing."

"But biscuits and bacon are the stars of our show. I love that we do two things really, really well and bolster their power with our supporting cast of baked goods and coffee, emphasis on *supporting*."

"I defer to your expert opinion. What if we made more flavors of biscuits?" Madison asked, imagining all the great things Clementine and Frankie might come up with. "Mint, plum, licorice."

"Oh, I can just see the line now for licorice biscuits."

Madison laughed. "Clearly, I'm out of my element and poking a little fun, but I bet you and your team could come up with some knockouts."

"That would require more ingredients. I have a feeling Frankie could come up with a killer chicken biscuit sandwich for breakfast. The sausage biscuit sells well. The question is, are you willing to shell out the cash, Ms. LeGrange?"

Madison blinked. "Oh, say that again."

Clementine's mouth fell open, but it also tugged at the sides. "We're in a business meeting, ma'am."

"It's really hot when you call me *ma'am*." She stood to join Clementine on her couch but was met with a finger in the air. Clementine then pointed back at her original seat.

"Uh-uh. Over there until we're done. I can't do this with you close and looking at me like that with those ridiculous blue eyes. We have business to conduct."

Madison's stomach twisted pleasantly. Other parts of her were awake now, too. "Fine. Then let's hurry." Clementine took out a printed sheet of paper from her bag, handed Madison an identical copy, and went over the bottom line with Madison, accounting for the new local sourcing. However, all Madison could concentrate on was Clementine's mouth, the shape of it, and the way her lip gloss hinted at a glisten. She missed her lips and counted the seconds until she could kiss them, nodding along like a schoolgirl, not paying attention in the slightest. She couldn't.

"But I think we stay the course and see if things even out. I feel like they will. What are your thoughts?"

"Hmm?" Madison asked, pulled abruptly from her rated R fantasy. She offered a weak smile. "You might have lost me at *Ms. LeGrange*. What did I miss? Was it important?"

"You're incorrigible. Fine. Meeting adjourned." Clementine crooked her finger. "Come over here."

The soft command sent a chill through Madison. Her skin prickled in the best way. Silently, she did as she was told and stood in front of Clementine who looked up at her from her spot on the couch. Her hands moved to Madison's waist. She lifted her shirt and softly and leisurely kissed her stomach, which had a huge effect on Madison's knees and their ability to support her. Clem's mouth was warm against her skin, her hair so soft in Madison's hands. "I love how smooth your skin is," Clem said, taking Madison by the hand and pulling her down to the cushion next to her.

"Moisturizer," Madison said. "I'm a firm believer."

Clementine laughed quietly and leaned in. "And a straight shooter," she said, just before capturing her mouth in a sizzling kiss. If Clementine showed signs of insecurity in her everyday life, they flew right out the window when it came to sex. With Clementine's tongue in her mouth, Madison felt her back hit the couch moments before Clementine was on top. Nothing could have felt more satisfying. Lies. Clementine's fingers were on the button of Madison's jeans, and she was no longer satisfied at all, her anticipation and longing shifting to off-the-charts. Her jeans were off, leaving her in her long-sleeve green pullover and black panties, already wet and desperate to be touched. Clementine's eyes had gone dark and the look of happy determination on her face sent a shiver all through Madison's body. Clementine placed a hand between Madison's legs on the outside of her underwear and pressed lightly, pulling a hiss from Madison, who damn near met the stars. This was so different from their last time together, slow and thorough. But Madison had no problem with either. Clementine began to stroke her, moving her hand back and forth, withholding the kind of pressure Madison desperately needed. "You wanna take it from here?" Clementine asked.

Madison understood her meaning, closed her eyes for a moment, and rocked against Clementine's hand, setting her own pace, her own rhythm, as Clementine watched in captivation. Every nerve ending cried out for release. She was in control but not, now moving quickly against Clementine's hand, nearly there when Clementine moved the square of fabric to the slide and slid her fingers inside. Madison moaned, and her hips rose off the couch as Clementine moved in and out, sending her quickly careening into an oblivion of pleasure that took its sweet time with her, over and over. As it ebbed, she relaxed onto her back and took a breath.

"Best business meeting of my life," Madison managed and tossed an arm over her eyes.

Clementine laughed quietly. "That's one way to keep the workweek exciting."

CHAPTER ELEVEN

It had to be after eight by now. Darkness had claimed the sky, and soft tunes played from the speaker in the corner. Clementine and Madison lay naked on the couch under an incredibly soft blanket, Clementine reclined with her back against Madison, who was propped up on a group of pillows. Warm and perfect. Clementine liked tonight a lot.

"Can I tell you something?" Clementine asked.

"Of course," Madison said, absently playing with her hair while Clementine's body hummed happily from the things Madison's mouth had done to her just an hour ago.

"I went and saw Brenda Anne to warn her about my father." It was easier to talk about something that felt so personal when she didn't have to look Madison in the eye. Her parents were not everyday conversation for her. In fact, they were her least favorite topic.

She felt Madison's arm tighten around her midsection. "You did? How did that go?"

"Not so great." She paused. "I think she's in deeper with him than I thought, and it has me very nervous. He's moved into her place."

Madison sighed. "Wow. They are serious. I'm sorry this is happening. So out of the blue, too."

"He was never one to go slow when he got an idea in his head. I ran into him on the sidewalk in front of the Nickel afterward." She shook her head. "I'd planned to stay the hell away from him, but if he's this close to Brenda Anne, I feel like I need to keep an eye on him. I agreed to have coffee."

Madison sat up, and Clementine turned around to face her. "Do you want me to come with you? Is he the violent type?"

"Not in the way you're thinking. Lying and cheating are more his thing. In the middle of the café, I'll be fine." She met Madison's gaze. "It's like he wants to prove to me that he's different, changed. What if he is?"

"Do you think it's possible?"

"Not really. No."

"Then keep your guard up, okay?" Madison slid a strand of hair behind Clem's ear. She'd done that a few times in the past, and Clementine didn't think she'd ever get tired of the caring gesture.

"Yeah. I think I have to." She stared up at the ceiling. "Things were feeling settled. Not that they were perfect. Some woman swooped in and bought my café, but it turns out she has a lot of other talents to offer, so I'm rolling with it."

Madison laughed. "Level with me, though. Are we okay in that regard? You're not secretly plotting to kill me in my sleep and this is all just part of your plan?"

"Not today, anyway." She winked. "I feel like we're starting to find our groove, working together. That's something. And maybe this just means that I'm meant to open my own place one day. I don't know."

"And leave me on my own with the Biscuit? No way."

"You can visit," Clementine said and kissed her hand. "Until I put you out of business, that is."

Madison's features twisted in horror. "This is getting worse by the second. I can't think about it anymore. Stay with me tonight and take my mind off it? Say yes. I don't want to say good-bye to you."

"Stay with a future competitor? That sounds like a conflict of interest," she said with a playful grin.

Madison placed a hand on her head. "Well, since we're already naked, we might have leaped that fence a little while ago."

Clementine glanced under the blanket. "So we have. Now what?"

"We eat another slice of that leftover pizza and go to bed. Together."

"Are these coming?" Clementine asked, looking down at Madison's amazing breasts. She exposed one and kissed it softly just above the nipple.

"Mm-hmm," Madison said, closing her eyes. "Guaranteed."

"Okay, but only since you're offering pizza and boobs."

Madison slipped out from underneath the blanket and stood, naked and gorgeous. "Who knew you were such an easy sell?"

Clementine watched in utter appreciation as Madison walked to the refrigerator and took out the cardboard pizza box. She took out a slice and took a bite, an image that Clementine would never forget. She took a mental photograph of the woman who was systematically rocking her world standing confident, naked, and enjoying a slice of cold pizza. Madison picked up a second piece and extended it in Clementine's direction.

That was too good an offer to pass up. She wasn't sure how she was lucky enough to end up here, but she wasn't about to take it for granted or miss a minute. She dropped the blanket and followed Madison, happier than she could ever remember.

That night they were more familiar with each other, yet still discovering new things. Madison, it turned out, was ticklish behind her knees and, when she was close to coming, got quieter instead of louder. A light flush came over her body when the orgasm hit and was gone in a matter of minutes after. The best part? Madison's appetite for sex matched her own, which might be a challenge to their basic need for sleep. Some sacrifices were worth it. She drifted off that night with her hand in Madison's hair, Madison's head against her shoulder, and a fullness in her heart. Dare she let it reach? She wasn't sure she had a choice any longer.

Madison pulled her pickup into a parking space in front of the Bacon and Biscuit. She usually ate a quick lunch on site at Tangle Valley and got right back to work. But today was the day Clementine was meeting with her father, so she'd pushed her lunch later so she could check in on Clem shortly before closing.

She took a seat at a booth and waited for the three-person-deep line to disappear, enjoying watching Clementine, who'd ravished her the night before, handle the customers with warmth and efficiency. At one point, she'd looked up and caught Madison sitting there. She broke into a grin and went back to work, affording her glances here and there that made Madison melt. She wasn't the type to melt. She was known as the clinical, practical one among her friends and family. Yet here she sat, gazing longingly at the woman who stole so many of her thoughts. She should say some of them to Clementine out loud, but the idea felt so foreign. She'd work on it.

"Just happened to be in the neighborhood?" Clementine asked, once Madison strolled up to the counter.

"More like happened to be starving." Madison surveyed the menu. She'd made it a point to sample just about everything, but the warm croissant with cheese and a side of candied bacon was her current go-to, so she ordered it. "And I remembered you were meeting with your dad today, so I thought I'd stop by, offer moral support."

"Hey-o, Madison!" Frankie called from the grill in the back. He flipped his spatula in the air and caught it. "Got your bacon coming up."

"Nice one, Frankie."

Clementine shook her head. "He's showing off."

"So, how's your state of mind?"

She dropped her voice. "Well, I'm a little sleep deprived."

"With good reason," Madison said, underneath the sizzle of the grill. "But you know what I'm asking about."

Clementine nodded, her smile dimming. "I've been a little on edge all day. Not gonna lie." She held up her hands. "Palms are clammy."

"My offer still stands to stick around with you. Be your sidekick. I don't have to say anything."

"I appreciate that, but no."

The look on Clementine's face told her that the idea was off the table, so Madison didn't press. "Okay, but will you let me know how it went? I'll be wondering."

Clementine nodded. "Of course." A pause. "And thank you. It's nice knowing that I have someone—you, I mean—looking out for me."

"Well, I am. Know that."

She held Clementine's gaze before taking her food to-go and giving her space before her meeting, hoping that Clementine wouldn't get hurt. While she didn't have all the details of Clem's past, she knew it hadn't been good and had clearly left a scar or two. All she wanted was to wrap her up and shield her from the world. If only she could.

❖

Clementine had wiped down every table in the café at least twice now. The physical activity helped her channel some of her nervous energy. She could probably get out the ladder and give some of the new wall decor a good wipe down, too. The newly painted walls were looking spiffy but required upkeep. She could take a rag to them while she waited.

There was a knock on the glass door that she'd locked once they'd closed for the day. She glanced up, rag in hand, and there he was, peering inside, his hand shading his eyes. She swallowed once, tossed her apron onto the counter, and unlocked the door. "Hey, come on in."

"Wow. Smells amazing in here."

"We had a good day. Lots of traffic."

He wore jeans and a tucked-in red and white plaid shirt. She noticed that peripherally because she'd yet to look at him full-on. She had to get over that and quick. This man held no power over her. If she said it enough, maybe she'd start to believe it. "Coffee?" she asked, forcing herself to look him square in the eye. "We have regular, cinnamon, and decaf."

"Regular is great. Black."

As a kid, she remembered making it for him first thing in the morning to try to get him to go to work. She'd been successful once in a while. "Seems nothing's changed."

He sighed, as if the past was weighing on him. "That's about the only thing that hasn't."

"Oh yeah?" She had a hard time believing it but hadn't agreed to this get together just to freeze him out entirely. This was a fact-finding mission, and okay, she was also a little curious herself.

She poured them two cups while he ambled around the café, taking in the details. "Got a lotta charm. I can see your touches."

"Thanks. I really like the place." She handed him his coffee and slid into a booth. He finished his lap around the restaurant and joined her. His hands dwarfed the mug when he picked it up. She remembered the back of one across her face for nothing more than asking an annoying question at the wrong time.

"You hear much from your mom?"

Clementine blinked. "Not since the day she dragged her suitcase down the street when I was twelve."

"Huh." He rubbed his chin. "I thought for sure she'd have reached out to you. She's got another kid now. A boy. Living down there in New Mexico."

Clementine nodded, numb to the details about her mother. She'd never been overly attentive to Clementine, but she had gone to the trouble to feed and clothe her, occasionally asking a question about school. That had counted for something. She'd shown her small amounts of warmth until the day she walked out and took it all with her, never once looking back. Clementine sat on the steps in front of their home every day for months, hoping to catch sight of her returning. It had taken years for her to accept that she was truly gone for good. She wasn't sure which was worse, the parent who'd stayed and been awful, or the nicer one who'd turned her back without so much as a good-bye. Her stomach felt off, and she set down her coffee, rejecting its bitter taste.

"Anyway," her father said, when she didn't really bite, "I don't talk to her much either. That ship has sailed, as you know." He exhaled. "I do think about you, though. Wish I could have done a lot of things differently."

"Like what?" she asked, raising her gaze to his.

"For one, I wish I'd have been there for you more. Attended your school events. Like that one time when you got the award for the honor roll."

She remembered. The other students had had their parents in the crowded cafeteria, snapping photos and cheering as they climbed the stairs to the makeshift stage. She'd accepted her award, smiled, and walked home alone in the dark, placing it carefully on her shelf, a source of pride.

"That would have been nice," she said. "Do you know what also would have been nice? Keeping my award. You couldn't have gotten more than a couple of bucks for it. Just cheap metal, but it mattered to me."

He lowered his head. "I was a bad guy. I know that. And I hate the things I did back then. I was selfish and focused on all the wrong parts of life."

She picked up her coffee again, feeling stronger. "We agree on that. So, where have you been?"

"Jail. Then Oklahoma. Then jail in Oklahoma. Three years that time, and that's when I had to take a good long look at myself. Started going to some support groups inside. I got a job. You're not going to believe this—in the library. Isn't that where you used to spend all your time?" He chuckled, shook his head, and sipped from his mug.

She nodded. "It is ironic."

"I did a shitload of reading. I didn't start out a fast reader, but with time on my hands, I turned into one. Read lots of biographies. Those were my favorites. Baseball players, world leaders, all types. Made me see that I didn't like who I was, and I had a real nice counselor who thought I didn't have to be that guy anymore. Turns out he was right."

Okay, so she had to say something supportive, even if she carried doubt. "Sometimes it takes meeting the right people at the right time."

"That's true." He shook his finger to emphasize the point. "I wouldn't have been ready to hear any of it just a year earlier. But God saw my struggles and opened up my brain. I believe that."

"What happened when you got out?"

"It was rough at first. Bounced around. Then I found some assistance programs that helped me get started with a landscaping company. I worked real hard and made some valuable contacts and was lucky enough to have one of 'em lend me the money to start my own business. Paid him back in full last spring. Damn proud of that. Company's been profitable, and I hope to make the leap."

"Here?"

"Why not? Nice to be back in my old stomping grounds. I have fences to mend here and there, but all in due time. Plus, you're here."

The whole idea made her itch, but she refused to show weakness. She met his gaze evenly. "I'm happy for you. You seem to be doing much better, which is great." She sat back in the booth. "But here's the thing. I've worked incredibly hard to create a life for myself here, a reputation that I value, and—"

"You're afraid I'm going to swoop in and stomp all over it."

She exhaled. "Yeah. That's exactly it."

"Not going to happen. If anything, I'm here to cheer you on." He lifted his mug. "And maybe grab a cup of coffee once in a while. Would that be so awful?"

"And Brenda Anne? What's the angle there?"

"Hell, I don't know. We hit it off. She's fun and lighthearted. I needed a little bit of that in my life, and well, she seemed to like me back. Not sure why." He flashed a grin, and she took a deep breath.

"Please don't hurt her. She's my friend and a really nice person."

"Listen to me, okay? You have my word," he said.

What was strange was that she actually believed him. Well, for a moment anyway. He was certainly convincing. That much was true.

"But I understand that nothing I say is gonna matter as much as what I do. My actions. This may take time, but I plan to show you, Clem, that I'm really working on myself. I only hope you'll give me that chance."

She nodded. "Yeah, well, I don't know. Let's just take things one step at a time."

He knocked on the table. "On that note, I know the worst thing I could do is overstay my welcome." He slid the mug to the side. "Thanks for chatting with me. Can't wait to stop in for some breakfast one day, if that's okay with you, of course."

"We're open to one and all."

He beamed. "Well, that's me then."

He didn't move to hug her, and she appreciated that. It had never been their way. Instead, he nodded and pointed back at the table. "Good coffee, too. See you around, I hope."

"See ya," she said and waved from her spot next to the booth. Once he'd gone, she looked down at her hands and saw that they were shaking. In fact, every part of her was, right down to her core. She took a minute, stood with hands on the back of her hips, gaze trained on the floor, to gather herself.

The door to the café opened, and she lifted her head to see Madison standing there. "I saw him leave." She gestured behind her. "Just doing some work in the parking lot. Not at all waiting around to make sure you're okay. So…are you?"

Clementine felt the damn tears spring into her eyes without permission, and the uncomfortable lump in her throat wouldn't let her actually speak, even when she tried. It didn't matter, though. Madison's arms were around her in a flash, and that somehow provided the safe haven she needed to let go. She sank against Madison's body and let the emotion leave her.

"I've got you," Madison said. "It's okay. I'm right here."

And in that moment, Clementine had never been more grateful for someone in her life. Madison did have her, and with Madison's arms around her, it felt like she was going to be okay. In the midst of all the fear she carried, she knew it in her heart. She was no longer wandering the streets alone.

"Thank you," she managed, loosening her grip. "I know I sent you away, but I'm so glad you're here."

Madison pulled back and found Clem's eyes. "Well, get used to it, okay?" She cradled Clementine's face, dried her tears with her thumbs, and placed a soft kiss on her lips. "Because I'm not going anywhere."

"You're not?"

Madison shook her head, and the world felt steady for the first time in a very long while. She was cared for. She mattered to someone. Silly tears sprang into her eyes all over again, this time for a very different reason.

"Hope you like wine."

Clementine laughed and pulled Madison's lips to hers so they could kiss like they were made to kiss.

CHAPTER TWELVE

Though Madison loved Thanksgiving, the Christmas season was the one that stole her heart. She'd stayed at Tangle Valley for the big turkey day, rather than joining her parents in Florida. They'd FaceTimed midday, and as always, her parents paid very little attention to remaining onscreen.

"I can only see Dad's hairline," Madison had to explain to them. "Can you guys adjust the camera so that—?"

"Is this better?" her mother had asked, framing her whole face, and booting her father off altogether.

"Sure. We'll go with that," Madison said with a laugh, picking her battles. Two minutes later, they were sideways on her screen. She missed them and her mother's special stuffing recipe, but this was her first Thanksgiving with Clementine, and she was not about to miss it. Gabriella had been good enough to cook them all a fantastic meal, and after, they'd gathered in their comfy clothes for a viewing of *It's a Wonderful Life* in a cottage recently vacated by a farmhand.

"I've never seen this film before," Clementine whispered, as she snuggled up next to Madison on the mass of blankets they'd brought with them. It had been the coldest night of the year so far.

"How is that possible?" Madison whispered back.

"Maybe I was supposed to wait until tonight. With you." They smiled at each other and shared a soft moment and a kiss.

"Mayday. The new couple is kissing again," Becca said.

"They do that a lot," Ryan said, passing Becca a grin.

Gabriella squeezed Ryan's arm. "It's adorable. I applaud any and all cuteness, on movie night especially."

Joey looked around. "I feel a lot of pressure to be cute now."

"I can't imagine why," Becca said, nuzzling her hair. "Look at you."

Clementine grinned and shook her head. She'd seemed so much lighter lately, and showed it off. "You guys always make me laugh."

She stayed over that night, and Madison lit a fire in her small fireplace. They'd stretched out in front of it and played Christmas music to usher in the holiday season. "I love how excited you are," Clementine said, kissing Madison's jaw. "Like an adorable kid. You're always so put together, so this is new."

"I'm not put together about Christmas," Madison said, getting excited all over again. "It's my weakness. I want to soak up every minute of the season before it's gone again."

"Okay. Why don't we make a point to do that?"

Madison kissed her because it was the best idea ever. "We absolutely will. Christmas lights. Hot mulled wine. I can't wait for Wassail Fest." That's when it hit her. "Wait one damn second. You always dress up with those Dickensian carolers. Oh my God."

Clementine reclined back on her forearms. "That's true. I'm an untrained alto with heart. Definitely not the star of the show, but I like to sing."

"I've never been more attracted to you," Madison said, approaching like a cat on all fours. "Can you bring the bonnet over after the fest? Say yes."

Clementine lowered herself onto the blanket and let Madison top her. She looked skyward. "I'll consider it, but I'm not making any promises."

"Are there long gloves, too?"

Clementine's eyes danced. "There are."

Madison slid her hips between Clementine's legs and grinned down at her. "What else?"

"There might be a hand muff," Clementine said and exhaled slowly, pressing up against Madison.

"Well, now I'm gone. Death by hand muff," Madison said, seizing Clementine's mouth for a searing kiss.

With three weeks to go until Christmas, everything felt utterly alive. The town of Whisper Wall did not hold back when it came to decorations. Main Street sparkled with twinkling lights, red and green decorative bells and stars, and a giant Christmas tree in front of the courthouse. Madison's personal favorites, however, were all the elves peeking down from awnings, around benches, and on signs. What made it even better was having someone to share it with. She popped in on Clementine at work once a day to pick up the bank drop and always made sure to linger for a stolen moment or two.

"I know you hate my suggestions, but hear me out."

"I'm listening," Clementine said, hand on her hip. "But the chances of me adding meat pies to the menu is a no-go. We've talked about this."

Madison backed up and waved a hand through the air, beckoning Clementine to picture the headline. "An espresso bar. Right over there." She pointed to the coffee station.

"Huh," Clementine said. "As in lattes and mochas and iced fancy stuff?"

"Exactly. Seasonal flavors, too. We could capitalize on the pumpkin movement. What do you think? You know this business and the customers. Will it float?"

Clementine looked thoughtful. "I'm sold. If you'll pay for it."

"Wait. It's that easy? You shoot down all of my ideas. What's happening?"

"It just so happens that it's something I've thought about a lot. For a while I thought the customers preferred our simplicity and didn't want the fancy stuff, but the more I watch, the more I think the market kind of demands it. If we're a legitimate breakfast establishment, we need to up our coffee game."

Madison pointed at her face. "I'm beaming right now. We should start shopping for equipment tonight."

Frankie came out of the kitchen. "We're getting mochas and shit?"

"We are," Madison said.

"I gotta tell Jun. She'll be up here every day."

"See?" Clementine said. "We just doubled Jun's business. You're apparently not awful at this."

Madison nodded. "Not awful is so much better than *How dare you pillage my dreams?*"

"Isn't it, though?"

"I'm still mulling over a giant inflatable strip of bacon on the roof." Madison scratched her head and stared at the ceiling.

Clementine blinked and smiled sympathetically. "Well, keep mulling that one, okay? Definitely no rush there, boss."

"Are we doing dinner and that hot chocolate stroll?" They'd talked earlier in the week about dinner out at the Cabernet Club followed by a leisurely walk through town to take in the holiday lights at night. The streets were always so beautiful when lit up.

"I've been looking forward to it all day," Clementine said, delivering that cute-slash-sincere combo Madison had grown to love. She also loved the way her voice dipped in volume to accompany the declaration.

"Me, too. I'll pick you up at seven. Tell Toast to prepare for head scratches."

"He will begrudgingly accept approximately three. His limit. In his contract."

Madison quirked her lips. "I'm gonna shoot for four. My parents have always said I was tenacious."

"God, they were right, and they haven't even seen you"—she dropped her voice again—"taking someone's clothes off."

Madison laughed. "They just get in the way."

After dinner that night, the sidewalks of Whisper Wall did not disappoint. The shops were open an extra hour or two to accommodate the influx of tourists and locals doing their holiday shopping. It was more than a little cold out, so Madison had worn her purple puffer coat and white knit gloves. Clementine's black peacoat and red scarf made her look cuddly and chic at once. They walked the main drag, enjoying the sounds of the Happy Guys, Madison's favorite local quartet, who wore Santa beards and stocking caps and played carols for all to hear from their spot in front of the Christmas tree. They'd stopped at the nearby chocolatier's, the Dark Room, for a decadent cup of hot chocolate and marshmallows to enjoy on their walk.

"I'm just hung up on how you can possibly get that wonderful pine smell from a box," Madison said.

"Candles work," Clementine said with a shrug. "And then you don't have to deal with all those needles on the floor."

"We have plenty of holiday candles at the Nickel, you know."

They turned to see Brenda Anne, her arm looped through Len Monroe's. "And they're on sale until Thursday."

"Hey there, you guys," Madison said. She smiled at Len. "I don't think we've officially met. Madison LeGrange."

"Len Monroe. Pleased to meet you. A friend of Clementine's?"

"We're dating," Clementine said evenly. She exchanged a smile with Madison. They'd not declared themselves a couple out loud to other people quite yet, but there was no doubt in Madison's mind that they were. They spent most of each week at each other's houses, had learned each other's habits and what the other liked on a sandwich. All the important things.

"I kinda wondered," Brenda Anne said, giving them a chastising finger shake of fun. "You two have been looking extra cozy and, now that I think about it, would be a really good fit." Brenda Anne bopped Len on the shoulder. "You don't know Madison yet, but she's very kind, level-headed, and smart."

"Well, that makes me happy to hear. Clementine deserves all those things." He nodded at her and she nodded back.

"You guys out to see the lights?" Clementine asked, squeezing Madison's hand.

"Len picked me up from work, so we thought we'd take a walk and listen to the music."

"They're sure doing a lot more with this town than ever before," Len said, gesturing around him.

"It was always pretty Christmassy. We just never spent much time in town," Clementine said. To her credit, the comment was a gentle one.

"You got a point there. What a mistake that was." He whistled and smiled, seeming in good spirits. He was a charismatic guy, and Madison could already see why Brenda Anne was drawn in. "Maybe someday the four of us can get together. Share a meal."

"I'd love that," Brenda Anne said.

Madison let Clementine answer that one.

"Sure. That could be fun. Why not?" Clementine said measuredly.

"Well, we don't want to horn in on the younger folks' night. Let's get outta their hair before I start in on my *Golden Girls* trivia." Brenda Anne laughed a little too hard at her own comment, and they all smiled, because she was endearing in every sense, a truly good and quirky person.

"Enjoy your night," Madison said and sipped her sinfully good hot chocolate.

"Good night, guys," Clementine said.

Once they were a safe distance away, Madison glanced at her. "That went okay, didn't it?"

"Surprisingly, yes. It was probably the most mundane encounter I've ever had with a family member of mine." She shook her head, mystified. "What in the world is happening?"

Madison shrugged. "Maybe he's really trying."

"I was going to say that crazier things have happened, but I'm not sure they have. Monkeys could fly off that roof, and it would shock me less."

"Well, that wouldn't be very Christmassy," Madison said with a frown.

"Should we just change your name to Mrs. Claus?" Clementine asked. "Is that the direction we're headed?"

"Now that could be hot," Madison said, feeling thoughtful. "I mean, called out at the right time, that could really send me places."

Clementine laughed. "You are ridiculous."

"About you? Why, yes, I am. Let's get more hot chocolate. Christmas is only once a year."

❖

The damn espresso machine from Satan was clearly plotting against Clementine. When the company installed the thing, they'd taken an extra hour to train her and her small group of employees. It had seemed simple enough, the way the woman doing the training whipped the parts and levers around like a pro, the hissing and whirring following her every command. Not so easy in reality.

"You got that fancy machine under control, or does it have you?" Maude asked, having arrived a few minutes early for the morning gathering of the Biddies.

"The jury is still out," Clementine stated over the sounds of the sizzling candied bacon. "The usual for you, Maude?"

"That'll do."

Clem rang up the butter biscuit and a medium coffee, lots of cream. "I noticed you all haven't been in much this week. Everyone busy?"

Maude pursed her lips and looked down at the billfold she clutched. "Birdie's not been feeling well."

"Oh, I'm sorry to hear that," Clementine said. "It's that time of year."

"Just didn't feel right to get together without Birdie."

"Of course not," Clementine said, nodding.

"But she's feeling much better, so we'll get back to our chats and stir up some trouble. We're known for it around here," Maude said, as if it was new information.

"I've heard," Clementine said with a laugh. She glanced back at the espresso station. "And one day, maybe you'll try one of our new drinks."

Maude made a *tsk* sound from her throat. "If you ever figure the machine out."

"Oh, ye of little faith," she said, just as the oven timer reminded her that they had a new batch of piping hot biscuits to introduce to the world.

As the other women arrived, she took their orders and admitted to herself that sweet Birdie didn't look quite like herself.

"You feeling better today, Ms. Birdie? I heard you were under the weather."

She accepted the white bag with her biscuit inside. She smiled, kindness touching her eyes. "I'm on the mend, as they say. Thank you for checking on me, Clementine." She turned to go and paused. "I heard your dad's back in town and over at Brenda Anne's." She frowned and raised her gaze. "Are you doing all right? I worry a little about you."

She softened and passed Birdie a small smile. "I am."

Not a ton of people knew about her struggles at home when she was younger, but the Biddies made a point to know everything, and in this instance, she couldn't say she minded. It was nice to be checked on, and it was clear Birdie meant no harm. This wasn't fodder for their gossipy Instagram account.

"Well, you promise that you'll let me know if you ever need anything?"

"I promise."

"Even if it's just an ear. I got two good ones." She tossed her head in the direction of the Biddies' customary table. "You got a group of old broads over there who will go to the mat for you anyway." She reached across the counter and covered Clementine's hand with hers, holding on tightly. "You're a good egg, Clementine, and don't you forget it."

Clementine swallowed back the lump in her throat and attempted to rally as her hands shook. She stilled them. "Thank you, Ms. Birdie. I will remember that."

"Anytime, sweet girl."

Their exchange had been a short one, but Clementine carried it with her throughout her day. She'd lived most of her life feeling like a leaf in the wind, not really noticed by too many people and affecting even fewer. Yet, in the past few months, she'd begun to feel like she'd been wrong all this time. Maybe she wasn't as forgettable as she once thought, and that made her heart and her spirit soar. Her life wasn't perfect, and there was much work to be done on herself, but Clementine felt like there might just be a shot for her to live a life bigger than she'd ever dared dream. Hope was a big part of that, scary as it was. She carried hope that what she'd found with Madison was real and long-lasting. She hoped the glimmer of redemption she'd seen in her father was authentic. She even wondered if she'd someday have an actual relationship with him. She hoped her newfound collaboration at the Biscuit would lead to bigger and better things for the place she loved more than any other.

Most of all, she hoped to matter in this world. To make an impression, a difference.

She forced Toast into a makeshift cuddle session that night as she listened to quiet Christmas music in her apartment with a smile on her face. While he huffed about it in his customary manner, he curled up into an adorable swirl on her lap and, with a deep sigh, was out like a light. Madison was catching up on her workload, which, Clementine was honored to say, had backed up due to the large amount of time they'd been spending together. She enjoyed her peaceful evening as she mentally prepped for Wassail Fest that Saturday. The Biscuit would have a small booth in which they'd sell butter biscuits and cinnamon biscuits until they sold out, generally by midafternoon. She'd take the first shift and had her staff staggered for two-hour blocks after that, freeing her up to sing with the carolers and maybe even enjoy some hot mulled wine from the Tangle Valley booth with someone special.

Who knew, maybe they'd even find a little mistletoe? "What?" she asked, as Toast raised his head and stared her down. "I can kiss who I want to kiss." In the moment, she placed a smacking one on his head.

CHAPTER THIRTEEN

Madison shimmied her shoulders to the sounds of the brass band blowing out "Joy to the World" as she handed off another cup of hot mulled wine to a grinning customer. Wassail Fest was hopping this year with more attendees than she'd ever seen. She stood shoulder to shoulder with Joey in the Tangle Valley booth, and their line had been pretty constant. Next door, in the Tangled booth, Gabriella yelled, "Who wants a hot Italian doughnut to go with that wine? We have zeppole over here, a favorite of old St. Nick."

"I keep thinking she's advertising an actual hot Italian when she shouts that," Joey said. "Takes me a minute."

"That might be why her line is longer," Madison whispered back.

"Speaking of lines, you're not doing so bad over there," Joey said, handing over a steaming cup of wine to Powell Rogers, who grabbed the provided orange slice and gave it a squeeze. "The Biscuit has done well."

"They always do. People have one of those flaky things, and they come back for a second one, every time."

"Are you guys going to hit the fest together?" Joey asked in a singsong voice. "You're off in an hour. Free to frolic."

"Yeah. I've been looking forward to today for weeks." There was a brief lull in customer traffic, and she turned to Joey. "I have a girlfriend, Jo." Madison shook her head. "I can't stop thinking about her, and it's Christmastime. I'm still letting that sink in."

Joey beamed and hugged her through their puffy jackets like a couple of sumo wrestlers. "This is by far the happiest I've ever seen you. And Clementine, too. She walks around like a new person, just as kind but with this new level of confidence that makes her radiate, and she was already beautiful."

"I couldn't agree more."

"And you called her your girlfriend. That's the first time I've heard you say it."

Madison laughed. "I think it's the first time I have."

"I'm missing gossip," Gabriella called over to them. "I can feel it. Get your hot Italian doughnuts!"

"Made by a true hot Italian," Joey yelled.

"I second that," Ryan said, approaching the booth. She and Gabriella grinned like people in love and shared a quick kiss. "I'm gonna kill time with Billy until you're free."

"Deal, but have zero fun without me."

"I can easily agree to that." She waved at them all and disappeared into the throng.

People in love. Madison mused over the words again. "How did you know you were in love with Becca?"

Mrs. Rokowski raised an interested eyebrow as she handed over her four dollar bills.

"She might be falling in love," Joey whispered.

"She's getting ahead of herself," Madison counter-whispered. Once Mrs. Rokowski moved on, Madison turned to Joey. "Stop outing me to customers."

"Fine."

They stole bits of conversation between sales.

"You know how I knew? When I woke up in the morning thinking about her before anything else," Joey said. "When I tried to live without her and just couldn't. When I preferred to risk everything rather than go another second without her. What can I get for you, Stephen?" she asked their buddy from the Moon and Stars Ranch.

"Two cups of the good stuff."

"You've always had the best taste."

They exchanged money for wine, and Madison nodded to Joey. "Good to know."

"Are you there with Clementine?" Joey asked. "Hi, Carla Cortez. I miss your face. We need to grab dinner soon."

"Yeah, we do," Carla said, her hair pulled into a long dark ponytail. "But let's ditch our significant others and catch up just us."

"Now you're talking." Carla was Becca's assistant manager at the Jade Resort and had always been a big fan of Joey's. She happily accepted two cups of hot wine.

Madison turned to Joey for the 3.3 seconds they had before the next customer shuffled forward. "We're a couple. That much, I know. But I haven't figured out much beyond that."

"Lies. You're just being measured. Madison the pragmatist."

"A new nickname?"

Madison's head swiveled at the sound of the familiar voice. There was Clementine, standing there with none other than her father, the two of them next in line.

"Hey, you two," Madison said, grinning like an idiot because she wondered how much Clementine might have heard and wanted to play it off. No big deal. Nothing to see here.

"We just ran into each other," Clementine said. "Just as we sold out of cinnamon biscuits. Frankie and Jun are working on killing the last rack of butter biscuits."

"I had one. Amazing," Len said. He hooked a thumb at Clementine. "She's showing me around the festival a bit until you're free. Then I'll get outta here and find my gal. She's in a wreath-making session in town square."

"Sounds awesome." She meant it. While Madison was surprised to see them together, the sight also made her heart squeeze for Clementine. Even though she'd never say so out loud, she knew how badly Clem wanted things to go smoothly with her father. So far, it seemed like he was surpassing her expectations each step of the way, which made Madison a happy, though cautious, cheerleader.

"Here you go, you two." Joey handed over the goods. "On the house. Enjoy."

"Thanks, Joey," Clementine said. Her gaze flicked to Madison. "And I'll see you soon?"

"Yes, near the tree on the right?" Madison asked, referencing their plan. A grin took over her entire face just thinking about it.

"That's the spot." They held eye contact for a long moment, and just like always, Madison felt her stomach do an excited dance.

"Did it just get hotter out here?" Gabriella called over once

Clementine and Len had gone. She fanned herself playfully. "The fake snow is melting."

"Uh-oh. The hot Italian just got hotter," Joey called to the masses playfully.

Madison laughed and memorized the moment. Her friends, the beauty of the day, and all it still had in store. These were the kinds of moments Madison lived for.

❖

This wasn't how Clementine imagined spending her time at Wassail Fest. There were moments in life that sneaked up on you. She firmly believed that. And defied any and all kinds of planning. That's exactly how she would describe the moment her father appeared outside the Biscuit's booth just as Clementine handed the reins to Frankie.

"Hey, Clementine."

She stared up at her father, surprised. "Oh, hi. Didn't see you there," she said, coming around the booth. She shoved her hands into her pockets and took in his apparent appreciation for the biscuit Frankie must have just sold him. He chewed slowly, grinning the whole time.

"Damn." He shook his head like the thing had just whooped his ass. Her goal with every customer, actually. "Who knew you could do this?"

"I did," she said with a smug smile. "But I can't take all the credit. Frankie and I are a team."

Frankie shrugged from behind the table. "I'm more the grill guy. She's got the biscuits down."

"You both do a fabulous job, then." He turned to Clementine. "I was hoping I'd get to try a biscuit and now, extra lucky, I've run into you. Wanna walk around?"

He said it so casually, like they were two people who might take a nice stroll together. She'd been dragged behind him at the grocery store before, or sent to the gas station to pick up a packet of cigarettes when she was underage, but strolling like two people was new. She decided, what the hell?

"Yeah, okay. I'm off now."

Because she was juggling nerves, Clementine took on the role of tour guide, talking way too much, which felt better than awkward silence. She pointed out the different booths, vendors, and offered updates on what all their neighbors had been up to since her father had last been to town.

"Wait," he said with a laugh. "You're telling me that Bunny Boy Benjy now sells insurance? Nah. Can't be."

"Well, we just call him Ben, but he's there for all your car, home, and life insurance needs. One-stop guy."

"Bunny Boy Benjy is now Insurance Ben. Huh. Times sure do change. We used to smoke cigars behind the gas station and shoot the shit."

"The good old days," she said with a hint of sarcasm. "How's your business coming along? Any luck establishing yourself?"

He nodded enthusiastically. "Ah, yeah. It's been great. Brenda Anne's put me in touch with some folks who need work. Got three clients already."

"Seriously? That's great." She was shocked by how fast he was moving.

"Yep. Did the estimates this week and was hired for all three jobs. Even picked up a couple of guys for my crew. We go out on our first one on Tuesday."

A kernel of pride took shape in her chest, and as they walked on, she felt it blossom. He was really trying. She could see that now. Showing up and following through. That had to count for something. She carried a lot of baggage from her childhood, but if her father was actually putting in the time and effort, maybe she should try and meet him partway. "I'm really proud of you," she said and passed him a cautious smile. Everyone needed encouragement now and then.

He looked at the ground and then back at her. "That means more to me than you know." He nodded a couple of times, absorbing.

To pull them out of the sentimental puddle they'd stumbled into, she laughed and pointed ahead. "That's Knead Me. Slight competition for the Biscuit, but also not. We're more breakfast oriented, and they're more multipurpose bread in general."

"Lots of different types of bread out there." His eyes were still misted up, and that had her eyes misting up.

"We're a couple of idiots," she said, referencing the obvious emotion at play.

"It's that time of year," he said, giving her a quick sideways squeeze. He'd done that before when she was younger. A thanks for an errand she'd run or a meal she'd cooked.

After they'd stopped for mulled wine, they'd finished the final loop of the tour, and she'd dropped him with Brenda Anne, who was finishing her wreath-making class.

"Thanks for the walk," he said, lifting his cup to her. "Highlight of my day."

Clementine lifted hers back. "I had fun, too."

"Hey," he said, walking back toward her. "I know you likely have plans for Christmas, and I don't want to screw any of that up...but I got you a little something." He shrugged. "Something small, and I wondered if maybe I could see you the day before. Or even the day after. Brenda Anne said you could come by our place. Bring Madison if you like."

"Oh." Her mind scrambled to process the request. She wasn't accustomed to seeing family at the holidays. Usually it was just dinner at Frankie's place, but this year was certainly shaping up differently. "Why not?" she said, warming her hands on her cup. "I'll talk to Madison, but I bet we could make Christmas Eve work."

His whole face transformed in celebration, and Clementine smiled, feeling a combination of happiness and unease. Such new territory.

"Yeah. Okay. This is great." Her father nodded. "I'll tell Brenda Anne. She's gonna be thrilled." He held up a hand to wave. "Enjoy your day, kiddo."

"See you soon." She waved back and watched as he approached Brenda Anne and made a big deal over her wreath. Clementine took a moment to survey the bustling sidewalks and closed-down streets full of people. Families walked together, laughing and sipping wassail to the sounds of the brass band. She checked her watch, realizing she only had a short time before her hour of caroling started. With a spring in her step, she hurried to city hall to suit up and warm up her voice with the others.

❖

Madison stood near the Christmas tree in the exact spot Clementine had ordained. It was the final spot on the Dickensian carolers' route, and it would give Madison a perfect view of the action. She heard them approach singing "Good King Wenceslas" in perfect harmony, sending the hairs on her arm standing up straight. She scrunched her shoulders in enjoyment, grinning and craning her neck to spot Clementine in the twelve-person choir. There she was. In a green bonnet and red gloves and full-on Dickensian getup, she stole Madison's breath and she'd be lucky to ever get it back again. She joined the crowd in applauding the carolers' arrival and happily listened to their performance of "Hark! the Herald Angels Sing," "O Christmas Tree," and the finale, "Silent Night." A gust of wind hit on the final line of the song, and Madison hugged herself, very aware of how special today was. She applauded heartily, so proud she could burst.

Clementine came right over at the conclusion of the performance and it took everything Madison had not to make out with her then and there. "That was amazing," she said instead, kissing Clem's lips softly. "You guys are so good."

"*They're* good. I'm just backup."

"There's nothing backup about you," Madison said. "It was all so perfect. I'm in awe right now. And don't get me started on the reaction I'm having to you in this outfit." She laughed. "It's everything I've ever dreamed of, you know."

Clementine stood taller. "Is that rightly true, Ms. LeGrange?" she asked in her best British accent.

"You stop that right now," Madison whispered, her cheeks heating against her will.

"I certainly cannot." More British. "I do believe you've got a blush."

Madison closed her eyes. "And now I'm done for. A goner."

Clementine dropped the character and leaned in slyly. "Looks like I have a new secret weapon."

"Please. Like you needed one."

"Christmas and English people are your kryptonite. I've cracked the code."

"Keep that under your hat."

"Do you mean my bonnet?" Clementine said in her ear.

"Are you sure you want to explore the festival?" Madison asked, blinking. "I could skip it. I really could. So boring around here."

Clementine laughed. "No, no. We're sticking around, but I need to get changed and get these clothes back to Marjorie, our director."

"Pity."

"I'm sure she'd lend me the outfit whenever, if I asked." With a wink Clementine disappeared, and Madison made a conscious effort to check her libido, which had never been on such high alert as it had in the past couple of months and showed no signs of dying down. Clementine had her under a wonderful spell.

They spent the next two hours moving through every inch of the festival, holding hands, sampling the wassail from each booth, and arguing over the best.

"Yeah, but the citrus in this one is killer," Clementine said.

"You are such a sucker for fruit infusion," Madison said, shaking her head. "Don't fall for it. It dominates and squashes the other flavors."

Clementine nodded. "Rightfully so. They can't steal the spotlight from the orange. It needs a pedestal. Much like mayonnaise."

Madison closed her eyes. "You're impossible."

"I'm a rabid orange fan."

"Well, who am I to deprive you? Maybe I need to up the citrus game in our pinot grigio."

"It's like you're finally seeing the light."

Madison laughed, enjoying herself so much her face hurt.

Later, they joined their friends to explore Santa's workshop and reindeer, an outdated display that still stole Madison's heart, reminding her of when she and Joey would race straight to the workshop when they were kids, staring in awe at the slowly moving animatronic reindeer.

"Remember when we asked if we could camp out here?" Madison asked Joey, with an arm slung around her shoulders. "Sleep with Blitzen and friends? Be a part of the gang?"

"My dad said not unless Santa called and invited us."

Madison nodded glumly. "So we sat by the phone all weekend in footie pajamas."

"He stood us the hell up." Joey sighed.

Becca laughed quietly. "The saddest sight in all of Whisper Wall. The Santa Claus castoffs."

"This is breaking my heart," Gabriella chimed in. "You two could camp out tonight and right this sadness. I'll stand watch. I don't even mind."

"Tempting, but no," Madison said, squeezing Clementine's hand.

She had another kind of sleepover in mind. "I think time has healed all Santa wounds. Back on good terms with the big guy."

They closed the festival down, drinking too much of the hard stuff and laughing their way home on foot, all staying on the Tangle Valley property that night. When Clementine emerged from the bathroom before bed, she wore a bonnet and not a shred of anything else.

"Gasp," Madison said. Her breath went shallow and her pulse kicked into overdrive. "You stole the bonnet, you magnificent grifter."

"Righto, I did, Ms. LeGrange," she said, sweetly, posing with a hand on the curve of her hip. God, Madison adored the hourglass shape of her body. The sight made her center throb and the rest of her tingle pleasantly.

"Please come here and let me explore England. Maybe give new meaning to the phrase *The British are coming.*"

Clementine grinned. "I thought you'd never ask."

Madison went up on her knees and caught Clementine's breast in her mouth as she approached the bed. That pulled a happy murmur as she sucked her nipple and then swirled it decadently with her tongue. Clementine, she had learned, didn't mind her getting a little aggressive with her breasts, so Madison sucked harder, cupping Clementine's bare ass with both hands. When Clementine began to slowly rock her hips, whispering as Madison showered her other breast with the same kind of attention, she bit softly, pulling louder sounds from Clementine. She cupped her face and kissed her lips, pushed her tongue inside, and melded their bodies together. "On the bed?" Madison said, coaxing. Clementine, her long hair falling from the bonnet, obliged, lying on her back. Madison pushed her legs apart, tasted her, explored with her tongue slowly. Finally, with Clementine squirming beneath her, she pushed her fingers inside. Clementine moaned as Madison took her time, moving slowly inside Clementine as she pushed back, asking for more. She picked up speed and watched as Clementine's breasts bounced to the rhythm. So sexy. So perfect. She cried out, coming quickly. Clementine's body, beautiful and bowed, went still, and she rode the current of pleasure with sounds Madison had grown to adore.

Finally, she touched the fabric of the bonnet and placed a kiss on Clementine's lips. "Best Christmas present ever," Madison whispered.

Clementine pushed herself up onto her forearms behind her.

"Oh, you ain't seen nothing yet." She kissed Madison soundly and switched their positions, all the while happily humming, "O Come All Ye Faithful."

"You're bad," Madison said with a grin.

"Do you like it?"

"I love it."

❖

"Can I offer you each a cinnamon stick for your tea?" Brenda Anne asked, scurrying around the small living room, doing everything in her power to make sure her guests were happy. It was late in the afternoon on Christmas Eve, and Clementine and Madison sat next to each other on the sofa across from her father, who wore a bright red Christmas sweater with Rudolph on the front. Clementine wouldn't have been shocked to hear that Brenda Anne had knitted it herself.

"I'd love one," Madison said. Clementine smiled at her, still amazed at her beauty, to be sitting next to her like this. The soft curls with the touches of blond. The blue eyes that never quit. And that radiant grin. The past few weeks had been beyond what she could have hoped for. Sometimes it just didn't feel real. She wondered if it ever would. Was she playing make-believe?

Clementine raised her hand. "I'll take one, too."

"Hell, I'll take three," her father said, grinning. The group laughed. "Not to rush, but this is for you." He slid a medium-sized box to Clementine. "Too excited to wait."

"Thoughtful of you," Clementine said and removed the paper. Inside she found a framed watercolor of a familiar grouping of ash trees. "Wait." She squinted and leaned in to the painting. "Is this what I think it is?"

He nodded. "Got a guy in town to paint it."

She stared at the scene, the very same grouping of trees that she used to fondly refer to as her reading forest as a kid. They were located just down the road from their home. She'd sit among those trees for hours, lost in whatever book she'd grabbed from the library that week. Other times, she would just daydream. "Thank you," were the only words she could manage as she stared down at the gift in amazement.

"This is an incredibly thoughtful gift." She gave her head a shake. This was so unexpected. "I didn't think you'd remember something like that."

"I got the important stuff," he said and tapped his head. "Anyway. No big deal, but I thought maybe you could hang it up at your place, so you could always hold on to it."

"I will do that." She turned it around and explained the meaning of the painting to Madison.

"Oh, wow," Madison said, taking the frame in her hands. "I see why this would mean a lot."

Brenda Anne had taken a seat next to her father after dropping off those cinnamon sticks. She had her hand over her heart. "Isn't it just the sweetest idea? It made me mist up when I heard what he'd done. Oh, and this is a basket of goodies for the both of you." She handed over an overflowing wicker basket full of spices, snacks, trinkets, and ornaments with an adorable red bow across the front.

"Oh, you didn't have to do this," Madison said, examining the bounty.

"Yes, I did, because I'm obsessed with making baskets these days. I just love gathering each piece and making it tie in to the rest. I made this one with the both of you in mind."

"Well, you're great at it," her father said. "I'd never in a million years know what to put in one of those things."

Madison had gifted the two of them a sampler basket of Tangle Valley wines, including their special mulled wine for heating on the stove. Clementine had arrived with a box of butter biscuits and the newest Groffman novel for her dad, and some fancy yarn for Brenda Anne, who loved to knit. The afternoon was truly shaping up to be a nice one. Their conversation flowed easily, and she and Madison wound up staying much later than they'd planned, listening to Brenda Anne tell stories of Len figuring out what to do with the feminine touches around the house.

"Even the placemats have a lace finish," he said with a laugh. "And we don't even get to eat on them. There are hand towels for guests and different ones for us. They have to stay separate." He laughed. "I'm learning all the rules."

"See what I'm dealing with?" Brenda Anne said with a giggle. They really were kind of cute.

By the time she and Madison left, Clementine had relaxed. In fact, as they walked to Madison's truck, she was on a high.

"I feel like that was a really nice get-together," Madison said, once they were in the truck.

"I can't believe I'm going to say this, but I agree with you. It felt…like a normal visit. Something regular people do to celebrate the holidays. Cookies, warm drinks, laughter." She played it all back again in mystification.

"It was. Trust me. And they seem to genuinely like each other, those two." She started the ignition. It was dark out, and the sky was as clear as could be, stars shining brightly overhead. "Plus, it's Christmas. The perfect time for coming together with the people you haven't always seen eye to eye with."

Clementine marveled. "I've seen it in movies. I just never imagined it would happen to me."

Madison leaned over and kissed her. "Might be time to start believing." She sat back in her seat and grinned. "Merry Christmas, sweetheart."

Clementine kissed the back of her hand. "Merry Christmas."

CHAPTER FOURTEEN

I'm amazed right now."

It was a cold afternoon in February, and Madison stood in the middle of the old barn at dusk, along with Gabriella, Joey, and Ryan, as they surveyed the finished renovated product. Ryan and her crew had worked steadily even in the midst of a few setbacks to get the place ready for the spring events Joey had lined up, and damn, it had been worth the wait.

The barn had been cleaned, the floors redone, the rafters replaced and reinforced, the side walls now slid away, and a whole new automated lighting system gave them more options than they knew what to do with. There was now a staging station walled off for caterers to prep, and a serving area for meals. A permanent stage had been erected on one side of the barn for bands or DJs to work their magic on the crowd. It felt new and open and offered fantastic views of the vineyard's breathtaking hillside.

"People are going to love it here," Joey said, folding her arms proudly. "Once we get a few weddings and parties under our belt, and the guests get to experience this place, the bookings are going to start pouring in. We may even need to hire a part-time coordinator."

Gabriella wrapped her arms around Ryan's waist and grinned up at her. "You hear that? You're a rock star. They love it."

"I'm glad," Ryan said, showing her dimples and demurring. She wasn't one to show off when it came to her work. If anything, she downplayed how talented she was.

"More than love it," Joey said. "We have just under a month before Loretta and Bobby's wedding. Plenty of time to get done what we need to. Now we get to relax and enjoy the hell out of the final planning stages."

"She's so excited," Madison said. "I've never seen her glow like this."

Gabriella grinned. "She came up here yesterday and cried when she saw how beautiful it is."

"She did?" Madison asked. Not a ton of things made her sentimental, but Loretta with tears in her eyes was one of the few things that could send her.

"Look at you. Madison LeGrange feeling the feelings. Rare. Does anyone have a camera?" Joey asked with a smile.

"I'd deny it in court, but yes, Loretta gets me here," she said, covering her heart. "She's like our honorary mom in so many ways."

"She's a keeper. That's for sure," Gabriella added. She poked Madison in the arm. "And dare I say that sentimentality looks good on you? You should try it more often."

Madison scoffed. "Nah, I'll leave the emoting to you guys." She checked her watch. "In the meantime, I'm gonna swing by the café and meet the new hire. Kevin, the coffee whiz, is taking over as resident barista each morning, so Clementine's bringing on more counter help."

"How's the new coffee business going?" Ryan asked. "I ordered a latte yesterday and was impressed."

"I'll pass that on." Madison grinned and rocked on her heels. "They've been working hard to perfect the process. Clem wants everything at the café to be the best you've ever had. Her personal motto, and lately she's been putting in the extra effort."

"I think she can be safely trusted to accomplish that at the café," Joey said. "I think it's because she finally feels supported. Rothstein was always her nemesis."

"And now she has you," Gabriella said with a winsome smile. "Her very agreeable boss and sex kitten."

Ryan and Joey attempted to smother their grins but weren't exactly successful. Madison just shook her head, immune to their jokes. She was simply too happy. "Laugh if you will. I own my boss-slash-girlfriend combo status."

"Well, you should," Joey stated and patted her arm. "It really seems to be working all the way around. You two are clearly loving life, and the café has never been better." She shrugged. "I think Clementine just needed someone to believe in her."

"Me, too," Gabriella said sincerely. "The sex kitten part is just bonus."

"A kitten, though?" Madison asked. "Can't I at least be a panther or a lioness?"

"I back that," Ryan said.

Gabriella sighed. "Fine. You can choose your own sensual feline."

"Big of you," Madison said.

"And how are things going with Clementine's dad?" Joey asked, inclining her head. "I didn't want to pry, but I saw them having lunch the other day, and everything seemed very relaxed."

"They are. She's never really had family around, so this is a new experience."

Gabriella nodded. "Oh, that makes me so happy for her."

"Me, too," Madison said. "I feel like she's really letting go, allowing herself to enjoy life more."

"Well, a lot of that is thanks to you," Joey said.

Madison shrugged.

"No, no. It's true. You make her happy."

Madison's cheeks went hot. She glanced away to avoid eye contact, not always comfortable showing off her softer side. "Well, she does the same for me, so…"

"You know," Ryan said, looking around and placing her hand on one of the new beams. "I hear there are a few spring bookings left in this barn. You could always grab one, make it official."

"Yeah, no." Madison's mouth fell open. "Let's not get crazy." Things with Clementine were both exciting and comfortable, which was the best combination possible. No reason to change anything. The two of them were different enough to keep life interesting yet came with the same value system, something that was important to Madison. And don't get her started on their ridiculous chemistry. She longed for Clementine on the nights they spent apart, waking up several times a night and touching the empty pillow next to her. Maybe that was something to unpack later. "Right now, we're enjoying ourselves. No reason to rush, right?"

"No reason not to," Joey said with a wink. She then touched Madison's arm. "I'm just being playful because I happen to love the two of you together. Apart, you're amazing people. As a couple, you're off the charts."

"Thanks, I think," she said with a laugh and accepted the kiss Joey planted on her cheek with a loud smack. But she understood exactly what Joey meant. She did feel like a better person with Clementine in her life, a more complete human. And now she couldn't wait to swing by the café and see those beautiful blue eyes. She waved with both hands to her friends as she backed away. "Congratulations on a fantastic job, everybody. I can't wait to see this place bustling with people."

"Hug Clem for us!" Gabriella called. "Tell her I'm already working on my right arm for softball."

"And maybe bring back some cinnamon biscuits," Joey added.

"Both things I can do."

❖

They were thirty minutes from closing, and the time couldn't tick by fast enough. It had been a whirlwind day at the Biscuit. Clementine had spent the morning training their new hire, Monique, who worked hard and liked to say, "I got you," a lot. She was also an excessive nodder, which was good in terms of checking for understanding but also had Clementine wondering how her neck muscles kept up.

"A vanilla latte with extra foam," Kevin said in his customary flat tone and slid the beverage across the counter to the waiting customer.

"Remember to stay friendly, upbeat," Clementine said to him once the customer was out of earshot.

"Right, that," he deadpanned.

The door opened, and the bell rang. Clementine glanced up, hopeful to see Madison, who would be stopping by to meet Monique and pick up yesterday's bank drop. It wasn't Madison, however. It was Becca. Clad in jeans and a green leather moto jacket, she made her way to the counter and grinned happily at Kevin.

"Kevin, it's great to see you."

"Hello," Kevin said, with a curt nod.

"I miss you at the fry place."

"You always struggled with the rules," he said matter-of-factly.

"Right. I never seemed to grasp that you only sold fries. I'm getting better, though. In fact, I'll take some crinkle cuts."

He blinked. "We don't serve fries."

"What? And here I am, finally grasping the rules."

Clementine rolled her lips, trying not to laugh. Kevin really did make it too easy. He was like a grumpy old man in a college student's body.

"Sad day. I had a hankering. Hash browns then?"

"Please consult our non-potato-based menu above."

Becca nodded and studied the menu as if it was the first time she'd seen it. "Very helpful, Kevin. You're always on top of it. I'll take a BLT from the lunch menu."

"Good. We have those."

Clementine cleared her throat and Kevin tried again. "And I'd be happy to put that in for you."

While Becca waited on Frankie to prep her sandwich, she turned to Clementine. "So, we're having the huge flower bed on the north side of the property completely pulled out and redesigned. I'm not thrilled with the original company we used and got approval to start taking bids. Your father dropped his card off."

"Did he?" Clementine said and slid a strand of hair behind her ear. "I know he's trying to establish his company one client at a time. The Jade is a big job, though."

"It is. I wanted your take before I went any further with him." What Becca wasn't saying because she was too polite was that she'd heard he'd had a troubled past.

"Three months ago, I would have been worried about his reliability. But from what I've seen, he seems like he's hardworking and set on turning things around."

Becca nodded. "Okay, good to hear. I like the idea of giving someone who needs it a chance." She knocked on the counter once. "I think I'll give him a call and see what his proposal looks like."

"That's very kind of you. I can't guarantee that he's the one for—"

"Nor do you have to," Becca said, waving off the idea. "Say no more. If he seems like the guy for the job, I'll hire him. If not, I'll go in a different direction."

"And there will be no hard feelings at all," Clementine rushed to explain. While she believed in her father's ability to turn over a new leaf more and more as the days passed, she still wasn't comfortable offering any kind of guarantee. He'd have to prove himself to his clients over time.

"Good to hear that," Becca said, retrieving the bag Kevin slid across the counter. "Thanks, guys. See you soon." She passed Kevin a look. "Stay out of trouble. I'm serious. No fry shenanigans."

"Gotcha." He blinked. And blinked again. "Gotcha. Enjoy your day."

Becca and Clem exchanged a smile at his lack of enthusiasm, and she was on her way. It wasn't more than five minutes before Madison popped in like a blast of fresh air, wearing a forest green sweater and skinny jeans tucked into her tall brown boots that were both functional for work and stylish. With her hair pulled up, some of her curls had escaped and fell around her face as if she totally meant for them to do that. She was blessed with great hair.

"Hey, you," Madison said, beaming across the counter. "The grapes say hey."

"Always so neighborly, those grapes."

Madison shrugged. "Just how they were raised."

Clementine laughed. "What can I get you?"

"What a question," Madison said with a raised eyebrow. They'd spent the last two nights apart, so the tension that built up from missing each other was palpable. "I will remain the utmost professional, however, and ask for a dozen cinnamon biscuits and the bank drop."

Clementine wrote up the ticket and began assembling the box of biscuits. "You didn't get too busy to swing by today."

"I feel like it might not be the smartest of me to leave cash in the building for days on end. I'm trying to be better about that, but some days it's easier to get here than others."

"Totally understandable. One moment..." Clementine disappeared and returned with the bank bag. "I can always drop it by the bank for you if you're ever too busy."

"No, I like this routine. Gives me an excuse to stop by and see you in the middle of the day."

Just then Monique emerged from the kitchen where she'd been restocking the fridge with their latest delivery. Clementine introduced them and Madison smiled.

"Well, we're thrilled to have you on board."

"Thank you. I already love it here. The food alone is…amazing." At the mention of the last word, her eyes drifted to her right to Kevin, who was busy cleaning the espresso machine. What in the world? Clementine shot Madison a look and saw that her eyebrows were at her hairline. She'd noticed, too. Did new-hire Monique have a crush on bored-with-life Kevin? Well, well. The Biscuit might have just become a soap opera for the college aged.

"We're glad you've found so much here to admire," Madison said, beaming. "And I will definitely stay tuned to your journey at the Biscuit. I have a feeling great things will come of it."

"You're so nice," Monique said. "Everyone is." Her gaze shot right back to Kevin, only longingly this time.

This time Madison looked Clementine square in the eye, and they shared a wide-eyed moment. "Well, I'll get out of the way." She retrieved the bank drop and the box of biscuits. "Tonight?"

"Oh, most definitely," Clementine said without hesitation. "I'll text you later."

"Thank God."

CHAPTER FIFTEEN

Clementine was on her knees between her legs and Madison couldn't see straight. Clem had her pressed against a wall and writhing within ten minutes of walking through the door of her cottage, another testament to the fact that they couldn't keep their damn hands off each other, and sleeping apart for two nights seemed to have certainly inspired Clementine. Madison couldn't complain. She pushed against Clementine's mouth, relishing the movement of her tongue, searching for sweet release, but also never wanting this torturous attention to end. With her hands flat against the wall where Clementine had requested them, her hips pumped more and more with each passing second. The pressure built until she thought she would explode. When Clementine pulled her into her mouth and sucked, Madison hissed and bucked as pleasure rained down on her. Her body went tight, and she heard herself cry out as Clementine continued to take her higher and higher with her mouth, her hair tickling Madison's thighs. Sweet heaven, she was done for. Owned. Transported to a new level of release.

"I really enjoyed that," Clementine said, looking up at Madison with a proud smile.

"You should try it from here," Madison said, struggling for air. "In fact, I insist."

The fun continued. Eventually, they made it to the bedroom, after they'd thoroughly enjoyed each other. She stared across the bed at Clementine propped up to a sitting position, her back against a pillow. The sheet covered her to the chest, leaving the tops of her breasts visible and gorgeous. "You're painting-worthy," Madison said, admiring the view. "If only I could paint. Now a deep regret of mine, because stick figures wouldn't do you justice."

"You never know. I could sit just like this and hold a basket of biscuits."

Madison laughed. "This idea is really taking off."

"We're going places." Clementine slid down the bed so they were face-to-face, lying on their sides. "Speaking of, I think Becca might hire my dad to design some outdoor flower beds for the Jade." Her eyes were lit up in excitement.

Madison took a moment before responding, choosing her words carefully. "That's great. Are you concerned at all?"

Clementine considered the question. "Yes and no. I should be, given what I know about his tendencies, but I can finally admit that he's not the same man. I see that more and more. He's talkative and interested in what other people have to say. Entirely different guy." She met Madison's gaze. "I believe him when he says he's changed. Do you think that's crazy of me? Be honest."

"It's not." Madison brushed a strand of hair off Clementine's forehead. "But I know it can be dicey when you're in between a family member and a friend."

Clementine quirked her lips in a way that said she didn't necessarily agree. "But what about getting out of someone's way who is trying to do the right thing? I couldn't tank his chances before he even met with Becca. That wouldn't be fair."

"No. That was probably the right call. I just don't want to see you in a rough spot, and from what you've told me about him, I worry." She was treading on thin ice now. Clementine had embraced her father back into her life, and here was Madison, raining on the good fortune. "Maybe I'm being overly cautious."

"I think you're being Madison. You assess risk and process data and outcomes before making any decisions for yourself, and that's what you're doing for me."

Madison closed one eye. "You make me sound like a machine. I'm not that cut and dried."

Clementine exhaled. "You're definitely not a machine, but you are very analytical. Sometimes I wish you'd show…"

"What?"

"A little more of your emotional side, some vulnerability. Lead with your feelings for once. Get mad or sad. How do you feel about us, for example? It's hard to know. I can infer a lot, but you don't actually say the words. Have you noticed?"

Madison kissed her. "How was that? Does that clear up my feelings?"

"It helps. But words would, too. I know that we enjoy spending time together." A pause. "I just wonder sometimes where your head is in regards to us, the present, the future. All of it."

Madison nodded and stared at the ceiling, a fish out of water. These kinds of conversations were always challenging. "I struggle when it comes to articulating emotion. I know that about myself. I try, but the big outpourings are not something I'm good at. I'm more of an intrigue, less of a rom-com kind of person."

"I know. You're the manager of other people's feelings, but not comfortable when it comes to talking about your own."

She covered her eyes. "It's sounds so stupid when it's boiled down to that, but I guess I lead more with my head and less with my heart. True."

Clementine winced and Madison understood why. It sounded like she just said Clementine didn't have her heart. Not at all what she meant to convey.

"No, not like that." She tried again. "The feelings are there. I just tend not to wallow in them."

"Not your feelings, but *the* feelings?" Clementine frowned. "I'm not sure this is going well."

"But I'm going to work on it because I like us."

"Me, too," Clementine said. "Was that so hard to say?"

"No, but doing this"—she kissed Clementine again—"is so much more to the point."

"I'll take a combo deal."

Madison sighed. "And you deserve it. So I'm going to work harder at telling you that you're here." She touched her chest.

"Where is that?" Clementine asked with a challenging smile. She was not letting Madison off the emotional hook anytime soon.

"My heart."

"I'll take it," Clementine said and passed her a soft smile. "Because you're in mine, too."

❖

Clementine did something that she didn't often do. She reached out to Jun. While it was Frankie who she was closest to in the world, Jun was someone she liked a lot, and she wanted to see if maybe she could expand her friendship pool. Frankie always said Jun liked *her* a lot and that they should get together. She was ready to stick her toe in the water and give it a shot after feeling more confident lately. Maybe picking up a few more friends wasn't such a crazy idea, because it turned out Clementine had a lot to offer, too.

"I'm going to narrow it down to two," Jun said, flipping between books in her stack of about eight. She had her dark hair pulled back into a ponytail, which signaled she meant business. "I'm glad you got me here. I've been meaning to read more. I need more killing in my life."

Clementine raised an eyebrow. They sat at one of the community tables in the middle of the fiction racks at Whisper Wall's town library. Jun had zeroed in on the mystery section and went to town, scooping up prospects like a squirrel gathering nuts for the winter. "Well, you can always come back once you finish the first two. That's what's great about this place. They never run out of books."

But Jun was busy deciding. "This one is about a murder on a train. I'm down for train murder." She moved it to the maybe pile. "This one looks like a regular old house murder. Too mundane." The book was shoved to the discard pile. She had an effective system, and it apparently revolved around the originality of the murder. She knew her needs. "Want to come over for some homemade soup tomorrow night? Grandma Hee's recipe. Supposed to be a cold one out. You can bring Madison."

"Yeah? That sounds like fun. Count us in."

"Done. I've decided to go with three books." Jun held up her selections. "Train murder, farm murder, and college murder."

"A winning trio."

Jun sat back as if exhausted but satisfied with her work. "How are things going with you two love doves? I saw you holding hands on the sidewalk in front of the Dark Room."

"Madison loves chocolate." Clementine set down the copy of Margaret Atwood's newest that she planned to check out. She'd already read it but was all set for a revisit. "Things are good. She's been working a lot. Gearing up for the release of the new chardonnay. Once it's off to bottling, I think she'll breathe a little easier. She says it's like sending her baby off to college."

"But with the two of you? Things are good?"

"I think so," Clementine said. She thought a minute. "Sometimes I wonder what goes on in her head. She's great about telling me about her day, or how the wine's doing, or that I look pretty, but she's not huge about opening up." She shrugged. "I don't know what scares her, or what she's like when she's sad."

Jun held up one of her novels. "She's a closed book sometimes."

"Yeah, that's a good way to put it." She pointed at the hardcover. "A mystery."

"You just have to solve it is all. If she's a keeper, don't give up. You give her time to open up."

"She's a keeper," Clementine said, smiling. "And you're right. I just need to be patient and let her know how I feel and see if she reciprocates. Terrifying."

"And how do you feel?"

She swallowed. "I'm falling in love, Jun. I know that as sure as I'm sitting here, and I don't see any stopping it."

Jun's eyes went wide. "This is a reason to celebrate. I'm doubling the soup quotient. Two bowls for everyone. Maybe three." Jun grabbed her arm. "You have to tell her."

Clementine smiled, bolstered by Jun's exuberance. "I think I will. Soon. Life's too short not to. Don't you think?"

"I do," Evelyn said, strolling past with the book cart, her red hair in a braid down her back. She was on a reshelving mission and must have overheard their conversation. "You and Madison are adorable together. I've seen you on the Biddies' Instagram. You're their favorite, you know."

"I've never felt more famous in my life," Clementine said, not nearly as mortified by the attention as she once would have been. In fact, now she enjoyed showing off her happiness a little.

"Sad about Birdie, though."

"What?" Clementine asked, her heart clenching in her chest. "Is she okay?"

"I'm not sure. She was hospitalized this week. Fluid around

her heart and lungs, they say. She was weak and dizzy and a little disoriented. I'm going to send some flowers from the library and just hope she improves."

Clementine deflated. Not Ms. Birdie. Sure, she was nosy and knew it, but she was the sweetest of the gossips, and a fixture in Whisper Wall. She just had to get better. She was one of those life forces that you just couldn't ever imagine going out. It was unthinkable.

"She'll be okay," Jun said, sobering. She placed a hand over Clementine's and nodded.

"I hope so. Mornings at the Biscuit wouldn't be the same without her."

"I'll say a prayer tonight," Jun said. "But for now, we are going to remember all of our blessings."

"A good reminder." Clementine forced a smile. "Because I have a lot of those lately."

"Let's take our books and run," Jun said. "I have some death to rip through."

Clementine laughed. "Can't delay the bloodbath a second longer."

"This is why we're friends."

❖

Later that week, Clementine swung by the tasting room after work, at Joey's invitation, to sample the new spring blend they'd just added to their menu.

"Limited release," Joey said, pouring Clem a two-ounce taste. "Only available here at the vineyard. Nowhere else."

"I feel so important."

"You are." Joey gestured to the glass. "As you enjoy, you'll notice hints of grass and melon with a citrusy finish. Madison was going for whimsical and light. Something you can enjoy on the back porch in spring, once the temperatures start to warm."

"Well, I do love citrus," she said with a smile. Clementine swirled the liquid in her glass and took a deep inhale, already picking up on all Joey described. She took a sip and let the wine settle in her mouth and roll to the back. She'd learned early on in her wine-tasting days to never size up a wine until your second taste. That gave your mouth a chance to adjust to the new acidity before it could discern the individual notes.

On her second taste, she got a lot more. Not only was the wine crisp, it was good. "Oh, I really like this."

"Yeah? Me, too. Madison was really pleased with the balance on this one, and I think she's right to be. More?"

"Please," Clementine said, sliding her glass forward. After the pour, Joey excused herself to help another set of guests who'd arrived for a tasting. It was late in the day, but the tasting room still buzzed with activity from several different parties all at different stages of their tasting journey. She watched a man and woman gaze at each over a bottle at a table across the room just as someone draped an arm around her.

"Hey, stranger."

Clementine looked up. "Becca. Hey." She was dressed casually today in jeans, a white T-shirt, and a maroon hoodie.

"My day off," Becca said. "So I like to help out around here. Off the clock now, though. The new blend?" she asked, gesturing to Clementine's glass.

"Yeah. I love it."

"So do I. Super light. Did you hear what they named it?"

She shook her head.

"Oh, um, dammit." Becca snapped her fingers. "It just flew out of my brain. We can ask Joey when she frees up. In the meantime, I meant to tell you. I met with your dad, and he showed me the plans he drew up. They looked fantastic. I hired him." Becca grinned.

"You did? Oh, that's great. I'm glad you two saw eye to eye on the project." She made a mental note to send him a congratulatory message.

"He has bright ideas and a passion for the work, which are the two things I like to see in someone I partner with. They're getting started next week."

"Thanks, Becca. I'm hopeful you'll be happy."

She grinned and squeezed Clementine's hand. "I think I will."

Right then, the door to the tasting room opened, and Clementine quirked her head. Walking through the door was a figure that vaguely resembled Madison but more accurately matched a creature from the black lagoon. Madison's face was splattered with mud, and her clothes were caked in the dried stuff.

"Oh, my," Clementine said as she approached. "Who did you get in a fight with?"

"A busted irrigation hose, that's who, and the thing won." She looked across the bar to Loretta, who'd rolled her lips in not to laugh. "I owe your fiancé a debt of gratitude for killing the water before we flooded the whole vineyard. Kiss?" she asked Clementine.

"Hmm. Tempting, but I've got this blend going, and it doesn't pair well with mud," she said, lifting her glass. To prove she was only kidding, she placed a delicate kiss on Madison's lips anyway. No way she could resist.

"What do you think?" Madison asked, her eyes twinkling bright blue, in nice contrast to the smudge of dirt across her cheek.

"It's fantastic. I'd like to purchase a bottle."

"Doesn't seem fair you should have to pay for that one."

"Why is that?"

Madison, adorable and muddy, nodded at Loretta, who picked up a bottle and turned it around so the label faced them. She placed it on the bar in front of Clementine.

"Wait. What?" Clementine stared at the gold lettering and grappled, trying to understand. "Clementine?" she asked. "I don't understand."

"Madison's chosen name for the blend," Loretta said gleefully. "I happen to think it's a perfect match."

"Refreshing, relaxing, fun, satisfying, and memorable. All traits that remind me of you. I wanted to commemorate that," Madison said.

Clementine still hadn't found the words. "And this is real. It's on more than one bottle?"

"All of 'em," Loretta said, picking up two from behind the bar. She jutted her chin at the couple Clementine had been studying earlier. "Those two just took one with them. Couple hundred more in the storage room behind me."

"I can't believe you did this," Clementine said to Madison, her heart bursting.

"One of the perks of having a girlfriend who is also a fancy winemaker," Becca said.

"What am I missing?" Joey asked, stalking over. "I hate missing anything."

"Clementine just met Clementine. They're in the midst of their meet-cute," Becca said. "It's going well."

"Awesome." Joey beamed. "I didn't want to spoil the surprise until Madison was here."

Clementine scooped up the bottle and showed Joey. She knew there were tears in her eyes, but she ignored them. "I love it. Nothing like this has ever happened to me. I feel famous."

"Well, you are now," Loretta said.

"People are ordering you left and right," Joey added. "You're the new fad at Tangle Valley this spring. Let me package you up a couple of bottles."

As she walked out with Madison by her side and two bottles of wine named after her in a bag, Clementine felt ten feet tall. "Thank you," she said, meeting Madison's eyes. "You were right. You do have your own way of showing me how you feel."

"Aww, shucks," Madison said. "Will I see you tomorrow?"

Clementine kissed the back of her hand. "Counting on it."

Madison walked her to the car, and because there was still much to be done on the vineyard, Clementine spent the evening on her own, curled up with a good book and the perfect glass of Clementine wine. Nothing had ever tasted better. Last year at this time, her life had been nothing but a series of waiting-in-the-wings moments that never manifested into anything. She hadn't truly been living anywhere but on the pages of other people's stories in books. Tonight, she felt like she had a story of her own and a true say in how it would end. "Life can sneak up on you," she said to her glass. "Little me. Who would have thought?"

CHAPTER SIXTEEN

"What do you need from me?" Madison asked, from her seat at the Round Table of Planning. That's what she called it when they all gathered in the Big House to iron out the details of Loretta and Bobby's wedding. She hadn't been given much to do other than her role as one of Loretta's bridesmaids. Carly, Loretta's daughter, would act as maid of honor.

"Can you be the wine shepherd? I'll be serving as the representative for the venue, which probably means a lot of running back and forth to make sure everything runs smoothly. If you could take over managing the bar staff, that would help a lot."

"Now that I can do," Madison said, scribbling a few notes.

"Becca, what do you need from us in terms of the out-of-town guests?" Joey asked.

"Not much. We've already booked tons of rooms on our block, which I've set up with a nice discount. The link is still live should we have more takers."

Joey scribbled away. "Fantastic. And we'll deliver those welcome baskets the Thursday before."

"Great. We'll have them waiting for each guest along with a bottle of wine from the vineyard."

Joey turned to Gabriella. "We all set on the menu?"

"With one exception." She sat back in her chair. "Bobby, bless him, has requested his favorite food, French fries, and though they don't exactly mesh with the menu I've designed with Loretta, I thought we could do a separate Tuscan fry station with a variety of aioli and toppings for folks to have fun with, and they customize their own. Thoughts?"

"Love it." Joey paused, marveling with a grin on her face. "I feel like we should be official wedding planners. We're good at this."

"We would wear berets and eat lots of pastries during our meetings," Gabriella said, clearly inspired.

Madison quirked her head. "Are we French wedding planners then?"

"Maybe we should be," Gabriella said, seeming to consider her options. "Seems sexier that way."

"All right," Becca said. "I'll pencil in my new French job during my off time."

They wrapped up the meeting, agreeing to meet the next week for final touches.

"Hey, Maddie," Becca said, walking out with her. "You seen Clem's father around lately?"

She squinted. "Not since last week. Why?"

"Not a big deal, but he started the beds for us out at the Jade. Did the demo on the current beds, dug them all up, but hasn't been back. That was three days ago, and it's just not the look I like for our guests. I wanted to see if he could come out and finish the job, but he's not returned my calls."

"Huh." Madison's stomach clenched, and she hoped this was not a glimpse at his reliability. It would kill Clementine. "You know, I haven't heard anything, but I can casually ask."

"You know what? Don't go out of your way. Just had my radar up."

"Of course. Probably took on too many jobs at once."

"Which is understandable," Becca said, always the perfect picture of professionalism.

Madison wished she felt as nonchalant, but alarm bells were sounding in the distance. She ignored them and refused to jump to conclusions. When she met Clementine for dinner, she informally mentioned her conversation with Becca over the Manchego croquette appetizer.

Clementine looked thoughtful. "Well, that's not a good look, tearing up the landscaping and then taking the next few days off the job. I bet you anything he bit off more than he could chew."

"I was thinking the same thing. Do you want to check in with him or let it go?" Madison smiled as the server topped off her cabernet.

"I'll ask the next time I see him. Frankie said he stopped by the Biscuit earlier after I'd gone home. He closed for me because I needed to let the maintenance guy fix the hot water issue at the apartment."

"You could always stay with me more. I don't know if you're aware, but I have some of the most awesome hot water in all of Whisper Wall."

"Well, now you're just sweet-talking, and damn, you're good."

Madison leaned across the table. "Tell me there's an overnight bag in the back of your car and that you're coming home with me tonight."

"With free hot water dangling on the string like that, how can I not?"

But Clementine was clearly off-kilter the rest of the night, and Madison could track the moment the shift occurred right back to when she'd brought up Becca and her dad. She was quieter and a less assertive version of herself.

"What's going on in there?" Madison asked later that night, touching Clementine's temple as they lay in bed listening to the branches of the trees rustle.

"Just thinking through the week. I feel like I have a lot of odds and ends dangling at the café, and I need to get Toast in for his yearly shots. He hates any sort of travel."

"That's all?"

"Yeah," Clementine said unconvincingly. "And I'm tired."

"Then let's sleep," Madison said and kissed her lips softly.

"Good night," Clementine said. She opened her mouth as if to say something else but then closed it. Long after Clementine had faded into the rhythmic breathing of deep sleep, Madison couldn't help wonder about those withheld words, knowing in her heart what they might have been and knowing she would have likely said them right back. As sleep eventually descended, she drifted off warm and happy and protective of the woman in her arms. The woman she…very much wanted to spend more and more of her days and nights with. She smiled. The words would come, wouldn't they? All in due time.

❖

Clementine was behind by at least three trays of biscuits, which would keep her customers waiting and her line longer than it ever should be. She'd already overpoured two cups of drip coffee and ruined her attempt at a nonfat almond latte. Kevin wouldn't be in until eight that morning, and Clementine felt like she was drowning, unable to keep her head in the game.

The news from Madison about her father abandoning the jobsite at the Jade was slowly chipping away at her. This felt all too familiar. The excuse she'd made for him was what she wished was true, but not reflective of what she feared most. When she'd arrived for work that morning, she just had a feeling she couldn't shake. Her father had been by the day before. Frankie had mentioned he'd asked to drop something for her in the office, a gift. She'd stood outside the office door earlier that morning, willing herself to go inside. She didn't find any gift for herself, but she had discovered the safe that held three days of bank drops had been pried open and emptied. Her brain hadn't worked right since then.

"I'm sorry, Monty. Can you repeat your order one more time? I must not have heard you."

"Sure. Just my usual."

She knew his usual as plain as she knew her own name, except today she didn't. Today, nothing worked. "Right. And that was a…"

He frowned, concern crossing his features. "Oh, just a butter biscuit with a side of jalapeño bacon."

"Right. Of course. Just a strange morning." She forced a smile, feeling stupid.

"I have them all the time," Monty said, sending her a supportive smile. By late morning, she'd regained her footing, and with Kevin on espresso duty, she could gather her thoughts. Perhaps that wasn't a good thing, because the more she ruminated on the missing money and her father's inevitable involvement, the more nauseous she became. The idea of telling Madison what had happened was almost unthinkable. She wanted to crawl into a hole and never emerge. Her hands shook, and her heart thudded way too fast.

"Hey, Clem? You're pale and quiet and I think maybe you should sit down," Frankie said from his spot at the grill in the midst of a lull.

"I'm fine," Clementine said, trying to project normalcy, but even her voice sounded strange. "Might have eaten something weird is all."

Frankie frowned. "We can cover things here if you want to take the morning. Kevin's a pro—aren't you, Kev?"

"Yeah," Kevin said with a one-shouldered shrug. "That's totally me."

"No, no, no. I'll be fine," she reassured them.

By the afternoon, full understanding of the situation took disastrous hold. The disbelief that had behaved like a makeshift shield had faded away, and she was left with the stark reality of what was happening. She was right back where she was as a kid, helpless and duped. Only this time, there were other people to think about. Who in this town had that man made promises to? Had his connection to Clementine fostered people's belief in him? That had certainly been the case with Becca. What about others? She was horrified for her friends and guilt ridden. Plus, her reputation mattered a lot to her. In fact, she'd worked for years to carve out a place for herself in this community, and in a blink of an eye she felt it dissolve. But one person's name rose straight to the top of her concerns. Brenda Anne. She needed to get to Brenda Anne and let her know what was going on before she got in any deeper.

Strangely, the Nifty Nickel was closed when Clementine arrived on the sidewalk out front. That didn't make any sense. It was midafternoon on a weekday, but the popular store was dark and locked. This didn't bode well.

Without hesitation, Clementine drove straight to Brenda Anne's house and knocked on the door. When she got no answer, she knocked harder and waited. After what felt like an eternity, Brenda Anne opened the door with bloodshot eyes and swollen cheeks that said she'd been crying. "Hi, Clementine," she said in a raspy voice. She looked awful.

"Are you okay?" Clementine asked, fear prickling the back of her neck.

"It's gone. All of it." She stared at Clementine, blank faced.

"What's gone?" Clementine asked.

"I should have known better. All my friends said to go slow, but everything was so great, ya know?"

Clementine nodded. "I know. I know exactly."

"And we made these wonderful plans, and I believed in them. I was finally happy. Do you know what that feels like? To be happy after so long?"

Clementine nodded, tears springing into her eyes. "I do." She reached out and squeezed Brenda Anne's hand. "Where is he now?"

"Oh, long gone. Left a note that said that he tried, but it turned out he wasn't much for settling down." She shook her head in disbelief. "Took every damn dime I had." Her voice broke. "That was my retirement money. Over twenty years of saving. Now what do I do?"

Clementine closed her eyes. The news crushed her and was so much worse than she had feared. "I'm so sorry, Brenda Anne. You have to file a police report."

"I still can't figure out how he got my bank passwords, unless he went through my desk down to the very bottom drawer in my recipe box."

Clementine sighed. "I guarantee he went through your desk and probably a lot more."

Brenda Anne stared at her with questioning, watery eyes. "Was it a scam from the beginning? I just can't believe that."

"I honestly don't know. Maybe not." She paused, reconsidering. "Maybe so." All Clementine knew was that she was hanging on by a thread. She felt like every step forward she'd made recently—every new revelation about herself, her life, her place in this world—had now crumbled around her. There was a clock ticking very loudly in her ear, counting down the moments until she split apart at the seams. Everything around her seemed too loud, too bright, too garish, and too unreal to be true. And yet, it was. She hadn't realized how much of her sense of self was wrapped up in her past, where she came from, and how she overcame it. But now it felt like she'd been yanked right back to where she'd started. She needed to be alone so she could find a way to breathe again, to see straight. Yet she knew there was one stop she had to make first, even though everything in her roiled against it. She offered Brenda Anne a hug that wouldn't change anything and made the short trip out to Tangle Valley.

Ten minutes later, she stood in front of Madison, who beamed at her, wearing gloves and standing alongside one of the tall metal tanks.

"Well, this is the best surprise. Hi." Madison leaned in for a kiss that Clementine had a hard time returning. The world felt too upside down.

"Can we talk?" she asked, indicating Madison's office nearby.

Madison's entire face shifted to concern. "Of course. Are you okay?" Madison nodded to the members of her crew, who seemed about to take over. Once they were safely behind the closed door, Madison turned to her. "Tell me what's up. Here, sit. You're so pale."

Clementine swallowed, declining to sit. She didn't plan to be there long enough. "You were right. My dad took off."

"Oh no," Madison said, moving to her. Clementine took a step away, and Madison blinked in confusion.

"It gets worse."

"Okay."

"Not only did he stand Becca up and run off with Brenda Anne's retirement savings, he also broke into the safe at the Biscuit and took the last three days' worth of bank drops."

"Oh no."

"I know. I'm so sorry."

Madison shook her head, squinting. "Why in the world are you sorry?"

"Because he stole from the café." The tears came whether she wanted them to or not. "From you. I'm horrified."

"But you're not responsible."

"I let him into my life. We had Christmas with him at Brenda Anne's, which is pretty much an endorsement in her eyes. I knew better, Madison. I was the only person who should have."

"Hey, it's okay. Look at me." It was hard, but Clementine did, meeting the blue eyes that she no longer felt she deserved. "You're really shaken up, and that is to be expected, but you didn't do any of these things. A really awful human did, who had nothing to do with you."

"He's my father."

"Not your choice."

The logic was there. She heard Madison's words, and they should have computed, resonated, and effectively made her feel better. They didn't. "Anyway, I'm going to go. I'm so sorry about the money. I'll repay you. I promise. I have a little savings."

"That's crazy. I don't need to be repaid. We're going to be fine at the Biscuit. But we do need to contact the police."

Clementine nodded. "Right. We do. I'll get on that." She headed for the door, the nausea taking over. She had to get out of there. She could tell Madison was on her heels.

"Hey, let me drive you home. I can take the rest of the afternoon off."

"No," Clementine said, whirling around. "If it's okay with you, I need some time on my own to absorb all this."

Madison paused, probably feeling out of options. She was always the problem solver, and this was one problem she couldn't fix. "Okay, well, I'll check on you tonight."

"Okay," Clementine said, already walking away. The farther she got, the faster she walked, as if needing to escape the farce she'd created. Nothing felt real anymore.

CHAPTER SEVENTEEN

The tasting room wasn't quite open for business when Madison busted in looking for Joey, who emerged from the storage room moments later.

Madison did away with good morning niceties and got right to it, her nerves in a ball. "Frankie called. Clementine didn't show up for work this morning. I'm going to head over to her place. Just wanted to let you know I'd be off the property, in case you needed me."

"What?" Joey said, her mouth falling open. "That is not like Clementine at all. She's dependable. I don't think she's missed a morning in years. This is about her dad?"

"Yeah." Madison sighed. "You should have seen her yesterday. She looked like she'd seen a ghost and was completely walled off."

Joey's eyebrows rose. "Definitely go, go, go. We're all good here."

"But I was supposed to speak to that tour group in an hour, and I don't know that I'll be back."

"I'll have Deacon do it."

Madison frowned. Her assistant winemaker was knowledgeable and bright but didn't always explain himself well to guests. Something they were working on. "Deacon repeats himself a lot and gets off on tangents about things like pesticides. People sipping wine don't want to hear about pesticides."

"Then this will be good practice."

"Valid point."

"And I'll put pesticides on the no-fly list with him. Now get out of here, and let me know how it goes."

"I will."

When she landed on Clementine's doorstep, she already had a foreboding feeling. Clementine was in a dark place, and she had to figure out a way in. She knocked loudly and stepped back. Nothing. She'd also received no answers to the texts she'd sent that morning. She knocked again before finally calling through the door. "Clem, it's me. I need to know that you're okay." Silence. "Please? I'm worried about you, and so is Frankie. Not like you to not come in." Nothing. She waited a few minutes, not sure what to do. "You have me really worried right now. If you don't come to the door, I'm going to call the police to make sure you're okay."

Just like that, the overhead light flipped on. A signal.

"Okay, so you're alive. Good." She covered her heart, hoping it would slow the hell down. "Now, can you open the door?" She wasn't exactly surprised when that didn't happen. "Tell you what. I'm gonna take a seat out here then. Cute alcove. And I'm not leaving until I talk to you."

And that's exactly what she did.

With her back against Clementine's door, Madison sat there waiting. She watched the sun reach the highest point in the sky and then begin its descent over the hills in the distance. She intermittently carried on a one-sided conversation, hoping to get to through to Clementine in some way. "Don't worry about the café. Frankie and Kevin covered the morning and were able to call Monique in to help. Apparently, she's a quick study and has done great." A pause. "You probably already know that."

It had been close to three hours before she heard the latch click behind her. Her legs were stiff, and she nearly fell over when the door gave way. She looked up to see Clementine staring down at her with honest-to-goodness circles under her eyes. She hadn't slept. She offered Madison her hand, which she happily accepted. "Thank God," Madison said.

"I'm fine. I promise. You don't have to hang out on my doorstep all day. You have work, I'm sure."

"Of course I don't have to, but I'm worried about you, and there's nowhere else I would possibly be."

"Well, I'm telling you I'm okay." She gestured to herself standing upright. "See?"

"You didn't come to work."

"I know. That's not like me, but I needed some time. In fact, I may need some more."

"Okay," Madison said, her brain trying to keep up. "We can have some of the part-timers fill in."

"Thank you."

"The police said they talked with you, and I followed up first thing this morning. So that's all taken care of. Brenda Anne, too. I checked in on her."

Clementine nodded, not seeking any extra information, so Madison left it there.

"Thank you for checking on me. On Brenda Anne. I promise I'll be fine."

"Okay," Madison said, knowing that pushing harder would only make things worse. "Can I get you anything? I could pick up dinner."

"I have plenty to eat here. Just gonna get my head together. Sweet of you, though. All of this."

"All right," Madison said, sliding her hands into her back pockets. "You'll call if you change your mind?"

"Mm-hmm." Unconvincing to say the least.

Clementine didn't come into the Biscuit at all that week. She rarely answered text messages, and Madison felt like her own life was spinning wildly out of control and she had no ability to stop it. She pulled a couple of counter shifts at the café herself, impressed with her progress behind the register. But the place didn't feel at all like itself without Clementine, its heart and soul. Frankie also seemed out of sorts, stressed and quiet behind the grill like he'd lost his other half. The customers didn't chat as much, and the Biddies had been notably absent from their customary table. The biggest damn scandal this town had seen in a decade had hit in the form of Len Monroe, and the Biddies had been eerily silent. The chatter around town was down, and their social media account sat dormant.

As for Madison, her heart hurt for Clementine, but also for herself. She missed Clem more than she could articulate, and a part of her was terrified of how this would permanently impact Clementine, as well as their future.

She kept herself busy at Tangle Valley as they moved toward harvest for the chardonnay. With the extra time she was putting in at the café, she could almost trick herself into staying busy enough not to focus on the ache in the center of her chest.

To her surprise, Clementine took a second week off, too. Madison had heard that she'd picked up some books from the library, and that was a good sign. She answered phone calls and texts more these days, but with as few words as possible, and the more Madison checked in on her, the more distant she became.

"I'm worried about her," Madison told Evelyn when she stopped in at the library, just hoping to run into Clementine. No such luck.

Evelyn took off her glasses and neatly folded them on the desk with a sigh. Her red hair was down today, and longer than Madison had realized. "I can report that she's definitely more withdrawn, nothing like she's been the past few months, which had been so nice to see. So full of life lately, talkative, and smiling. I hate that all this has happened, and that she seems to have taken it on herself."

"That's the thing. This asshole comes in and screws a bunch of people over, and it has nothing to do with her."

"I'm not sure she would agree. Sometimes our sense of self is too closely tied to where we come from."

Madison thought how lucky she was in that regard. Her family had been wonderful and supportive, if not a little overbearing about things like grades and responsibility. She had no idea what it must have been like growing up with none of that warmth. "So what do we do? That's my question."

"My advice? Give her what she needs for now. Space. She'll come around."

"I hope you're right."

But then she did, quite literally, come around moments later, appearing in the entrance of the library and walking a handful of books to the desk.

"Hey," she said, quirking her head at Madison as if surprised to see her.

"Just hanging out at the library," Madison said.

"Since when do you do that?" Clementine asked. Was that a smile? God, it was good to see.

"Oh, any chance I get. Big fan of books. Isn't that right?" she asked Evelyn.

"Madison has been coming in more and more." Not a lie. *Well done, library lady.*

"What brings you in?" Madison asked.

Clementine gestured to the books. "Blew through these. Need reinforcements." She inclined her head toward the stacks and took off for them.

Madison followed. "Feeling any better today?"

"Yeah," Clementine said. "I am. I think, if it's okay with you, I'll come back to work on Monday."

"We'd love it, but whatever you need."

She glanced at the floor. "I don't want to even ask how you've been covering for me. I'm so sorry."

"Don't be. You deserve time off. We've all pitched in. Even me. I'm a whiz on counter now. You'd be proud."

Clementine's face fell. "You're busy enough. I didn't mean for you to have to do that."

"Why? I own the place. The least I could do is help it run smoothly."

She shook her head, ashamed. "Still."

"Can we have dinner tonight? Catch up."

"I don't think so." Clementine met Madison's eyes when she said it, but she didn't see the Clementine she knew. She saw regret, sadness, and maybe even resolve. That part was terrifying.

She flexed her fingers and curled them into her palms. "Tomorrow, then. The next day. You decide."

"Madison." Clementine closed her eyes as if this was the hardest thing in the world, when it really didn't have to be. "No. It feels like I was pretending to be someone I wasn't. That wasn't me."

"Yes, it was." The words were like the worst kind of slap, stunning and unexpected. They left a sting. "What are you talking about?"

Clementine swallowed. "That's the thing. I don't think I even know anymore, and that means I need to take a step back and figure it out."

What in the world was happening? Madison felt like she was losing her grip on the situation. "This isn't you talking. I know you."

"No, you don't. That's the problem. Not the actual me, and this whole thing was the worst kind of reminder. Maybe I needed it, though. It was only a matter of time before everything came crashing down. I don't know why I'm surprised."

"Listen, I get that this unfortunate scenario with your dad has rattled you, but don't throw away everything good in your life, the people who care about you and love you."

There was that word again, love. She meant it, too. She hadn't exactly said it in unequivocal terms, but it was there all the same, and that had to count for something.

"I think I need time on my own."

"For how long?"

"I don't know."

"That sounds like forever."

Clementine didn't say anything, which actually spoke volumes. Everything in Madison went still and eerily cold. She understood the message even when she didn't grasp the motivation. She wasn't one to fall apart, beg, or plead her case when the writing was so plainly on the wall. She dealt in facts, and the fact of this matter was Clementine, in a move she never would have predicted in a million years, had just ended things between them. "Well, I'm shocked." She heard herself speak the words.

"It was only a matter of time. We're so different, Madison."

She nodded. "Okay. Now I know." She glanced behind her, trying to remember what came next. "Right. This is my cue, then."

"I hope this won't affect anything at work, but if it does, I understand."

How could Clementine talk about work right now? How was that even a possibility? "Your job is fine. It's yours, always."

"I appreciate that."

"Yep." Madison turned to go, feeling like she was living in an alternate reality of the worst kind. "Anyway. I'll go."

She only got a few feet away before Clementine's voice stopped her. "Madison."

"Yeah?" She turned back, numb and frowning.

Clementine opened her mouth to speak, then closed it again. "Nothing."

Madison nodded and walked out of the library an entirely different person than when she'd walked in.

❖

Gabriella had been talking nonstop since she'd plopped into the chair across from Madison's desk. First it had been about something funny that Ryan had said, and then an anecdote about dinner service the night before, and now she was on to something about fish and their feelings.

"I just wonder if they know they're less sought after and how they might feel about it."

"Who?" Madison asked, blinking at her.

"You know, the less desirable fish. Monkfish, for example. They're awful, but do they know it?"

"Of course they don't know it." Her tone was harsher than she meant it to be.

Gabriella paused. "You seem hostile. Do you have fish hostility I don't know about?"

"I don't have any particular feelings about fish."

"Well, that was curt, so you have feelings about something. Did you and Clementine have a fight or something?"

"Nope. And we won't be in the future either."

Gabriella squinted. "Why? Are you guys immune, and how does one achieve immunity from couple squabbling? That's part of it."

"We're over as of two days ago. Her choice."

Silence.

"No. Wait. What?" Gabriella asked, dragging her chair forward. "You're going to have to back up, because I don't understand what you're saying. Does this have anything to do with the whole dad scandal?"

"It seems it was the catalyst for a larger self-evaluation. I didn't make the cut, so that's that."

Gabriella balked. "That's that? Why are you being so businesslike right now? This is not the end of a partnership with a wine distributor. This is your life. You have to be hurting."

Madison nodded. "Well, sure. But what can I do about it? Throw myself on my bed and cry? That won't make anything better, so I focus on what I can control."

Gabriella sat there a minute, absorbing, that shocked look still on her face. "I'm so sorry, Maddie."

"Me, too," she said, not looking up from her laptop.

Eventually, at a loss, Gabriella drifted away, probably on a mission to let Joey and whoever else know, and that was fine. At least she didn't have to go through the motions of informing each new person because that process sliced at her all the more.

Her new goal was to keep moving forward, bury herself in her job, and not leave a lot of time to think. Her thoughts, the myriad what-ifs, would be the end of her. She'd experienced the most unexpected kind of happiness. She knew what it felt like now, and that was perhaps the most dangerous knowledge there was.

It was gone, and she was here.

Alone.

❖

"That'll be five fifty-two," she said to the nice man in glasses before bagging his order and moving on to the next customer. Clementine was rusty but found her groove soon enough, shrugging off Frankie's fanfare at her return, accepting his hug but not encouraging him further.

"You don't know how much I've fucking missed you," he said, grinning like a kid. He continued to smile like that through the rest of the morning, and Clementine came to understand how much the two of them depended on each other. Frankie and Jun were important to her, and she now clung to the parts of her life before Madison had bought the Biscuit, when her world moved wildly into a lane that had never been hers. She was the kid eating lunch outside with a book, not at the boisterous tables inside. The second she'd forgotten that, the world fell out from beneath her. Dramatic? Maybe. But this was about survival.

"Hey. I'm really glad to see you, too," she told Frankie once the breakfast rush eased.

"You doing okay? I know all of this hit you hard. Can't say I blame you."

"I am," she lied. She hadn't been sleeping much and missed Madison more than she'd ever allow herself to fully absorb. She was embarrassed about the scandal her father had thrust about the entire town and wondered what everyone must be saying behind the scenes. Clementine's plan was to do her job, lie low, and to stop reaching for things that weren't meant for her. "Just needed to step back and adjust. Better now."

"Your dad's an asshole, by the way."

"Yeah, I know."

"Which in no way makes you one."

"I know that, too, but thanks, Frankie."

"And I was chatting with Madison when she filled in for you, and it turns out, we were right. The homemade jam? It's working. We're up eighteen percent on pastries, which she says makes it worth the extra cash. At last. Several people have mentioned the kick-ass jam on the survey cards. They use different words."

Clementine felt the corners of her mouth tug. She needed a victory like this one. "Yeah? That's great."

"Since we've switched to locally sourced bacon? Up another twenty-two percent." He rolled his shoulders. "I've been feeling it on the grill, too. People are ordering more, telling their friends."

"That's amazing."

"That espresso machine has almost already paid for itself."

Clementine tried not to mist up as she clung tightly to the fact that she'd done something right. The Biscuit was thriving.

"So the asshole taking a little money didn't matter at all. Fuck that guy. We're ahead."

"Yeah," she said, unable to hold back the smile. Probably the first one in a while. "Fuck that guy." A pause. "Hey, have you heard anything about Ms. Birdie?"

Frankie shook his head. "Not a word. The Biddy, the one with the voice?"

"Maude."

"Yeah, Maude's been by once or twice but takes her order to go." He adjusted his bandana. "Kinda sad when you think about it. Those ladies not doing their thing here anymore."

Her gaze flitted to their customary table, now empty, as worry squeezed her heart. She wasn't up to much these days, but she had it in her to seek out Ms. Birdie and see how she was doing. As annoying as they could be, the Biddies were a fixture in this town, and it didn't feel the same without their opinionated meddling.

She called ahead to be polite and was informed by the kind voice at the nurses' station that Birdie said she would be happy to receive her as a visitor. The medium-sized hospital was located down the highway a good twenty miles. Clementine made the drive and took a deep breath before heading inside with her box of biscuits. She tried to always bring a gift when visiting someone, knowing that if it were her, she'd be touched by the sentiment. Ms. Birdie's room was located on the fourth floor. It was small and private with lots of sunlight streaming in from the large picture window, making the space feel cheerful.

Birdie turned to her as she entered the room. "Well, never did I expect you to come all this way to see little old me," she said, sitting up and smoothing her hair.

Clementine set the biscuits on the wheeled table near the bed. "It had been too long since I'd seen your face, and I needed a little cheer in my world, so here I am." She made a point to smile widely. She was here to spread cheer, after all.

Birdie waved her off. "I would have thought you'd be glad to have me out of your hair for a while."

"Not at all. I miss you troublemakers. The other three don't gather at the café anymore."

Birdie seemed surprised to hear that. "Well, I'll be giving them a good talking-to. No sense giving up what they love just because I'm sidelined. What's new in town?"

"Well, spring is in full bloom."

"That's lovely, dear, but what's the dish?" Birdie laughed, her eyes glistening.

Clementine smiled. "I'm a little out of the loop, but if I'm being honest, most of the town is talking about my father and how he swooped in, charmed everyone into thinking he was a great guy, and then stole a bunch of money. He's gone again now, of course."

"My, my," Birdie said. "That's sad to hear. Are you okay?"

Clementine nodded. "I wish I'd stuck to my instincts about him. I got charmed, too."

Birdie patted her hand. "It happens, and when it does, you can't beat yourself up for expecting the best out of someone. Your daddy let you down. You didn't let yourself down."

Clementine raised her eyebrows. "I don't know about that." A pause. "Tell me how you're doing. I've been worried."

Birdie hesitated. "My heart's not so good, and sometimes it just does whatever in the whole wide world it wants to."

"Well, that's no good. Do you think you'll get better?"

"I hope to. Got a lot more to do in this life. Maybe in a nicer way, though. Been giving that some thought while I'm stuck in this room."

"What have you been thinking about?" Clementine gave her hand a squeeze.

"The gossiping. Maybe we've gotten a little carried away as time has gone on. It's the best kind of fun to know all the news, but maybe it needs to stop there. Knowing is one thing. Spreading is another. Thelma was the internet savvy one who got us the Insta-something account, but looking back"—she shook her head—"that maybe wasn't the nicest of us."

Clementine closed one eye. "Maybe not."

"I think I'm going to talk to my friends when I get out of here. Maybe change up our ways some."

"I like the initiative you're showing," Clementine said, grinning. "It looks good on you."

"When you face your own mortality, you realize what's important. My advice to you is not to wait until you're in my shoes to wade through all the unnecessary garbage that gets in the way of the good stuff. Eat lots of sinful food, and stay out late."

Clementine laughed. "I can work on that."

"The most important part, though, is find the people who make you smile the most, and don't spend too much time away from them."

Clementine's spirits dimmed, as she knew full well she'd just taken a giant step away from the very person who made her smile most. "Well, Ms. Birdie, I wish it was that easy for me."

"That's the garbage part I'm talking about. When you come up with dumb reasons to not be happy, that's garbage in the way. We all do it." She pointed her finger at Clementine. "But don't anymore. We're not here long enough to be precious about who gets to hold our hand and why. Find the best people out there and stick with 'em. That's all there is to it."

"Well, thank you for the advice," Clementine said. "You've given me some things to think about."

"Is that about you and the winemaker? Boy, I tell you. You ought to see the way she looks at you. I know that look. My Vincent used to look at me that way. Wish I hadn't wasted so much time saying no to him until I finally said yes. Think of all the memories we missed. Don't make that same mistake with Madison."

Clementine didn't know what to say, because Ms. Birdie seemed to know way too much.

A nurse peeked her head in the room. "Excuse me, ma'am, but they're here to take you for your scans."

Clementine stood. "Guess that's my cue to get out of your hair."

"I'm so glad you came, and I can't wait to have one of those biscuits. I've missed them so much. Maybe I'll even give one to one of my new nurse friends."

"I think that sounds like a great idea." She placed a kiss on Birdie's soft cheek. "You get better and come see me at the café soon, okay?"

"Now there's an offer I can't pass up."

Clementine stood in the doorway a moment, sharing a smile with Ms. Birdie, who looked tired, but happy. Clementine was glad she had come. "See you soon, Ms. Birdie. You stay strong."

"Oh, I will. And you stay focused on what matters, you hear me? Say hi to the sunshine. I miss it."

"You got it."

CHAPTER EIGHTEEN

It was a beautiful day to get married.

Home from the champagne brunch Joey had thrown at the Big House to usher in the day, Madison stood in front of the large window in her bedroom, soaking in the sunshine and trying her best to feel nothing but happiness for Loretta and Bobby, two people who deserved only the best on the afternoon of their wedding. Today was about them, and as much as Madison's heart ached painfully, she needed to stay focused on the event at hand. *Be happy, dammit*, she ordered herself.

With a fortifying deep breath, she slipped into her turquoise bridesmaid's dress with the lattice back and then into her cream-colored strappy pumps. Loretta's daughter Carly had assisted Loretta in picking out the dresses and, with her killer fashion sense, had done a fantastic job. Madison pulled her hair half up and let the loose curls trail down her back just as they'd discussed with the stylist Joey had hired. A drop necklace with a single diamond and matching earrings, inherited from her grandmother, topped off her look.

"Here goes nothing," Madison said to herself in the mirror and forced a bright smile. Upon inspection, she deemed it believable enough and set off for the Big House, where Loretta would be putting the final touches on her hair and makeup.

"Oh, wow. You're gorgeous," Madison said, as Loretta turned, on a short break from taking her pre-ceremony photos.

"Can you believe it's little old me?" Loretta asked with wide eyes. "I don't even recognize myself. I feel like Cinderella on her way to the ball." Everything about Loretta glowed. Her hair had been swept up and the subtle makeup made her green eyes pop.

Madison laughed. "Well, you are. You're the bride, and today is your day. It's Cinderella time."

"I've never seen her happier," Carly said, placing an arm around her mom.

"Nervous, too, though," Loretta confessed to both of them.

"Nothing to be nervous about," Madison said. "Every last detail has been taken care of by Super Joey over there. All you have to do is say *I do* to that man of yours and then dance a little with your friends and family. Eat some fries at the fry station."

"Now that part I can do," she said with a laugh.

The old barn looked like anything but when Madison took her place for the procession. Canon in D, played beautifully by a single flautist, kicked them off. When it was her turn, Madison made her way slowly down the center aisle as the faces of their friends and neighbors smiled up at her from the white wooden chairs assembled into neat rows. She kept her eyes trained ahead and took her spot alongside Gabriella down front and waited for the rest of the wedding party.

It was only a few moments later when her carefully placed smile went still. Seated about ten rows back, Clementine stunned in a maroon cocktail dress, her hair down and curled. As if sensing Madison's gaze, Clementine raised her eyes and met Madison's briefly before dropping her focus to her lap. Today's theme was love in the form of forever, and they'd failed in that regard. Still didn't seem possible. They'd fit together perfectly. Their lives. Their bodies. Their ideas about the world. Madison shook herself out of it and focused on the here and now.

When Loretta appeared, and the congregation stood, her heart overflowed. This was the kind of moment that she would forever remember, Loretta beaming and Bobby shifting his weight nervously as the woman he loved approached. He wasn't the kind of guy who said a whole lot, but his heart was as big as the whole state, and he would move heaven and earth to make Loretta Daniel happy. Correction, Loretta Wilder, in just a few moments.

As the vows were spoken, Madison couldn't help it. On *to have and to hold*, she stole a glance at Clementine, who, if she wasn't mistaken, had tears on her cheeks, which meant she was every bit as moved by the day's event as Madison was. So maybe the problem was Madison herself. Clementine just didn't feel for her what she should in order for their relationship to continue. At this point, it was the only explanation. Resigned and sad, she made sure not to show it. Not today when everyone was rightly celebrating.

While the guests mingled in the dwindling sunshine, the onsite crew transformed the barn into a picture-perfect reception site, moving the white chairs around beautifully decorated tabletops. The dance floor emerged, and the live band warmed up for a night of dancing and fun.

Madison sat with Gabriella and Ryan and, of course, Joey and Becca for a fantastic meal prepared by the team of Tangled chefs. She even hit up the fry station, which had been the best idea. When the lights were dimmed and Loretta and Bobby led them into an evening of dancing, Madison relaxed. With the bar stocked and under control, she could now fade into the background and sip a glass of the reserve pinot, which she'd been looking forward to all day. Maybe even find a way to slip out of these heels. She stood along the edge of the barn, staring out into the vineyard below as the party played on behind her.

"Hi."

She turned to her left and saw Clementine standing there, holding a cocktail. "Hey," she said, trying not to notice how beautiful Clementine looked tonight, and failing dismally. Her chest ached just being in close proximity. "Having a good time?"

Clementine nodded. "I can't get over how gorgeous this place is. You guys really outdid yourselves."

"All Ryan."

They stood there a moment as the song changed to a slow one. She turned and watched as the guests coupled up on the dance floor, Joey melding perfectly into Becca's arms as they shared a smile. Why wouldn't they? Those two had everything. Here she stood alongside the woman she loved, and they felt like strangers.

"How have you been?" Clementine asked. She looked over at Madison, who kept her eyes trained ahead into the night. "Am I allowed to ask that? The rules are a little blurry."

"You can ask, but I'm not sure I have an answer." She shrugged. "I don't allow myself to dwell on questions like that these days. I stay busy, instead. That's always been my thing anyway." She met Clem's eyes briefly. "But I'm good. Promise. Don't worry about me."

"Oh, okay. Well, I'm glad to hear it."

"What about you?"

Clementine exhaled. "I guess I've been a little all over the place. You know that much. But I'm finding my footing again after… everything. I was rattled more than I ever would have expected to be. It helps to get back to work. Reset my life to what it was, which was more manageable."

Back to before Madison. That resonated, the knowledge hanging heavy and uncomfortable. She forced herself to breathe. She was okay. "Any news on Len?"

"The police have an open investigation and have talked with the officials in Portland as well, but no. Nothing I've heard. We may never hear from him again."

Madison turned and faced Clementine fully. "Is it weird to you? Us talking like this?" Madison asked, no longer able to ignore the elephant in the room. They'd shared so much and now stood here making small talk as if none of it had ever happened. It felt surreal and wrong and made her want to disappear under a table. All she wanted to do was erase the recent past and go back to who they used to be.

"No. Of course, it's not easy for me," Clementine said, shifting her weight. "But I wanted to try for some normalcy for the both of us. Keep our working relationship easy, and maybe one day we can even be friends again. What do you think?"

"Yeah, friends. That sounds fantastic," Madison said flatly. She was failing miserably at this conversation, yet there was nothing she could do to change that. Faking it was no longer feeling like an option.

Clementine studied the ground. "I'm really sorry about everything. I got caught up and lost, and somewhere along the way, my feet came off the ground. He ripped me right back down again."

"You don't have to soften it. You don't feel for me what I feel for you. I can't come up with any other explanation."

Clementine stared at her, mystified. "Why would you say that? I just told you the reason. This is about me."

"Am I right or not? Just say it. Makes this a whole lot easier."

"No," Clementine said. "You're not. Every word I said to you was true."

"Then this makes no damn sense." Madison shook her head and walked away. She found a spot at a corner table and did her best to smile and raise a glass anytime anyone looked her way. When the wine kicked in and her buzz hit, she even indulged in a dance or two with her group of friends, which allowed her to lose herself in a haze of lights and music.

The next time she surveyed the room, Clementine was gone.

Madison stayed until the end of the party, cheering with the rest of the well-wishers as Loretta and Bobby ran through a blaze of sparklers to the Rolls-Royce Becca had hired as their wedding present. They looked in love and perfect as they waved through the window on their way to the Presidential Suite at the Jade before flying to Jamaica the next morning.

The site crew they'd hired handled the majority of the cleanup at Tangle Valley, and Gabriella and her staff took care of the catering teardown.

"You're all set, Maddie," Joey said, giving her a warm hug. "You can head home if you want. You don't really seem like yourself."

She wasn't wrong. Madison hadn't been all that talkative, as much as she'd tried to be lively. "Just been a long day."

"I think it's more than that, and that's okay, you know?"

"Yeah."

Madison, left with very little to do, walked alone and barefoot back to her cottage, where she promptly did something completely unlike herself. She closed the door behind her, slid to the floor, and sobbed, allowing herself to feel every single emotion, each one taking its turn with her. She didn't shove them to the side, or busy herself with this task or that one. She faced her feelings head-on. Wallowed in them, even, as one racking sob overtook another. Her body shook. She'd held her friends when they'd cried before. She'd been there for them, but she'd never been on this side of it, where it felt like the world was ending, and the breathable air had floated away. She placed a hand against the wall for support and realized that she'd never been more alone.

An hour must have passed. Maybe more.

The skin on her face felt swollen and stretched out. The tears had dried up, but her cheeks remained wet. Blinking and not sure how to pull herself out of this, she quirked her head at the sound of a quiet knock behind her. And then there it was again. It didn't make sense. It was too late, and the day had been such a long one.

She stood slowly and pulled open the door.

"I was worried about you," Gabriella said with a shrug. She'd changed out of the turquoise dress that had matched Madison's and wore her comfy black sweats and those ridiculous fuzzy slippers. "Stand back. I'm coming in."

"No, no." Embarrassed and wiping her face with windshield wiper hands, Madison balked. "Sorry, but this is not really the best time."

"I can see that, which makes it the perfect one." Gabrielle brushed past her, undeterred. "Let's sit. Can we do that?"

Madison stared after her, the doorknob still in her hand.

Gabriella gestured to the empty spot on the couch with command. "You heard me. C'mon. Get over here."

Madison closed the door, swallowed, and due to an utter lack of direction of her own, did as she was told. Staring at Gabriella from the opposite end of the couch, she felt her vulnerability return. Her bottom lip wobbled, and to her horror, the emotion rose up all over again. "Oh no," she whispered, closing her eyes in defeat.

"Hey," Gabriella said softly and slid down a seat, facing Madison. "It's okay. Let it happen. We're alone in your house." She grabbed one of Madison's hands and held it tightly as the tears slid down Madison's face once again.

"I don't get it. I'm usually more in control."

"I know. I'm well aware, which is why I'm here, because these things do happen to me. I'm a crier, which is totally okay." Madison nodded because it was hard to find her voice. "Your heart is broken, Maddie." She nodded again, too exhausted to put up the brave front and apparently incapable anyway. "And it's not fair, because you didn't do anything wrong. Neither of you did."

"I'm not what she…" A pause for more tears. "Wants," she spat out.

"I don't believe that," Gabriella said. "I think Clementine has had a hard go of it most of her life, and just when she'd finally managed a little patch of happiness for herself, the universe swooped in to convince her she wasn't deserving."

That was the part that mystified Madison. She'd considered that option, but it didn't seem like a possibility. The logic didn't fit. "How in the world could she think she's undeserving?"

Gabriella offered a soft smile. "Here's the thing. You've always been a confident, self-assured person for as long as I've known you, and talking to Joey and your parents, I think you've been that way since birth."

"I guess that's true for the most part."

"Now imagine having none of that. Zero."

Madison tried, but it was hard.

Gabriella continued. "Clementine is a kind, wonderful person, but she doesn't come with that same rock-solid sense of her place in this world. She doesn't assume success. In fact, she assumes the opposite. She's not unflappable, and this thing with her father has affected her more than we probably can comprehend. It's shattered what little self-worth she had going for her."

Madison shook her head, trying to fully absorb all of this, because the way Gabriella framed it made sense. "It's hard to not be able to put myself in her shoes and see the world the way she sees it."

"Because you've always been a very logical, data-oriented person, and this stuff that we're talking about now? Can't be quantified."

"Right. No, it can't."

"I think it's perfectly okay for your heart to be broken, but believe me when I tell you that I don't think this has anything to do with Clementine's feelings for you."

Madison sat back against the couch, thoughtful and helpless at the same time. "So she's wrestling with her feelings about *herself*."

Gabriella nodded. "That's what it seems like to me. She's in survival mode."

"What am I supposed to do about that? That's not okay. She's the most amazing person I've ever met, and she has to know that."

"I'm not sure there's much you can do. Be her friend. Be patient." Gabriella's smile faded. "But there is something you can do for yourself."

"Tell me," Madison said, feeling desolate.

"You can stop walling off your emotions. You've trained yourself to do it, and it's time to reverse course. Let them flow for the good or bad."

She laughed sardonically. "Easy for you to say."

"Try it. Cry when you feel like. Celebrate the good moments like a crazy person. Let it out." She shook Madison around on the couch.

"Just not something I'm used to." Madison exhaled slowly. "No. It's even worse. Do you know how terrifying that sounds?"

"I do. But I know you, and you're not scared of anything except what's right here," Gabriella said, placing a hand over her heart. "Time to conquer it once and for all, and if love ever comes around again, you'll be ready."

"Two a.m. logic from someone who wears fuzzy slippers."

"And don't you forget it." Gabriella pulled Madison into a hug that once again had her leaking from her eyes, a foreign concept. "I'm literally down the path if you need anything. We all love you—remember that."

"I love you guys back." Madison pulled away and smiled. "See? Emoting already."

Gabriella gave her chin a small shake. "You're a champ. Now get some sleep. You need it."

Once Gabriella had gone, Madison locked up and did what she was told, feeling safer and not so alone after Gabriella's visit, almost as if some unseen force had sent her friend to her in the very moment she needed her most. And maybe it had. Friendship was a powerful thing, and she was blessed in that department. As she drifted off, she allowed herself to cycle through her feelings of sadness for herself and for what Clementine might be going through. While it wasn't easy to face those emotions, she also found it rather freeing to explore and release them. Was it possible that Gabriella, soft and sentimental, had been right?

Madison decided then and there to find out.

An experiment, an important one, was about to commence.

CHAPTER NINETEEN

The biscuits were hot, the bacon was crisp, and the Biddies, all *four* of them, were back at their customary table. "I can't tell you how it's made my morning to see you back in your old chair," Clementine said, encircling Birdie in a gentle hug from behind. "I knew you'd get better. I saw the fire in your eyes." The other three women beamed, happy to be a foursome and back at it once again.

"Well, I couldn't very well leave these three to take care of this town," Birdie said. She was thinner, but just as bright and cheerful.

"And we certainly wouldn't want you to," Thelma said, looking just pleased as punch. "Who would keep us from going over the edge?"

"We're going to pull back on the Instagram," Maude said, looking a little conflicted. "Birdie's suggestion, but it's likely a good one. We voted and it was unanimous."

"We get carried away," Janet said, jumping in.

Clementine nodded. "Is that right? Well, I like the new direction."

"Me, too," Birdie said with a small grin. "Good for us."

Things were starting to feel normal again. Clementine almost had her feet beneath her for the first time in weeks. She rang up the last few breakfast customers, knowing the lull was near, and that meant she could scarf down a quick bite before gearing up again.

Kevin gave his head a shake. "So many lattes. I'm going to dream about them."

"I think it's safe to say that the espresso drinks have caught on like wildfire," Clementine said, still shocked at how much money people were willing to pay for one of those drinks. They sure seemed to love them and their new availability at the Biscuit. In fact, townspeople who'd never really stopped at the café were now swinging by to pick up a coffee to go. They asked for a biscuit just because and were hooked from there on out. "People are going to start calling you Coffee Kevin around town. How will you handle that?"

He blinked, not reacting. "I've been called worse."

"Fair enough," Clementine said. "I won't ask about that."

"For the best," he deadpanned.

"I got a butter bacon biscuit with your name on it, Clem," Frankie said, sliding her plate across the counter between them. "Eat it while it's hot." He rang the bell.

"You don't always have to ring that thing," she said, knowing she'd never stop hearing it in her sleep.

"Yes, I do," he said, ringing it three more times.

"You are a fantastic man sent from God when it comes to food, but you got a bell problem that needs Jesus." She lifted the plate, inhaled the wonderful aroma of fresh biscuit and bacon before seizing the sandwich and taking a sizable bite, too big for her own mouth.

"Hey, guys."

Clementine turned with a mouthful of food and nearly choked to see Madison eyeing her curiously.

She pointed at her mouth. "Sorry." But the word didn't sound remotely like *sorry* or any word, really. She took a moment to chew and swallow like a normal human while the seconds ticked away at a shockingly slow pace. Embarrassment rained down on her like a storm of shame. Once she recovered and ignored the fact that her face felt hot and had to be bright red, she faced Madison. "It's the lull when I eat."

"I noticed," Madison said as if it was no big deal, which was kind. "Just stopping by for the bank drop."

Clementine held up a hand and retrieved it quickly from the newly repaired and reinforced safe in the office. "Here you go." It had been a couple of days since they'd seen each other at the wedding, and no matter what Clementine did to try to get Madison's face that night out of her head, it hadn't seemed to work. Their conversation hung over her like a rain cloud she couldn't shake. She hated the strange new dynamic between them. Her body behaved entirely differently when Madison was in the room, having no idea it wasn't supposed to react anymore.

Her mind perked up like the day had just begun, betraying her with each encounter. Getting over Madison was proving to be damn near impossible, and all she could do was hope that time would help.

"Everything going okay here?" Madison asked.

"We're boppin' along nicely." Frankie passed her a thumbs-up from the back. "Thanks for the approval on that bacon order. I think we've got it balanced out for this season. We were running out too early in the day."

"No problem. I trust you, and you haven't let me down yet."

Yes, this was good. Talk about the café. Clementine clung to any kind of normal conversation about the running of the business. It kept her head where it needed to be. "We've really found our groove with the espresso menu, too. I'm even capable of putting together a pretty mean latte all on my own when Kevin's not around."

"Oh yeah? I'll have to see for myself," Madison said. "Can I get one to go?"

Clementine raised her eyebrows. "Now?" She glanced behind her at the machine she'd gotten to know pretty well. "Of course. How about a little vanilla tossed in?"

"I won't say no." Wow, those blue eyes didn't quit, did they? They seemed extra bright on Madison today, probably because of the blue button-down shirt she wore open on top of that black cami that showcased the spot on her neck where she loved to be kissed. Dammit. Not the kind of thoughts she was allowed to have anymore. She'd have to work harder.

Kevin seamlessly took over the register, and Madison followed her down the counter to the coffee station, which gave them some space from the others. As she prepped the latte beneath the loud whir of steam, she felt Madison's gaze on her. Not too long ago, she would have loved the effect. Now, she felt like a failure who'd not only upended her own life, but Madison's, too. Going back to who she'd been before also hadn't proven as easy as she'd hoped. Maybe because she wasn't the same anymore.

"Today, I'm missing you a lot," Madison said. "Yesterday, I felt like maybe I'd find a way to breathe again without you, you know, if I tried hard enough, but now I'm not so sure."

Clementine went still, the to-go cup in her hand suspended in midair.

"You don't have to say anything to that. I'm just trying to be more expressive with how I'm feeling. Voice it out loud. New thing I'm doing." She shrugged. "So that's how I'm feeling today. I miss you. It's that simple."

With shaking hands, Clementine returned to making the drink with a nod, but the back of her neck prickled hot and her palms were sweaty. "One vanilla latte made with care," Clementine said, presenting her creation. She paused, holding Madison's gaze. "And I think it's great that you're expressing your feelings more." There was so much that she wanted to say, yet those unspoken words died from her brain to her mouth. For the best.

Madison smiled and sighed. "Time will tell, I guess. Sorry for the blurting. I guess I'm still finessing my delivery. Have a good one," she said, raising the latte. Moments later, she was gone, though Clementine still stared after her, her heart hammering away. Part of her held tightly to the knowledge that Madison thought about her still, missed her even, while another part knew the dangers of entertaining those kinds of notions and slapped her wrist for doing so.

"Why isn't my life going back to normal?" she asked Evelyn later that afternoon at the library. "I used to live a very manageable, if possibly boring, existence. Why can't I get back to the unexciting?"

"You mean since Madison?"

She nodded.

"Because when you meet someone important, you're forever changed by them. You can't go back to who you were. That person doesn't exist anymore." She studied Clementine, her green eyes doubtful. "How do you not know this after reading all those stories your whole life?"

Clementine sighed. "I thought that's all they were. Stories." She shook her head. "Who knew it could be this hard?"

"If it was easy, it wouldn't be love."

She paused. "I did love her, Ev. We never got to the part where we said it. I think words like that are hard for Madison. She's not someone who dwells on emotion. Well, at least she didn't used to be."

"I loved this one," Jun said, arriving next to her at the desk. They'd agreed to meet at the library for another round of books. Jun held up the college murder book. "An entire sorority terrorized and I never saw the ending coming."

"It was one of the sorority sisters from within, wasn't it?" Clementine asked.

"How did you know that?" Jun asked, mystified.

"I've read a few of those kind of stories, too," Clem said, grinning at Evelyn.

"Well, I'm still new, so consider my mind blown. I'll need more of these things," Jun said, looking between them. She was now a book junkie, and they were her dealers.

Evelyn smothered a smile. "Good thing we have thousands of books here."

"This could take a while," Jun said, appearing thoughtful.

That made Clementine laugh, which she very much needed.

"Am I interrupting?" Jun said. "Here I am just bursting onto the scene, making demands, and it looked like you were in the middle of a really good chat session."

Evelyn demurred, as it wasn't her life to share.

With a sigh, Clementine relented. Jun was a friend after all. "I'm having trouble hitting reset after Madison."

"Well, yeah, you are. You don't meet the love of your life and then pretend it never happened. How in the world could I un-know Frankie? That little bugger is in my system. I couldn't get him out if I tried."

Evelyn straightened. "My feelings exactly. Though, I must say, you illustrated more vividly."

"It's the books. I'm telling you, rubbing off on me." She turned to Clementine. "But you just keep trying. Tell yourself it wasn't meant to be, and that it's safer far, far away from Madison. I'll be over here telling myself the sky is green."

Clementine winced. "That seems harsh. I'm not that delusional."

"Do you know what I think?" Evelyn asked. "Life is too short to get in our own way. So you have a few personal hang-ups. Obstacles to overcome. We all do, but why deprive yourself of happiness at the same time? Can't you work on the hang-ups and be happy with Madison at the same time?"

"I don't think it's that simple," Clementine said, feeling more at sea than ever.

Jun held up her book. "Do you think the sorority sisters thought it was simple to find the killer? No, Clementine. It was terrifying, but they didn't give up. You don't either. There. I've spoken." She smiled to soften the aggressive rally cry.

Her friends had been helpful and maybe pointed out a little bit of her own faulty logic, but when Clementine searched her soul for direction later that night, Ms. Birdie's words were the ones that floated to the surface. *We're not here long enough to be precious about who gets to hold our hand and why. Find the best people out there and stick with 'em.*

If only she knew how to execute such a plan.

❖

"I'm feeling grateful for you and our friendship," Madison said to Joey, who stared at her from behind a large pot of homemade mashed potatoes. She'd popped by the Big House after work to hang out and see what Joey was up to.

The declaration seemed to give Joey pause. "Are you angling to stay for dinner? You know you're always welcome."

"No, I'm ordering in. Been planning on a pizza all day. Just wanted you to know how I feel. No big deal, right?"

That did it.

Wielding the large wooden spoon covered in potatoes, Joey turned to Madison fully. "Today, you're grateful for our friendship. Yesterday, you wanted to thank me for sticking by you as a teenager when you realized you weren't straight. Don't get me started on all the declarations you made last week. Are you moving away? Did you get some sort of awful diagnosis? What gives?"

Madison relaxed. "I'm just making a point of telling the people who matter to me what's in my head and heart. I have all these thoughts, and it occurred to me that I never actually say them. Okay, it didn't occur to *me*, it occurred to *Gabriella*. But she's right, fuzzy slippers and all. And as someone who was once in a relationship with me, she probably knows how hard it can be not getting that verbal validation."

Joey stared at her. "You're emoting on purpose."

"Yes. Definitely." She paused. "I think I have to work on my delivery, though."

"You might. But there aren't exactly rules." As she talked, she waved the spoon of potatoes around for emphasis, realized what she was doing, and dropped the spoon back in the bowl. "The potatoes have opinions, apparently. I apologize. But I think all of this is great."

Madison leaned back against the counter. "I suppose I could acknowledge my own thoughts and feelings and then pick the right moments to share them. Spouting them willy-nilly seems to catch people off guard, but I have to say, it's good practice, this experiment, and the reactions are amusing."

"I bet. Sounds like the experiment is going well."

"It gets easier the more you do it." Madison shook her head, marveling at the difference she felt just by letting her thoughts flow freely. "I'm so much lighter for it. I had no idea what a relief it would be to have so much off my chest."

"Does this have anything to do with Clementine? I stopped by the Biscuit, and she seemed a little more like herself."

"Yes and no." Madison chewed her lip. "I don't know that Clementine and I will ever make our way back to each other, but if we do, I want to be better this time around. If not, well, then I'm just more open in general, and maybe that's not a bad thing."

Joey's face transformed into a sentimental grin. She opened her arms and pulled Madison into a hug, abandoning her pot of potatoes. "I'm so proud of you, Maddie. You've had such a rough time of it lately, and yet you still look for the good in any situation."

"I don't know about that," she said bashfully, hugging Joey back. "But this experience has opened my eyes to how important other people are, and that makes me want to work on myself. To be the best version of me possible." She sighed. "I'd be lying if I said I didn't think about her every day. Correction. Every hour. I should have paid more attention, seen all of this coming. If I'd been there to catch her, maybe she never would have fallen."

"No. You can't do that," Joey said. "Speaking as someone who's fallen herself, Clementine has to go through this process on her own. It's her journey."

Madison nodded. "When did you get to be so wise?"

"Loss does that to you." Joey smiled, ruefully. "I have that in common with Clementine, which is why I root for her. And I haven't given up on the two of you, either. This movie isn't over." She offered a wink, which Madison took to heart.

What if Joey was right? The glimmer of hope she carried with her seemed to glow a little brighter today.

Patience, she reminded herself. *Patience.*

❖

It was the Muskrats' first practice of the year. With softball season in Whisper Wall kicking off in just three weeks, it was time for Clementine's team to knock the rust off in preparation for their first big game against the Gophers. She'd taken over management of the team two years prior and truly enjoyed her role as organizer and head motivator. Last year, with Gabriella joining their team as a ringer, they'd even taken home the championship, a first for the team.

"What's up, Muskrats?" she said to the gathered group, which, of course, prompted the team of twelve to make the required muskrat face, complete with little claws out. She always got that little flutter of nerves when she spoke to a group of people, but she'd learned if she pushed through, it got easier. "We have nine games scheduled this season, followed by the championship match, which I fully expect us to play in."

"Muskrats win! Muskrats win! Muskrats win!" the team chanted.

Somewhere in the midst of their shouting, Clementine caught sight of Madison in the stands, and from that moment on, nothing felt the same.

"She came with me. Maddie," Gabriella said, thirty minutes later. She'd just rounded home following batting practice. "She was done with work for the day, so I told her she should come along and watch."

"Oh, cool," Clementine said.

"You don't seem it," Gabriella said. "You should say hi later."

"Of course I will," Clementine said, like it was the smallest deal ever. When Madison cheered for someone on the team, Clementine felt her voice all over. When she glanced in Madison's direction, her body responded to what it saw, Madison in shorts and a pink T-shirt, curls down and beautiful. How had they gotten here, and why couldn't she be happy with the decision she'd made?

Because maybe it was the wrong one.

She blinked, feeling nauseous with confusion and self-doubt.

At the end of the practice, Clementine stood along the bleachers while the rest of her team packed up their gear in the dugout.

"Not too shabby," Madison said. "Lucinda is turning into a great left fielder. Keep an eye on her."

"Yeah, I will. She told me she's been practicing catching fly balls in the off season."

"You're hitting with more confidence, too," Madison said.

She felt the heat hit her cheeks. "Taking out a little aggression maybe."

"I think that's earned," Madison said with a quiet laugh. "I saw Brenda Anne yesterday. She was smiling again, and that made me happy."

"Yeah, she's really rebounding."

"Are you?"

Clementine opened her mouth and closed it. "I don't know. Some days, I think yes, others, no."

"Fair enough."

"What's new with you?" she asked, sliding onto the bleachers, one row below Madison.

"Well, I was proud listening to you coach the team." A pause. "And I think you look fantastic in athletic wear. That's something."

Clementine scoffed and looked down at her old Muskrat jersey from two seasons ago. "This dusty old thing?"

"That would be the one." She studied Clementine. "Speaking of the dust, it got kicked up pretty good out there." She leaned down and, with her thumb, wiped away the dirt from Clementine's cheek, leaving her speechless. "Oh, looks like Gabs is all set. I'll see you soon, hopefully." And with that, Madison hopped off the bleachers and took off with her friend, Clementine watching her go. She rolled her eyes at the old habit, at herself, and at her dangerous desires.

Stay in the safe zone.

Stabilize your life.

Simple is best.

If only she could keep herself convinced for more than a few hours.

CHAPTER TWENTY

Spring was Madison's favorite time on a vineyard, especially in the western part of the country. She gaped in awe, as she always did, at the dormant vines as they woke. She walked the rows of the vineyard daily to inspect the progress, examining the early buds and shoots as they elongated more and more each day. Soon, blossoms would appear and fall off, and little buds of first fruit would make their first appearance. Then she'd have a new group of grapes to tend and care for as they matured, changed color, and burst with sugar. The life of the vines was cyclical, and this was the clean-slate part. Something about it brought her comfort this morning, the idea of starting fresh, and doing it better than you did the time before. That's what she planned to do with the grapes, and maybe with her own life, too.

"You're smiley today."

She glanced up from her pruning to see Bobby approach. The man still glowed like a newlywed should.

"Yeah, well, they're coming to life again," she said, indicating the vines. "Looking good, too. Averaging about an inch every two days."

He nodded. "Warmer temperatures are definitely helping, though I wouldn't mind a little rain."

She stared at the sky. "Oh, it's coming." She shielded her eyes. "How's it feel to be off the beach? Thrust back into the real world."

He shook his head, taking his time. Bobby was definitely not a chatterbox, but what he said tended to matter a lot. "Best thing in the world is regular life. Even better now with Loretta. I'm lucky."

"Was it hard at first?" That was a question Madison might not have been bold enough to ask not long ago, but her own new start had her speaking up more often.

"Ah, yep. We liked each other but weren't so good at the communication part. Mostly my problem. She was patient." He grinned. "I'm a work in progress, but she stuck with me."

There was that word again, *patient*. And weren't they all works in progress? She filed that little nugget of wisdom away and did something new. She gave herself permission to daydream about Clementine. No rules about keeping her hand off the bruise. She cycled through all their wonderful memories together and reminded herself of all the things she loved about Clementine. There were so many. Her generosity. Her quiet determination. That smile. Her uncanny intuition and, of course, her huge heart. She'd give everything she had to a stranger in need.

"Do you know how amazing you are?" she said to Clementine later that day as they stood in the Biscuit's parking lot. She'd popped by the café to go over the books. They were steadily pulling in a healthy profit, and Madison couldn't have been happier with Frankie's and Clem's suggestions, which had been right on the nose.

Clementine paused next to her car, hand on the door handle. "Why are you saying that?"

"No reason, except that I think it every day."

Clementine laughed. "Well, that's nice of you."

"I'm being serious, though."

This time the placeholder smile slid from Clementine's face. "Okay." A pause. "Really?"

Madison nodded. "I spent a part of my afternoon today just listing all the great things about you. This town, all of us"—she raised a shoulder—"we're lucky to have you. That's all. You make everything better." She raised a hand. "See you soon. If not tomorrow, I'll swing by the next day."

Clementine hadn't moved. Finally, she raised a hand and attempted to wave back. Madison wanted to run to her, pull her into her arms, and tell her a million times that she was amazing and worthy and smart and beautiful. Instead, she nodded and pulled away, content that she had been honest and open.

❖

It had been ten minutes since Madison had pulled out of the parking lot. Clementine knew because she checked her watch from where she sat behind the wheel, but she still hadn't mustered the ability to drive home. Madison thought she was amazing and told herself so daily? She shook her head, wondering why she would devote that kind of energy, after all Clementine had done to them.

A knock on her passenger-side window made her leap in her seat. She covered her heart and exhaled slowly, seeing the friendly face of Ms. Birdie peering in at her. She popped the lock, and Birdie opened the door.

"Scared ya, didn't I?" Birdie grinned widely.

"Oh, I'd say that you definitely did that."

"I was walking past." She held a small bag in her lap. "Finished up my shopping at the Nickel and saw you daydreaming in your car. You doing okay, sweetheart? You had a strange look on your face."

"I'm in a tough spot lately," she admitted.

"I can tell. One reason I stopped by. Want to see my wares?" She opened her sack and removed several packages of sunflower seeds. "Brenda Anne got these in last week, and I had my eye on them. Gonna plant them in my garden and watch them grow."

Clementine nodded her approval. "Those will be beautiful."

"Did you know that without water and sunlight, a flower like this will wilt and fade?"

"I did hear that somewhere."

"Some flowers aren't used to sunlight. They haven't had access to it, and that takes a toll. Doesn't mean that they won't thrive when they get the nutrients they need."

Clementine turned her cheek against the car seat to face Birdie. "Is there a metaphor here, Ms. Birdie?"

"Maybe a little. You just strike me as the sweetest flower is all, and I want you to let that sunshine in."

She squinted. "Who sent you here?"

Ms. Birdie laughed. "I'm an old lady who makes my own damn decisions." She covered her mouth. "Didn't meant to say *damn*."

"Oh, that's okay. Would you like me to drive you home?"

Birdie considered her options. "I think that would be nice. I've had a full day on the town."

Clementine turned on the car, popped on some quiet tunes, and followed Birdie's directions to her quaint little home on a side street of one of Whisper Wall's more popular neighborhoods. "Thank you for the lift," Birdie said as she exited the car. She held up her packages of seeds. "I'll get to work on these tomorrow."

Clementine smiled and waved. "And thank you right back for your words of encouragement."

Birdie feigned confusion. "No idea what you mean. See you soon, Clementine!" They shared a smile and Birdie shuffled up the walk.

The next day, Clementine forced herself to do the very thing she'd been putting off. It was time to check in on Brenda Anne. They'd seen each other a handful of times since her dad had fled town, but looking her friend in the eyes was a harsh reminder of all that had transpired and the guilt she carried. The Nifty Nickel was fairly quiet when Clementine popped in.

"Oh, hi, Clementine," Brenda Anne said. Her eyes were red, and she turned away behind the check-out stand, dabbing at them. Her spirits plunged seeing Brenda Anne still in such pain.

"Hi there. Thought I'd stop in and see how you were. It's been a bit since we chatted."

"It sure has. But honestly, I'm doing okay. I think I'm getting my swagger back and my money, too."

"You are?"

Brenda Anne sniffled and nodded. "I had some protections on my bank account, apparently. Ones I didn't even know about, but once the police report went live, they kicked in."

Clementine felt a weight lift off her shoulders. "That's fantastic news. I had no idea." She paused. "When I came in, you looked so sad."

Brenda Anne's small smile dipped. "Well, I am. I heard some very unfortunate news. Ms. Birdie Jenkins passed away at her home overnight."

Clementine stared at her. She played back the words but they didn't make sense. "I drove her home yesterday afternoon. She had her sunflower seeds ready to go."

Brenda Anne nodded, tears filling her eyes entirely. "I couldn't believe it myself. She'd just been in here to purchase them, so excited about spring." She paused. "I guess her heart just finally gave out on her after giving so much of herself to this town." Brenda Anne promptly handed her a tissue.

Clementine hadn't realized it, but tears were streaming down her cheeks. "Thanks," she said, her voice strangled. Not Ms. Birdie. No. She gestured to the door, and Brenda Anne nodded. In light of the news, they seemed to agree their conversation could wait. Not knowing what else to do, Clementine drove the streets of Whisper Wall with shaky hands, missing her friend, the sweetest, kindest soul. "Oh, Ms. Birdie," she whispered, still in disbelief. Because she needed to, she found herself driving past Birdie's home. She paused when she saw a man with short dark hair and bright eyes similar to Birdie's exit the house. Something came over her, and she stopped. Seeing her pull over, the man paused his progress and waited.

"Hi," she said, knowing she must look a wreck. She touched her hair absently. "I'm Clementine, a friend of Birdie's. Are you a member of her family?"

"Her son, Kenton. The youngest of two," he said with a sad nod. "I live in Seattle but have been down quite a bit since she went sick. Do you run the, uh, biscuit place?" She nodded. "I thought your name sounded familiar. Mom told me about you. You visited her in the hospital and made her whole week."

She smiled at the memory, and that made the lump in her throat grow. "I'm just so surprised. I drove her home from town just yesterday afternoon. She was excited to plant her new sunflower seeds."

"Thank you for doing that." He glanced behind him at the house. "Wait here a second." He hurried inside, and when he returned, he held the packages of seeds. "On the kitchen table. Something tells me she would want you to have these."

She accepted the packets and held on to them like a lifeline. "Are you sure?" she asked.

"I am."

"Thank you." She paused. "I'm so sorry you lost your mom. She was always a source of joy in my life, even when it felt bleak."

He grinned through his own grief. "Sounds like her. Thank you for telling me." She nodded and let him get on with his day. With a last look back at Birdie's house, she drove herself home, clutching tightly to those seeds.

CHAPTER TWENTY-ONE

Madison waited in line at the Biscuit, her work notebook in her arms, and her laptop tucked away in her messenger bag. After word traveled about the loss of Birdie Jenkins, she made the decision to work at one of the booths at the Biscuit. Most of her workload that morning was administrative in nature anyway, and she had a feeling Clementine could use a friend in her corner today. She thought the world of Birdie and had often said so.

When she reached the front of the line, she met Clementine's admonishing gaze.

"What have I told you about waiting in line?"

"That I own the place and don't have to. Hi."

"Hi." Clementine quirked her head. "So why did you do it anyway?"

"Feels wrong to cut, so I wait, like a good customer."

"What'll it be?" Clementine smiled but it was brief. A show. There was a heaviness about her today, which made perfect sense. She was sad, and all Madison wanted to do was gather her into her arms and help her through it. In the absence of that kind of permission, she'd send support from a nearby booth.

"Can I have two butter biscuits and a vanilla latte?"

"You certainly can." Clementine produced her double biscuit order piping hot, and after Kevin delivered her coffee, she found a spot. Before getting to work, she surveyed the dining area. The Biddies' table sat empty, a sad testament to the town's loss. What was even more touching was that throughout the morning, not one person sought to occupy it—the table itself carried reverence, a reminder of a woman lost to them.

Ninety minutes later, as Madison tried to keep from drowning in unreturned emails, she looked up to see Clementine standing next to her booth. They'd hit the famous lull in the latter portion of the morning. "Want to sit?" Madison asked, clearing off the far side of her table.

"Why are you still here?" Clementine asked. She looked so tired, as if she hadn't slept. "Not like you to linger on a workday."

"I decided to turn this very booth into my office, and honestly, it's worked out nicely. I'm getting all my loose ends tied up after spending too much time in the sun." She smiled. "Hard to stay indoors on a vineyard in spring."

Clementine shifted her weight and dialed her facial expression to doubtful.

"Okay." Madison sighed. "The truth is that I was worried about you after the news about Birdie and thought it might be nice if you knew you had a friend nearby"—she looked around—"literally in your corner. So here I am. I promise to stay out of your way."

"You're doing this for me," Clementine stated quietly, almost to herself.

"Well, yeah, of course." She gestured to her empty white paper bag. "And the biscuits. I might order a third."

Clementine walked behind the counter and, with a few words to Frankie, returned with a biscuit for Madison and a bacon biscuit, iced coffee combo for herself and slid into the booth. "Hi," she said, with a tentative smile.

Madison relaxed a tad at its appearance. It meant Clementine was holding her own, and that's all she wished for. "It's good to see you."

Clementine exhaled. "I can safely say the same." She jutted her chin in the direction of Madison's pile of work. "What's new at Tangle Valley today?"

Madison knew her cue. As Clementine ate, Madison rattled off every little detail about her emails, the blossoming vineyard, and the wine production challenges she'd faced with the not-quite-in-balance tannins. Her goal was to offer Clementine a much needed distraction, and from the looks of it, her endless monologue was working.

"I've always enjoyed listening to you talk about wine. You get this look in your eye when you're fired up."

"Do I?" Madison asked, not surprised. Sometimes she had trouble tamping down her passion for her job.

Clementine nodded and popped the last bit of her bacon biscuit. "I never get tired of it." Her eyes scanned the room until they landed on the empty table at the front of the café.

"Do you think they'll be back?" Madison asked.

Clementine exhaled slowly and blinked. "I hope so. It's what she would have wanted." A small smile appeared, as if she'd just drifted somewhere pleasant. "Ms. Birdie always urged people to live their lives to the fullest. It was her thing."

Madison sat back. "Then I have a feeling they'll be back soon."

Clementine nodded, tears now apparent in her eyes. "Me, too. We owe it to her to grab hold of whatever time we have here. She was a smart woman."

"And feisty," Madison added.

"And she had a great sense of humor."

"The best. To Birdie," Madison said and retrieved her cup, holding it in the air.

Clementine grabbed hers and joined in on the cheers. "To Birdie."

❖

The watercolor of Clementine's reading forest, the one her father had gifted her for Christmas, had been placed in a drawer, facedown, after his rushed exit from Whisper Wall. It was a reminder of a man she didn't need or want to think back on. She'd wasted enough of her time on bad people, and it was time to do just as Birdie had said, and put every ounce of energy into the good ones.

She gathered what few gardening supplies she had and set out with a book tucked under her arm.

It was a beautiful spot, her reading forest, and though it had been years since she'd spent any real time beneath its branches, in many ways, it felt just the way she'd left it. She walked the small stretch of land before the trees became too thick, touching their trunks fondly, saying hello to her old friends. There was an open patch of grass that pulled in good sunlight a few feet from the grouping of ash trees. She knelt down and got to work, taking time to plant the seeds properly and with great care. When she was finished, she sat back and studied her work, the fruits of which she wouldn't see for at least a couple of months. She'd come back and water them as needed and nurse those sunflowers into the world. They'd always remind her of Ms. Birdie Jenkins and also of the promise that Clementine now made to herself, to live her life with tenacity and passion, no matter how daunting a task that might be. She smiled at the spot of the newly planted life and sat beneath one of those big, beautiful trees to read a little of her book. The serenity of the space had her wondering why she didn't visit more often, knowing full well she would from this moment on.

The next morning, she felt more at home in her own skin than she had in a very long time. She could breathe easily and, at last, saw a clear path for herself. Midmorning, the very person she was looking for presented herself at her counter.

"Hey, Joey. I was hoping to run into you today."

Joey beamed. "Well, I'm happy to be run into."

"Your usual?"

"Yes, please."

She popped a white bag, ready to load up Joey's half-a-dozen biscuit order with a side of maple bacon, of course. "I was hoping to impose upon you and ask for a favor."

Joey rocked on her heels, her blue eyes bright with intrigue. "Do tell."

"Well, do you have any events scheduled in the new barn tonight? It's supposed to be a nice one."

"In fact, we do not." She eyed Clementine sideways with a smile as she waited for more.

Clementine couldn't hold back her excitement. Butterflies played in her midsection, but she ignored them, too determined to care. She was on a mission and would not screw this up or get in her own way. She refused. "Let me tell you what I'm thinking."

CHAPTER TWENTY-TWO

Madison sat with a pen, a notebook, and an early bottle of their pinot from two harvests ago. It was primitive at this early stage but still gave her a good sneak peek at what they could look forward to with the new vintage, which would move into bottling in just a handful of months, giving it a little more time to mature. Alone at her desk, she sipped and made notes, understanding that beyond the natural processes there wasn't a lot she could do to change the wine's direction at this point. But that didn't matter. She was pleased that the result was reminiscent of past vintages, and recognizable as a Tangle Valley creation, but also complex enough to stand on its own, an individual. She sat back and analyzed. It was a jammy wine with pleasant hints of vanilla spice and smoke. "I like you," she said to the wine, practicing her new open and honest communication.

She sat back and exhaled, her workday coming to an end. The weather had been nice today, sunny and warm. Now that the sun was slowly making its descent, temperatures were cooler. She decided to take a walk and enjoy the early evening before it slipped away into total darkness, but she wouldn't have long.

Madison corked the wine and stood, just in time for Joey to come skidding to a stop in front of her office door. "You run places now?" Madison asked, looking behind Joey to see if she'd been chased.

"Only when it's very important. I need your help."

Madison frowned. "Is everything okay?"

"Nothing to panic about, but can you come with me?"

"Well, you were running."

Joey searched for a way to explain. "Perhaps that was an overreaction."

Madison nodded. "I see."

Out of nowhere, Gabriella came sprinting into the barrel room like the world was on fire. "Madison! There you are! Thank God." She skidded to a stop next to Joey, who looked at her in annoyed confusion.

"What are you doing?" Joey asked quietly. "I already did that."

"I thought I was gonna run in," Gabriella whispered.

"No, you were supposed to be the go-between. Just…never mind."

Madison had to work hard to hear them but couldn't have been any more confused. "Does someone want to explain the running and whispering act you have going, Lucy and Ethel?"

"There's an issue with the barn."

"A big one."

"An important one," Joey corrected.

It couldn't be too horrible, Madison decided, because Gabriella was grinning like an idiot. "All right then. I suppose I'll check it out."

"You're so bad at this," she overheard Joey whisper after she'd passed them on her way out of the barrel room.

"I am not. I sell it."

She heard her friends continue to bicker at who was worse at whatever game they were playing until their voices trailed away, and she was left with the setting sun and a curiosity about what the hell was going on. The quickest way to the barn was to cut through the pinot and angle to the right, something she'd done a hundred times over. She inspected the vines as she walked, pleased to see the early signs of small buds appearing. "Hey, little guys," she said. "Looking good."

When she emerged from the vineyard field, she looked up at the large barn, pleased to see it still standing, and not in any kind of structural danger. The moon hung big and beautiful in the sky, and interestingly enough, the white twinkling lights were on in the barn. Joey must have done that, for her to see by, perhaps. Though the fluorescents would have been fine.

As Madison approached, she heard the soft sounds of music playing from the sound system, which was odd, to say the least. What was going on? Some sort of event she'd forgotten about. The walls had been slid back, but there was no crowd inside. She made her way up the three steps and into the barn to find Clementine standing there. Madison paused and took her in. Her hair was down with a slight curl, and she wore a simple turquoise sundress that had to have been made just for her. Madison quirked her head as she approached, still trying to understand.

"Hi," Clementine said with a smile. Her lips glistened with gloss and her eyes matched her dress. God, she was stunning.

"Hi." Madison looked around at the beautiful ambiance, took in the music and the way Clementine looked. "What's going on?"

Clementine gestured behind her. "I asked your friends for a little help. I've never done anything like this before."

"You look beautiful, but I feel a little underdressed." She glanced down at her jeans and blue Tangle Valley polo.

"You're perfect," Clementine said. "I've thought so ever since the first day I laid eyes on you in freshman biology. I knew you were the prettiest girl I'd ever seen in my life, and when you opened your mouth, I found out you were the nicest one, too. I spent years too shy to speak to you for very long because you made me nervous."

Madison smiled. "I had no idea back then."

"How could you? It's not like I gave off any signals." She swallowed, and it was clear to Madison that she was nervous. "But then you did something that to this day I believe was meant to be. You bought the café. I thought it was the worst thing that had ever happened to me, but I was wrong. It was the best. After all that angry tension I carried around subsided, I got to know you."

"Uh-oh," Madison said with a smile. She shifted her weight, wondering where this was going. Her heart thudded, but she ordered herself to relax and take this ride with Clementine, whom she was so happy to see.

"There's no uh-oh. You surpassed my every expectation. Being with you changed me, and I'd never been so happy." She took a small step forward. "But I doubt myself a lot. It's something I'm working on, but it's there all the same, and when my father…did what he did…that lack of self-love pulled me under, and I was drowning." She shook her head regretfully. "I'm sorry I ran away from us, from you. I couldn't quite see myself fitting into your life, and the idea of always feeling like a failure, an imposter, was too much for me."

"And now? Do you still feel that same way now?"

It felt like a lifetime before Clementine answered. "I took a look at myself through your eyes. It was hard. I didn't want to, but a good friend reminded me what's most important in life, so I did it. I remembered how you looked at me, and it was everything. I was startled by the way it made me feel, and I wasn't willing to waste more time." She shook her head. "We don't have all that much of it to waste."

Madison didn't even hesitate. The words had been on the tip of her tongue for a while now, and it was time to say them. "I looked at you like the woman I loved."

Clementine's lips parted, and she studied Madison as if trying to understand.

"I'm so in love with you that you're the first thing I think about when I open my eyes in the morning, and the last person I want to speak to before I close them. You're everything to me. Everything. Do you hear me?"

Clementine nodded, her eyes brimming with tears. "I didn't know that."

"How could you?" Madison said, borrowing Clementine's line. "I should have said it all along, but it doesn't make it any less true."

"I love you, too," Clementine said. "I just had to clear a lot of garbage away first. Ms. Birdie's wisdom."

"Then I certainly owe her a great debt. So what now?" Madison asked, daring to hope, but not wanting to push.

"I just want to be with you," Clementine said. "I don't know how you feel about that given the way I left. Maybe you want me to leave you alone, and I'd get that. But I promise you that I don't have any more plans to run."

"I'm sorry. I'm too busy reveling in the fact that we're in love. Did you say something?"

Clementine laughed and tilted her head, holding Madison's gaze. The look in her eyes said everything. She missed Madison. She wanted her back. And best of all, she loved her.

"Why don't we dance while you think it over?"

"Out here?" Madison asked. She marveled because there was a time when she would have balked at the over-the-top cheese factor, but now nothing sounded better. Clementine held out her hand, and Madison took it, pulling Clementine slowly to her. Something soft and sultry played on the speaker, a female singer, and as Clementine's body touched hers, Madison closed her eyes and relaxed. No place on Earth felt better than this. They danced silently, cheek to cheek at first, until she had to see Clementine's eyes. She pulled her face back just a tad and found them.

"God, I've missed this," Clementine said. "Touching you this way. The way you look at me. The way you smell." She buried her face in Madison's hair.

Madison's heart sang. She touched Clementine's cheek softly, then cradled it. "I think this is meant to be. I've never been more sure about something, someone." She leaned in, let her lips hover just shy of Clementine's before going in for the kiss she'd been dreaming about for so long. Clementine's lips clung to hers, and they kissed slowly beneath the twinkly lights of that old barn. At some point, the song came to its conclusion, but they didn't care. Madison could kiss Clementine until the end of time and, in fact, planned to do just that.

"I love you," Clementine whispered against her lips.

Madison shook her head. "I've never been more happy to hear three simple words. I love you, too." She grinned, understanding that her world was right side up again. She had the woman of her dreams right there in her arms, and she would spend every waking moment showing her how wonderful she was, how loved. "Come home with me," she said, before going in for another kiss. Clementine nodded and smiled and kissed her back.

They found their way back to the cottage slowly, pausing along the way to steal glances at each other, soft touches or a kiss beneath the looming moon. In fact, Madison couldn't stop touching Clementine, to make sure she was actually here, that all of this was real. The warmth of her skin and softness of her lips guaranteed that Madison wasn't dreaming.

Without hesitation, Clementine took the lead, taking Madison's hand and leading her down the hallway to the bedroom. While Madison was anxious to get her hands on Clementine, she was captivated by the look on Clementine's face as she slowly undressed Madison, revealing her body one piece of clothing at a time. The determined look on her face was incredibly sexy, and Madison quivered beneath her touch. As Clementine made love to her, she was slow and measured, reverent even, kissing Madison's skin with a newfound tenderness that drove her wild with anticipation. When pleasure ripped through her, she clung to Clementine, knowing she'd found where she belonged in this world. "I love you," she whispered, taking Clementine's face in her hands.

"Maybe you could show me," Clementine said, her eyes dancing with desire.

"You don't have to ask me twice," Madison said, palming Clementine's breast and taking her nipple fully into her mouth. Clementine gasped, and they were off.

In the dim light of morning, Madison woke with a smile already on her face. She was naked in her bed with Clementine's arms around her from behind, their bodies pressed together, warm and perfect. She covered Clementine's arms with hers and brought them even closer together with a squeeze. Clementine sighed and placed a kiss on her bare shoulder before drifting off again. With a heart overflowing with love, Madison gave thanks for all she had. Wonderful friends. A job on the most beautiful vineyard on Earth. And now the love of a woman she could hardly believe was hers. Her life was full, and her heart overran with gratitude, so much so that she couldn't keep the words inside for a moment longer. "Thank you," she whispered to the early light of day. "Thank you."

CHAPTER TWENTY-THREE

Madison was up early because she didn't want to miss a moment of the day. She brewed two cups of coffee, tried her very best at some lopsided pancakes, and popped a few colorful candles right in the center of the less-than-perfect stack. When Clementine poked her head around the corner looking for Madison, she began to sing.

"Happy Birthday to you, Happy Birthday to you." As she continued singing, she watched as Clementine's face transformed from surprised to touched to sheer happiness.

"You got up early and made me breakfast?" She was adorable standing there with her sleepy grin in Madison's T-shirt. "I don't think anyone has ever done that for me before."

"Taste the pancakes first. You may never want anyone to again. Good morning, sweetheart." Madison kissed her lips and pulled her in. Clementine, as always, fit perfectly. "What are you going to do with your day off?"

She appeared thoughtful. "There's a lot I should do back at the apartment. I still need to finish in the kitchen before Tuesday when I have the cleaners coming." Clementine had been staying at the cottage with Madison for months now, and it just felt silly to keep paying rent on an apartment she never used. So they'd made it official and moved in together. Clementine was now home for good, and nothing could have made Madison happier. The past year of her life had been the best she'd ever experienced. She woke up happy and went to sleep even happier alongside the woman she knew, without a doubt, had become the love of her life.

"I think birthdays should be more about what you *want* to do," Madison pointed out, joining Clementine in a bite of pancakes. Not bad at all.

"What I'd really like to do is swing by the library for a new stash of books and read one of them outside."

"Well, there you go. That's exactly how you should spend your day. And then tonight, we celebrate." She'd made a dinner reservation at the Jade Resort's fancy rooftop restaurant, the Crown Jewel, and invited Joey, Becca, Gabriella, Ryan, Frankie, and Jun to join them.

Clementine lit up. "I sneaked a peek at the menu on their website. I'm so excited for this dinner."

"Good. We're going to eat all the best food and maybe even taste some fancy wine."

Clementine kissed her. "I love today and I love you."

"I love you, too."

That night everyone arrived at the restaurant looking like a million bucks. Becca arranged for a large round table by the window that showed off the view of the vineyards surrounding the resort. As night fell, they drank and laughed and celebrated Clementine. The twin custom-made bookcases Madison had commissioned to house Clementine's books were too large to wrap, but Ryan had taken photographs of her work for Madison to present instead. Clementine stared in awe at how beautiful they'd turned out.

"These are really for me?" Clementine asked.

Madison nodded. "I thought they'd go perfect along the back wall in the living room. You can fill them with all your books."

Clementine stared at the photo, unable to take her eyes off the bookcases, which made Madison's heart swell. Everyone else took their turn presenting their gifts, all thoughtful and very Clementine, right down to the Biscuit Queen apron and chef's hat from Gabriella. As the dessert dishes were cleared away and everyone settled in for one final after-dinner drink, Madison took an envelope with a red bow on top out of her bag. "Just one more birthday celebration," she said and slid the envelope over to Clementine.

She stared at Madison with curiosity and then regarded the envelope. "What's in there?"

"You'll have to open it and find out."

Clementine opened the envelope, took out the paperwork inside, and studied it. "I don't understand." She looked at Madison and down at the ownership papers.

"I just need your signature on a few of those, and the Biscuit is yours."

Clementine swallowed, scanned the faces of their friends, before training her gaze back on Madison. "I still don't get it."

"That café has always been yours in every sense. It belongs with you."

"You'll sell it to me?"

"We can handle it any way that makes you the most comfortable. A gift, a sale, or a magic wand. If you ask me, it's only a matter of a time before our bank accounts become one." They'd talked about marriage, and both were very serious about making that lifelong commitment. Madison couldn't imagine waiting much longer. "But the main idea is that you and the Biscuit belong together. It's yours." Their friends applauded, and she joined them in ushering in what was always meant to be.

Clementine's hands were shaking, and the tears were already on her cheeks. She reached for Madison and held on to her. "Are you sure?" she whispered.

"Absolutely. I bought the place because something was guiding me to it, guiding me to *you*. My purpose with the café has been fulfilled because here we are." She dried Clementine's tears with her thumbs, and when she looked around at the smiling faces of their friends, there were very few dry eyes.

"What can I say? I'm a sucker for special moments," Gabriella said, referencing her emotion. Ryan pulled her in for a squeeze.

"We're so happy for you," Becca said, kissing the back of Joey's hand.

"I can't think of a better person for the job," Joey said.

They formalized the arrangement that next week, and the Bacon and Biscuit Café became Clementine's.

"I can't believe this is real. I still feel the need to pinch myself," Clementine said, as they stood in front of the building, staring up at it. Because she'd insisted, she'd purchased the business from Madison officially and would make monthly payments in addition to the chunk she'd put down up front. Well, at least until it no longer mattered anymore, which Madison hoped would be sooner rather than later.

"Pinch away, because it's not going anywhere."

She looked over at Madison. "Does this mean I won't see you every other day for bank drops? I always look forward to those stolen moments. Highlight of my day."

Madison gave her waist a squeeze. "I don't really see those going anywhere. Not sure I could stay away. The biscuits beckon."

"Hey!" Clementine said, wounded.

Madison quieted her with a kiss. "I love you and plan to see you just as much as before. Maybe more. No possible way to keep me from it."

"So much better," Clementine murmured against her lips. Another kiss that made Madison flash back on their celebratory morning in bed, and her cheeks went hot.

"How many hours until tonight?" she asked.

"Too many," Clementine said with a smile. "But we'll get there."

Why had it taken Clementine so long to give in to this? Domesticity rocked, especially when it was Madison she got to gaze at dreamily across the house every day. She lounged on the couch, lost in the latest Groffman mystery, dimly aware that Madison studied the ice cream sundaes she'd constructed for them with the scrutiny of a true artist.

"Why do they look so much better in the photo?" Madison asked, holding up the laptop and the Pinterest page she'd found and bookmarked. She'd taken up a handful of new hobbies lately, vowing to be adventurous if it killed her. It was adorable, really.

"You're asking me? The person who loves any and all ice cream creations? I think they look wonderful," Clementine said, hoping to move the process along and dig into that gorgeous dessert alongside the gorgeous chef. "You just happen to be a perfectionist in all things. You also rock an apron. It's like ice cream porn for me."

"Perfectionism is overrated," Madison said with a sultry smile and added a big dollop of whipped cream that destroyed the picture-perfect aesthetic. "Working on moving out of that tendency. Keeping the apron, though." She winked.

"Do you know how impressed I am with you right now?" Clementine grinned, pushing herself into a sitting position and placing her book on the end table. Madison carried over the sundaes and took the spot next to Clementine on the couch.

"Voilà. Made with love."

They shared a soft kiss that lingered, and Clem dug in. "Oh, my, I like the strawberry addition."

"I thought you might."

Clementine savored the rich hot fudge, turning her spoon over to be sure she got all of it. "What?" she asked as Madison eyed her.

"You make ice cream eating sexy. Who does that?"

Clementine knew she was blushing but didn't stop. Couldn't. It was too delicious. "Stop undressing me with your eyes mid ice-cream eating."

"You don't know that's what I was doing."

"Do so." Clementine pointed at Maddie with her spoon, circling it. "I know that look."

"Fine, but you eating a hot-fudge sundae topless is not an awful idea. Just throwing that out there."

Clementine undid one button on her top for good measure.

Madison laughed and shook her head. "Such a tease."

"What shall we do tonight?"

"I need to take a final walk through the vineyard before we lose the sun altogether. Make sure the new hoses aren't oversaturating the soil. Then maybe later we can rent a movie?"

"Sold. Can I walk with you?" Clementine asked with a soft smile.

"I'd love it."

Hand in hand they walked through the vines of Tangle Valley as the sun faded into a glorious pink on its way to bed. It startled Clementine how normal it all felt, how comfortable, yet still amazing. This was her life now, and the doubts she'd carried had slowly floated away the more she gave herself over to Madison and their commitment to each other. They talked through any bumps in the road these days, and Clementine always felt stronger for it afterward. She wasn't sure that she'd been a believer in fate before Madison bought the café, but she was now. She was right where she belonged and no longer felt on the outside of anything. On shaky legs, she'd claimed her life with bravery and humility, and it had been the best decision she'd ever made. At long last, Clementine knew her place in this world. She squeezed Madison's hand as she looked over at her, Madison's blue eyes glistening in the waning sunlight.

"I love you," Madison mouthed.

She grinned and kissed her right there in between the vines.

Clementine was home and she was happy.

EPILOGUE

The days, weeks, and months that followed only got better. After living with Clementine for a month, Madison knew it was meant to be. She had never known this kind of excitement for life, and it felt like once she let herself fully feel and emote and express herself, the entire scope of her love for Clementine and the love she received back came raining down on her in wonderful payoff. She knew with utter certainty that until Clementine, she'd been limping along in life, missing a part of herself.

Never again.

They got up early together every morning and met back up for dinner at the cottage or a local spot in town where they'd see their friends and neighbors. They never heard from Clementine's father again, and that was for the best. Though they both wondered what had become of him. Brenda Anne eventually started seeing Powell Rogers until each was rarely seen at public events without the other. To her credit, Brenda Anne even managed to get Powell to adjust the band on his ball caps so they didn't perch so high on his head. It was nice to see them both so happy.

The Biddies continued to biddy, trading gossip with each other and dropping hints of it all around Whisper Wall. Since the loss of their fourth, Birdie, they did so with a softer touch. Photos on their Instagram account were more of a commemoration of the town and all its happenings and less about spreading sensational rumors. Birdie would have been so proud and was likely smiling down on all of them.

When Clementine got down on one knee and proposed to Madison nine months to the day after her birthday celebration, Madison said yes with every fiber of her being, tears in her eyes like a happy cliché. She wouldn't have wanted it any other way. They weren't the first of their friends who would exchange vows, however. Joey and Becca beat them to the altar just a few months prior in a beautiful ceremony the town was still talking about. Gabriella had officially moved in with Ryan out at the lake house, and together, they'd adopted Goofy, a retriever mix, from the Moon and Stars Ranch. Goofy was a more energetic brother for Dale, who led him on lots of new adventures. Madison knew it was only a matter of time before the couple added a child to their family. They talked about adoption more and more these days.

As for Clementine, the Bacon and Biscuit had been named to Oregon's list of Best Breakfast Spots. She'd happily hung the certificate they'd sent her right next to the door of the café and smiled at it every day. They were semi-famous!

Madison was pleased with Tangle Valley's ever-growing business and reputation in the wine world. They'd discussed expansion, but slowly and over time. Joey had no desire for mass commercialization, and neither did Madison. But as the vineyard slowly gained more and more respect and attention, they saw their profit margin grow. Not a bad spot to be in.

"What now?" Madison asked, in her meeting with Gabriella and Joey. She sat back in her chair after hearing the good news of their profitable quarter. There were so many options and directions they could take the vineyard. She felt like this was the perfect time to capitalize on their momentum. Knowing Joey, and her ever-turning list of ideas, she likely agreed.

Joey looked from Gabriella to Madison. "I don't know how you guys feel about this, but I was thinking a movie night tonight?"

"Oh, with tons of popcorn, too," Gabriella said dreamily.

Well, that was that for business talk, apparently. Madison laughed. "I'm in. Clementine was just saying it had been a little while since we've done one."

"I'll bring my slippers and the popcorn, of course," Gabriella said. "Ryan, too, for cuddling purposes."

"Don't forget the good butter," Joey added. "I'll bring the wine and my wife."

"Cinnamon biscuits and my fiancée?" Madison asked and held up her hands, palms to the sky.

Joey nodded. "Sold."

So much had changed in their lives over the past three years, but the good parts remained untouched. The way they looked out for one another, nudged each other when they needed it, or simply enjoyed the friendship they all shared. Tangle Valley, along with the people who worked there, was a special place, and Madison sent up thanks every day for all she had been blessed with. She often wondered about the vineyard and what little bit of fairy dust the Wilder family had sprinkled across the land that made it such a unique and magical place. She knew on an essential level that she'd remain there for a very long time. There were so many memories yet to be made, so many toasts to raise up a glass to, and—most importantly—so much more love to give.

About the Author

Melissa Brayden is a multi-award-winning romance author, embracing the full-time writer's life in San Antonio, Texas, and enjoying every minute of it.

Melissa is married and working really hard at remembering to do the dishes. For personal enjoyment, she spends time with her Jack Russell terriers and checks out the NYC theater scene as often as possible. She considers herself a reluctant patron of spin class, but would much rather be sipping merlot and staring off into space. Bring her coffee, wine, or doughnuts and you'll have a friend for life. www.melissabrayden.com.

Books Available From Bold Strokes Books

Fleur d'Lies by MJ Williamz. For rookie cop DJ Sander, being true to what you believe is the only way to live…and one way to die. (978-1-63555-854-8)

Guarding Evelyn by Erin Zak. Can TV actress Evelyn Glass prove her love for Alden Ryan means more to her than fame before it's too late? (978-1-63555-841-8)

Love's Falling Star by B.D. Grayson. For country music megastar Lochlan Paige, can love conquer her fear of losing the one thing she's worked so hard to protect? (978-1-63555-873-9)

Love's Truth by C.A. Popovich. Can Lynette and Barb make love work when unhealed wounds of betrayed trust and a secret could change everything? (978-1-63555-755-8)

Next Exit Home by Dena Blake. Home may be where the heart is, but for Harper Sims and Addison Foster, is the journey back worth the pain? (978-1-63555-727-5)

Not Broken by Lyn Hemphill. Falling in love is hard enough—even more so for Rose, who's carrying her ex's baby. (978-1-63555-869-2)

The Noble and the Nightingale by Barbara Ann Wright. Two women on opposite sides of empires at war risk all for a chance at love. (978-1-63555-812-8)

What a Tangled Web by Melissa Brayden. Clementine Monroe has the chance to buy the café she's managed for years, but Madison LeGrange swoops in and buys it first. Now Clementine is forced to work for the enemy and ignore her former crush. (978-1-63555-749-7)

A Far Better Thing by JD Wilburn. When needs of her family and wants of her heart clash, Cass Halliburton is faced with the ultimate sacrifice. (978-1-63555-834-0)

Body Language by Renee Roman. When Mika offers to provide Jen erotic tutoring, will sex drive them into a deeper relationship or tear them apart? (978-1-63555-800-5)

Carrie and Hope by Joy Argento. For Carrie and Hope, loss brings them together but secrets and fear may tear them apart. (978-1-63555-827-2)

Detour to Love by Amanda Radley. Celia Scott and Lily Andersen are seatmates on a flight to Tokyo and by turns annoy and fascinate each other. But they're about to realize there's more than one path to love. (978-1-63555-958-3)

Ice Queen by Gun Brooke. School counselor Aislin Kennedy wants to help standoffish CEO Susanna Durr and her troubled teenage daughter become closer—even if it means risking her own heart in the process. (978-1-63555-721-3)

Masquerade by Anne Shade. In 1925 Harlem, New York, a notorious gangster sets her sights on seducing Celine, and new lovers Dinah and Celine are forced to risk their hearts, and lives, for love. (978-1-63555-831-9)

Royal Family by Jenny Frame. Loss has defined both Clay's and Katya's lives, but guarding their hearts may prove to be the biggest heartbreak of all. (978-1-63555-745-9)

Share the Moon by Toni Logan. Three best friends, an inherited vineyard, and a resident ghost come together for fun, romance, and a touch of magic. (978-1-63555-844-9)

Spirit of the Law by Carsen Taite. Attorney Owen Lassiter will do almost anything to put a murderer behind bars, but can she get past her reluctance to rely on unconventional help from the alluring Summer Byrne and keep from falling in love in the process? (978-1-63555-766-4)

The Devil Incarnate by Ali Vali. Cain Casey has so much to live for, but enemies who lurk in the shadows threaten to unravel it all. (978-1-63555-534-9)

Secret Agent by Michelle Larkin. CIA Agent Peyton North embarks on a global chase to apprehend rogue agent Zoey Blackwood, but her commitment to the mission is tested as the sparks between them ignite and their sizzling attraction approaches a point of no return. (978-1-63555-753-4)

Journey to Cash by Ashley Bartlett. Cash Braddock thought everything was great, but it looks like her history is about to become her right now. Which is a real bummer. (978-1-63555-464-9)

Liberty Bay by Karis Walsh. Wren Lindley's life is mired in tradition and untouched by trends until social media star Gina Strickland introduces an irresistible electricity into her off-the-grid world. (978-1-63555-816-6)

Scent by Kris Bryant. Nico Marshall has been burned by women in the past wanting her for her money. This time, she's determined to win Sophia Sweet over with her charm. (978-1-63555-780-0)

Shadows of Steel by Suzie Clarke. As their worlds collide and their choices come back to haunt them, Rachel and Claire must figure out how to stay together and, most of all, stay alive. (978-1-63555-810-4)

The Clinch by Nicole Disney. Eden Bauer overcame a difficult past to become a world champion mixed martial artist, but now rising star and dreamy bad girl Brooklyn Shaw is a threat both to Eden's title and her heart. (978-1-63555-820-3)

The Last First Kiss by Julie Cannon. Kelly Newsome is so ready for a tropical island vacation, but she never expects to meet the woman who could give her her last first kiss. (978-1-63555-768-8)

The Mandolin Lunch by Missouri Vaun. Despite their immediate attraction, everything about Garet Allen says short-term, and Tess Hill refuses to consider anything less than forever. (978-1-63555-566-0)

Thor: Daughter of Asgard by Genevieve McCluer. When Hannah Olsen finds out she's the reincarnation of Thor, she's thrown into a world of magic and intrigue, unexpected attraction, and a mystery she's got to unravel. (978-1-63555-814-2)

Veterinary Technician by Nancy Wheelton. When a stable of horses is threatened, Val and Ronnie must work together against the odds to save them and maybe even themselves along the way. (978-1-63555-839-5)